THE FOURTEEN POINTS

THE FOURTEEN POINTS

ARTHUR B. REEVE

INTRODUCTION BY

ROBERT H. DAVIS

COVER BY

LEJAREN HILLER

STEEGER BOOKS • 2021

TABLE OF CONTENTS

MR. DAVIS PRESENTS
THE AUTHOR

IN THE SCIENCE of detection Scotland Yard has reduced its formula to the simple phrase, *"Find the motive."* Paris Sûreté, thriving in an atmosphere of romance, has for its battle cry, *"Find the woman."* The author of *The Fourteen Points* which make up this volume summons to his aid a simpler dictum, "Find yourself."

Voltaire in *Zadig*, the first story in which analysis and elimination were brought to bear upon the scheme of detection, proved the theory, unwittingly, perhaps, that reason was a key equal in importance to the clue.

The mind recognizing no mathematical limitations defines its own frontier. A great detective must possess, along with his authority, his familiarity with the existing evidence, his knowledge of human frailty, one perfectly good set of brains. Otherwise the enigma becomes insoluble.

What of the genesis of the author of this book? Turn back the pages of the record to 1907, at which time the writer of these lines was editing a magazine carrying a mixed table of contents.

Enter Arthur Reeve, young, blond, blue eyed, full of youthful illusions and collegiate learning. This was prior to the days of the leather portfolio which in later years came into vogue and bulked tremendously. An author's entire output could be carried easily in his inside coat pocket. The market was limited, in spite of which the demand exceeded the supply.

"I would like to submit a manuscript," said my young visitor.

"Fact or fiction?" I asked.

"Both, in a manner of speaking. It deals with certain established facts through which the reader finds himself led into the higher atmosphere of boundless imagination."

I took the manuscript impatiently and turned to the first page. The title of that manuscript written by the then inconspicuous Arthur B. Reeve, now known throughout the English-speaking world as the creator of Craig Kennedy, was *Greatest of Mysteries—The Human Brain.*

This isn't the time or place to quote any part of that essay except to record that it treated of the manifold complexities of the mind, the tricks of memory, its capacity for cataloguing the priceless and worthless reflections, to say nothing of its myriad ramifications, detections, conclusions, visions, and vagaries through a human lifetime, and last but not least the mystery of its illimitations.

He had taken the thinking machine apart, examined it, put it together again, and offered it at the market rate, seventeen years ago.

At that time Craig Kennedy, scientific detective, had not been thought of, or else he was so far back in the dim recesses of the author's inner consciousness that articulation had not begun, and yet it was not improbable that the foundation was being laid subconsciously in that "greatest of mysteries," to which the young collegian had addressed himself.

FEBRUARY, 1924. Enter the creator of *Craig Kennedy,* middle-aged blond, blue eyed, *sans* youthful illusions, but with a trace of dignity and perhaps thirty additional pounds of adipose tissue careful distributed. This time he lugged a large portfolio under his arm. It was bulging with the paraphernalia of authorship: his own books, other people's books, manuscripts, a volume on chemistry, reports from Scotland Yard, tracts on prison reform, a steel engraving of Bertillon, three pamphlets written by Lombroso in his youth, to say nothing of numerous memoranda and notes for stories in process of acquiring birthright. Whereupon I took his picture in the act of invading my privacy.

"I have nothing to sell," said he, an observation which placed me instantly at ease and was probably the reason for the more or less flippant dialogue that ensued.

I invited him to sit down and rest his portfolio.

"What's the matter? Is old Craig Kennedy written out? Have you emptied your box of tricks?"

"No one man," responded Mr. Reeve, setting his glasses firmly on the bridge of his nose, "can empty a receptacle into which the entire human race is pouring its best suggestions."

He sat down rather languidly, doffed his Fedora, and passed a plump hand across a high, slightly bald forehead. My mind flew back to the occasion of his first visit, the period of his heyday, since which time he had made for himself a reputation that had both prospered and sobered him. Nevertheless, there lingered in the blue eye that gleam which comes only from men who are born with imagination.

In spite of the fact that this mild Anglo-Saxon dreamer had made a fortune transmuting the baser passions of the world into entertaining, golden fiction, I had the feeling that perhaps he could do something else better—an utterly insane conclusion, of course. What he was best fitted to do he did, and yet there is a certain pleasure in being irreverent in the presence of one of the apostles. To wit:

"You have exhausted hate, love, vanity, pride, jealousy, revenge, and the kindred passions. Chemistry, pseudo science, radiography, speech and transmission of pictures by wireless, have just about come to an end. What are you going to do next?" I paused for his reply.

"Every second," said he, with a soft voice and his white hand rummaging through his scant hair, "a new set of events accumulates, wavers, shatters, and reassembles. Kaleidoscopically the whole thing falls suddenly into perfect geometrical harmony.

The missing ingredient is found. The most casual word, the simplest detail, and—*Eureka!* What would you suggest?"

Without intending to ignite the fuse that led to the powder magazine of Craig Kennedy's imagination, I struck the pose of a schoolboy and recited in a high-pitched voice the following thirteen words:

"North, east, south, west; air, earth, fire, water; seeing, hearing, tasting, smelling, feeling."

The author of *Craig Kennedy* cradled his occipital protuberance in the hollows of his palms, looked aloft for a few moments, and made this amazing retort:

"Not a bad idea, but you've left out one of the senses."

"For example?"

"The sixth—common sense. Now with the points of the compass, the elements, and the six senses we've got fourteen points. *Very* much obliged. Seven thousand words on each of these separate subjects means ninety-eight thousand words. Just the right length for a book. The return of Craig Kennedy!"

He purred the last sentence.

"Can you use these tales at the rate of two a month?"

The blond gentleman had suddenly become a colossus. Dazed, yet aware that something important had occurred, I offered my hand as a sign that a bargain had been concluded.

Exit the blue-eyed man who had shown such incredible speed and dexterity in the merchandising of his imagination.

A PREFACE is a dangerous thing, the more so because it appears in the same volume with the material that inspires it. It is like a cross-word puzzle; when it seems perfectly all right in the horizontal it is imperfect in the perpendicular. Some day a magnificent preface will be written to a book that has never been printed, and under the circumstances the book never should be printed.

In the present instance, however, the prefacer makes bold to say that in these Fourteen Points lie concealed mysteries, plots, themes, situations, and tableaux calculated to satisfy the most exacting student of the great unsolved.

These stories began to flow into my office within three weeks after I had accepted them alone on their titles. The first to arrive was "Air" and the last "The Sixth Sense." It would be inadvisable for me to disclose any of these mysteries and inappropriate for one to expect it.

I may, perhaps, be forgiven for calling attention to the amazing ingenuity displayed by Mr. Reeve in the story that appears under the title "South." It would be perfectly reasonable at one point in the story to assume that the clue came from the East and then slipped over to the West, but when a certain character involved in this story crumpled beneath the gaze of Craig Kennedy and confessed guilt, the conviction came up from the South.

"Water," from the standpoint of the chemical formula H_2O, is perhaps the driest tale ever written. Notwithstanding, when the mystery is solved the establishment of guilt gushes upon the reader like a cloudburst.

"Taste" is the quintessence of suspense. There is a situation in this story in which it seems that the author has lost all sense of direction and purpose; that he is responsible for the sterility of every clue. Do not be down-hearted. Mr. Reeve touches the steering wheel of his kaleidoscope, the scattered fragments fall together in geometrical perfection, and paradoxically an absent thing becomes present only because of its absence.

The whole volume is a departure from conventional forms of detective fiction. The title of each tale is carried out in its development as the warp and the woof combine in textile creations. No concessions are asked of the reader, nor does the long-bow of coincidence twang its flagrant discord.

The last of the fourteen manuscripts, "The Sixth Sense," was completed within twelve months of the date upon which the series was begun. In this story, the handy Jameson, Craig Kennedy's "shadow," comes magnificently into his own and justifies a career fraught with patience and self-elimination.

I rise to make genuflection to Mr. Reeve, who in these "Fourteen Points" proves conclusively that the greatest of mysteries is the human brain, more especially his own, which is self-contained in that it has developed in a conservatory of mysteries, none more engaging or more artful than the "Fourteen Points" that comprise this volume.

He has "found himself."

New York City,
Nov. 24, 1924

Robert H. Davis.

NORTH

"**IT'S MIGHTY FINE** of you fellows, but I don't deserve this welcome." Stanley Kane, an old classmate at the university, had invaded Craig's laboratory, and Kennedy and I were delighted at the old-time reunion. "Really, I don't. I've been rotten, showed mighty little interest in you both since college. But war—and a wife kept me busy, you know."

"War and a wife?" repeated Kennedy.

A rather bitter smile flitted over Kane's face. "Yes. Doris and I have agreed to disagree. You know I married a beauty, a mighty fine girl, I thought. But now I'm living at the club; Doris is out at the old house, with the children. We don't seem to mix. Common enough story, these days, I guess. Things began to go to the dogs a couple of years ago. I suppose I wanted an old-fashioned wife, and Doris was too used to the freedom and privileges of married women during the war—and since." Kane had lighted a cigarette and dropped into an easy chair. "But that's not what I'm here for, Craig. I've been robbed. The Kane jewels have been stolen."

"Stolen? When?" asked Kennedy.

With a droll smile Kane stood up, flicking his cigarette. "Doris said the first time she missed them was last Friday night when she was dressing for the opera. She opened the wall safe and, to her horror"—another fleeting smile swept over his expressive face—"the jewels were gone—all of them, everything! Some of them were family heirlooms, too, valued above their mere cost in money—but all are gone. Here it is Monday afternoon—and not a clew, yet." He spread out his hands in a sort of mocking manner as much as to say, "That's her story—but I don't believe it!"

Stanley Kane was tall, blond, and handsome, the kind of man, too, who knows he is tall, blond, and handsome. I regarded him rather closely. Certainly "war and a wife" had not aged him appreciably, nor brought any lines on his face. He looked, however, a little too absorbed in himself, too self-centered, I fancied, to make any woman really happy.

"Do you see your wife, Stan?" asked Craig.

"Gosh, no! We always fight when we meet. So Doris keeps out of sight when I go to see the children. I do that once a week—Wednesdays—to keep my eye on how things are going." He ended with a weak smile.

"Are you thinking about a divorce?" pursued Craig.

"Doris is going to get one, I believe. She and the children are going to Nevada, or Oregon, or some place, as soon as she can make up her mind. Kennedy, I don't like it. She is too blamed anxious for this separation, and all that. I don't believe it's all a gentle wounded spirit hurt by neglect and going on a rampage. I think there's a man in the woodpile—if I could only find him." His skepticism caused him to flick the ashes of his cigarette again so viciously that this time they went all over himself.

"He loves Doris Kane yet; he is jealous of her," was my own mental observation.

"How much were the jewels worth?" inquired Craig.

"Oh, I should say a quarter of a million, at present prices. The pearl necklace was worth over half of that, alone."

"Insured?"

"Yes," said Kane bitterly. "I paid the premiums. Insured for a hundred and fifty-five thousand. The All American Insurance Company."

"I see." Kennedy was considering. "You say she kept them in a wall safe? Why not in a safety deposit vault?"

"She did. But the pearls—that was the big thing—she was

going to wear them to the opera, had them out of the bank, the day before, for some reason." He scowled. "In the wall safe, in her own boudoir, in the old Kane mansion where we lived before I went to the club here in the city."

"Have you seen the safe since the robbery?"

"Oh yes. When Doris is in real trouble she kindly gives me a telephone call. That is the sort of husband I am to her. I was interested enough, naturally, to go right out there to Hempstead. Doris wasn't in, of course, when I entered my house, but the children and their nurse were home. I went up to the safe in my wife's room and looked it over. The queer thing about it, the part I don't understand at all, is that there is no evidence of tampering with the safe. It hasn't even been touched by a 'can-opener,' or 'soup,' or anything, as far as I can see."

Kennedy said nothing; just waited. Often I have seen him sit quietly and let the other people do the talking. Their rambling explanations of domestic unhappiness, of business troubles, furnish clews to many cases. Craig is a good listener.

One could easily see that Stanley Kane was not happy. When he spoke of his old home and of the children, there was an undertone of dissatisfaction, of unhappiness, in his well-bred inflection. And there was bitterness, too, a peeved bitterness, as of brooding over wrongs that were acts of omission rather than of commission by his beautiful and popular wife.

Kane leaned back in the chair, smoking another cigarette, thoughtfully. "It's this way, Craig. My wife has devilish extravagant habits. It takes a Kane fortune to keep her going—and she's not getting all of it, any more. But she has remained just as recklessly extravagant. So it seems, anyhow. Now, where is the money coming from?" He looked from one to the other of us shrewdly.

"I've done something you fellows may think I'm a cad for doing," he went on at length as Craig said nothing.

"But, by Jove! I feel so up in the air that I'm trying to get my marital crisscross puzzle solved in almost any way—for the benefit of the children."

He paused and Kennedy asked, "What have you done, Stan?"

"Hired the nurse of the children to watch my wife. I suppose you'll call it spying and all that. But I want something to make out a counter suit. I think I'm entitled to it."

"Have you got anything yet?"

"No. Either she is careful—or there's mighty little to get. Louise Layton—that's the nurse—tells me my wife never entertains any men at home and never confides in her or even her own maid, Lucille, as to what she does or where she goes when she's out."

"How many children have you?" asked Craig with a smile.

"Two. Two wonders. A boy and a girl. Stanley is five, born after the war, you know. We call him Junior. Dorothy—'Dot'—is only three. That's one big reason. Craig, I hate to think about those missing jewels. I wanted Dot to have those old Kane jewels when she grew up." He leaned forward eagerly.

"I'll have to see the place, Stan," remarked Craig. "I want to get in without anybody knowing that I am even interested in the jewel robbery. Keep that as quiet as possible. I'm glad the papers haven't found it out yet."

"I can give you a letter to Louise Layton, the nurse. She is working for me, anyhow. I'll tell her you are coming out to help me on my case against Doris. I'd better write it on the club stationery. I'll send it around, tonight."

"By the way," hastened Craig, "we'd better go out there under other names. Call me Carson; and Walter, oh, well, call him Johnson. And no one must suspect we are even from the insurance company, either."

Stanley Kane soon left. He was too restless to stay in any one place long. It was easily seen, I felt, that he was still in love with his wife and too proud to tell her so. Many a marriage has gone on the rocks for that reason. He would let her go her way. That was big and sounded generous. He wouldn't stop her. She should be happy in her way. Yet he was secretly raging at Doris because she didn't come to him and fight to keep him. I thought of the millions of women who would feel a glow, a thrill, if their men were not quite such icicles. Such a girl would feel flattered if the man with the lofty modern generosity would forget it, come to her, take her arm as if he meant it, and whisper: "I love you! I need you! I won't take 'No' for an answer!"

"Poor old Stan!" exclaimed Craig as the outside door banged. "I wish I could help him find his jewels—and his happiness."

"What first?" I asked, with an eye to the case. "The insurance company?"

"Yes. They might have found out something by this time that they are not telling Kane."

At the office of the All-American Insurance Company, late in the afternoon, we found the usual personnel. Two detectives assigned to the case had fortunately come into the office to make their reports. Schneider and Watson were both the usual type of exalted flatty, sure of themselves as sleuths.

"But how do you think it was done?" flattered Kennedy, after a few moments of conversation.

"An inside job!" exclaimed Watson, positively. "I s'pose you know the scandal in the Kane family? She has some expensive habits." The detective paused, hinting that Mrs. Kane might have done it herself for money sorely needed. "This here mah jong ain't no improvement on bridge, y' know, either. She used to have some big debts, they tell us, in her bridge. Well, the East Wind can sweep away money just as fast!" He laughed immoderately at his own imagination.

"I see." Craig was absorbing the detective angle of it.

Schneider leaned over confidentially, "You know this Jack Rushmore?"

"The actor?" nodded Craig.

"Yes. In that play, the society melodrama, 'The Ear in the Wall'? Gee! what a scene in the third act where he takes the dictograph that's been put in to catch the wife and opens the safe with it, listening to the fall of the tumblers by the microphone, until he gets it right!" He lowered his voice. "Well, Jack

Rushmore is an intimate friend of Mrs. Kane," He drew back. "Did you know that?"

"No," confessed Kennedy.

"Well, he is. A high flyer, too. Birds of a feather. You can exercise your own imagination!"

Kennedy thanked them very courteously, but even to me made no comment. Outside of a visit on the way uptown to Third Deputy O'Connor, our old friend at headquarters in charge of the detective force, and a confidential chat before we went to dinner and to a show, I could not see that Craig had the case on his mind at all.

It was not until the next morning that Kennedy seemed disposed to take it up. Along in the forenoon it was that we were approaching the fine old Kane mansion, out in Hempstead.

"I'd like to see Miss Layton—Louise Layton—if you please," Craig inquired at the door that seemed to be in the servant's quarters.

A pretty, saucy little face peeped over the broad shoulder of a substantial-looking cook who had come to the door. "I'm Louise Layton," she said, with the easy informality of the service end.

Kennedy bowed. "I have a letter to you, Miss Layton, from a friend." Careful not to let the cook see the club monogram or the handwriting, he passed to Louise the letter Stanley Kane had sent around to us the night before.

Louise glanced at it "My word! Just when I'm busiest! It's time for the children to get dressed for that birthday luncheon party at the Walcotts'. Oh, well, I don't break rules—often. Come in."

The cook laughed good-naturedly. It was evidently an event to see visitors at the house, even at the service end.

"Come with me." Louise led us into a little room used by the servants for receiving their friends. "I guess you know I'm the nurse for the Kane children."

Now that she was alone, she read the note more carefully. A calculating expression on her piquant face betrayed the fact, I thought, that, in behalf of her real employer, she was not averse to spreading the net for Doris Kane's entanglement and embarrassment.

"It's this way, Louise," explained Craig in an undertone. "Mr. Kane wants some quick action and he has asked me to help you get the goods on his wife. Are you willing to help me?" Kennedy could be persuasive.

Louise felt the charm of his personality. "Certainly I'll help—if Mr. Kane wants me to help. But I have two children to dress for a party. They are up in their nursery waiting for me this moment. Mrs. Kane isn't coming home until just before lunch time to get them. You may come up to the nursery with me—for a few moments—while I get the children ready."

"I'd like that," agreed Craig. "It's a long time since I have played with kids."

"Well, these kids are brought up by rule and regulation. Strangers are tabooed. Germs and kidnappers come with strangers. There's only one thing their parents agree on. That is that the children must have the best of everything." Louise shrugged her slim little shoulders. "And that includes the best of care."

Even before we reached the nursery we could hear the merry sound of children playing, gay shrieks of delight intermingled with full round tones of laughter, a mirth too deep for words.

"They sound happy," I ventured to Louise.

"They ought to be. Everything in the world they want. Their father would try to get the moon for them if they asked it." Louise said it proudly. There is a feeling among the help of a family of wealth, a detached feeling of pride in the welfare and good fortune of their employers, that sets those who work for such families a little higher in the world of domestic employment. Louise was proud of the Kanes. Their marital unhappiness was just a little spice in an otherwise monotonous routine of cares and responsibilities.

"I don't believe all that good nature is inherited," remarked

Kennedy. "I imagine you spread some of that about you." He looked at the girl with evident approval, almost admiration.

Louise was not exactly beautiful. But her face was irresistible. Her features were too irregular to win a beauty contest. Yet I doubt whether any successful contestant would have got a second glance, afterward, if this pretty little nurse stepped into the room. She had that elusive quality of an attractive personality that is able to touch lightly each feature with a glow and radiance of feeling, life, romance, the stirring of the emotions that causes people to do things in this otherwise prosaic world.

Just a moment ahead of us Louise skipped into the room, almost like one of them to romp with the children.

"This is going to be your first party. Junior. I'm going to get you ready in a few minutes. But I want you to meet some friends of mine first. Come, Dot. I have brought you some visitors."

Taking the little ones, each by a hand, she led them up to us. A grave bow and a curtsy were our greeting.

Junior was serious, dark-eyed and brown-haired. Tight ringlets that held something of the glint of the sun in their highlights curled about his tiny ears and sun-browned neck. His was a countenance that showed ability to concentrate, even at that age. Dot was a merry golden-haired little girl hardly out of the chubbiness of babyhood. Both were dressed in little white play suits. It was hard to tell which of them was the more charming.

"What a tragedy!" I whispered, aside, to Craig. "Two youngsters like that—and not to be able to live with them!"

The nursery was a large room with four big windows. Three of these made up one side of the room, a group under which was a window seat and toy boxes. About the room were toys enough for a department store or a kindergarten. The woodwork was a deep ivory and the walls showed a departure from the usual banal nursery decoration one sees in every department-store barber shop for children or the "nursery beautiful." The ceiling was of blue, the color of robins' eggs. Stars, golden stars, gleamed down on the children as they played. Also there was a glorious rainbow painted on one side wall arching over the single window. In front of this window rows of prisms hanging in the sunlight reflected the prismatic colors on the floor, on the wall, moving with the wind-blown glasses. By the bookcase was a painting of their mother, beautifully done. In her hand was a book, opened, and with the other she was beckoning the children to come and share the delights of the book world, represented in the little, low, well-filled book shelves below.

The walls were covered with plaster board and in various panels were shown simply the wonders of nature. All were beautiful, inspiring. A large square table, with very short legs, stood on one side of the room, up against the wall. On this was a shallow zinc tray with a rim about three inches around it, backing up the wood. Here the children could play in the sand, making mountains and hills, valleys and caves, as their imaginations stirred them. About the floor, under the table, were scattered the sand toys of Dot, just as she had left them.

On the other side of the room was Junior's manual-training bench, well equipped. Everything to amuse and stimulate the mind of a healthy, growing child seemed in that room. Doris Kane might have failed as a wife. But certainly there was judgment and discrimination in evidence here. She was a model society mother.

Mrs. Kane was late, but the children did not in the least mind waiting, in such a room.

"Mister, will you play smoking island with me?" Two big brown eyes were pleading with Craig. "I love to play with boys!"

Kennedy laughed outright. "Surely, my boy. Tell me how you play it." He leaned over and listened at tentatively.

"So! Right away he ropes you into that game!" Louise exclaimed, with an amused laugh. "Well, you see, he has had *Swiss Family Robinson* read to him so much that he imagines he is Fritz seeking the girl on the volcanic island. Come, Dot. I'll get you ready first, while brother entertains Mr. Carson and his friend."

Dot left the room under protest. She wanted to join in the search, too. "Let me see smoke, too—please! Don't knock it down!" she called back over her shoulder as Louise pulled her gently out of the room, upstairs in this wing of the house.

"Now, little man," asked Craig, "how do you play it? Show me."

"My daddy uses a cigarette. I'll show you." He ran to the sand table by the side of the wall. Pulling up his little sleeves, he turned. "Now I'm going to make a big mountain."

The sand was piled quickly in a heap. "Light a cigarette, mister. There! Push it 'way down in the top—not too far. Here! It keeps on smoking. See! I have a volcano—a smoking mountain!"

Delighted, he jumped about as Craig carried out his directions. "Now this is all water." He swept clean the bottom of the big sand table. "Here comes Fritz! I'm Fritz—finding the girl lost on this island. Oh, don't you just love that book? Louise reads it to me every day."

So engrossed had I become in the game with Junior that it gave Craig a chance to observe the nursery, the general layout of that end of the house, the inclosed sun room like a sleeping porch, the grounds from the windows, and the hall outside the nursery, before Louise returned with Dot all ready to go to the birthday party with her mother.

"Come, Junior," hastened Louise.

While she was getting Junior ready, our chief trouble was to keep Dot up off the floor and from getting dirty. Dot soon tired of the smoking mountain in the clean sand. Hers was not an adventurous disposition, at least not for that kind of vicarious adventure. She inclined to the maternal instinct. Dolls were the crowning attraction to her. Soon we were surrounded by her family, all sorts and conditions of dolls.

As for Louise, it was a diversion, it seemed, a treat to her sense of humor, to have two strange men sent by the husband of her mistress to watch the latter—and now busily engaged playing dolls with the daughter of the house. It was interesting, too. Here were two men with whom she might find some entertainment. She was making the most of it while it lasted.

Junior's party preparations were soon over. Back to us he hurried, eager to be with men. I was sorry for that boy, sorry for that father. Each was missing the other.

Tired, even of seeking the lost lady on the island, Junior led Craig and me on a tour of inspection in which Dot joined. There were toys that talked, toys that walked, toys that flew. Kennedy entered into it with his whole soul.

Louise looked at us with amazement. "You should come to see me often. Say, I could leave you for a couple of hours to amuse these kids. They wouldn't even miss me. Where did you take your course in child training?" she laughed.

"Oh, look! Look what my father just bought me!" Out of a drawer Junior pulled a box still tied up. "Do you want to see it? What's in it? Guess!"

Craig stood in deep thought. "A Teddy bear—or a big dog."

"No!" in disgust. "My father wouldn't buy me a Teddy bear— or a toy dog or horse. Not now. I'm too big for that. Wait!"

Quickly Junior worked. String and paper flew about, in his keen excitement. He drew the things forth from the package proudly as he sat on the edge of the sand table—a Boy Scout uniform, many sizes too big for him yet. But that was of small importance to Junior.

With a smile aside to us, Craig asked, "Do you belong, Junior?"

"No," he replied sadly. "I have to wait until I'm twelve, father says. But I'll be ready to join."

In the sand box the rest of the equipment had dropped— knife, hatchet, aluminum cooking utensils, and a compass—as he held up the hat and uniform. Craig looked at them all closely with a satisfying interest for the boy. As it slipped off his lap the glass cover over the compass came off and the needle dropped off in the sand. Kennedy was a long time cleaning it and putting the needle again on its pivot, adjusting it.

"Louise! Louise!" Up the stairs came a maid's voice. "I want you to sign for something from a New York store. Come down."

The nurse hesitated a moment, then decided we were worthy to be left alone with the precious children.

It was Kennedy's opportunity. "Ever play tag?" he asked Junior.

"All right," accepted the young gentleman, eagerly.

Like a flash Craig had tagged him and was in the hall. "Where is your mother's room. Junior?"

"Right next to the nursery," was the answer.

"Catch me. Junior, if you can!" Away darted Craig.

He allowed himself to be cornered; then took refuge in Doris Kane's room. Dot and I followed. It was the boudoir. Kennedy glanced over at the wall safe, as indicated by Stanley Kane when he visited the laboratory, then at me. I had to use diplomacy and help him.

Watching every movement he made, in case he needed immediate assistance, I managed somehow to divert the attention of the children from Kennedy to me. I made all the funny faces for which I was famous as a boy. I had the children red in the face from laughter.

Quickly Craig worked. With the combination which Stanley Kane had confided to him he opened the wall safe. No part of it he seemed to miss. Every mark, every inch of surface, inside and out, he examined, now and then tapping it. I was looking, too, and saw nothing wrong about the safe. It was more than strange. Some one must have taken the jewels who knew the combination—and most ladies with jewels do not recklessly publish about the combination of the safe. I wondered.

Looking about me, I realized the amount of money it must take to live like this. Certainly Doris Kane had an incentive to take the jewels. In that respect I felt the insurance detectives might be right. I half expected to see a framed photograph of Jack Rushmore. But there was none—nor of Stanley Kane.

Craig was silent, thinking. It was only for a few seconds.

Once again he was the jolly playmate romping in the hall and back to the nursery. There we were making more noise than was necessary and apparently did not hear Louise when she came back from downstairs. Her face now wore a slightly harassed expression.

"Mrs. Kane has come home—unexpectedly early!" she whispered—"She'll be sure to find you. Then I'll be in bad—with both of them. I'm going to call you my brother, Walter," she added, with a nervous laugh.

I nodded quietly. Already I could hear the click of high heels coming down the hall and stopping quietly for several moments before the open door of the nursery.

"Louise—I—don't understand."

"Madame, my brother Walter. He is going to sail soon with his friend—and he wanted to see me before he went away for so long a time. He has a good job. The family are taking him abroad with them, as a courier. This is his friend, Mr. Carson, a commissioner."

Craig and I bowed. It was really homage to beauty. Doris Kane was one of the most beautiful women I have ever met. She was the most beautiful little girl of my childhood memories, the most bewitching comic-opera star of my college dreams, the most marvelous Madonna I saw in my rambles through the cathedrals and art galleries of Italy—all in one dainty woman.

She had eyes that, while she stood quietly before us, showed childish curiosity, a teasing luster of the dilated pupils, a snap and fire possibly over our intrusion, and yet with the gentleness of the mother as she looked at her children, as well as at the assumed sisterly affection Louise was bestowing most generously on me.

It was Craig who smoothed things over deftly. "Mrs. Kane, we shouldn't have bothered Louise. But Walter sails Thursday, and he cares a great deal for his sister. He hasn't seen her much for years. We heard the children and begged to see them. They are irresistible. We forgot, and were children, too. They are wonderful. I trust that we may be pardoned?"

It was Craig's way with the ladies. I who try so hard to attract, to please them, see all my efforts wasted, when a few words from Craig in his own inimitable manner make them forget my very existence.

"I'm sorry, Louise. I misunderstood. It will be all right for you to see your brother. You are entirely welcome. I shall be ready in about quarter of an hour, Louise."

Doris Kane's hair was like that of her son, dark and curly. Dressed in a quaint pink organdie with a large but soft-brimmed hat trimmed simply with a wreath of roses, she looked like the spirit of youth. No wonder the children ran to her with outstretched arms! I would have liked to do that, myself.

Some people one remembers with difficulty. Others it is easy to recall. Doris Kane was one you could never forget, one of those souls that possess that essence of life which they seem to radiate about them. I thought, What a woman!

Intermittently that evening and the next morning Kennedy seemed at work in his laboratory on some analysis, both chemical and with a super-microscope. It was not until the middle of the following afternoon that he received a telephone call from O'Connor and turned to me after a hasty conversation, his end of which I could not make out.

"I'm going out to the Kane mansion, Walter," he decided. "I'd like to have you come along. You know to-day Stanley Kane visits his children. I'm going to try to arrange things to meet Doris Kane."

I had been thinking of the differences between Stanley and Doris. "You've dealt yourself a job that needs tact and diplomacy, I'm thinking," I ventured. "You may be successful in detecting crime. Do you think you're going to be capable of making other folks detect a love to which they willfully shut their eyes, which they refuse to see?" I was skeptical. As a bachelor I made it a point to keep out of the difficulties of my married friends. I believed in playing safe.

Craig begged the question. "I hear Doris Kane is going to a mah jong party this afternoon. That will leave me free to do a little more looking about in her rooms before she gets back."

I regarded Craig silently. Had he made any progress at all in this case? To me he seemed more interested in the reunion of the Kanes than in the robbery. Possibly he thought that if Doris and Stanley were reunited the jewels might turn up of themselves. The motive to sell them would be lacking. All of the Kane money would establish the managing of the Kane mansion on a sound basis. It was too much for me.

Stanley Kane himself must have been expecting us, for it was he who let us in the house. He was even more excited than when he had visited us first.

"Well, Craig, what did you find?" he asked, anxiously. "Louise has told me you were here yesterday."

"Two mighty fine children, Stan, and your beautiful wife—as well as a very devoted nurse and a good-natured cook."

"H-m! We're alone, Kennedy. Find anything about the robbery?"

"I saw what you saw. Apparently, just as you said, the safe had not been tampered with. I opened it without any trouble, using the combination you gave me. You didn't see any sign of violence about it, did you?"

"No," admitted Kane. "I told you that."

He was about to continue the quizzing. It was nearly five o'clock. Up the walk came Louise and the children.

When Dot and Junior caught sight of us, nothing could restrain them. Dot catapulted herself at me with a violence equaled only by Junior's impetuous reception of Craig. Louise nodded, colored a little, and proceeded indoors.

Both the children refused to let us go. "Come up—come up and have supper with us!" Junior pleaded with Craig as we went in.

It was hard to resist. Louise was a little shy in the presence of Stanley Kane and held a neutral attitude on the idea of the invitation. She neither urged nor objected.

Kennedy settled it. "All right, Junior, I'll come up. I hope you have a good supper. I'm as hungry as two bears!"

With screams of delight the children ran ahead, while Louise stayed below to order supper for two nursery guests.

Stanley Kane followed us up and stood in the door, watching. Craig always had been supple, athletic, kept in training. Cart wheels, handsprings, and standing on one's head may not seem good form in a sack suit, but the thrills they furnished Dot and Junior more than made up for the lack of gym clothes. Louise was almost run over by Craig as she entered the nursery door. He was giving the children a new kind of ride, for them. On his hands and feet, with head up, toward the ceiling, and back to the floor, with both Dot and Junior on his chest, he was walking about the room. It was no easy task, at best. Handicapped by the weight of the children it was a feat. Even Louise had to applaud.

I was amazed at Kane's face. It was most serious, as if he felt that Kennedy should have been working openly on the case, instead of performing gym stunts for the children. Possibly he might have been envying Craig's versatility, though.

Louise soon had the children dressed in their night clothes. It was an attractive sight to see the kiddies frisking about in their little white sleeping garments.

Then Louise made them sit down quietly a few minutes before eating. But it was hard to suppress them. They were ready for a lark.

Meanwhile, the supper was brought up. When Stanley Kane saw that preparations had actually been made for us to eat with the children, his disgust was intense.

Passing me, he confided, quietly: "What's the matter with Kennedy? He may be a detective that loves kids. But as a detective that solves cases, he is getting nowhere. He hasn't a thing yet on—anybody." I felt sure he was going to say "Doris," but had checked himself and changed it in time. "Tell him if he wants to talk over the case with me when he is finished playing with the children, I'll be out there on the porch. I'm going to have a smoke." With this last fling of irony he disappeared, and I could hear him walking heavily on the sleeping porch adjoining.

"Mister, you sit next to me." Craig laughed and allowed himself to be appropriated by Dot.

Junior next drew up a table before them. Silently we watched this methodical little old-fashioned boy. He pulled another chair over to the table and called: "Louise! Louise!"

"Not now, Junior. Let me wait on the table to-night. We have guests, you know."

Then he nodded to me. With a profound bow I accepted. We were all seated.

It was a simple meal—soup, graham bread, milk, and fruit. But the hospitality of the children was pretty. It was so evident that we were welcome.

"You had better join us," I coaxed Louise. "Sit down in my place and let me wait on you."

"No; I can wait. I don't feel hungry to-night, anyhow. No, Junior, you finish. Louise has no appetite." She looked at me nervously and whispered. "I hope Mrs. Kane is late, doesn't find you here to-night, too. She will be furious with me for allowing such a thing while her husband is here. Mr. Kane never stays as late as this, either—and when they meet there are fireworks!" A pretty shrug of her shoulders indicated her apprehension of the impending pyrotechnic display of tempers.

"Don't worry, Louise," assured Kennedy. "I'll smooth things over with Mrs. Kane, as I did yesterday."

But Louise refused to see it that way. She showed plainly that she wanted us out before her mistress returned.

Craig refused to take the hint. Instead, he turned toward Junior and Dot. "Who can get to bed first? I'll give the one who gets under the sheets first a big dollar!" He was balancing a shining cart-wheel silver dollar.

The children jumped about with excitement. "Just a moment. Junior. Dot's the smaller. I think a big boy like you ought to give her a handicap. Here; you start from the table; let Dot start from the door."

Craig gave the signal as soon as Louise had reached the sleeping rooms. There was a wild scamper up the stairs. A moment and we heard Dot's treble calling down in triumph: "I'm in bed! I'm in bed"

It was followed by Junior's call. "I let her win! She's a girl. I had to let her win!"

We were alone then in the nursery with Louise. She was fidgeting, but sat down on a little chair, waiting for us to go. I felt that there was little chance now for Craig to enter Doris Kane's boudoir again.

Suddenly the face of Louise startled. There was a slight slam of the outer door below, then the sound of light steps running up the stairs.

"She's here already! Now see what I get!" Louise looked reproachfully at us in a manner demanding that, as we had placed her in such a false position, it was up to us to get her out of it.

Doris Kane was standing in the doorway, a picture of offended dignity. With a haughty glance she swept the room, passing us with no sign of recognition. I dropped my eyes before her indignation. Louise was sullen. Craig was silent.

Doris Kane was about to reprimand Louise for our second intrusion into her children's nursery, when she stopped suddenly. The slight quiver of her sensitive nostrils showed plainly that she had caught the odor of her husband's cigar wafted in from the porch. For a second or so she stood with a frightened indecision as she saw Stanley Kane's tall form pacing up and down the porch. Then a suppressed gasp following a flash of anger startled us. She clutched the breast of her gown almost frantically. Her face was colorless. In her eyes I fancied I discerned a pitiful look, almost like one asking for help. Her emotion roused my sympathies. Was this her fear of being trapped? Had she discovered, intuitively, that we were detectives, and not the relatives and friends of Louise, the nurse?

Without a word she turned from the doorway. Up the stairs to the bedroom of the children she hurried.

"Dot—Junior—are you all right?"

The answer must have been satisfactory. It seemed only a few seconds when we heard her flit desperately back to her own boudoir. She slammed the door shut, but it did not catch; it was not tight enough to prevent the sound of something like sobs from being heard in the nursery.

There was an awkward, constrained silence among us all, as if we were waiting to see how Stanley Kane would expose his pretty young wife. Kane had stopped pacing the porch. But he did not come in.

Kennedy seemed to be the only one who maintained his poise or his ability to act. It was like a bit of a dramatic pantomime, that entrance and exit of Doris Kane. And, like most classical pantomimes, it wasn't clear. What had been Doris Kane's feelings, what conflicting emotions had prompted her anger and her apparent fears? We needed an explaining pamphlet of the play.

I felt like a fool, personally. Here was Craig, with no evidence that I knew about, holding the center of the stage. I hoped that he had at least in his keen mind the ability to save this home from going the way so many others have gone in these days of easy divorce.

Nonchalantly Kennedy walked over toward the sand table. He raised the lid of a box. Without turning back toward us he remarked, "It seems that Junior's father has been initiated into the mysteries of the Boy Scout's uniform and equipment, too."

Smiling to himself, he lifted slowly out of the box all the boy's treasures, so recently acquired—knife, hatchet, cooking utensils, compass, everything.

Thoughtfully he picked up the compass and examined it, played with it, much as a small boy might play with a compass, keeping up a constant fire of remarks on the children, their toys, as if to divert us from our own disturbing thoughts.

Several times, carelessly, the compass dropped from his hands into the sand table. The situation was so tense that I actually started each time it fell.

"I say, Craig, don't break it before he has a chance to use it!"

It seemed as if the five of us in that house feared to leave the positions we were in, feared we would start the thing, whatever it was, that seemed as if it must happen any minute.

Absent-mindedly Craig picked up the compass. I was amazed to see him take off the glass cover, lift the needle carefully off the pivot. What was he going to do next? He looked at the little needle carefully and at length. What was there in that thing that demanded so much attention? Louise was sitting quietly near me. The sobbing from the next room was stilled. The aroma of cigar smoke was still wafted in from the porch outside, but the pacing had ceased.

Suddenly the little needle dropped into the sand.

I was exasperated. "Now you have lost it for the kid!"

Kennedy leaned over calmly, with a smile, hands in his pockets, seeking where it had fallen. He took one hand from his pocket, poked around the sand with his finger, pushing the little needle about.

Suddenly he tired of that diversion and just stared at the wall before him—vacantly, I thought. The table happened to be placed against the wall, on the boudoir side.

His coolness was exasperating. Even Louise began to feel tired of the childish actions. Stanley Kane on the porch was becoming more restless. He might have been wondering how he was to make his get-away without those customary verbal pyrotechnics. He had taken to coughing, a dry, significant cough. He wanted to go—but was afraid of starting a fight, hysteria, trouble of some kind. No man lightly starts something he knows he is unprepared to finish.

Again Kennedy leaned over the sand-box. I moved across impatiently, by his side, touched his arm.

"Let's beat it," I whispered. "We are in a devil of a position!"

Craig merely looked incomprehensively at me. "This is interesting, Walter. I haven't played with a compass like this for ages. Look in the sand box."

Bored, I leaned over impatiently. I could see nothing thrilling or particularly entertaining in that table of Band and a needle. I was fed up on nurseries.

Everything was so quiet that even the softly modulated tones of Craig's voice were carried out of the room. I knew, because everything was so quiet on the porch that the occupant of the porch must be listening to every syllable that was said. Of one thing I felt sure. He wasn't hearing much. Nor was the occupant of that boudoir, listening through the slightly open door.

"See how the sand sticks to that needle. Isn't it interesting?"

I looked again. It was true. Three or four particles of black sand had adhered to the needle. Kennedy was studying the particles carefully.

"It's only the usual black sand one sees in the white beach sand," I remarked. "Nothing very wonderful in that. I used to go down to the shore with my horseshoe magnet, when I was a kid, and pick up the black sand grains in the white."

Craig regarded me, absorbed in the needle and the sand, apparently oblivious to the drama that was going on in the old Kane house.

"Yes, it is black sand. Black sand has some iron in it. That's what makes the magnet pick it up. Yes. But not the usual black sand. I noticed it yesterday when I was here, too, when the top of the compass fell off and the needle dropped in the sand. It gave me an idea. I picked off several grains, under my finger nail, analyzed a few of the particles up in the laboratory, this morning. These," he added, with provoking calmness, "are little vanadium steel filings. And Mrs. Kane's safe is made of vanadium steel!"

If it had been quiet before, the silence now was such that one could feel it thunder.

"What!" I exclaimed, sharply, impulsively, in surprise.

My exclamation sounded like the bursting of a shell, to my own strained feelings. I fancied, too, I heard some one in the next room, the boudoir. Doris Kane must be near the door. Was she listening in palpitating fear? Even Louise seemed interested at last. She had turned and was watching Kennedy as closely as I had been. Out on the porch I could almost feel the constraint.

Kennedy was through with the sand box. He sauntered over to the manual-training work-bench, his interest now seemingly galvanized on the tools. Some he picked up and discarded quickly. Others he left in a little pile by themselves.

"These tools don't belong to the other set," he motioned, as he pointed with a quizzical smile to some he had placed by themselves. "You see, these are really for children. But these—are rather mature—and not so new. Quite a heavy hammer to have for a boy. And this chisel has had recent strenuous use—possibly not by a child."

Fascinated, I watched Kennedy. I might have known him better. Always before, when his actions had seemed most vapid, most stupid, he had suddenly burst forth with a brilliant light that dispelled the darkness.

"Even Junior noticed the presence of these alien tools, as I may call them, although he said nothing about them to me, when he was showing me about the nursery."

I listened to the sounds in the next room. Some one there was evidently straining to listen better through the crack of the door.

"When he came to the work-bench he quietly separated the tools, as I am doing now. His he put away. These he left to be put away by some one else later, as he thought, evidently. Even a child will lead us to a clue." Kennedy smiled gently toward Louise and me, the only ones in the room he could see or talk to, directly.

My patience was being strained to the breaking point. I

wanted to know who had taken the jewels. Would he never get to it?

Quietly he picked up the hammer and the chisel from the little pile of tools he had laid to one side. He walked slowly across the room. Suddenly he hit the plaster board a sharp blow. It sounded ominous—a fateful blow for some one involved in the crime. I expected Doris Kane to shriek. Instead there was a significant silence on the other side, in the boudoir.

"This plaster board is easy for some one with determination, a fair amount of strength, persistence, and a sufficient motive to take down—and put up again—as has been done here....

"You see, Walter, this has been tampered with. The lath has been removed—and then replaced. I'll show you."

Stepping lightly up on the sand table, Craig set to work. In a short time he had removed the section of plaster board that was on the other side, back of Doris Kane's wall safe. Plainly now, as he had reasoned, could be seen the work of the thief.

"The back of the safe has been drilled with an electric drill," he pointed out. "Some one must have reasoned, 'Who ever will look closely at the back of a wall safe?' From this side the jewels have been removed. Then the back has been replaced, cemented on, merely, held there from the outside, the whole back."

He wiped his face slowly with his handkerchief, then turned to us. "Now, I know I'm right. It was an inside job!"

With cool deliberation Kennedy stooped and picked up the little needle from the sand in the sand box at his feet. He replaced it on its pivot, still with the grains of steel filings on it. It swung again, slowly, but without difficulty.

He stepped off the table. In a second Kennedy was the man of action, the quick thinker.

"Jack Rushmore's valet,—the gentleman's gentleman,—has a record as a cracksman." He bowed. "Your husband, Louise— *alias* Layton. You have a little record, too, at headquarters. My friend, Deputy O'Connor, with the description of the jewels from the insurance company, has located, identified the pearls, unstrung, and the other stones, unset, in the possession of old Mandelbaum, the fence. Mandelbaum says they were sold to him by a man and a woman, Sunday afternoon. Sunday was your day out. The descriptions tally, too."

He was not looking at Louise. Rather he seemed absorbed in the needle of the compass, watching it until it came to rest.

"This needle points north—and north of this city, up the river, is Sing Sing, too!"

For the first time he looked her squarely in the eye, the bobbed-haired safe-cracker.

"Go get your hat, Louise!"

The girl trembled, held her hands nervously to her face, stood hesitating.

"Please don't tell anyone! Don't let my mistress know!" Some think of curious *non-sequiturs* in a crisis.

"All right," gravely agreed Craig. "Get your hat!"

Louise started up the stairs to her room, beside the children.

"Craig," I whispered, fearfully, "she'll get away!"

He shook his head. "No other exit in this part of the house."

"She may commit suicide—jump," I persisted.

He shrugged, as if he would leave that open if she preferred it.

From out on the porch came Kane, his eyes now fairly bulging, his cigar out.

"O'Connor assures me," forestalled Craig, "that the police will get the stuff back, all of it, from the fence, Mandelbaum." He paused. "But even that won't settle things… will it?"

Stanley Kane was still frowning unhappily. "N-no," he admitted, reluctantly.

Kennedy put his hand on Kane's shoulder. "Stan—for me—please go in—tell Doris—tell her how you really feel—not your pose, Stan—how you really feel."

Kane was still frowning uncomfortably, undecided.

I could hear the nervous step of Louise coming back down the stairs.

The door of the boudoir moved, then stopped. A hand had pushed it out. But the hand did not close the door again.

There was the light sound of the sleeping children, above.

"Kennedy, you're a brick!... I will!"

SOUTH

"I'VE SENT FOR you first, Kennedy, first, even before the police, I own this building, live in it. It's always been above reproach. And I want it known that Jerry Watkins is always on the watch for the safety of his tenants. If it was a prowler, a thief, no matter who it was, I want him caught. I want criminals to understand that there is a deadline about my properties beyond which they must fear to go!"

It seemed that the very stairs of the Studio Building palpitated as I followed Kennedy from creaking tread to creaking tread. Ahead of me, Craig was following a rather stout, florid individual, this same Jerry Watkins, owner of the building.

We were mounting to the top floor, where the famous artist, Norman Norcross, had his studio—mounting toward what?

The janitor had told Watkins; Watkins had got in immediate touch with Kennedy; and Kennedy and I had hurried downtown.

For the janitor had caught just a keyhole glimpse of Norcross, lying on the floor of his studio, motionless, in a pool of blood.

Jerry Watkins opened the door with his pass key. The heavy drapes at the windows were still undrawn. No light penetrated through the darkness to lift the somber shadows of tragedy. It was still—too still. Almost, I imagined, the man's spirit might be hovering about to assist us in the search for the murderer.

Where was he?

It was Kennedy who relieved the tenseness. His pocket flash

swept a quick semicircle of light about the studio floor. Light should have overcome the morbidity. It merely seemed to accentuate it.

There, on the floor, eyes staring up at the ceiling, arms outstretched like a human cross as if he would still have protected the picture he was painting, lay what only a few hours before had been gay, debonaire Norman Norcross.

Dark hair, thick and curly, the kind women love to run their fingers through, fell about his forehead in a tangled mass. This man had loved life. But here was death overtaken him, death in its grimmest form.

Watkins found the switch and flooded the room with light.

Evidently Norcross had been painting when the murderer appeared. There was all the evidence, too, of a terrific struggle that had ended so tragically for the artist.

He still wore his smock, covered with smudges of color that he had used in his work. But, crying out above all the marks of his work, were the vivid stains of the artist's life blood as it had trickled down from the wound in his breast—red—deep red.

"I must keep things as they are for the police," muttered Craig, busily absorbed in his examination of the body, everything that surrounded it. Nothing seemed to escape him, though he touched nothing.

"I wonder what was used to kill him?" I murmured, bending over, after Craig.

"Here it is. It has been thrown in this pile of drapery."

I moved over in Kennedy's direction. There, as if thrown in either fear or horror, was a quaint dagger, a dainty work of metallic art, picked up, no doubt, in some antique shop. It was lying in the folds of a beautiful pile of rose chiffon and gauze. The blood was coagulated but still moist on the cold metal blade. What a setting for so ghastly an object!

"He must have been working on this picture. Some of that paint is scarcely fixed." Craig called my attention to the canvas on an easel.

In spite of the horror of the surroundings, I paused, fascinated. Never had I seen a more beautiful girl than the one taking form on the canvas before me.

"Do you know who that is?" Watkins asked it with the tone of one who himself knew.

"No," I admitted, only to be interrupted by Craig, with his wide acquaintance and uncanny memory for faces. "I heard her sing last week. At the opera. Marcel Loti. Not only can she act. Loti can sing. She had created a furore. They tell me that next season her *répertoire* will include all the coveted soprano roles."

Watkins nodded.

"So," I repeated, "that is Marcel Loti!" Still gazing with a sort of fascination at the canvas, I added, "Think of having a face, a form like that—and the voice of a nightingale!"

Watkins nodded again. "Yes, Loti. She used to come down to see Norcross every day. They seemed to be wildly in love with each other. They were like two children. I never saw Norcross like that with any other girl—and I've seen him with a good many!"

I was watching the face of Watkins keenly.

"Did he have many visitors?" asked Kennedy.

"I should say he did. He was the kind of man who made many friends. The women all liked him. But the men—well, there have been many rumors of trouble. Maybe you have heard some of the gossip?"

Kennedy nodded. As for me, I was too engrossed now in the portrait of Marcel Loti to pay much attention to the ramblings of Watkins.

Marcel Loti had youth, and Norcross had caught the spirit of it. It breathed in the exquisite modeling of her arms and hands, the very posture of the graceful body, and the fairy-like lightness of the slender limbs suggested through the folds and draperies of the pink chiffon.

"Look!" I exclaimed, coming back to earth. "She is draped in the same chiffon! That pile of stuff where the dagger is must be what Marcel Loti wore when she was posing."

Kennedy nodded, then looked inquiringly at Watkins.

Watkins understood. "Yes, Kennedy. Now I come to think of it, I've seen that dagger on the little desk Norcross used over there in the corner. He used it to open letters and as a paper cutter."

My eyes wandered back to the picture, avoiding the THING now on the floor.

Hair that was golden, but not too fine, the kind I have seen some women have which seemed charged with electricity. No two hairs would keep together. It made a delightfully golden fluffy mass like an aureole. The eyes were beautiful—great dark eyes of rich brown, with a hint of witchery, fascination, passion—eyes that one would expect to see in Sicily or in Spain in the very young. They seemed to glow with a tender questioning of life, as of a dream unfolding. What messages must have been flashed from the eyes of Norcross to those of Marcel in these intimate sittings!

I shook my head. "If a girl ever looked at me like that," I exclaimed, "I'd never be able to paint!"

She was standing out of doors in the sunshine, the wind inflating the folds of her draperies like the sails of a bark. A tender smile on her parted lips showed a line of ivory teeth gleaming between the roses.

She was holding in her hand a bitten peach. One could see the marks of her teeth on its painted surface. Casually, the remarkably natural color of the peach struck me.

Back of her and above her the deep blueness of the sky and the dazzling white of the clouds combined to set off the girl. What a marvel Norcross was with color! This portrait was as fresh, as full of vigor as morning, as youth itself.

The studio was a large room, with a wall of glass for the prized north light.

About the sides, on three other walls, ran a narrow gallery.

Everything suggested success. On the walls were many paintings and works of art, collected by Norcross abroad while he was studying under the best teachers in France and Italy.

One end of the studio was devoted to work. Here were unfinished canvases, cases for colors, and art materials. Thrown about in artistic confusion were palettes, brushes—all the things used in his work. And Norcross was a worker.

Critics had called Norcross the "thinking artist." His work pulsated with life, breathed culture. Always these qualities predominated above mere manual dexterity.

Old tapestries, rare embroideries, and rarer laces, some, no doubt, filched from churches and monasteries centuries ago during turbulent religious struggles, were draped or hung about the walls or suspended from the gallery rail. Their arrangement and manner of draping were so skillfully accomplished, done in such an exquisite way, that it seemed to me a pity that the artist's ability in this direction had been confined to his own studio and not loaned to some of the larger collections in the city. Furniture, bronzes, and old ivories, all of them fit for museums, rivaled one another in interest and beauty and profusion.

I saw why women of wealth and culture delighted in visiting Norcross. His charms and persuasive qualities, his gentle deference to women long past the age of romance had opened wide the doors of the socially elect.

I picked up a memorandum book pushed under the base of a lamp on the table. It seemed to contain notes and information about his work.

Among the things written last on its pages, evidently uppermost in his mind, were some scribbled thoughts on the elusive qualities in Marcel Loti's beauty that evidently he felt he must attempt to transfer to the canvas. There was the suggested title of the picture, "Peaches and Cream."

My glance strayed from the vibrant beauty of the singer so wonderfully depicted in marvelously chosen and blended pigments to the tragic figure on the floor. Those eyes gazing up seemed still to be seeking the love light gleaming in the eyes of

Marcel Loti. Even the film of death could not conceal the fact that death had come and ended his one last endeavor to win and keep his sweetheart's smile.

The pallor of his face and hands had robbed his body of that virile look, but one could imagine in life the hard muscles now stiffened in death. Those arms had clutched frantically and held close for the last time the beautiful girl in the picture.

Kennedy came close to me and peered long at the portrait. "Norcross *could* paint women!" he muttered. "He was *the* woman painter!… But there is more than skill in this portrait. If ever Norcross put his soul, his life into his work, he has done it here. That girl made Norcross give of himself. It's the best thing he has ever done. Before, his work was for the material rewards of life, ambition to succeed. But this is a work of love. It was born in the greatest emotion the man had ever known—and executed by fingers touched with a tender skill. It shows through. You can see that."

On the floor near him was a palette, evidently the one he had used last.

"Look!" I exclaimed. "There are the colors he was using for that peach! No wonder the girl smiles over that bite. I've never seen a peach in life look like that!"

Kennedy's back was to me. "Don't say again you never saw a peach like that. Here is one. It's lying here on the floor. Did you ever see more exquisite coloring?"

One side of the fruit, not too large, but unusually well developed and apparently juicy, seemed to have absorbed all the red and orange and yellow of many sunrises and sunsets. It was perfect, flawless. And out of it only one bite had been taken— the counterpart of the bite portrayed in the picture.

There it was, under a table, as if it had been knocked over in the scuffle that must have taken place before Norcross had been stabbed. Or else it had been flung there, as the dagger had been tossed into the chiffon.

Then I noticed about the floor broken brushes, tubes of color, cloths, all the paraphernalia of a working artist. It seemed as if some one in indignation had swept the table clear and in an ungovernable rage had trod on the mute objects of its wrath.

Craig continued his search about the room, in the corners, under the furniture, about the walls. He even opened the drawers of the desk and peered into chests about the room.

"I notice one thing characteristic of Norcross. He was worldly wise—or else somebody has beaten me to it. I can find no old letters."

Watkins shook his head. "Kennedy, Norcross never kept anything like that. I have talked with him a lot. Always he was intimate, free with women. But over them he possessed a cynicism that used to make even me furious. He smiled and used women for his own advantage. But he never allowed them to use him. You couldn't get that man to write a sentimental note or letter—and he never kept those he received."

"I see." Kennedy nodded reflectively. "His philosophy of conduct toward women was not very flattering to the sex."

"I should say not. And the worst of it was, the women never knew it. But every man could see it. That's why he had so few personal friends among men. Most men thought him a cad."

"But how he could use a brush!"

Watkins nodded back. "I heard him say once at a luncheon of a woman's club," he went on, recollecting, " 'Every woman is loved by a lover, a husband, or a son—some one whose tenderness discovers in her a charm, an attraction to which others may be insensible. I ask myself, when I undertake to paint the portrait of a woman, how to please her.'"

"Yes," agreed Craig, "and he usually ended in making them love him. But he caught their elusive personality. He always made good on the portrait—even though the heart of the subject might break afterward!"

Watkins shook his head vigorously. "But it wasn't that way with Marcel Loti. He loved her, I tell you, desperately. I could see it. He was furiously jealous of her. He raved over any attention she received from other men. I have watched them. She would laugh at him. He would storm about in anger. Then Marcel would put her arms about him tenderly—and the storm would be over."

Kennedy was following intently. "At last he was in the position he had placed many other men and was feeling the heart aches he had made many women feel."

"But this is—awful!" Watkins shivered, almost, as he looked again at the dead artist.

Suddenly Craig stooped over and picked up what looked like a piece of glass from the floor not far from the body. Curiously I watched him as he took it over to the light. It seemed to be a piece of a broken lens from an eye-glass.

"Norcross never wore glasses," exclaimed Watkins, excitedly.

"But," I jumped to the conclusion, "that is a piece of lens from somebody's eye-glasses... possibly from the murderer's!"

It was the only clue, to my knowledge, that we had found so far, this piece of lens. I was keenly excited about it. Craig rather disappointed me in his merely casual interest in it, however.

"What are you going to do to trace it, Craig?" I urged.

He merely smiled. "I might go to every lens maker and oculist in New York. But then there would be those of Los Angeles— and possibly London. I might find the prescription in the first place—or out in Kalamazoo But I'll keep it. It may help."

He was back again, admiring the peach in the picture. He drew my attention to the naturalness of the coloring through the fuzz.

In fact there was such a display of artistic criticism about the peach—and none about the girl—that I was restive. I felt anxious to do a little detecting on my own concerning that lens. In that, it seemed to me, he had a clue, perhaps a difficult clue, but nevertheless something real, tangible. Now I was expected to listen raptly to a rhapsody on a tinted peach in a picture!

I might have been more willing to let the lens wait in order to listen to an appreciation of Marcel Loti. But that was not forthcoming. Nothing but peaches.

"Craig," I interrupted at last, a bit exasperated, "there on that canvas is a girl—in my vernacular, a peach of a girl. In her I am interested. But peaches—I can buy a basket at the first fruit stand, yellow Albertas, Delaware peaches, wonderful California peaches—for three dollars—maybe less."

There was no more use for Canute to order the tide to halt than for me to try to curb Kennedy in his raving enthusiasm over the talent of Norman Norcross in painting peaches. It couldn't be done. I had to listen. In fact, I had to like it. Almost, I felt, I could have sat down and painted that peach. There wasn't a tint, an outline, a shadow that Craig failed to expatiate upon.

When he had finished, I exclaimed, "Well, now, what about the lens?"

He stook his head absently. "There are probably thousands of them in the world just like or nearly like this one. Try it yourself."

I felt suddenly chagrined about my good idea. There is nothing that so takes the wind out of one's sails in a case of this sort quite like, "Well, try it yourself!" I was silent.

Kennedy had been regarding the portrait, his mind, however, now on the girl of it.

"Did anyone ever visit the studio with Marcel Loti, do you know?" he asked Watkins.

"Yes. Not long ago. A man… I think his name was Bullard. Yes. He came with Miss Loti to see the picture. Norcross was violently angry. Bullard didn't stay long. Bullard and Norcross loved each other like a couple of wild cats."

"So—there was a jealous man!" I exclaimed.

"Lee Bullard, a construction engineer, rather famous," nodded Watkins.

"I'm going to see Marcel Loti," remarked Kennedy, thoughtfully. "Watkins, you had better get the police in now. I have done all I can—here."

Kennedy began by looking up addresses. It did not take long to discover that Marcel Loti lived in the Opera Apartments.

It was more of a surprise to me, then, when I found that Kennedy was bending his steps to the Felton, a well-known new bachelor apartment. I understood the reason when he asked the hallboy for Mr. Lee Bullard.

"Mr. Bullard left on the Midnight Limited for Chicago, sah," was all he could get out of the boy.

Still another cross-town trip brought us to the Grand Central section of Park Avenue where the architects and builders and engineers hold forth. Craig was calling at the office of the Craven Company, contracting engineers, where Bullard was next in control.

In as business-like a tone as if he had under his arm a million-dollar construction job to let, he asked for Mr. Bullard. A very efficient young lady appeared.

Here, too, the answer was the same as at the apartment.

"I am Mr. Bullard's secretary. Mr. Bullard left last night for Chicago, on our Lake Shore job. Is there anything I can do for you, Mr. Kennedy?"

"Thank you so much. No, I'm afraid not. By the way, when did he leave?"

"At midnight, on the Central."

"I see. Too bad." Kennedy, while we were standing in the reception room, had been studying vacantly a flashlight photograph of some engineers' dinner. His eye wandered toward it again. "Is Mr. Bullard in that?" he asked, casually.

"Yes—right... there he is." The secretary laid her pencil on the figure of a rather athletic young man in evening clothes seated with some others at one of the white tables. There was a bit of distortion and some halation, as in many of these dinner pictures. But we could make him out well enough. The face was that of a man accustomed to rule men, from even days of prep school football captaincy.

I stared at just one thing, however. He was wearing big horn-rimmed glasses—"cheetahs."

Kennedy said nothing, bowed himself out, and outside remarked, merely: "Now for the Opera Apartments. I have satisfied myself of one thing."

At last we were waiting in the little reception room at the apartment of Marcel Loti. The maid had disappeared into an adjoining room, ostensibly to work, but, somehow, I had the uncomfortable fancy that we were being watched.

Soon down the hall we could hear footsteps and a wonderfully sweet voice singing softly a little French *chanson*.

At the door Marcel Loti halted, making one of those quick little bows that delighted the audiences every time she appeared after an *encore*.

She laughed lightly as she intuitively identified Kennedy in the pair of unpardonably early visitors. Her beautiful teeth showed a glint of ivory between her coral lips.

There was an air of expectation, a spirit of exhilaration, that seemed to permeate the very room which she entered and lifted the spirits of us both buoyantly. The richness of her full, carefully enunciated tones betrayed the singer's training. Her words, the commonest of them, had life.

Kennedy and I bowed to her beauty, her grace. She was young, about twenty-two, I fancied, the most radiantly beautiful creature I had ever seen. Some orchid-colored morning gown illuminated her face, spreading over its creamy whiteness a flush of rose.

As she stood, Kennedy moved over and placed a big chair. There was nothing presumptuous about it even in a stranger. It was done as thoughtfulness.

"May I ask you to be seated while I talk?" he anticipated. "I fear that some of what I have to say may be hard to bear."

Marcel startled suddenly. Her dark eyes glowed with anxiety as she regarded Craig. She clutched her heart dramatically.

"Wh-what is it?" she asked, suddenly. "I want to know—and

yet I have a feeling it is bad news for me. Why does a woman's heart betray her so? Is it—about Norman—Norman Norcross?"

"Are you strong, Miss Loti?" Craig looked her steadily in the eye for a few seconds before he replied, sympathetically: "Yes, I have come from Mr. Norcross. He—"

She rose in her excitement. "He has sent for me? Call Celeste. I'll go right away."

Kennedy raised a warning hand. "No, Miss Loti, he hasn't sent."

Marcel's eyes opened wide in sudden terror. Then she covered her face with the same beautiful hands I had admired in the picture.

"Not sent for me? Then—Norman must be too ill. He would want me." It was said with the dignified simplicity of a woman sure of her lover. Suddenly a new idea seized her. She took Kennedy's arm in her agitation. Almost in a whisper she asked: "What is it? Is he—" She could not finish the sentence. Death and Marcel Loti were so alien to each other that her lips even refused the word.

Kennedy's continued silence told her the answer. The color faded from her cheeks. She swayed slightly, but with an effort regained her poise for the instant. "How?" she asked, simply.

"No one knows, Miss Loti—not even the police. They have just been summoned."

"Police?" she cried.

Craig nodded.

"Why the police? Has he been hurt?"

"Miss Loti, Mr. Norcross is dead. He died before your portrait. I have heard you were... lovers. So I came to tell you first—and to try to get your help.... Can you tell me whether he had had any quarrel with anyone recently? Have you ever heard that he feared anyone?"

"Fear anyone? Norman was afraid of nothing!" She said it in pride in spite of her agitation. Still it seemed as if she could not realize that her lover had been taken away from her. She looked at Craig helplessly, hopelessly. "I was to have luncheon with Norman—to-day!"

The tears rolled down her cheeks now, unheeded. Her hands were clasping and unclasping each other alternately. She seemed as if she hardly knew what to do next. It was pitiful to see her grief. Regardless of appearance, she sank into the big chair, her face buried in its broad arms, sobbing and listening alternately to Craig's story. He told her as gently as he could. But such a message, no matter how tactful the bearer, is like piling a weight on the heart of a woman who loves.

"Is there—anything I can do for Norman now?" She finally lifted her tear-stained face and cried.

"No. They wouldn't let you, yet. But I want to ask you a few questions. I wonder whether you could tell me something about the relations between Norman Norcross and Lee Bullard?"

Marcel Loti colored slightly, but faced Kennedy quite frankly. "If I say anything, it might hurt Lee Bullard—and I don't know enough to permit me to say anything that would hurt anybody else!" She stopped abruptly.

I wondered at her reticence. Could she be shielding Bullard for some unknown reason? I wondered, too, if she knew that Bullard had left town.

It was evident the girl was hurt sorely at the news. Yet it was strange she could think of Bullard's safety at the time of her lover's death, I thought—when Bullard might possibly be the murderer, also. Women were a puzzle to me. When I began to study their psychology I was beyond my depth.

"But Lee Bullard was jealous of Norcross, was he not?" persisted Kennedy.

She looked at him still tearfully. "All the men I know very well were jealous of Norman. But he was more jealous of them. He wanted me only for himself—and I was willing. Of course it made hard feelings. But I never saw anything that might have suggested—murder." She shuddered.

"Didn't Lee Bullard and Norcross have a fight once in his

studio while you were there?" Craig put the question kindly but firmly.

"Yes," she hesitated, "they did—and over me. What of it? It wasn't the first time men have fought over a woman."

"And Bullard threatened Norcross that he would get him, didn't he?" Craig was building. But she did not know that. His information seemed rather to worry her.

"He threatened Norman only after Norman had called him everything on the calendar—and ordered him from the studio." Marcel was trying hard to justify both. "But Norman didn't mean those things. I was an obsession with him, I suppose.... And I loved his jealousy—although it worried me, too. It delighted me to think I was loved so deeply by such a wonderful man—and then when I stopped to think about it, I wondered where it was all going to end... Now it is over... I... I feel... lost!"

"When did you see Lee Bullard last?" asked Craig.

"Last night, for a short time." She said it reluctantly and seemed to cut it short, perhaps to have told it before she thought.

"Did he mention Norcross, anything about him?" went on Craig.

"Y-yes, in a way. He wanted me to give him up, of course. He wanted me to marry him. But I loved Norman deeply. I could do nothing but refuse Lee, again."

"Was he angry when you parted?"

Marcel shook her head wearily at the continued questioning. "Of course he was. He always was when I refused him... But, Mr. Kennedy, I am weary, broken-hearted. I feel as if I have been the cause of Norman's death, as if he had died for me. Now please don't make my words condemn another man to death. Don't twist them. Let me be alone—with my grief. I can't stand much more!"

The girl showed the strain of her sorrow. Her eyes were wells of tragedy. The flaming redness of her lips was the only color visible on her beautiful face.

"And I must sing to-night!" she repeated, forlornly.

She rose slowly, called her maid, and left us. I watched her as she passed up the hall, every step the poetry of motion—but the poetry that brings the tears, rather than the smiles.

We were silent as we left the place. Kennedy asked me finally whether I had noticed the apartment. I stopped to think of the strangeness of the fact. For once I had met a woman whose personality was so charming, so overwhelming, that it transcended her mere surroundings.

"I've talked to Watkins, his landlord, and Marcel Loti, his lover," considered Craig. "If Bullard had been in town I should certainly have talked to his rival. I won't go back to that studio. The police are there by now, messing things up beautifully, and Watkins doesn't know anything more than he has told, I am sure. He seems to have a gossipy knowledge of some of the women Norcross knew, but very little about the men. Surely Norcross must have had some friends among the men in his own profession. I would like to learn something of the man's past, something about him when he was in Europe studying, or even before that, before he had made good."

"Why don't you stop in at the Berkeley Gallery, then? Berkeley always exhibited the work of Norcross, was always delighted to get a finished piece from him. It meant a quick and profitable sale." This much I could tell Craig with certainty. The art critic on the *Star* would thrill for a week over a new canvas by Norcross. "Let's stop in. Berkeley will know, if anybody knows."

In a few minutes we were in Berkeley's private office.

"I can't believe it, Mr. Kennedy!" gasped the amazed art dealer. "It doesn't seem possible that that genius has been cut down in the beginning of his career. He would have gone far!"

"I want to work fast on this case, Mr. Berkeley," explained Craig. "I don't want the murderer to cover up his tracks successfully. I want to find out who the intimate friends of the artist were besides Marcel Loti. You can get important evidence from those who know the life and habits of a man."

Berkeley knitted his brows. "Oh, he had several friends in

his profession—Gruby, A.C. Lawrence, and Micello, the young Italian."

Kennedy was jotting the names down on a card.

"Any of those men could tell you more about him than I could. They knew his habits, his manner of living, much about his intimate affairs. Then, of course, there is Harriet Amory. She recognized his ability from the first, you know," Berkeley advised as an afterthought.

"You mean Miss Amory, the daughter of old Jarvis Amory, the banker?" I asked.

"The same. She has befriended many a poor devil in the Latin Quarter. Over in France so much of her time, you know. She makes it a business to help those Americans who show real talent. Norcross was poor, but a genius. She just pushed him along, provided the best teachers, gave him money to travel a bit, to sit at the feet of the old masters, as it were, and learn from their marvelous creations. His success verified her judgment. She rarely goes wrong. She has been a big sister to many a struggling American artist, has won their love, belongs as an honorary member to all their clubs and organizations, and all that."

Kennedy nodded. "I have often heard about her. She did a lot toward rebuilding devastated France after the war, too—sort of good Samaritan to everybody in hard luck —quite the opposite of her father down in the Street. I think you're right, Berkeley. I'll try to see her. She is more likely than anyone else to know just the things in his life that I want to find out about."

Berkeley nodded. "I know she's out at her country-place now. I saw her in her car on the Avenue shopping last week. She's down near Southampton. Wonderful place there."

Kennedy jumped up. "I'm going right down there, before it occurs to the police to get to her. They will learn of Harriet Amory, just as they have no doubt of Marcel Loti, already. They'll get her antagonized by their methods; she'll shut up like an oyster—won't say a word." He shook his head. I knew he was thinking how things must be going by now with the hammer-

and-tongs quizzing of Marcel. "I want to keep just a jump and a half ahead of them. It's the only way."

"I wonder if the news will precede us—or shall we have that all over again?" I considered, as we started in Craig's roadster.

Kennedy merely shrugged.

As we turned into the wonderful driveway of the Amory estate, I looked about me in admiration. Straight from the gate for a long distance was a beautiful hard yellow-pebbled road bordered on each side by rows of trees uniform in size and symmetrical in shape. The lawn on each side of the road was dotted profusely with the vivid orange of the butterfly weed, making a brilliant contrast with the bright green of the well-kept grass.

Up the road we sped. Around a turn, we found the tree-bordered drive led directly to the white-pillared mansion.

A porch extended the length of the house. In the rear the grounds sloped down in terrace after terrace. A profusion of shrubbery, evergreens, and flowers, had turned the spot into fairyland. It was a high brick Colonial mansion betraying wealth, distinction, hospitality.

Harriet Amory was decidedly informal. She met us outside, in her garden, evidently coming in from some real work. I must admit I was startled at her appearance. I had half expected to see a woman dignified, well along in years, overburdened with the weight of social position and many charities.

But Harriet Amory was cast in a different mold. The war had brushed away every shred of social stiffness and class distinction. Her mingling with youthful artists, painters, musicians, had given her a viewpoint on life that refused to allow her to grow old. Her hair was decidedly gray, but abundant, and she wore it in a buoyant bob. Deep, throaty, but unusual tones booming with good nature characterized her greeting of us. Her eyes were blue, deep blue, surmounted by the blackest of lashes, a striking incongruity, I thought, with the grayness of her hair.

Harriet Amory's personality was such that khaki knickers in

the afternoon created no surprise. She had been working, had adopted working togs, and somehow she and those clothes gave dignity to labor.

Brushing her hands lightly, gleaming white teeth parted in a smile of welcome, she remarked to Kennedy, "If I had expected callers from the city this afternoon I should not have gone out to work. But do come into the house. You see, this garden is my hobby out here in Southampton."

We followed her into the cool depths of the house. Everywhere one looked, Harriet Amory's personality seemed to invite. Cool, sturdy, reliable chairs, suggesting the woman herself, were about.

"Now, Mr. Kennedy, what is it?" she asked, as we settled ourselves. "Your face is so serious, I know you have something of importance to tell me. Don't hesitate. I know the signs. I have been the confidante of many a fine boy over in France."

There was a detachment surrounding Harriet Amory that seemed to lift her and her personal affairs out of the ordinary. She seemed to be like a guardian angel hovering solicitously over the lives of others, with no entanglements of her own life to interfere with her benefactions. Yet she seemed a warm-hearted, big-hearted woman.

"My news isn't public news yet. Miss Amory," began Kennedy, as if in some doubt just how to break the shock of it. "You see, Mr. Berkeley of the Berkeley Galleries suggested your name to me—as one who might know something of the life and friends of the artist, Norman Norcross."

She nodded curiously, with just a suggestion in it to proceed. Kennedy cleared his throat. But before he could go on she interrupted him: "Mr. Norcross is a genius. A few years more will see him received as the greatest painter the States have produced in this generation. I am an enthusiast over the work of Norcross. Over there is a picture he painted of me. He was much younger when he did that."

We looked. There Harriet Amory was, in the golden age of

woman. She was attired in the costume of a French nurse. Out of her eyes shone a compassionate understanding for all the woes of Europe, and a desire to relieve them. There was a directness, an intangible quality of strength in the lovely face that suggested a reservoir of energy and nerve force. Our engrossed silence told her better than words our appreciation of the portrait.

"It's my favorite portrait of myself—a delightful age for a woman to be in—and an exciting time in which to live," she commented, a bit pleased at us, I fancied. "Now I like the quiet on my place here, where I can putter about. When I get tired drawing the best out of my young friends abroad and in New York, I come down here to see what I can do with my flowers and fruit. I am never satisfied with them as they are. I always want to improve them. I yearn for the skill of Burbank."

Craig seemed at once fascinated by Harriet Amory. I could not criticize him, at least, for that. Her cosmopolitan training, her breadth of vision, and her supreme intelligence made her a woman apart. It was a joy to listen to her.

"But *my* hobby isn't *your* hobby. You have something to tell me. What is it?" she asked, directly, again.

"I'm interested in Mr. Norcross," began Kennedy again, seeking a way of breaking the news. "Will you tell me something of his friends and his habits?" he asked, quickly, feeling about.

She looked shrewdly toward me. "Well, good publicity hurts no one. Mr. Jameson, being a good newspaperman, will probably give Mr. Norcross a good write-up, eh? I don't mind telling you what I know about him— His is an interesting life— It takes me back several years—more than I like to think about. Age is the bogie-man of every woman, you know." She rose, gave a slight tug at the bell pull. The butler brought refreshing beverages and some cigarettes.

I couldn't keep my eyes from her, as she sat casually in a big chair, a deep red in color, her striking locks with an impressive background. She leaned far back in the chair puffing for a few minutes at the cigarette. She did not speak until it was time to flip the first ashes. Then an amused little laugh broke her reverie.

"I still smile over that first meeting, Mr. Kennedy. It was early evening when I drove down to the *pension* where he was staying. I was late for an appointment and was running up the dark stairs, when I almost fell over him at the turn. We both laughed, but I was surprised to hear in the darkness the voice of the girl I had come to visit. She was in trouble and had appealed to me. I couldn't do anything but come to the child's assistance.

"She was impetuous and zealous in her work. Her model had become tired of posing, but she hadn't become tired of painting. There was an argument; it ended in a fight and a demand for money on the part of the model. The girl had only a few francs, not enough to satisfy the model. I was late and the model was insistent. In despair my little friend had appealed to Norman Norcross to help her. There they were on the steps, counting their francs like two puzzled, impecunious children. Well, the model was bought off.

"Mr. Norcross asked me if I wanted to see his work. I agreed to look at it, and I recognized his genius even then. It was some simple theme, an old mother, wrinkled and bent, in a rocking chair, alone. In her hand she held a baby's shoe. But one could see the memories in that dear old face. The thing I marveled at was the way his skilled fingers drew her neck. One could almost see the emotion pulling at those withered muscles and filling her throat with suffocating sobs. He has never lost that ability. Just look, when you see his pictures next. The throats and necks of his women are perfect. There was nothing for me to do then but to encourage that young man—and he has gone far beyond my expectations."

I sat back in my chair, charmed by her reminiscences. What stories she might tell of struggling artists, hungry and away from home! Craig was now silently listening.

"In those days young Norcross was such an innocent. He had three or four very good friends besides myself. It was like a family, that little group of happy, industrious, ambitious boys and girls. They knew I was glad to see any progress in their work, and they would come to me for approval and advice. But of them all, young Norcross had the genius, the untiring zeal, the ability to concentrate which the others lacked.

"Then, he had a way with him. Moments when he was discouraged, he would come up to see me and to talk of his parents. When Norman became sentimental over his mother and father, I knew something was wrong. He would finally end in telling me the trouble—the inability to proceed further in his art through lack of funds, generally.

"There was something fine about the boy, too. All that I loaned him he has paid back to me long ago. Always he accepted assistance as a loan, never as a gift. I didn't want to take the money back, but I felt if it helped him in his opinion of himself, I would not be the means to destroy that in the least.

"Nights we would take rides about the city streets. Paris at night was a joy to me. There would always be a gay party of us. I enjoyed the society of these young people. While I was very little older, still it seemed I was of them but not like them. I think I felt their sorrows and triumphs more keenly than even they did.

"The lights, the happy people, the rush and whir of motors, the excitement of seeing others some of us knew, the gay repartee, the artistic atmosphere in which I lived with these young folks, were like a tonic to me. They were like me in one respect. They could see beauty, something in almost every contact of the day. I have been out with them at times when the smallest bit of beauty would inspire a theme for a picture.

"I remember Norman one night getting an idea for a picture that brought him many medals and much honor. I hadn't heard from a friend for some time and we agreed to look the boy up, to see what might be the trouble. We walked over to his studio. Near the building was a florist's. Suddenly Norman touched my arm, stopped. 'Look!' he whispered, quietly. I saw what he meant in an instant. It was a study in contrasts. Only a man with a soul could have seen it and grasped it.

"By the window was a girl, richly dressed, holding some orchids which she had just purchased. Even her admiration was dull, satiated with the rich things of life. By the cellar door on the sidewalk, where the waste was kept, was a sprig, I think it must have been yellow forsythia, a touch of spring which had blossomed through the crack of the side of the cellarway. It was only a few inches high, just one little tiny branch trying to obey in its own way its purpose for existence. Over it, crying with delight, was a dirty little waif, with the dirtiest of faces and the most beautiful eyes imaginable. She could not have been more than six or seven. But there she was dancing up and down in her glee, clapping her hands. Face alight, she leaned over and tenderly drew the sprig out of the crack beside the cellar door. She hugged it to her heart, held it up and kissed it with fervor and all the grace that only a little French child can command.

"Norman's face beamed with sympathy. He hastened to that child and asked her if he could paint her. He gave her a franc to buy more blooms. She gave us her address, and her thrifty parents allowed her to pose for him. The flower-filled windows of the shop were the background. He caught the happy spirit of the child, fresh and eager for simple delights, and the ennui of the young lady, surfeited with the luxuries of life. Those were his themes, all inspiring, nothing debasing.

"And every picture was better than the previous one. His were the singing colors, the wonderful technique, the spiritual outlook on life that existed not in painting Madonnas, but in uplifting ideas that inspire beautiful conduct." She stopped for a minute and drew her hand lightly over her forehead. "It's warm in here, don't you think? I wonder if you would care to walk in my garden with me while I tell you more of his later life—his later work?"

Craig rose, and I was just as delighted. Tempting vistas of those gardens had been the only thing that had distracted me from our charming hostess.

"But don't you think. Miss Amory, with your own poetic soul, your love of the beautiful and fine served as a wonderful inspiration in that early impressionable part of his career?" I asked her. "I wonder if those pictures were his ideas of the world as he saw it through your eyes."

"Possibly my influence helped. I hope so. But to do what Norman Norcross does, one has to have the divine gift of seeing things beautifully, born in one."

Down one of the paved terraces we stopped and gazed about us. To the left was a rock garden gloriously rich and luxuriant. Away in the distance, as much like nature as artificiality could leave it, was a bit of woodland. Here during the progress of the year were found the wild flowers common to Long Island.

"That is my joy in the spring," she exclaimed to us, "All the arbutus I want to look at—and then leave alone. Later the fringed gentians that are appealing to so many wasteful fingers—and down there," indicating with a graceful sweep of her arm, "are my fruit trees—my hobby of all hobbies."

"Do you see much of Mr. Norcross now?" began Craig again, attempting to get at the purpose of his visit.

"Not as I did in France. The artistic atmosphere is so different over there. There is a camaraderie that is strangely lacking here even among the same people. Until recently I have been away. My other interests demanded my time and energy over there. Norman was painting over here. He has had several important commissions and seems extremely busy."

"Do you—er—know his American friends as intimately as those he made over in France?"

"Frankly, no. Partly for the reason I explained, and partly because they are of a new circle. The older one gets, the harder it is to make new intimate friends. I have met many of his friends. But on this side of the water my social duties preclude giving much time to art except as individual cases I hear about need help."

"Do you know Lawrence or Micello?" I asked, thinking of Berkeley's information.

"Micello I like very much—the true artist. He is a young Italian who has struggled to make good and has succeeded. His specialty is landscape work. Lawrence is more versatile—as to both art and morals—not always a good influence. Naturally an artist needs money. Lawrence needs it all the time—always broke. He dabbles with the girls who care for the wild life, and it is already having its effect on his work. If Norman doesn't leave him and his ways alone, his own work will be affected." Harriet Amory was thoughtful.

"Do you know what Norcross is painting now?" asked Craig.

"He told me a short time ago he had an unfinished picture. I believe he thought it was his sincerest work. The portrait he finished last, before that, he received more for than for any other he has ever done. It was a success financially. But it lacked that greater quality, to me—improvement. There is something wrong when a man's work stands still."

Craig nodded in agreement. For a moment the conversation lagged. We were wending our way slowly about the artificial pool. Its lights and shadows as it reflected the shrubs and flowers about it focused our attention.

"Has Mr. Norcross given you permission for this interview about himself?" Miss Amory asked of me. It seemed as if she placed the responsibility for our presence on her estate on my shoulders.

I hesitated and looked quickly at Craig. I did not want to tell a deliberate lie. Such a woman commanded too much respect, too, for deliberate deception. Neither did I want prematurely to betray Craig's purpose in seeking information.

Craig relieved my embarrassment. "No, Mr. Norcross does not know of our visit."

Miss Amory arched her eyebrows suddenly.

"Well, I wonder if he would like it—these intimate things I have told. Possibly he would. Sometimes when one grows great there is a delight in boasting of humble beginnings. It makes the man seem the greater. Then others like to conceal an ordinary origin. That, to me, is a sort of mental degeneracy." Over the rail about the pool she leaned, looking reflectively into its green and silver depths. The breeze tossed her hair lightly and her cheeks glowed with color. "For what publication is the story written, Mr. Jameson?" she asked, in the manner of a woman desirous of entertaining strangers with whom she had little in common.

"I'm not going to have anything published, Miss Amory, as far as I know. I have merely come out with Mr. Kennedy." I smiled.

She looked next at Craig curiously. "Why do you want this information, may I ask? I'll tell you more if you give me a reason."

Kennedy cleared his throat. "I want to know the friends of Norman Norcross because of a grievous wrong that has been done him. Can you tell me about any of his enemies?"

"Wrong? What wrong has been done to him?" She asked it with a sudden anxiety in her tone. Before Craig could enlighten her, she added: "Norman has enemies, of course. Anyone who puts his head a little higher than the multitude invites a club. But his enemies are jealous rivals in his profession. Their enmity would consist in unkind criticism or bickering. Norman has the strength of character to rise above that, to disregard it."

"If it were that alone, he might," Craig added, then went on, solemnly: "But Norman Norcross is dead. His jealous rivals will be troubled no more by his spectacular work."

"Dead! *Dead!* I can't believe it! I will not believe it! Surely you must be having a practical joke!" She half whispered it as her knuckles hardened under the pressure of clutching the rail.

"No, Miss Amory; it is too true. Norman Norcross was killed some time last night. That is why I am so anxious for you to tell me of his associates—all those you know he knew. Were you acquainted with any of his women friends here in America? Anything at all may help."

She seemed to wish to avoid answering that question. As she

struggled with the shock of her emotion, her face became sad and pensive.

"Little did I think, when I rebuked him over that last completed picture when he asked me to see it right after my arrival home, that my plain words would be my last advice to him. I couldn't go against my better judgment. But now I wish I had. His last memory would have been kinder to me, perhaps. It looked like a made-to-order picture, not one inspired—and I told him so."

She turned from the pool and walked silently ahead of us. Of course we respected her grief. Had she not watched over this artist's phenomenal progress quite like a successful horticulturist with some new flower whose beauty he is watching develop from day to day?

Down the steps she walked silently, almost blindly, through a wilderness of flowers. All the flowers I had ever heard my grandmother mention were here in this garden. Old-fashioned coriopsis was wind-blown over snapdragons and zinnias, a riot of colors, a stimulation to the eye. But Miss Amory saw nothing of it. Her thoughts were on the stricken life of her protégé.

Some women take their grief with noise, a hurricane of emotion. Others bite their nails and suffer in silence. But Harriet Amory's expression of grief was quite masculine. She smoked in silence.

"Shall we leave you for a while?" Craig asked, thoughtfully. "You can rejoin us later, at the house."

"No, don't." She turned to us with a sad, sweet smile. "I'm down here, unconsciously, with the things I love best. When I am troubled or pondering some question, I come here. You may consider yourself honored. Only my intimates get past the lily pool."

I looked about. Here was a new method, to me, in vineyards. The grape vines I had known grew on arbors either arched or upright. But these vines were planted with single arbors for each vine. There seemed to be more than a hundred of them, all with the promise of a wonderful harvest.

"That is the way they do it in France," explained Harriet Amory. "You should see the sketch I have of this little vineyard Norman painted for me. It is most exquisite."

Then, I saw, came the fruit trees, a novel scheme for them, too, I thought. They were trained to grow on a wall. How beautiful they looked now. But how much more beautiful they must have been in the springtime in blossom.

"You are surprised at my wall garden? It is common in the old gardens of England, in France, and in Germany. Over there wall fruit is no novelty. And what a price you have to pay for it in the markets!"

Smoking incessantly, but glowing with a certain pride at her possessions, she turned at length to Craig and pointed to some beautiful purple and red plums, extremely large fruit, growing with the branches of the trees trained like vines against the wall, and fastened here and there by pieces of leather to it. One could see how carefully these trees had been set away from the wall then trained toward it, how the soil had been prepared. I remembered now the wall on the outside as we came along the road, where, in its shade, ferns and Alpine flowers grew bordering the estate.

Now as I looked about I felt that this garden might make an Englishman think he was in an estate at home.

Suddenly she turned again to Craig. "You asked me if I knew Norman's friends among the women here. I have met one or two. But I can't say I knew them."

"Who were they?" pursued Craig.

"One was Katherine Holt, the actress, a very charming girl. The other was Marcel Loti, the singer. Both have a wide circle of friends and it is not strange that Norman should be drawn to both." With a quiet smile she added, "I hear they do not like each other."

Craig was listening in silence. Now I noticed we had left the plum trees and were standing before a row of beautiful pears growing in the same attractive fashion. Kennedy waited, surveying them thoughtfully.

"Do you know, Miss Amory," I exclaimed, involuntarily, "this is the first time I have ever thought of fruit trees as anything else than utilitarian—just good for fruit, good to eat, in the fall—and, of course, to enjoy the blossoms for a week or two in the spring. But these are an asset to the beauty of any estate."

"There can't be a dozen wall gardens of any size in America, I imagine," remarked Kennedy. "Certainly none like this—although I believe it is just becoming a fad."

"Yes, some of my friends are adopting the wall garden. I have all kinds of fruit grown this way. It takes time and patience. Much pruning, a seemingly heartless amount of it, and rigid thinning of the fruit in the spring, too, make the wonderful results you see. One doesn't get them in a day. Work, vision, and time are what the wall gardener must possess."

Suddenly I stopped. What had been admiration before at the other specimens of fruit turned into wonder at the glorious sight now. Before us the wall continued over a hundred feet, a hundred feet of wall peaches, just ripening with the largest, most vividly colored peaches it had ever been my privilege to see.

Kennedy was in rapture over them. He seemed to recall the names from English gardens—the Early Beatrice, the Royal George, the Grosse Mignonne and the Sterling Castle, ripening in the order named.

He picked up a padded, cup-shaped fruit picker on a rustic table, with a short handle, toying with it as he talked.

"I suppose," he remarked, "I don't know what those peaches mean to you. Miss Amory."

She smiled wanly back. It was difficult to avoid the hint of Kennedy as he toyed with the fruit gatherer. She picked one, passed it wearily to him.

"Isn't that marvelous coloring?" she murmured. "These trees to me are priceless. Here, Mr. Jameson, is one for you. No, you don't know what these peaches are to me. I have never seen their equal anywhere. I have given of myself in their propagation. I brought them from England eight years ago. They are my pet hobby. Just look at that peach bloom!"

"Yes," murmured Craig, in frank admiration.

She was still holding the peach she had picked for me. Slowly Kennedy reached into his waistcoat pocket.

"It is even more marvelous through a lens!"

Craig passed her the broken piece of lens he had found near the murdered artist's body.

Harriet Amory stared silently at Craig. The peach in her hand dropped to the gravel path. Slowly she took another long puff at her cigarette. Then that fell to the path, too, bitten through in her agitation. Suddenly her eyes fell. The whole life of the woman seemed to depart.

"Miss Amory," began Craig, in a low voice, "you come here when you are troubled. You were here this morning. Were you troubled then?"

She did not answer. Nor did she raise her eyes.

"It rained last night. These half-smoked cigarettes, so many of them, lying about were used this morning—and they are the kind you smoke. I have bought them in France, too."

I didn't think a woman could age in a few moments as she had done. Her eyes shone mistily, tenderly as she looked once on the beautiful peaches.

Again she dropped her head, closed her tired eyes wearily. Craig waited silently. I was aghast at the sudden turn of events.

"My God, Mr. Kennedy!" she exclaimed, striding a step or two at length. "It was more than a woman could bear!" She raised her arms upward, hands clasped, the silent tears creeping down her cheeks. "I had made him, had loved him, given him all! My life and my fortune were his. My friends had helped him, through my influence. At first he worshiped me. Each new picture he painted brought us closer. They were beautiful, happy days and I forgot the world when I was with him.... But we each had our work. The thought of each other stirred us and thrilled us to accomplish great things—until he came back to America—and *she* came into his life!"

"Marcel Loti?" inquired Craig, with a touch of sadness.

"Yes." It was said bitterly. "She had youth, beauty—was a song bird—and I—I had nothing more to give. Norman was by now woman crazy—and I was cast aside....

"I endured his neglect, his silence, as long as I could. I went to see him, to plead for the return of the old days, the old happiness. He was working on *her* portrait. He was painting his new love, painting this beautiful new sweetheart—with my peach in her hand—the peach of the old! *My* peach—from a basket I had sent him! I looked at that picture—and something seemed to snap in my brain. *That girl* had bitten into my peach. It was like biting into my very heart. That peach, that lovely peach turned to acid! I raved. I tried to destroy the picture. I had picked up a paper cutter to slash it—and was going to strike, when Norman tried to stop me—I saw red—and—"

"Why are you telling me this, Miss Amory?" asked Craig, leaning over.

"Because I knew you knew when you came here!"

She paused a moment. The gust of her passionate remembrance had passed. Now she faced cold reality.

"I don't know what you're going to do with me, Mr. Kennedy. I don't care. The sooner it's over, the better—because—oh, Norman, I love you—still!"

Silently now her lips were calling her murdered sweetheart's name—and there was no answering call. It was her worst punishment.

"Every clue had been obliterated," murmured Kennedy, almost to himself, "except the fragment of the lens—and there might be thousands of them all over the world. But the moment I saw that peach I knew there is only one wall garden, in America, with the Royal George, grown with the characteristic exposure—to the south—nowhere else. I, too, knew you knew when I came here!"

She faltered, swayed, caught at a tree to save herself, dragging it down from the wall.

"I doubt, Mr. Kennedy, if I even live to face a mortal judge!"

EAST

"**WHY DON'T YOU** take a hand in the case of that Morehead maid, Jeanette Lafitte, Craig?" I urged, as tactfully as I knew. "It's a wonderful setting for a mystery—this pretty girl dead in some strange fashion, found in the sun room of a millionaire mansion on top of a Fifth Avenue skyscraper. Why, one can build theories all around that!"

Kennedy merely smiled. "No one has called me in. I'm not exactly interested. You know, I never take a case just because it is a case, not even a murder case—unless there is some element of interest in it that gets me personally."

"Well," I persisted, trying to think of some other handle to take hold of, "what do you think of it, then?"

"I don't know anything about it—except what you have told me."

"I didn't mean what do you know. I asked what you thought. Nobody knows anything, yet. There doesn't seem to be a clue, inside or outside the place. Only, I thought you might have an opinion."

Kennedy was not to be betrayed into expressing anything half baked. He smiled again indulgently at my enthusiasm. But that was all. I felt it incumbent on me to keep the idea alive, in the hope that he would commit himself to something.

I had met the Moreheads and it was really at a hint from them that I was feeling out Kennedy. Mrs. Morehead I admired greatly. She was like many of the very wealthy women of to-day, not content just to enjoy an idle, luxurious existence. She had devoted her life to numerous charities and she had never surrendered her artistic interests, while at the same time no one could ever accuse her of neglecting in the slightest degree her family.

I had heard the particulars of the death of the maid only the night before and had called up the Moreheads immediately. Spencer Morehead had confirmed what little was known, just enough to put the idea in my head of getting Kennedy interested in the case. In fact, I could tell from Morehead's manner that nothing would please him more just now than to have Kennedy take hold of the mystery that surrounded the death of the pretty maid, Jeanette.

Scarcely a year before I had seen that the Morehead place had been given a whole page in the Sunday *Star* magazine. Old Morehead was a queer mingling of progress and reverence for the past. The push northward of business in the city had made great changes in his realty holdings. On the site of the Morehead mansion on Fifth Avenue, with its stables down the street, in the rear, had been built this wonderful apartment hotel. On the upper floor Morehead had established his own apartment. And on the roof he had actually laid out a garden, in the midst of which was a great glass sun room, ceiling and side walls of glass, a veritable crystal palace in miniature. It was there that Jeanette Lafitte, the French maid of Mrs. Morehead, had been found.

I had seen the pictures of Jeanette. The face of the girl was the face of an idealist—big eyes, serious and questioning, which, in the photograph, even, seemed to have the quality of haunting one. The eyes, of themselves, had fascinated me. I felt that here was a girl who with proper lighting and direction might have made a motion-picture star. Her oval face, with tiny, shell-like ears peeping from under her boyish bobbed hair, must have been distracting, in life. Her mouth was saucily firm. No one would deny the spirit of this girl, even from merely a newspaper photograph.

"Have they any idea how she died?" asked Craig, casually.

I was encouraged by even this morsel of interest. "From what I could gather from Morehead's conversation over the telephone, they think she was poisoned."

"Poisoned? By what?"

I shook my head. "They don't know. Nor do they know just the time it actually happened. But the medical examiner suggests, I believe, that the death was by some exotic poison. He even hinted that it might be an exhalation, possibly, from some exotic plants in the sun room itself."

I thought that that would fetch Craig. But it didn't. I turned to a pile of Sunday papers which I had not had time to look over and began running through them, not so much to see what they contained as to give my mind a chance to evolve from the subconscious another angle of attack by which to get him interested.

Turning hastily the pages of the rotogravure section of the *Star*, I was startled to catch a picture that might have some remote bearing on the case in that it would enable me to reopen the subject.

"H'm! This is curious, Craig," I prefaced, bending closer. "Look what the *Star* published yesterday. Here's part of an air map of New York—the Central Park area, showing Fifth Avenue. There's the Morehead Apartments, just as distinct as if you were up over them."

Kennedy leaned over the picture with me, then took it up and held it to the light. It was his first real interest in anything I had been saying.

"That's really wonderful, Walter," he remarked, moving over where the light was still better and taking up a lens from the table as he studied the air map. "Aerial photography has certainly made advances since the war—and I thought then some of the photographs were pretty near the last word in the art, when they were enlarged. Who made this?"

"I think you'll find the name on it, in the small type underneath. The Aerial Photo Company."

Kennedy nodded. "I'd like to see the negative of this picture. It has unusual definition. But a good deal has been lost in the process printing. Do you know these Aerial Photo people?"

"Yes. They are down on Longacre Square."

I felt that nothing was too remote if I might use it to fan Kennedy's interest. The fact was that I had a selfish purpose in it, also. I was thinking not only of the Moreheads, but of Walter Jameson. It had been some time since I had put over a really big story for the *Star*. I was ready to make a flight myself with a camera if conceivably that might fix Craig's interest.

Thus it was that in the forenoon we dropped in at the office and studio of the Aerial Photo Company.

They seemed to be doing a pretty large business, for there was a growing demand for photography from the air, rather unique views of cities and towns, estates and buildings.

My connection with the *Star* enabled us to secure attention, and soon the negative of that particular section of the New York air map was produced, as well as prints and enlargements from it.

"You've reduced this thing to a science," complimented Kennedy, studying all three with his glass, as if checking up on them.

What could possibly interest him I did not know. Nor did I care greatly. All I wanted was for him to interest himself in the plight into which the unexplained death of the maid had thrown the Moreheads.

"When was this taken?" asked Craig of the manager, without even raising his eyes from his intent study of the negative.

His absorption in it was complete and my hopes for his taking up the case were rising every second as I watched him.

"About six months ago. You remember when we waked the city up with a story about possible danger from air raids, the air defenses, and all that? It was the beginning of our advertising campaign. I had a great deal of work to do then. They're getting back again to walking in their sleep—but we're getting business, too. So I guess everybody's happy—except the Air Service."

With his glass Kennedy was searching the negative that showed the sun room on top of the Morehead Apartments.

"This is a mighty strange sun room, Walter," he commented, "filled with antiques. Most of the sun parlors I have seen have been filled with easy chairs of wicker or with bright painted furniture. This might be a gallery in a museum!"

I nodded. "And do you see that conservatory that connects with it? They tell me the body was found at the entrance to that, or not far from it."

"Do you mean where that little rug has been placed?" Kennedy was looking sharply at the spot as if he might find some unexpected hiding place where the girl's assailant could have concealed himself.

Craig squinted and focused all his attention on the negative. I could see nothing more than the details of the furnishings, so sharp was the picture under a lens. But I knew from his manner that something unusual was there in this old picture, something that had given him a scent for the chase. I waited expectantly for him to tell me what he had found. But he ventured nothing. Still, I was not surprised at that. Kennedy never confided in anyone until his ideas were put into sure and logical shape. I knew I would hear all sometime. What heartened me most was the look on his face. I was familiar with that look. He was interested in the case and would never rest until he had found the truth. At least, I felt, the Moreheads would have his services.

I was confident enough to put the wish into words. "Will you go over to the Moreheads'?"

"I'll go with you, Walter," was his laconic response.

As for myself, I had to take that glass, give the negative a study myself, trying to find out what had influenced him so unexpectedly to take up the case. But I could see nothing unusual—only caught a smile on Craig's face as he watched me to see if I saw what he saw.

"These Moreheads, do they travel much?" asked Craig as we started across and uptown again.

"Not nearly as much as you would think. They aren't professional globe trotters. They go abroad, but not every year as so many people in their social position do. To tell the truth, they do the States more than they do Europe."

Kennedy was evidently thinking things over quietly as we rode across. Occasionally he would ask me something about the family, but my information was not very comprehensive. "How many children? Are they being educated here? Have they any foreign tutors? Has Mrs. Morehead any relatives? Do they live here or abroad?"

I knew so little that I was a bit exasperated. "Wait until you see the Moreheads. They can tell you better than I can. What is it you are trying to find out?"

"Just trying to find out about the family before I meet them," he replied, in an absent manner.

As we came into the neighborhood of the apartment house, I was hoping that Craig's insatiable curiosity would not antagonize Nancy Morehead. I knew her for a high-spirited and independent woman who would be questioned only to the extent that pleased herself, not others.

"Craig," I admonished, "it needs tact with Mrs. Morehead. She is temperamental, but one of the most charming women it has ever been my privilege to meet. She will talk if you let her think she is talking because she wants to talk—and not because you want her to talk."

"I'll be a good listener, never fear—and then she will feel disposed to tell what she knows."

We pulled up before the Morehead Apartments and Kennedy leisurely locked his car and got out.

From the sidewalk the apartments towered above the other houses. In spite of its height there was a Colonial aspect to this building of brick and stone. Only a stone balustrade seemed to surround the roof. There was no other indication that there was virtually another house atop of this skyscraper.

The entrance was simple with the simplicity which denotes

artistic judgment. We passed through and an attendant met us in the lobby. He, too, was uniformed in rich simplicity. There was not a superfluous wrinkle or mark on his clothes, not an unnecessary gesture or word in his manner, not even a smile. He might have been a Morehead automaton.

"Whom did you wish to see, sir?" the attendant asked Craig.

"The Morehead apartment. Mr. Morehead, please. Mr. Jameson, with Mr. Kennedy."

The man turned to the house telephone. A moment later he motioned to the elevator.

Even the elevator was finer than any I had ever seen before, with its mirrors, upholstered seats, imported floor covering, and with fresh flowers that suggested the kind of tenants in the building.

"Is this the Morehead elevator?" asked Craig of me.

"No. They have a private lift, for the family and intimate friends. In the rear, too, is the service elevator for the help."

The top floor was set off from the rest by an artistic iron grill-work. In it was a massive iron door. As we approached, a servant opened it for us.

It was evident that we were welcome, for no sooner had we entered than Spencer Morehead himself greeted us. He nodded to me, did not even wait to be introduced to Kennedy.

"Very glad to see you, Mr. Kennedy," he began. "You know, a thing like this shakes the nerves of a family dreadfully. My wife seemed quite relieved when she heard just now you were willing to interest yourself in the case. Woman-like, she fears that perhaps there may have been some mistake on the part of the murderer. She fears for the life of some one in the family—that poor Jeanette, her maid, may have been mistaken for herself, for instance."

He laughed leniently at the supposed woman's weakness. I could not, myself, help repressing a smile at the idea of anyone mistaking Jeanette Lafitte for Nancy Morehead. To myself I thought of Morehead as obsessed by the "protector" complex.

Those men get away with it, and their money and position enable them to buy courage and real strength from others to impress their women.

We had come to a marble staircase which led up into the Morehead apartment. The interior was much like that of many of those high-class apartments built for people who have tired of living in big houses and going the weary rounds of employment agencies to get servants to take care of them.

At every turn was evidence of the wealth of this family. Beautiful old furniture, valuable paintings, rare ornaments and china, were on every hand, the evidence of culture. Everything was compact, yet nothing for comfort, convenience, or beauty had been omitted.

"I want to present you to Mrs. Morehead, Mr. Kennedy," bowed Morehead as his wife appeared and greeted me. "Mrs. Morehead can tell you more about Jeanette than I can. My wife is a sculptor and it was Jeanette who took care of the studio, among other things, for her. They were in close personal contact."

Kennedy listened, and I took it as a cue and did the same, as our host preceded us into a wonderful studio.

Nancy Morehead was herself a beautiful woman, though of a type quite different, of course, from Jeanette. She was small, with a slenderness almost as of youth, in spite of her two quite grown-up children. She had big brown eyes that snapped and sparkled, hands that gesticulated in rhythm with each varying emotion, white teeth that glistened, and a wealth of chestnut hair that curled.

Mrs. Morehead had seemed scarcely able to wait for the introduction. As she came forward she slipped her little hand under her husband's arm and with the other motioned us to seats.

"Mr. Kennedy," she hastened, "which do you want first—to go up to the sun room or to hear about Jeanette from me?"

"Both," smiled Kennedy.

"Well," she said, leading the way, "Jeanette was my wonder maid. Was she not, Spencer? She had so much intelligence."

We were following Mrs. Morehead's quick, nervous steps up to the very top, the roof garden and its solarium in the center.

The sun room was different from any other sun parlor or solarium I had ever seen. Its size made me think of the inclosed verandas in some hotels I had visited in winter resorts where hosts of guests were to be made comfortable.

Mrs. Morehead smiled at my surprise. "You needn't apologize. Everyone gasps when he sees this for the first time. It really is incongruous, I suppose. But when one studies the incongruity, it is at least distinctive and pleasant."

Spencer Morehead was listening and watching her closely.

"You see, my husband and I differ in the sources from which we get inspiration. I get mine from the skies. I am as moody as the clouds. But somehow—it may be childish—the heavens make me think of the future. I think of the future. But Spencer comes from such an old family, is so proud of his ancestry, that beautiful relics of the past affect him most. That is why you see so much glass and so much of the sky—and so many antiques."

In fact, one entire side of the solarium, with the southern exposure, had wide glass shelves built across it running from floor to roof. On these shelves reposed a fortune in early American glass and rarer pieces brought from abroad by the various collecting Moreheads. Through these colored glasses the sun filtered, reflecting their beautiful colors in streaks on the marble-tiled floor.

"Aren't they beautiful?" Nancy Morehead asked, impulsively.

Craig agreed, with enthusiasm.

After the first surprise at seeing such a peculiar sun-room, I studied the many different old-time pieces of furniture. Craig was observing them carefully, too, but I knew our reasons were divergent—mine because it was a sort of hobby, a joy to see some rare bit of old cabinet-maker's art, Craig's, no doubt, in the hope of finding some scrap of evidence.

It all seemed so hopeless to me, the solving of this mystery. There was nothing I saw that pointed to anyone or even suggested an idea. It was like a spherical safe—no corner on which to take hold. Some time had elapsed, too, since they had found the body. Many people, including the police, had come and gone, leaving new marks and perhaps mixing up the possible clues, if there had been any. I felt that if Kennedy had only been called in at first it would have been a different story.

Every moment my thoughts on the case were interrupted by catching sight of some valuable old table, or a chair that sent me into a rhapsody of appreciation. Spencer Morehead and I were getting along famously. He saw my delight unfeigned, and while Nancy Morehead did most of the talking about the case in her breezy, inimitable way with Craig, the host and I discussed furniture. Still, I must confess that I was listening to Kennedy and our hostess, too, hoping to get something new on the case.

There were several butterfly tables made of pine and they had come down, stanch and firm, from early American days. Here was a small mahogany Pembroke table with its drop leaves and inlaid-work. I could hear Morehead saying, "This is a real Hepplewhite; he favored this design." There was a Jacobean love seat, a small upholstered settee about the size of a double chair. Evidently some Morehead in the past had romantic inclinations.

Mrs. Morehead saw me admiring it. "Little did its past owner dream of the tragedy it would witness some day! Oh, if these old tables and chairs could speak, what secrets we might hear!"

"Yes," I agreed, "and that highboy over there. I wonder how many girls in the past have fluttered with excitement as they took out their daintiest apparel to dress for their lovers."

"This is one of my favorite pieces," Mrs. Morehead went on, taking up her own views on the hobbies of her husband, "this *poudreuse.* It was made in 1679 and a great lady of France saw herself beautified before it each day. I just adore it. Do you know, Mr. Kennedy, Jeanette used to love these things, too? She was a mimic. I have seen her sit before it and pose and act like some grand dame of old. I have heard her say, 'How I would like to be surrounded by such old, beautiful things! Some day, perhaps. Who knows?'"

There were many kinds of chairs grouped about the place. Most of them came over from England years ago. Here was a perfect type of Yorkshire ladder-back, common in Georgian times. There was a ribbon-back, a shield-back, wheatsheaf-back, and the oval backs favored by the Brothers Adam.

Next that caught my fancy was a *fauteuil*, a French armchair. Its history dated back to 1650 and in those times it was a sumptuous piece of furniture, generally covered in the richest fabrics and found only in the homes of the great.

"But this is the irresistible piece of all. A little delicate new-moon-shaped table. Jeanette and I had an idea that this piece was uncanny. It moved so easily; sometimes when it seemed you had scarcely touched it it would slide an incredible distance."

"Nancy Morehead!" Her husband was interrupting. "The Moreheads never kept anything that seemed possessed of the devil! Just because Jeanette with her foolish, superstitious ideas made it seem alive did not make it so!"

Nancy Morehead kept her temper, with a shrug. "I can't help it. When I sat down before it I always felt uncomfortable, as if I were being crowded. Jeanette used to tell me she believed some dashing lover of the past still used it and when he saw me would try to embrace me!"

Spencer Morehead frowned with dignity. But his wife was unabashed. "Jeanette had imagination," she pursued, "a touch of sentiment, and those qualities, with her beauty and wonderful form, made her an ideal subject to pose for me, at times, even. I shall miss her." There was a real pathos in the voice of the mistress of the dead maid. One felt that Nancy Morehead missed her more than as maid alone or even as model.

Morehead was not inclined to yield the privilege of talking about the antiques. "Mr. Kennedy," he interposed, "I can remember most of these things, except what I have myself added to them, from the time when I was a little boy—and they were old, then. They were all in the old house some hundred and twenty years ago—and a hundred and twenty feet below—where the Morehead mansion and barn were on Fifth Avenue in what was then the country, not even a suburb. They had been in the family for generations when that was built."

Spencer Morehead was proud of it all and showed it in every gesture and word. Kennedy was rather silent, and observant. I fancied he was looking about all the time sharply as if for something.

"What do you expect to find?" I asked, under my breath. "Fingerprints?"

He smiled. "Walter, when will you learn that I expect no particular thing? Only, there is the possibility of finding something. Nothing is too small or indefinite to overlook."

Some idea must have penetrated our host's mind that Kennedy would be more interested in hearing about the mysterious death in the Morehead *ménage* rather than about the Morehead possessions.

"Everything is just as it was when we found Jeanette," he remarked. "Of course, they have moved the body—from over there. But they took pictures of her on the floor, dead. Everything in detail can be obtained from the police. There was a man—I think his name was O'Connor—in charge. They were quite thorough."

Kennedy turned to Mrs. Morehead for confirmation. "You are sure nothing has been taken from the sun room since Jeanette was found here?"

"Oh yes! Nothing has gone out—excepting poor Jeanette."

Kennedy was silent again for a few seconds, thinking. He rose from his chair and was looking out of the glass walls at the city of towers and spires and at the blue sky above us.

"What are the directions here, Mr. Morehead?"

Spencer Morehead pointed them out to us. "Come over here. Do you see the Hudson? Well, that is west." It was a beautiful, inspiring view, and at night, with the lights of the city shining, it must have been like fairyland. "Now, over this way you can see the East River. In that direction is north; and of course that is south."

"I see." But there was absentness in Kennedy's answer. A moment later he added, "You were unable to give the conservatory a complete southern exposure. Do you find that it makes any difference?"

"Not in the least, up here. When the sun shines at all, we get it. Then the winds in the cold weather are stronger on a building facing west than they are on the southeast. We found that out in our country home and made use of it here."

Again Kennedy seemed reflective. I felt so, too. It was strange to me to be in a room and see the white clouds massing and tumbling, ever onward, over our heads. It was strange and beautiful. The atmosphere was so serene and calm that it seemed almost impossible to think of this wonder room with its delightful treasures as the scene of so recent a tragedy.

"There is one thing you haven't spoken about yet, Mr. Kennedy," remarked Morehead, slowly, "and that is a thing I am deeply interested in. This doctor who was here on the case, who is like the coroner used to be. I gather, has disgusted me." Morehead wound up by speaking rapidly to get Craig's attention.

"What is it you have in mind?" asked Kennedy.

Morehead cleared his throat. "Another hobby of mine is flowers. In that conservatory which I and my family visit every day I am raising some beautiful plants. The door to the conservatory was open when they found Jeanette dead. Now that doctor hinted that an exotic poison might have exhaled from these plants, that that was what might have done it."

"Exotic?" repeated Kennedy.

"It is ridiculous!" Morehead exclaimed. "These flowers are just some lilies and orchids, some tropical plants that do fairly well up here. But they have never done anything to us—never affected Jeanette, until she died—if then, I don't believe the plants had anything to do with it."

By this time we were in the conservatory. "I can't see any of us gasping for air yet," smiled Nancy Morehead. "Do you feel any faintness, Mr. Jameson?" I confessed that I did not; rather an exhilaration at my surroundings of country aloft in the city.

"How long had you had Jeanette?" asked Craig suddenly, as if he had entirely forgotten the flowers and the opinion of the medical examiner.

"About four years," Mrs. Morehead replied, promptly.

"Did she come from an agency or upon the recommendation of some friend?"

"I suppose you would say upon recommendation. I have a cousin who married an English nobleman. He was in public life and a great favorite with the royal family and other influential people. Jeanette went with them when she was little more than a child as a playmate for their own child. They thought that with a French governess and a French playmate the child's accent would be perfect as she grew older.

"Jeanette, I believe, was treated like one of the family, almost. She traveled with them, was with them through all their holidays, and apparently idolized them. Lord Frothingham was sent to Bombay on some political and commercial mission for two years and her interest in the family was such that she stayed the full time with them there. I mention that merely to show her devotion.

"After leaving Bombay they returned to London. Then Lord Frothingham, in some capacity in the diplomatic service, was much in Paris. Jeanette seemed delighted to be in France again. But suddenly she changed, my cousin wrote me, and insisted on leaving. No inducement could make her reconsider. She asked my cousin for references and help, to get located somewhere here in America. They thought of me right away, and when the girl left them it was to come direct to me, assured of a position.

I was more than pleased to get the girl, for her worthiness had become family gossip."

Nancy Morehead paused reminiscently. "She loved Lady Frothingham devotedly and rarely spoke of her without some show of emotion. It sometimes seemed to me that she bestowed on me the love and affection she had formerly given my cousin. One couldn't treat her like a mere servant; there was something that forebade it. Jeanette was keenly interested in my work. She had ambition. She was altogether admirable."

"Was she contented, toward the end?" asked Craig. "Had you noticed any change in her demeanor?"

"No, we had not, Jeanette always seemed the same, ready to love and serve us whenever we asked her."

Kennedy had moved out to the side of the room from which extended the conservatory, and was regarding the floor thoughtfully.

"It was right there, where you are standing, that Pierre found her," explained Morehead, "right in front of the door leading to the flowers."

"Pierre? Who is Pierre?"

"My man. I had been up here during the afternoon, left my glasses—forgot them. We went out to dinner that night. It was rather late when we returned. I sent Pierre for them. That is what he found!"

"Why Jeanette came up here at all after we left is a mystery to me, to all of us," put in Nancy Morehead. "Pierre locked the door below about seven, without coming up. So you see it must have been late in the afternoon that it happened—between six when Mr. Morehead went down and seven when Pierre locked the lower door."

"Were Pierre and Jeanette interested in each other?" asked Kennedy with a glance that showed his interest in any bit of backstairs romance.

"Not in the least," answered Nancy Morehead, quickly. "Why,

Jeanette was too superior a little person to be interested in plain old Pierre. She aspired higher."

"But what of Pierre?" asked Kennedy, bluntly.

She shook her head vigorously. "They were both excellent servants—but of different types. Jeanette's sparkling eyes and teasing smile must have been reserved for younger men than Pierre. But—of course—he may have aspired. Jeanette never looked down!"

"It was quite different with a chauffeur we let go recently," put in Morehead.

"Yes? Who was he? What was his name? Why did you let him go?"

"Benito. That was his last name. An Italian. Just plain William seems too ordinary, now, after the romantic name of Benito. This Benito was a handsome chap—but girl crazy. I had let him go when I found out his weakness. He was a married man, but that fact did not prevent him from paying ardent attention to Jeanette. She never took him seriously. But she did go out in the car three or four times with him after she had finished her duties for Mrs. Morehead. She always came back indignant, finally, then absolutely refused to go. Then when we heard about his wife, that was the end. We wanted no scandals among our help."

"Did he try to see Jeanette after that?" I asked.

Morehead frowned. "I have thought of that, Mr. Jameson. But Jeanette was secretive—very. Unless things concerning herself were apparent to us, none of us knew anything about her personal life. She was not exactly talkative, made no confidante even of my wife, although Mrs. Morehead was closer to her than any of us. To Mrs. Morehead she did at times admit possessing ambitions and desires far above her social status. Jeanette was no ordinary person, else my wife would not have made use of her in her art work so much."

"I see." Kennedy nodded. "Who are the other servants?"

"Well," Morehead continued, with a smile, "we have a cook whose main idea in life seems to be to save her soul for heaven when she is not feeding the family so well that there is danger we may be hurried there first. I think Amanda is absolved of suspicion—just a good, old-fashioned Southern cook, black as the ace of spades, with no inhibitions or soul scars."

"And our new chauffeur, Grimes—this William," Mrs. Morehead interrupted. "With a wife so vigilant and a family so numerous that the poor fellow is kept continually busy seeking means to satisfy the wife and provide for the children. Surely, Grimes is a rare find for us. He is industrious and works hard because he needs the money. Then, he is too old to be interested in a girl like Jeanette. Grimes is another of my husband's antiques."

Morehead did not take the quip with ill grace. Rather he was a bit proud of it. "You see, ours is a family where the help stays."

"How long, for example?" queried Craig.

"Oh, Pierre has been with me fifteen years, at least. And Javary, the butler, came to work for us when my wife and I were married, two years or more before I engaged Pierre."

"We have tried to keep our servants satisfied, happy," explained Mrs. Morehead, "and that means we cannot stand for anything the least bit—irregular."

"You have had other servants besides those mentioned?"

"Yes," Mrs. Morehead answered, quickly. "Amanda is not exactly an old servant, with us. She came to us about five months ago. We had a Hindu before that. I engaged him because he was such a splendid cook. Oh, what wonderful curries he could prepare I But he had never been so far from home before. He grew homesick, about five months ago, I think." She turned inquiringly to Morehead.

"Yes. Last spring. I bought him his ticket on the Cunarder, *Iberia,* and he sailed that week."

"And you have no other maid?"

I fancied Morehead was trying to flash a look at his wife. Was it a look of caution? I could not get whether she caught it.

"Oh yes. I have another maid, Renée, a French girl, too."

"Were Renée and Jeanette cordial to each other?"

She shook her head. "Jeanette never mixed with any of the others, as I told you."

But did Renée try to be friendly with her? Did they like each other?"

"I couldn't say that they did, particularly. But they got along. Jeanette was prettier, more graceful, and I had her with me more than Renée, naturally, in the studio. I think Renée felt a little slighted over that. She had been with me longer than poor Jeanette. Sometimes I did think she resented Jeanette being taken into my confidence as far as I took her."

"Did they ever quarrel openly?"

Mrs. Morehead did not seem to be one of those women to whom the servants are a never-ending source of conversation. "Mr. Kennedy, I hate to go into these facts. It puts Renée in a very bad light, makes me feel positively disloyal to the girl. I hate to tell anything that might react on a person whom I think would be incapable of committing a crime."

Kennedy nodded. "May I speak to Renée?"

"That's all right, my dear," interrupted Morehead. "It may be that Mr. Kennedy does not think Renée is capable of the crime—and still she may have been an innocent cause of it. I'll call her."

He pushed a near-by button, and in a few minutes Renée appeared. Renée was inclined to be defiant, silent, and looked askance even after Mrs. Morehead spoke to her.

"Renée, Mr. Kennedy is going to ask some questions of all the servants and he wants to speak to you now."

Only a sullen bow was the acknowledgment.

"Renée," began Kennedy, frankly, "when did you see Jeanette last?"

The girl raised her eyes guardedly, as if she feared Kennedy would see something she was trying to conceal under those lowered lids.

"That afternoon," was the short answer.

"What time?" encouraged Kennedy.

"It was a little after six. A short time before Mr. and Mrs. Morehead went out. I thought I heard a noise as if some one was in the sun room. I started up to see, and Jeanette was going up there. She was angry when she saw me, said something about being watched and spied on. I was angry, too, then. I said something and went to my room. That is the last I heard or saw her alive."

"Was she alone?"

"I can't say. Only, by her manner I should say she wasn't. At least she acted as if some one else was there or coming up there, and she was afraid I would see the person and tell…. You are the first one I have told this much too."

Kennedy lowered his voice confidentially. "Did you know any of Jeanette's sweethearts, Renée?"

The girl looked, gave a little, nervous, startled laugh at Craig's question. "I did not. She was mighty careful of her friends. I often wanted to go out with her. But she felt too—big, you call it, for me."

I caught a bitterness in the tone and thought that, even if Jeanette had been her enemy, she might have shown more compassion for the dead girl.

"Have you ever had words over anyone?" persisted Kennedy. Renée's face colored a trifle. "Over Benito?"

It was evident that they had. "I liked him—and she knew it. She didn't care for him. I used to think she went out with him just to make me jealous." Apparently she had succeeded.

"Do you see Benito now?" Mrs. Morehead interrupted, quickly.

Renée lowered her eyes, did not answer.

"Did you think Jeanette had Benito in the sun room that night when the family were going out to dinner?" asked Craig. "Was that why you were spying?"

"I tell you, sir, I was not spying. I heard a noise and was trying to see if everything was all right. It seems as if faithfulness to a family lets one in for a ragging, as they say in England. I saw no one—and what a person thinks is not evidence, sir. It would not be received in a court room, would it?"

"That's all now, Renée; you may go." Kennedy nodded a dismissal, then to us, as she went out, "She reads the papers!"

I think Nancy Morehead had the same desire that I had, toward the end of the visit, to find out whether Kennedy had any ideas himself on the case. But Craig chose to gratify neither of us.

However, I could no longer resist asking, as we were leaving the Morehead building:

"Did you find anything, get any idea?"

"I don't know, Walter—yet. But I have some things I want to look into this afternoon. I'll meet you somewhere for dinner. Do you think you'll be at the *Star* at six?" I nodded, determined to make a point of being there. "Well, then, I'll telephone about that time and tell you where to meet me. I'm in a hurry now. You're going down there now, aren't you? Well, keep in touch with the case, if anything develops."

So it was that I found myself in a state of actual suspense when I was called to the telephone at the newspaper office.

"Yes, Craig," I answered. "Where to?"

"Down in the Village, Walter. I've done a great deal, with the help of Deputy O'Connor, since I left you—and I imagine I must have spent an hour hunting for a place to eat, some interesting place, something different."

"Did you find it?" I was a bit annoyed. I thought he might have interested himself more in the case for that hour than in a new place to dine.

"Yes, I have. Meet me at the Arch. I'll be waiting for you."

Kennedy was most enthusiastic over the Village when I met him and I wondered what aberration had drawn him to this mint of aberrations.

"It's the greatest little place you ever saw, Walter. I had lunch there. Such camaraderie! Everybody knows everybody else. Dry agents would have a fat chance."

"I suppose I'll enjoy the novelty of it," I agreed, "but, Craig, I must get a story. In an unguarded moment I mentioned to the chief, down on the paper, that you were interested in the case, under cover, of course. It was with difficulty that I restrained him from putting the staff at your disposal. Now I've got to make good. I'm glad it's up to you—not to me!"

Kennedy smiled good-humoredly but still without giving me even a hint of what it was he wished to talk over with me at dinner. "I know how you feel about it, Walter. But if there were no intermissions, nothing but the daily routine of news for you, lectures for me at the university—no crimes to talk over—I'd be no good in a short time. Human nature demands variety."

By this time we had penetrated the Village and come to a rather dull, forlorn old brick building. I saw that it was one of the many bohemian restaurants, the Civet Cat, rather a well-known place, in its way, down under the shadow of the Elevated railroad, surrounded by Italian wholesale dealers in olive oil, every Latin delicacy, and, I felt sure, in some that were unconstitutional.

Craig was carrying a cylindrical package wrapped up, a couple of feet long and several inches thick. As we entered I noticed that he did not even trust it to be checked, but kept it with him as he selected a table.

The captain of the waiters seemed evidently to know Craig, for, although every table was occupied except two or three with a little sign indicating they were reserved, it was to one of these that we were assigned.

Moreover, our waiter seemed to be guided by the attention given us by the captain. The deference of his service as he laid the menu cards before us was unimpeachable.

Kennedy scanned the card thoughtfully while I divided my attention between it and getting my first impression of our surroundings in the Civet Cat. Suddenly Craig looked up from the card.

"Mrs. Morehead's remark about curries has set my mouth watering, if you'll pardon my elegance, Walter. How about it?"

"Very good suggestion." I felt more like suggesting getting back to the Morehead case, rather than thinking of dining, but I restrained myself. With the order attended to, perhaps Kennedy would come to it, himself.

He did not, however. And soon we were enjoying the curry. Never had I tasted anything better. I made a mental note that in the future I would come here often to enjoy them.

Once, when the waiter passed, Kennedy smiled at him. "One of the finest I ever ate." He nodded toward the dish.

"Thank you, sir. I shall be glad to tell the manager, sir."

"Are they always as good as this?" I thought Craig had let the curry go to his head.

"Oh yes, sir; famous. The *chef* will be pleased when I tell him what you say."

Kennedy looked up quickly. "I wouldn't mind telling him myself. Is there any objection?"

"I don't think so, sir—for you."

A moment later I found myself following Craig and the waiter down into the kitchen. I shook my head. I was beginning to think that perhaps, after all, Kennedy was not as interested in the case as I had imagined. Had my wish been father of the thought and was he only mildly interested?

Standing over the big gas stove in the kitchen, stirring vigorously the contents in a huge copper kettle, was the *chef*. He was so busy that he did not see us at first, not until we were close to a small table beside him where he could conveniently lay his spoons and dippers and huge forks.

Finally the obliging waiter called him. The *chef* straightened up and turned to us, slim and tall. His hair, what we could see about the edge of his headdress, was straight and dark. His skin was a deep olive, and his eyes large and lustrous. There was something fascinating about this face.

Kennedy smiled and moved a step forward. "The curry—it is the best I ever ate. I felt that I must tell you so."

The eyes of the man brightened at the praise, but his manner toward strangers seemed reserved and quiet. Even if he were a *chef,* he had a peculiar dignity.

"I must add my praise," I volunteered. "I shall come here often, just for that."

Kennedy had laid down his bundle for a moment on the table. "How do you make them? There are curries—and curries. But you have that subtle seasoning that can be found only in the land from which we get the best curries."

"It is not hard—if one knows. I grind my spices fresh every day. So much difference. I use ginger, lime juice, almonds, mustard, and poppy seeds, allspice, cardamons, chillis, cinnamon, cream and curds. I vary my curries, different days. There are so many good things to put in them."

I smiled at the agreeable answer which really revealed none of the secrets of the curry.

"From what part of India do you come?"

"I came as a little boy, years ago, they say, from the Punjab."

He turned away from us with a polite bow, to his pots and kettles. The interview was over as far as he was concerned. He had his work to do. The waiter looked at us to leave.

Kennedy was regarding with interest the man's costume. About his head he wore a *lungi,* bound round a red *kullah.* The *lungi* is made of cloth, generally blue, and has an ornamental border. The *kullah* is a tall red conical cap. The ends of the *lungi* hang down in the back and are called a *shimla.*

Just now the *shimla* had fallen forward over the *chef's* shoulder, hiding his face. He wore a white *kurta,* which is like the shirt of the European, only the sleeves are very long and fastened tightly by buttons at the wrist. The trousers were loose, of white cotton, and fastened also at the waist by a string.

Kennedy leaned over and touched the *chef's* elbow. "Are you a Punjabi Mohammedan?"

The *chef* turned impassive eyes on Kennedy. "Why do you wish to know?"

"One can generally tell by the costume from what part of India a man comes."

"You know so much, why ask more?" was the rather sullen reply.

"Did you ever know anyone by the name of Dass?" asked Kennedy, quickly. "I have news for him."

The waiter was about to speak, but a look from the *chef* checked him. The *chef* continued to face Kennedy, impassive. "Yes—I know Dass. He bought a ticket for England, then back on the P. and O., five months ago. I know him. He has gone long time."

Kennedy smiled quietly. "A ticket was bought for Dass, my friend, that is true. But Dass never sailed. I have been down to the steamship company's office. There is no record of any such arrival at Southampton. Dass never got off the *Iberia*, because he was never on it. He sold his ticket to a scalper on Whitehall Street."

The waiter now was watching the *chef* silently, and Kennedy was studying sharply both inscrutable faces.

"Dass!"

That was all Craig uttered. But it seemed to fire a thousand evil flames in the man's eyes.

"I am not Dass!" He repeated it several times.

Kennedy affected not to hear.

"You met her in Bombay, did you not, Dass?" He paused. "Jeanette Lafitte was beautiful, graceful, and you loved her. You wanted her for yourself. You knew her arms about you would comfort you, those slender, graceful limbs would dance for you, those dainty hands would serve you. You loved her madly, jealously—your little Jeanette."

Craig stopped again. The muscles of the man's face were

twitching. Could it be that merely talking of Jeanette was more than he could bear?

Still he repeated stubbornly: "I am not Dass. I don't know where Dass is!"

"But she did not love you, Dass." Kennedy's tone was as relentless as fate. "Not because you were not rich enough. Dass, you are a rich man, once a horse dealer, a very rich man in India. The British consul has found that out for me. But you were dark, and your society limited. Jeanette was ambitious. She wouldn't have you, scorned you, made sport of your religion—yet her mere presence worked you up to a state of madness between desire and jealousy."

"I am not Dass. I am not Dass." The man almost screamed the intonation now.

Craig kept on in his pitiless tone. "Those sweetly scented curls were too much for you. Those beautiful, haunting eyes lured you from your native land. You could not let her go. You knew that the Frothinghams were ignorant of your love for her, even though you followed her from Bombay to London and to Paris."

"I am not Dass. I don't know any Jeanette!"

But the hands of the man were now pressed in agony over his eyes as if to shut out the torturing beautiful vision of the dead girl. His fingers were pressing so hard that his knuckles were white with the tautness of the skin.

"Allah! Allah!" he cried, lifting his eyes heavenward.

"You threatened her life in Paris, too. You made her life cruelly unhappy there, with your unwelcome love. Dass, she fled from *you*—and came here to America. And now, Dass, I have found you—"

"I never heard of any Jeanette!"

It was almost a wail. But there was a longing and love in the tone in which he cried even her name.

"You followed her." Kennedy was inexorable. "By subterfuge you managed to become engaged for a while as cook for the Moreheads. But there, too, she hated you, repulsed you, infuriated you. Your love for her, her scorn for you, your race, your religion worked on your Mohammedan soul. You were ready to run amuck—to kill!"

"I am not Dass!" he moaned. "Allah! Allah! Help thy servant! Why do you call me Dass? You have no proof!" Again his subtle native courage was in the ascendant. A spirit of bravado seemed to urge him to this last defiance.

"Yes, Dass. I have the proof."

Kennedy reached down, carefully unwrapped the paper from the cylindrical package he had carried. I gave a gasp as he uncovered it. It was a rug, a prayer rug.

"You are a good Mohammedan, Dass. You prayed to Allah, dutifully, at dawn, at noon, before sunset, after sunset, and at the end of the day."

The eyes of the man were almost protruding with wonder and fright. He gazed at the rug, fascinated, hypnotized.

"It is beautiful, Dass. I admit it. The most beautiful little prayer rug, I think, I have ever seen. I admired the design the first time I saw it. Now I admire the coloring, the texture."

"Where did you see it? Where did you get it?" Dass burst forth with excitable voice that forgot his impassive pose.

Kennedy's quiet tone had been soul-slaying to his tortured mind.

"I found out that you were here, this afternoon, after going the rounds of all the Hindu restaurants in the city. There are not so many. I worked quickly. I found you had rooms near by, on Tenth Street. It was the easiest thing in the world, with the help of the police, to search them.

"I found the rug. It was the same rug I had seen in an aerial photograph taken about six months ago from an airplane at noon over the Morehead Apartments. It showed the sun room with its beautiful marble tiles, its wonderful furniture—and only one incongruity—this small rug not far from the conservatory door. That was queer, I thought. In some other place, downstairs, no doubt, its beauty would have adorned more appropriately. But here—it was not evidence. It was a hint. It set my mind at work. Why was it there?... And when I saw the sun room, it was not there. Nor had anything been taken out—except the girl. Some one must have used it, praying, at noon!"

Dass was now looking helplessly, hopelessly from one to the other, blocking flight. This trouble had come so suddenly to him in his fancied security. Why had Allah allowed this, from the unbelievers? Kennedy's voice continued, cold and clear. The silence was as the silence of a Judgment Day.

"I'm sorry, Dass! Sorry for you—more sorry for poor little Jeanette. East and West cannot meet. You should have known that. The fatalism of the East should have taught you to accept it....

"You could not leave Jeanette. You delayed sailing. Your heart was here, Dass. But there comes a last time with us all. You came one evening at sunset when you knew the Moreheads were out to dinner. You saw Jeanette. She tried to conceal your presence from the other servants, not that Jeanette was secretly in love with you, but she was afraid the family would find it out and dismiss her. They were particular about their servants, and Jeanette loved her mistress.

"Your religion, your color were not the religion, the color for Jeanette and her happiness. You pleaded, begged, threatened. But it was futile. In your mind you saw Jeanette loved by another, her arms about him. It crazed you. You tried to kiss her, to show her how you loved her, would cherish her. She repulsed you to the last—for the last time. In desperation you broke, in a hand-kerchief or something, the vial of poison for her to inhale as you held her, struggling. It was the subtle poison of the Hindu mancanilla tree, that exhales at night, which killed her. It was all over in a moment—just one of those moments between six and seven that night—and you fled down the stairway as you came, avoiding the service elevator. I suspected from the description of her waxy appearance. From the organs of the body still with the medical examiner I confirmed it by one chemical test."

Kennedy paused, reminiscent of the rapid work of the after-noon.

"The hint came first to me from the strange presence of the Oriental prayer rug in that picture of the sun room—and its absence later in the room. Each fact confirmed me. When Mr. Morehead told of one Dass, a Hindu, I was almost ready to act. The fact that Jeanette had lived in Bombay advanced it a step. The steamship records were another step. Then the mancanilla test of the organs—and the rug—clinched it!"

Kennedy had laid the prayer rug down on the floor as he spoke, and was turning it slowly, carefully.

"There—with the customary apex, that point in the figures of all prayer rugs, turned as it must be, Dass, toward the Holy City of Mecca toward the East!"

Dass seemed suddenly to realize that his game was up. As Craig placed the rug and left it, he dropped to his knees on it, for absolution from a sin, to be forgiven one of the faithful against an unbeliever, no matter how meritorious.

Kennedy leaned over.

"Your Allah may cleanse you of pollution, Dass—but that won't go with American courts! Come with me! You're wanted!"

WEST

"I'LL FIND OUT who murdered Jimmy Gurney. I'm working on it quietly. I got some clues I'm running down. It's going on two years, but I ain't give it up yet. No, sir!"

Eben Hawn, constable of South Elliott, brought his fist down on the arm of the old pew with emphasis.

Kennedy and I were on a little hunting and tramping trip in the mountains of New Hampshire, for relaxation rather than game. Sometimes we would take along some local nimrod as a guide; more often we would go alone. But at night we never failed to drop around and talk and smoke at Phil Smith's garage. The country garage has taken the place once held by the post office and country store as the center of gossip.

For example, above the watering trough at the South Elliott House, where we were staying, still hung the sign: "Water your horses—and don't forget yourself." Other times, other manners, had changed that. The cryptic point of the latter part of the advice had been amended. Now, too, there was no need to stop and water your horse at the hotel. You did not, likely, have a horse. Sooner or later everybody had to go to Phil Smith's garage. Gas and oil were indispensable.

In front of the garage, to one side of the big doors, back of the gas pump on the edge of the road, stood an old pew taken from a dismantled church. At night, one by one, villagers dropped around in their flivvers. It was their club. Just now there were three or four, including the constable and Phil Smith, on the "mourners' bench."

Kennedy and I had started out early that day, alone, over the hills, tramping for hours in solitude broken only occasionally by some jocular remark as to whether we would find anything to take back to the cook in the quaint little hotel.

We had gone several miles from the village and had reached an elevation known as Cobble Hill. Even the valley at its foot was not used much for farming. The soil was poor, and I recalled seeing only one farm as we came along. Cobble Hill was quite deserted this late fall afternoon.

About halfway up on the old trail we had come across a cabin, old from neglect rather than from time. It was unoccupied and there seemed to be an enveloping air of mystery about it, something sinister that provoked foreboding thoughts.

"Do you get it the way I get it Craig?" I muttered. "I don't know a thing about this place. But I wouldn't stay in it overnight if you gave me the whole hill."

Kennedy looked at me and laughed. "It does seem a bit forbidding, Walter—even spooky. I wonder why no one lives in it? It would make a comfortable home for some recluse."

We found the lock rusted and hanging, went through the cabin. But there was nothing that seemed to give any information concerning the former owner, except that, instead of sleeping in the one decent room on the first floor, he had seemed to prefer the attic, where a weather-beaten, sagging rope bed still stood.

"Recluse," I repeated. "Well, he couldn't have been very sociable, that's true, living 'way up here, away from everybody."

"It's getting late," suggested Kennedy. "Let's go back to the village and find out who owned the place, what is its story."

"All right," I agreed. Curiosity was not the mainspring of my desire to be on our way. Shadows were lengthening and I acquiesced in a manner quite agreeable.

After dinner at the hotel we strolled down to the little garage on Main Street.

"Get anything?" queried the monosyllabic Phil Smith.

"Not so much to-day," avoided Kennedy. "But we ran across something else that was interesting. It looks like a mystery."

"Mystery?" One of the men on the pew spoke up. "Where's there any mystery around here?"

"Oh," I answered, casually, "we were just wondering what was the matter with that old cabin up on the side of Cobble."

There was a quick, significant exchange of glances.

"Ever been here before?" Our interrogator from the far end of the bench quizzed with a shrewd glance.

"No; never been up in just this vicinity before," Craig answered. "Why?" He surveyed the group with interest. The heads of the villagers were wagging in a way that suggested untold intelligence.

"Funny you fellows should fall on the only mystery hereabouts." The garage man departed from his usual taciturnity. "You'd oughter ask Eben Hawn about that cabin. He knows more'n all the rest on us put together." Phil Smith jerked his thumb in the direction of our interlocutor on the far end of the bench.

It was thus that we formally met the village constable, and it explained his eager desire to find out whether we had ever been there before. His was the village mind suspicious of strangers. The others were suddenly quiet and Eben Hawn looked at us as if he still must be convinced. Hawn didn't answer immediately. I think he felt it was a put-up job on the part of Phil Smith to get him to talk. At least so it seemed to me.

"Well," Kennedy persisted, "bring on the mystery. Who was murdered? Did they catch the murderer?"

Hawn spat thoughtfully into the road. This was the one point that involved his honor. He must talk. "No, they haven't caught the murderer of Jim Gurney," he replied, a bit sullenly.

"But have the authorities given it up as one of those unsolvable mysteries?" I asked.

That was the question that seemed to touch to the quick his honor as a constable, that made Hawn so vehement in his remark that he would still find the murderer of Jim Gurney.

"I ain't give it up yet. No, *sir!*"

Up there in South Elliott they didn't know then who Craig really was, and they don't know it yet. In fact, I am telling this story because it deals with the last of the cardinal points of the compass, but, more, because the two principals in it, the murdered man and the murderer, are dead, and I feel at liberty to tell it for what it is worth.

Eben Hawn was a type, an individual who stood out most distinctly in that little group of the "Amen Corner" in front of the garage. Possessed of a rural pompousness, an aplomb derived from the confidence inspired by his connection with the law, he looked with a hurt dignity at any who challenged his sagacity.

Hawn was tall, thin, stoop-shouldered, the kind of man who always has deep wrinkles across the front of his vest. Time and weather had taken the color from his clothes and about his rounded shoulders this discoloration was most noticeable. He always sat hunched forward, hands flat on his spare knees, suggesting constantly that he was on the point of leaving.

At once Craig was interested in this unsolved mystery. He was anxious to hear the details. "Tell us about it, Hawn. What was the cause—robbery?"

"Not a thing taken, sir. When I drove over there about noon that day I found everything just as it should be, as far as that was concerned. None of his money had been taken. His watch was in the pocket of his vest on a chair. Nothing had been ransacked in the house. All was in order just as Gurney left it. No, I wouldn't say it was a case of robbery. If anything of value was taken it must have been something we didn't know anything about, like a valuable jewel or a paper." The tall constable stood up, stretched, and then sat down again.

"You say it was two years ago?" inquired Craig, prompting.

"Just about this time of the year," nodded Hawn. "How I knows, I was planning to go gunning, myself, when this murder happened and I had to stay home."

"What kind of man was this Jim Gurney?" persisted Craig.

It was Phil Smith who answered. "Not much of a man as men go, I guess. He was almost what you'd call a hermit. He didn't want to have anything to do with anyone. Just left us all alone—and, then, he was a tight-wad. He wouldn't buy a dog biscuit."

"Ever have any sweetheart?" asked Kennedy, with a smile.

Smith shook his head. "Years ago he might have had. But any girl who'd look at Jim Gurney in his later years would 've run away if there was any lovin' to be did. Women might a worked for him—but I can swear none of 'em 'd love him."

"How was he found?" Kennedy's curiosity was insatiable.

"Dead in bed, sir. He was up on the second floor, in the attic bedroom. It had only one window, too. If you remember, that little cabin has its back to Cobble. There wasn't one window or door lock that had been tampered with in the least—even the locks on the first and only decent floor was all in good working order, and working, too. It sure is a mystery."

"But just how was he murdered?"

Hawn smiled a superior, official smile. "That is one of the first questions I am asked, 'How did he die?'" He paused.

Kennedy waited.

"Well, tell him, then, Eben," spoke up Smith.

Hawn cleared his throat. "He was killed by a shotgun. Both barrels had been emptied into him, literally tearing his heart out. It was awful to go up there and find such a grewsome sight. I felt sorry for the poor devil—no matter what he was nor what he done."

With a careful use of diplomacy Craig had managed in the last few minutes to ingratiate himself in the good graces of the constable. Old Eben Hawn was answering almost everything, but if you rushed him he would shut up tight.

"Shotgun. All locked up. H'm," considered Kennedy.

"I got my own theory of explaining that," volunteered Hawn. "To my way of thinking, it must have been done from the bit of woods that runs down to the cabin clearing, from an elevation. It would'a' been easy to get Gurney that way."

"I admire your persistence, Hawn, your doggedness in holding to a case. Still enthusiastic after two years have gone and no one caught! It's very unusual. Most constables I have seen would have forgotten it all by this time."

"I never give up!" Hawn smiled. "I got some clues still, and I think when I finish a-running them down, I will land the murderer yet!"

So many of the villagers had criticized Hawn for his inability to fasten the murder on anyone, even ridiculed him, that he was really pleased at the sympathetic attitude of this stranger.

"I haven't forgotten a single thing," he confided to Kennedy. "I still have all the old evidence. Something may come of it some day. I'll land that murderer, yet. You needn't laugh, Phil Smith, either. The arm of the law is long. You all laughed when that fellow Springstein skipped with the traffic violation for speeding on the turnpike against him. Well, I traced him out to California, I did. You know what happened."

Phil Smith sobered. "You bet, Eben. He sent a money order to cover the fine; he did." There was a touch of local pride in the tone. Hawn knew the way to appeal, knew it every time he came up in the village election.

"When do you think the shot was fired?" Kennedy was back on the subject. "What time of night?"

"Say!" exclaimed Hawn, his eyes bright and beady. "You sure do like to hear about murders. Well, murder and hate stirs us all, even when we only hear about 'em. You want to know why I reasoned it out that that murder must have been done in the dark of the morning, eh?"

Kennedy nodded.

"All right. I'll tell you. It ain't no secret. You see, I went down to see that there Doctor Foote who lives in Boston. Ever hear tell of him? He's a police doctor that's made a study of medicine and crime. I seen him. I asks Doctor Foote that and he asks me can he examine the contents of the stomach. So I gets Doctor Morrill, here, our county physician, to perform an autopsy, and he does. Doctor Foote says in his report to me that the condition of the food in the stomach showed the time was early morning. By jingo! he even tells us what old Jim had to eat the night before, and we finds it was true by what's in the cabin. Can you beat that? How'd he know if it wa'n't all on the level?"

Hawn looked at the others. I found out later that the thrifty taxpayers had criticized him for incurring this bill, that one election had been fought out on it and Hawn had won.

I was looking at Hawn with astonishment and a new respect. I could see that he was making a favorable impression on Kennedy, too. No one could call Hawn a hayseed. He was just a shrewd New Englander with a lot of hard-headed sense.

"Were there any other suspects?" I asked.

Hawn looked at me fixedly. He was not one to be pumped. Yet at the same time he was human. And we had treated him like a man, in contrast to many of the small-minded critics about him.

"I'll tell you. I go on the theory that as far as I'm concerned they're all guilty until they can prove 'emselves innocent. If I had a good case, I'd make an arrest—and let the fellow fight his way out of jail, see? Suspects? Yes, sir; several." He paused as if enumerating them on mental fingers. "Some thinks his own brother done it. Others that Warren, his nearest neighbor, the farmer in the valley, had enough of a grievance to kill him. Then there's Mathieu, a French Canadian, lives just beyond the village line. Him and Jim Gurney couldn't get along, always scrapping whenever they met. It all started over Jim trying to keep Mathieu from trapping and shooting over that side of Cobble in the season."

"I see," considered Craig, taking things one at a time. "His own brother. Was it a case of fighting over money in the family?"

Hawn shook his head. "No. It's a rather sad story—the story of a beautiful girl who died of a broken heart—and everybody in the village blamed Jim Gurney for it, too."

Now I was interested. A murder with the glamour of love about it is twice as interesting from my angle as any plain murder. All one has to do is to watch the newspapers and see that.

"Who was the girl?" asked Craig.

"Zilpha Norton. Just as purty as a picter, too. Them was the days before these here bob-haired tomboys in short pants. Just a purty little old-fashioned girl, with lots of spunk and fun about her, too."

"Was Gurney jealous of his brother and this girl?"

"No, not exactly. I don't think so, leastaways." Hawn was gazing back in the darkness twenty years. "It all happened years ago when Jim and Leroy Gurney was quite young. Jim was the older brother and liked to be boss. And Jim was always a rather cantankerous cuss as a boy. He never made friends easily with either boys or girls. And when the engagement of Zilpha and Leroy became known, Jim was furious. He opposed the marriage in every way. I expect it was mainly because he didn't want no new boss to get his kid brother, maybe. People couldn't understand the opposition, anyhow, and they asked him to explain. But he was obstinate about that, too. In the meantime this Zilpha Norton was wearing herself out with worry. Her bright, happy little ways all seemed to be changed."

Hawn took off his hat, smoothed back his hair reminiscently. "Well, you know, that girl come from a fine family, people above the average in this village and around here. They were college-bred folks, had traveled some, were much higher than Jim Gurney socially and every other way."

He paused again and went on. "I can remember little Zilpha Norton as though it was yesterday in one of them rubber-tired runabouts that was so fashionable 'bout twenty years ago. She had a purty horse and useter go driving every fair day. She knew everybody and had a smile for everyone. The village loved that there girl, and Zilpha loved Leroy. When they went walking together she'd look at him kinder shylike, and he was so crazy 'bout her, folks passing uster nudge each other, especially any older married couple. It brought back their own courtin' days to 'em."

The constable was romantic, too. He stopped and seemed to be in deep thought. I wondered if memories of Zilpha had stirred his heart, too.

"Did Leroy marry Zilpha?" I couldn't help asking.

"No—he didn't. Jim kept right on opposing that match. He was questioned so much 'at finally he blurted out and told why. He said there was gossip about Zilpha, that she was being spoke lightly of, that when she went away to school one time she really went to a hospital instead and had a child…. Consarn it! You know how such gossip travels. It's bad enough in a big city. But in a small town it's terrible. There ain't no stoppin' it. All the women and most o' the men was discussing it before nightfall. Finally it reached back to Zilpha. It was too much for that little girl's proud nature, the way they was looking at her and hanging the scarlet letter on her. She committed suicide one night. Then Jim Gurney's brother, Leroy, he disappeared, went out to the Coast. After the tragedy, after them two lives was blasted by that there gossip, it was all found to be a mess o' lies, just plain lies, to break up the match."

"What did her folks do?" inquired Craig.

"Do? Her father thrashed Jim Gurney down in front of the post office to within an inch of his life, he did. But Zilpha was dead and Leroy was gone. He might have felt like shooting Jim Gurney, but old man Norton was the kind not to take the law into his own hands—much. Soon after that he died, and Mrs. Norton didn't survive him long. Zilpha was the only child.

"The only Norton living now is her cousin—a great naturalist. He keeps his home here, but he travels most of the time. Mighty fine man, too. Only he knows too much book knowledge for me. When I talks to him I always gets warm about the ears for fear of making mistakes. He lives in the big Norton house down in the other end of the village. You must 'a' seen it. You'd oughter go there sometime. They say the house is filled with strange birds, bugs, and beasts from all over the world. He ain't got a lot of money, but he's a regular globe-trotter, never could be contented, as long as I've knowed him, to stay in one place. Maybe you seen some of his articles in the magazines? Willis Norton? They won't keep you awake nights, but they're good."

"What happened to Jim Gurney after the tragedy?"

"Oh, Jim Gurney went away, got jobs in various places. He come back about three years ago; hadn't been back long afore this here thing happened. When he came back he took up living in that lonely cabin up on Cobble, over the farm of this Warren that'd once been the Gurney place and Warren bought."

"How did the villagers look on Gurney when he came back?"

"Oh, no one liked him no more'n they ever did. He left 'em alone, and that arrangement suited us to a T. If he had ever had a real enemy in the world, they'd outgrown the enmity, we allowed. An' I think as he got along in years time softened the despicable thing he done, somewhat. You know it has that effect on most things. He had been peculiar. We knew it. And when he come back none of us cared to investigate to see if he'd changed. We let him alone."

"Well, how does the brother become a suspect?" I asked. "Has he come back, too?"

Hawn thought a long time. "Not that I ever heard of," he said, slowly and deliberately, as if holding back, "but many people suspected at the time that he come back quietly from the Coast, after years of brooding over Jim's lying interference, and killed him."

Hawn said it with a caution that even Kennedy seemed disposed not to question. One must not quiz official caution if one seeks to get anywhere in an interview.

"It's a mighty interesting murder," remarked Craig, thoughtfully. "Did they ever get enough on anybody to hold him?"

"No; not after the coroner's inquest. But people have done a lot of suspecting, and it ain't been pleasant around here for Warren, nor Mathieu, neither. I think they'd both leave, only it looks too much like a confession. They're still here, glowering at each other, as if each of 'em thinks the other is responsible for the suspicion resting on him." Hawn laughed quietly.

"I told my wife the other day, if Gurney's murderer wa'n't caught soon there'd be another murder committed." Phil Smith's deep throaty chuckle revealed his twist of humor.

"What was Warren's grievance against Gurney?" asked Craig.

"Oh, Warren bought some of the Gurney property. It seemed that part of the acreage had been left to Leroy, but Jim settled it up with him when Leroy left. He sold the farm land to Warren, kept the upland. When he come back he said Warren had over-stepped, that his boundary fences was over on the upland. One morning Warren finds his fences all down and set back on what Jim Gurney says was the dividing line. Then there was a dispute and a law suit and everything. That scrap was going on in the courts when Jim Gurney was killed. Warren is a stubborn customer. He don't seem to care if he is in contempt. I noticed the other day his fences was all back on the line that Jim Gurney broke up. The case is still in the courts."

Craig seemed preoccupied. "What is there against this Mathieu?" I asked. "Did he ever have any trouble with Gurney?"

"Did he?" This was from the usually silent Phil Smith. "I'll say he did. That's what I had to tell at the inquest. I was gunning one day on Warren's place. Warren asked me up any time I wanted to have a little sport on his place in the fall. Some parts of his woodland that Jim Gurney didn't claim runs up into them parts that Gurney did claim, and along by what wa'n't in dispute at all, too. I heard voices and enough to know that it was Jim Gurney and Mathieu in some argyment over traps that Mathieu'd set on the side of Cobble. I was afraid my dog'd get caught in one of 'em, or shot, or something. So I called him and put him on leash. By the time I come out in the open I see there was Jim

Gurney and Mathieu having it hot and heavy over them traps.
O' course Gurney had the better of it. He was right. It was his
land. He maintained any fur-bearing animals onto it was his. I
dunno what Mathieu's argyment was, but just as they heard me
I caught Mathieu a-reaching for his knife. Of course when I
came on the fight was over right there. Mathieu slunk off in the
woods, and Jim was mad yet, cussing about 'that damn Canuck
trespasser'."

"That's a long speech for you, Phil," put in one of the chaps
on the bench. "I guess you must 'a' learned it for the coroner's
jury, to speak it."

"Oh, that wasn't the first fight," observed Hawn, changing the
subject before Smith could retort. "Mathieu knew he could get
Gurney's goat, and the devil in him made him trespass lots o'
times. They loved each other like a couple o' wild cats." Suddenly
Eben Hawn's arms were raised high over his head. His loose vest
stretched up, showing the white shirt between vest and trousers.
"I'm dog tired. I was up late last night. Rum runners. I'm going
to bed. If we talks much more about murders, you strangers'll
be askin' me for an escort back to the hotel."

This labored sally was a general signal to break up for the
night. We left with the rest.

"Walter," observed Craig, as we walked back alone, "I rather
like these people up here. There's a lot of hard-headed common
sense in most of them. Now, about this Gurney case. It rather
interests me. We might stay on a day or two, eh?"

"It suits me. I like the place. That man Hawn is nobody's fool."

So it was that bright and early the next morning we left the
hotel for another long jaunt without a guide. It was beautiful.
The hotel was on the side of a hill itself, but around us and across
the valley the greater hills and near-by mountains towered even
higher. It seemed so peaceful, so quiet, that crime in such an
atmosphere was an anomaly.

The country was inspiring. In the distance the little river
wound its way through the valley serenely placid. What jumpy

city people call "pep" and admire so inordinately sinks into proper insignificance compared with that detached, intelligent calmness bred of the hills and high places.

Over the hills the trees were getting bare and the ground under them seemed like a molten mass of color, a riot of yellow, orange, and red. Only the sky above us, slightly leaden in spite of the morning sun, preserved the quiet, gentle colors. Even the masses of evergreens luxuriantly covering the sides of the higher hills and mountains looming in the distance like sentinels were softened by a haze.

In the foothills rested the villages and small settlements tucked in one might think for shelter and quiet. Here and there we could see the early morning stirring-about of the inhabitants.

"I've been turning that Gurney case over in my mind. Craig," I ventured, as we plodded along. "What do you think about that brother? Do you suppose he came back quietly—and slipped away again in the same manner?"

Kennedy did not answer, and I knew from that that he was not ready to talk. But I felt a desire to talk that morning. "You know," I tried again, "Eben Hawn said they found no trace of Leroy since the murder. He must have got away quietly, got back again to the Coast, if he ever came here."

Kennedy was smoking, taking long puffs at his pipe as we slogged along. In that smoke he seemed to be seeking the solution of the lonely murder on Cobble Hill. It was no use. I left him to himself and followed the road behind him, quietly, too.

We passed people occasionally and received a pleasant greeting usually. Most of the men we had met at one time or another at Phil Smith's garage. This was an opportunity for us, too. We could stop and talk to them, and through the gossip obtain little scraps of information that might help.

We were now following the trail to Cobble Hill. Not that we intended to go to the deserted cabin again. The Warren farm was Craig's objective, and the ostensible reason for our visit was Warren's well-known interest in sports that demanded a gun and a quick eye. He was one of the best trap-shooters about South Elliott and had shot all kinds of game for years in those north woods.

Warren was out on his place when we arrived. Evidently our presence in the village was known to him, although he was not acquainted with our real names. Still, he knew that we hunted, and that bond was strong enough. He invited us in and offered us some of his apple cider that he had made himself. There was a tang to it that even the government seems unable to stop nature from bestowing.

"On the Cobble trail, eh? I kinda thought you would turn in here. Most people do since the tragedy up the hill. That place seems to drive people away."

"I didn't feel exactly comfortable on the place when I was there, either," agreed Kennedy, casually. "I was glad when we left."

"I'd like to buy the place, only the estate is asking too much for it. Old Gurney and I didn't just seem to hit it off—always in hot water over our boundaries. I let him have his own way most of the time." Suddenly he stopped and looked at us sharply. "You folks ain't thinking of getting it, are you?"

Kennedy shook his head reassuringly. "Not investing in real estate right now. Just out for our health and a little game. But it might make a nice little hunting lodge, at that."

Warren nodded. "Why don't you stay here and shoot to-day? No one else coming that I know of. There's only one man that has the nerve to come without asking, and that's Mathieu, the Canuck—and he can't come. He had a little accident the other day—hurt his hand—and I ain't seen him since."

"Mathieu?" repeated Kennedy, as if questioning.

"Yes. You know, he was mentioned in that Gurney case." The mountain farmer jerked his thumb over his shoulder toward the cabin. "People don't like him too much. Him and me agrees on one thing. We let the others talk about it, but we don't. Our attorneys told us that was the best plan. But, still and all, I can't help thinking a powerful lot that if I had a brother like that there Jim Gurney was, I guess I'd know something about it, or know them that did!" he concluded, triumphantly, with this cryptically veiled reference to Leroy.

"Where does this Mathieu live?" asked Kennedy. "Near here?"

"No. Quite a piece down the valley road, toward town." From the hill, looking down, he pointed to what looked like little more than a one-room shanty by the bend in the river. Kennedy gazed at it some time as if fixing it in his mind, while Warren gazed at him, noting it. "If you are going to see him," he said at length, "are you sure how he will greet you? Mathieu is a surly cuss—refuses to see even some of them that calls on business. He chased the letter carrier off last month, called him a damn spy."

The farmer laughed a cracked laugh at Mathieu's idea of visitors, and I could not help thinking there was malice behind the remarks he was making concerning the other men suspected. I wondered what that meant. Had he really anything to conceal and was that his method of diverting suspicion from himself? I thought it almost childish. Almost anyone could have seen through that.

We stopped and chatted for fully half an hour. In all the conversation, in spite of Jim Gurney's horrible end, there seemed in what Warren said to be an implacable hatred even of the dead man's memory. Surely, I thought, if hatred were the tutor of murder, Warren must have been a proficient pupil.

Out on the highway, down a little overgrown path, and then cutting our way through the brush and woodland, we came out at last on the little road that led to Mathieu's shanty. I was wondering how badly he had been injured. There was at first no evidence of him about the place except a little smoke climbing in a spiral ribbon from the chimney.

"Somebody's home, anyhow," was Craig's brief observation.

We went up toward the cabin. The ferocious barking of a dog greeted us from within.

"Shut up, Wolf!" came a voice, harsh, threatening, matching the dog's own growl in quality and temper. It silenced the animal. "What do you want?" continued the voice. "There's nothing no one has to see me about." The ungracious voice trailed off suddenly into an oath and an exclamation of pain.

Kennedy was not abashed or deterred. "Mathieu," he called back through the still locked door. "You don't know me, but I'm a hunter, too. I heard you were hurt. I've come to see what I can do for you. Call that dog of yours off, open the door and let me in."

Evidently the man was suffering intensely. His groans were pitiful, at least would have been in a man who did not repel one so. The poor dog, evidently scenting trouble of some kind, was now whining in sympathy. Kennedy listened intently.

"I'm a doctor. You never saw me before—and after this vacation you'll probably never see me again. Let me help you if I can."

There was a gruff response in a voice that was scarcely audible now from suppressed pain. "All right! Get under the table, Wolf! Keep quiet, damn you! Ah, my arm!" Followed a string of oaths half in English, half in Canadian French, that would have been a lexicon for any blasphemer whether backwoodsman or hijacker.

The door was suddenly flung open, revealing a man, his arm in a sling made out of an old flannel shirt, his other hand clutching at it in a frenzy of pain. His face was white and drawn and covered with a heavy beard. His hair had not been combed in several days and stood in disarray in thick mats about his head. On his forehead, in spite of the coolness of the weather, stood great beads of sweat—the sweat of pain, not from the small fire in the cabin. His brow was furrowed by deep lines and these lines were accentuated by the dirt that long ago had settled in the wrinkles. If that man had been well, I should not have cared to meet him if his mood were other than peaceable.

Kennedy was the kindly Samaritan seeking tactfully to help this man in distress. "Let me take a look, old man." This was said in a matter-of-fact manner as if a refusal were the last thing in the world to be expected.

Mathieu acquiesced. With deft fingers Kennedy undid the

bandages while I made some boiling water. Always Craig carried on our trips of this sort a little emergency kit for immediate aid in case of gunshot wounds or other injuries.

"I always take this along," he explained as he opened the kit, and, with a smile to Mathieu, finished: "I never know how many greenhorns I'm going to meet in the woods. Lots of game around here—if you can find it. But I've had a lot of fun."

Mathieu's sore hand was caused by an infected gun-shot wound. It needed attention desperately. "It's going to hurt some. I'll be as gentle as I can."

"He can't hurt no more than he does—so!" Mathieu answered, as he looked at the red marks of infection creeping up the veins of his arm. "Go ahead. Somehow I believe in you."

The least said about that dressing the best. It was painful, but after it was done and the wound had been opened and cleansed, there was a temporary relief. A salve and fresh bandage with a clean sling made life look brighter for Mathieu. We made him a little soup before we left, and by the time these things were done Mathieu had said many things and had not realized it.

"Mon dieu!" he exclaimed once, at a twinge. "If a little shot like this can hurt so much, what must it be that Zheem Gurnee feel when he have that hole in his breast, eh?"

The remark had followed our confidence that we had been shooting over Cobble. "Oh," returned Craig, "that was so sudden he probably never knew what struck him, from all accounts." Kennedy continued in a tone of perfunctory curiosity. "Who did it? Did they ever find out definitely?"

There was a quick glance and a frown, but evidently what Mathieu saw in our faces disarmed his suspicions.

"I think," he went on a moment later, "that hees brother, Leroy, he know more about that murder than anyone else know. You know, maybe, that that Zheem Gurnee keel his brother's sweetheart? No? Well what he do come to that, just the same. *Oui,* if I have been Leroy I would keel him long time."

Kennedy was silently listening. Mathieu, to me, seemed

nervous and to show it. But then one had to consider the weakness and nervousness brought on by the dressing and the sleeplessness before that. It might not all have been caused by emotion produced by our talking about the crime.

"I no like Zheem Gumee. Mean man. Nevair want no one shoot in hees woods. I have many trouble weez heem over zat. You hear, eh? Maybe. Many people think I might know more about eet than I say." He shrugged, tried to smile. "But, no."

Mathieu was grateful and showed it. "E-yah!" he ejaculated, still thinking of Gurney, as well as his own pain. "He maka trouble for all—especiallee the neighbor. I do no see how Warren stand eet. He quiet man, no say much, but"—he raised the finger on his well hand—"but deep!"

Kennedy without a word finished packing up his little first-aid kit, rolled it up, dropped it back into the capacious pocket of his hunting jacket.

"Eef you stay here long time for me get better, I take you where game *IS*. I have tramp about so much there no be many place I no find out myself. Some do no like. Pouf! This world she was made for ever'body—not just a few. Eh?"

I took it that this was both his philosophy to explain himself as well as his manner of showing gratitude. Kennedy wound up by advising him to keep quiet for a few days and we prepared to leave.

"Mathieu," he said as we parted, "I'm coming up to dress that wound again to-morrow—about the same time."

With a wave of our hands we left him, much more comfortable, standing in the doorway, and passed on down the rough road toward the village.

"Where are you going now?" I asked. "It's early yet."

"Wasn't that last visit enough?" Kennedy turned, looking over the country about us. "If I do any shooting about here, it will be poaching. These woods belong to people here in South Elliott. If we come to a new trail we can take that, see where it brings us out."

We threaded our way through the woodland. Birches growing in the little sociable groups so common to that kind of tree seemed to be leaning forward gracefully, inviting us to explore further in the depths of the forest. My spirit seemed to be in accord with the mood suggested by the trees in my fancy.

Imagine my dismay when I came to a huge sign nailed to a tree, "No Trespassing."

The beauty and appeal of the place were irresistible. I wanted to go on. So did Craig. But we were not lawbreakers.

We were debating what to do next, when a man's voice hailed us. I suppose we looked bewildered, rather lost. "May I help you? Are you looking for some one's place?"

The man was tall and slender, high-browed, with a wealth of heavy dark hair. He wore no hat. About his face he affected a close-cropped beard coming to a point at the chin, a Vandyke. His eyes were deep-set and kindly. I liked the stranger immediately. Mentally, I gathered, he was much above the inhabitants of the village I had met.

Kennedy smiled. "We're strangers—just a little mixed on the trails. We were exploring, and finally came up to this sign. We have just about decided to turn and go back to our hotel, perhaps start all over again. Whose place is this?"

"The Norton place. I am the owner. I see you are strangers around here. But if you care to walk through with me I will show you about, be delighted to do so. I'm very fond of it up here."

I murmured, thanking him for his kindness, but it was Craig who spoke up quickly. "Norton? Norton? I have heard them mention that name down at the hotel and the garage, in the village. Aren't you the traveler and naturalist?"

"I have traveled a bit—and possibly to a degree I might qualify as a naturalist," he smiled. "I have done much museum work, have been on various expeditions to South America, Africa, and Central America for the study of bird life and animal life in general. We must have our hobbies. That is mine."

"It sounds mighty interesting." I spoke up earnestly and

meant it. "I have often felt a desire to go on such trips, but my calling doesn't permit it."

Somehow we naturally fell in step with the man as he led the way about the beautiful place from which he was away so much, listening, as we tramped, to his stories of hunting big game in warmer and wilder climes.

"This must seem tame to you up here after your varied adventures," volunteered Craig.

"It seems quiet. But it is good. It's home. My travels have led me into all sorts of dangers, yes. I have had wasting fevers that have helped to undermine my health. I'll never be so strong again, I doubt."

"But you have lived!" I admired, spontaneously. I had been quite won by this cultured adventurer. He was so gentle and simple and knew so much.

"Yes, I have lived—and I have had my losses. I am practically alone as to family, except for a sister in North Elliott, who is married. Alone. That isn't good… It is hard to see all one loves taken from one." He was speaking sadly, absently. "There have been several distressing things that have happened in our family—and that is one of them."

We had strolled down a path to what looked like a little old-fashioned family graveyard such as one so often sees on the very old estates far from cities. He had touched a stone reverently, the nearest one.

"There they put my little cousin Zilpha when she died." He waved to two others alongside. "There lie my uncle and aunt. They were father and mother to me after my own died in a wreck."

He turned away quickly and we followed him at a brisker pace to the house. "Would you care to see my collection of curios?" he suggested.

We were eager to accept, and felt rather flattered over the invitation. Somehow I felt that an invitation was not given to everybody.

"You see," he continued, as if getting his mind off the gravestones, "I have a collection of photographs of beasts, birds, flowers, plants, trees from all over the world. They were snapped by a wonderful little vest-pocket camera made specially for me, with a German lens, a little Icarette. I always take it along on every trip. Then I can make enlargements from the snaps, better than you get from most of our large cameras."

The house, too, was old-fashioned. One could see at a glance it had been the home of those who in the past combined domesticity with culture. The grounds, the trees, the outbuildings were all in good condition, in spite of Willis Norton's frequent and long trips away. We spoke of it to him.

"Well, an old family like the Nortons up here generally manages to keep one or two faithful retainers, to say nothing of the splendid old Chinese servant I brought from Manchuria right after that war. I always leave some one behind to look after the Norton place when I go on a trip—some one who cares."

In the rear of the old house was a spiral staircase, quaint and beautiful. It went to the top floor of the house, where Norton kept his collection. In cases, arranged in groups significant as to habitat, were strange animals brought from the many lands out of the beaten track that he had visited.

Folios filled with photographs, his own and others, gave rare and intimate chance to study wild-animal life taken when the animals thought they were unobserved, a silent testimonial to the patience and endurance of Norton in obtaining and collecting them. Everything carefully catalogued by his own hand denoted painstaking systematizing of records, dates, places, whether taken alone or with other witnesses, the time of the day, any data for lighting or other photographic information of any possible interest. All had been saved and recorded. Then all was filed so that future reference would be easy.

It was fascinating, sitting before the huge fireplace that cool afternoon in the fall, listening to this much-traveled man tell thrilling anecdotes of his varied experiences. Kennedy was enjoying it, too. Here was a man brilliant, capable, refined, the last sort of person I had expected to meet when we started out that morning.

"Norton," observed Kennedy, "I can't say I blame you either, for being away so much or for having this wonderful place to come back to, after I hear your stories. You have lived, as my friend so aptly put it a while ago. I suppose you get the most fun out of life and studies in little-known areas, rather than out of what is so well known to us all here at home in the States."

The man was leaning back indolently in his chair, fingering the keys he had been using opening various chests and cabinets and compartments as he showed us his treasures.

"No; I would hardly say that. Of course, you know, what I have is commonplace in those, to us, strange countries. What to us is well known is just as strange and remarkable there." He paused. "No; I am intensely interested in what is about us here, too. I have showed you these exhibits only because I thought the strange things would be more appealing to you because not so well known. If you were an Eskimo or a Kaffir, I have things about us here just as strange to show you, comparatively. It is all a matter of comparison. Personally, I take a great deal of interest in native wild life, just that about South Elliott, for instance, or even domesticated life."

He paused again, thinking back. "You see, when I was younger I was photographing whenever I had the chance. I suppose that is what started me, beginning around here. But—times have changed. It doesn't seem so much like home. And I feel better in other parts of the world. I am now planning a trip with one of the expeditions sent out by a famous museum in New York. They want me along for my technical knowledge of photography and my knowledge of the birds we are going after."

The mention of the expedition by Norton drew my attention to his physical condition. He did not look strong, looked hardly robust enough to endure the hardships and rigors, to say nothing of the dangers of another lengthy exploration.

He saw me. "I know what you are thinking—that I don't seem very rugged. That is the reason I am going out this time with others, not alone."

He bowed his head as he spoke, then suddenly looked up. "Perhaps you would like to see some photographs taken about South Elliott. You know it all depends on how, with what eyes, we look on the very life about us, so familiar. I think I have taken a new angle; that is, new to most people. I'll show them to you. Since my folks have died I don't take the same interest here, though. Once in a while when I get over to North Elliott I feel a bit of the old enthusiasm. But it goes away. Not the same interest. I think I have mentioned that several times—but the repetition tells what a family man I am by nature—and that I'm getting old, too," he smiled.

Kennedy nodded sympathetically. "You know, Norton, I have heard about the sad case of your little cousin Zilpha. Her death seemed to stir the whole village. They haven't got over it yet. It's terrible, the disastrous lengths gossip can go.... Have you ever thought much about Mathieu and his relation to the murder of Jim Gurney, for instance? We just left his cabin. I heard he was suffering. He seems to be regarded with such general dislike about South Elliott that we ventured up to see what we could do for him. He surely is bitter against even the memory of Jim Gurney."

Norton raised his brows. "I know Mathieu when I see him. And I know Warren, the other man under suspicion in that Gurney murder. But I have taken very little interest in the case. All I could see in it was fate, retribution. The measure of hate a man bestows on another person in this world is meted out to him in some way before he is through living. Sort of a law of balance." He turned from us as if the subject were distasteful, as if it brought too many painful memories of the little cousin he had loved so dearly.

"Now here is a folio of domestic animals about South Elliott." He said it with a smile. "You wouldn't think of taking as much care with horses and chickens as, say, with the hartebeest in

Africa? I'll show you these first. Some of them you may at first think funny. We don't usually think of our pigs, horses, and cows as having romances."

He paused again, and instantly I was fascinated. The man had something romantic about him, a, to me, new romance. "But in these pictures I am showing you how they woo, the capitulation of the female, the beautiful mother instinct of preserving her young. To me, with my love of animals, it offers many a lesson to us humans. There is nothing flippant about it. It is a serious study, and mighty interesting."

The pictures proved the truth of what he had been saying. As he showed them to us in the order they should go, a new phase of animal existence right about us dawned on me. Those animals may not possess the convolutions of brain, the cells of gray matter. But they know the Law of Life. They are interpreting it faithfully and beautifully. Are not many of us humans out of tune with the Law?

All of these pictures were dated, too. Some had been taken years ago, marked the beginning of his career as a naturalist. Others were more recent, on down the years. Probably a few had been taken each time Norton returned to South Elliott from wandering over the face of the earth.

In many of the photographs the locations were familiar to me. Our tramping over the hills had taken us past many places we could identify in the pictures. Our own recent acquaintance with the background enhanced our interest in what Norton had caught in the foreground.

"H'm! This is rather interesting." Norton passed us a snapshot. It was only a picture of five cows in a field, grazing, over at what I took to be North Elliott, ten miles the other side of Cobble. They were grazing earnestly and all looking the same way. I could not see anything very wonderful about that. Many of the other snap-shots had appealed to me. This was just five cows eating as if their lives depended on it. My thoughts must have been expressed in my face, showing I was eager to have him go on and show others of his romantic animal studies. Norton spoke quickly. "Just about two years ago. Look at the date. That is the date of that murder you mentioned. The hour is that very morning, near dawn, taken soon after sunrise."

Now I was interested, even if it was taken miles away, hours of hiking over the hills. I looked at it over Kennedy's shoulder, five cows grazing, all facing the same way. It was easy to identify the location—Cobble in the distance, South Elliott beyond that, ten miles away, with the cabin of Jim Gurney on the South Elliott side of Cobble, far away from that lens.

"I had just come back from a little vacation in Labrador, was staying at the time with my sister. My brother-in-law developed those films for me that very morning."

Kennedy had been holding the print, studying it intently. Now he laid it down quietly, but still with his hand on it. Slowly he was shaking his head.

"When I was a young fellow in college, I spent much of my time every summer in Wyoming on a ranch," he remarked, slowly. "In the morning, the cows are lying down lazily, still chewing their cuds. Even when they get up they graze all over the field, in every direction, some east, some south, some north, some west. There is plenty of light for them to see by that time."

He paused, snapping the corner of the crisp print in thoughtful emphasis. "But at night they graze all with heads toward the westing sun. Any other way they are in their own light. And they graze frantically, for the very last bite before darkness lowers—just as these cows are grazing. They have all night to digest it. If you saw five hundred head of cattle, they would all be facing the same way at this time, and at no other time—just as these five.... This was taken the night before you started out, Norton—and you dated it the morning afterward, for your alibi, which you carefully prepared!"

I could actually see Norton, not physically strong, anyhow, weaken, crumple almost literally, his hand on his heart. His lips moved several times, framing words, but no sound came from them. Kennedy did not speak. He wanted it to sink in, wanted Norton to speak.

"These people up here, they will never understand!" Finally Norton had found his voice. Now the words were flooding out with a rush of pent-up emotion. "But you, sir, you are a man of the world. You will understand…. Yes. It was *hate*. That man *blackened* my family, my favorite, my only cousin. He murdered Zilpha with his damned lying tongue. You might as well call it that, call it what it was, in a community like this. It wasn't true. It was a lie. And it killed. I followed him. I searched for him. That was bask of my globe-trotting, really. Always I was too late. He had moved on!"

Norton was now standing, his hand on his breast, as if to witness the truth of each word.

"He did not know it. In twenty years he thought all had been forgotten. He came back, tired of wandering, took the cabin on the hill. I heard it, found him, back here. I knew the cabin, the window near where he slept in the attic room. I rested the old blunderbuss in a crotch of a tree. I was taking no chances. I let it blaze, both barrels! Shot him, like the dog he was! I meant it, to blast out of him that evil, lying filthy heart!"

Kennedy nodded.

"Yes, and this picture was to be your alibi, taken in the morning, that morning, you said, dated, developed by your brother-in-law, ten miles away. It got past Hawn, here…. But it was taken really in the evening, the evening before, not in the morning, near dawn. The cows are all facing *west*—the setting sun—and you, Norton, with your hand clutching that old heart of yours, the sun is setting on you, too, soon!"

AIR

KENNEDY HANDED THE powerful field-glasses to me,
I focused them on what had been to my naked eye not even a
little speck up in the sky.

With the glasses now I picked out by the red, white, and blue
concentric circles and the number painted on the wings what
I knew must be Wallace Knight flying a Curtiss plane in the
New York *Star* contest for altitude while carrying a passenger.

"Craig!" I exclaimed, "he is coming down!"

Kennedy nodded. "That's what I wanted you to see."

"Has he engine trouble, do you suppose?"

Craig shrugged. "If he has, he shows no nervousness."

I thought of the cheer for Wallace Knight when he had taken
off against Harper in the De Haviland, a cheer quite as much
also for Henry Gaines, his passenger.

A few moments and the speck was visible to the naked eye.

"Mr. Jameson! What's the matter?"

It was Adora Gaines, with us, who made the exclamation,
hands clasped tensely, peering eagerly up at the descending
airplane. Adora shivered as if a sense of premonition had swept
over her. She clutched my arm.

"If anything is wrong," she almost whispered, "it's Henry...
The plane is coming down too smoothly for Henry to be guid-
ing it."

I tried to reassure her, although I have long since ceased to
scoff at women's intuitions.

Our college classmate, Henry Gaines, had married a splendid girl, Adora Hollister, of Westbury. Kennedy had known
the Hollisters for years. Adora was only a child, very small, with
big blue eyes that scintillated. She was one of the most graceful
girls in the dance that I have ever seen who was still an amateur.

Gaines loved with an intensity of feeling. Solidity, a sense
of security, prevailed when he was around. It was that that had
first attracted Adora Hollister. When she had been with Henry
she had a good time—and knew there would be no come-backs
afterward. He was square, on the level. She had loved him and
married him.

Wally Knight was the type of athlete. He had been active in
all sports and it was with the greatest zest he had taken up aviation as the king of them all. Wally was a singularly handsome
fellow, of a long, rangy type, one of the born bird men. Today he
had been wonderful, at times like a knight of old in his helmet
drawn closely about his face emphasizing his clear-cut profile;
at other times an intensely modern figure, one of the few who
could affect with ease the slouch of sport apparel.

Henry Gaines was of a quite different type, quiet, reserved in
nature. Wally had been among the unsuccessful suitors for the
beautiful Adora Hollister. He had taken it like the sportsman
his friends found him. He had been the "runner-up" in the love
game. Henry had won. Wally had accepted it.

It was a wonderful afternoon for such an event. The hanging
on of summer in the early part of October, with its warmth, had
lured many people to the fields of Belmont Park. There must
have been fully thirty thousand. Acres of parking space had been
reserved for the cars, cars that totaled millions of dollars in value.

To me the crowd had been quite as interesting as the event.
Beautiful girls in sport clothes were everywhere, low trained
voices, musical laughter, the swish of silks, whiffs of strange
perfumes, as we mixed in the throng.

Up—up—up the planes had risen in long spirals, climbing,

climbing, climbing—until they were lost to the eye in the gray blue.

Now a murmur ran through the crowd.

"Too bad! Wally couldn't stay up long enough even to make a good try for the record!"

"Ticklish business—this flying!"

He was sweeping down now in long spirals as he had climbed, now volplaning to earth.

It became a silent, waiting crowd. Both Henry Gaines and Wally Knight were of them, at least of that portion who had, through my paper, the *Star*, helped promote and finance this meet for the prestige of aviation in America, the country where it was born.

Society was interested in this aviation meet, and especially in the altitude contest. It almost made me think of the polo games. Many of the same people were there. I must confess that I was consumed with a newspaperman's sense of delight in mingling with so many of the best known. Through the *Star* and Kennedy I found myself on good terms with most of them that were worth while....

They were frankly disappointed. All the faces showed it. There were murmurs of apprehension, too, as well as of annoyance. The De Haviland was still far beyond our unaided vision.

Knight rounded one of the pylons, swerved his machine dangerously toward a section of the paddock where about ten thousand people had gathered, then out over the field, down and running along the turf as three or four attendants ran after to catch up with him.

His propellers droned to a quick silence and we could see Wally rise, waving his arms frantically. He cupped his hands and shouted.

"Is there a doctor on the field?"

Kennedy broke from the crowd, over the fence, and ran toward him. I followed with Adora.

As I came nearer I could make out Henry Gaines, pale with

an exaggerated pallor, sprawled in his seat in the machine. A thin trickle of blood from his nose had already began to coagulate.

Doctor Nesmith pushed ahead of us.

"How high did you get?" he asked, speaking rapidly as he made a hurried, thorough examination.

"Only about fifteen thousand feet."

I thought hastily to myself. Only about three miles!

"Traces of pulmonary hemorrhage," muttered the doctor to himself. "Rapid breathing because of lack of oxygen in the rarefied air…. Heart didn't keep pace…."

As he turned he did not need to say anything. I knew that Henry Gaines was dead—strapped in his seat in the airplane!

For several moments Adora Gaines stood stunned. White and shocked, she looked helplessly at her husband. I hovered near, ready if she fainted. But it was not necessary.

She stood stunned, waited until they took him from his seat. Doctor Nesmith and Craig lifted him on a stretcher that had been hurriedly brought forward. I don't think that even then Adora accepted the doctor's verdict.

As they started to take him to one of the little rooms near the grandstand, Adora glided forward. "Wait!" she cried in a hollow voice.

She acted as if she knew her love to which Henry had always responded would call him back to consciousness. We could do no more than let her satisfy herself. I heard Wallace murmur, "Let's humor her. I know how she loved him."

She knelt on both knees by her husband, took his limp white hand, raised it to her trembling lips. "Henry—look at me—dear!"

There was no response. Adora shivered again nervously as she had before. Henry had never acted like that.

Wallace would not stand her grief as she bent over her husband. He left our party and looked over the aeroplane without seeing. As he passed he muttered to me, "I can't watch her agony, Walter!"

Taking her wisp of handkerchief she gently wiped her husband's lips and face. "Henry! It's adora. Please answer me! Shall I take you home now?"

Still no answer. She raised her eyes, startled, to Craig.

"Please, Adora, let me take you home. Walter and I want to help you, in every way. The others will do everything they can for—"

"Henry!" she added, brokenly. "My husband!... I don't care much where I go...."

Craig took her little hands in his and she staggered to her feet. "I can't believe he left me alone here.... It is all too sudden. Where is Wallace?"

I called him.

"Adora," he cried huskily, "I wish I had gone in his place. I feel—terrible.... I—I shall never fly again!"

"How did you know, Wallace? What did he say last?" Adora leaned forward tensely in utter tearless grief.

"I heard a cough. I knew then he must be in trouble. I couldn't leave the controls. I started back, down. I looked. I know as I watched her lips that he was saying, 'Adora!'"

"While I was laughing, gay, down here with you," she exclaimed, looking solemnly at us, "Henry was dying and calling me up there—and I didn't know it... I want to go home, Craig—to mother's."

"Do you think I had better go with her?" whispered Wallace aside.

Kennedy shook his head. "No, you would only suggest the tragedy more vividly to her. I want her to get a little quiet and comfort."

"I know... I'll do anything here I can...."

It was the day after the funeral—the most agonizing time of all. Then the emptiness of things is so appalling and the future seems so long.

I had not liked the burning wistfulness of Adora's eyes. Such grief kills. There was always a ghastly question in those eyes. Why had this thing come to her, just when she was so happy in Henry's love?

"Walter, we ought to go around to see Adora," remarked Kennedy thoughtfully. "She needs help."

"That's right. She'll brood and worry herself ill, alone in that big house Henry built for her."

"Later, I'm going to get the young people here to urge her to join in some quiet things, things that will keep her outdoors. Outdoors is what she needs. Nature has so much of death in the fall of the year that there has been something provided as an antidote, as it were. It's in the air. Adora needs it to overcome the melancholy. She may not want golf at the Country Club; but a good horse—a new car—anything—even breaking a few speed laws, would get her mind on something else."

We motored around to the Gaines house. As we entered the big hall, a maid handed Adora a huge bunch of white chrysanthemums. Adora looked at the card hastily and laid it down. As we followed her into the living room, I saw that the card was from Wally Knight and on it was written, "Just to let you know that the thoughts of your friends are with you to-day."

Adora Gaines was still not much more than a child. She had been only nineteen when she was married. Even the tragedy of the flying field had scarcely touched her real youth. The pallor of her face and the deep circles about her wonderful blue eyes were the only noticeable evidences of the inroads of harrowing grief. In her pleated white crepe dress falling in graceful lines about her slender, youthful figure she was entrancing.

"It's awful—to-day—Craig!" she half whispered.

"I know," he answered, his voice lowering. "That is why we have come to see you."

Suddenly she betrayed great agitation. She had been leaning against a big chair when a pitiful moan escaped her. She gripped the chair.

"Henry's chair! Oh. Craig, I can't bear it. The flowers are beautiful; my friends are so kind; you have been just what I would expect of one of my oldest friends. But none—compensates for the loss…. Oh, help me, Craig. You are so dependable. I think that is one reason why Henry cared so much for you." Somehow the girl could not cry. "Sit down and talk to me. This house is like an empty shell, now," she smiled sadly.

"This is a beautiful room, Adora," remarked Craig, changing the subject. "But I know a better place for you."

"W-where?" Adora asked it, startled.

"Out of doors—and as much as you can find time to be out. Get interested in work for some children. They always heal a wounded soul." She shuddered. I knew what her thought was.

The living room was indeed a room to inspire one. An old house in Andover had been stripped of all its golden maple panels, mantels, doors. The wide floor boards were in harmony with the softly glowing maple. Exquisite draperies, rare old pieces of maple furniture, museum pieces really, were placed about the big room. On the floor were beautiful old hooked rugs with their gay colors mellowed in time. The lights were fashioned of pewter and looked like the old pewter candlesticks of a century and a half ago. Everything was just right; nothing neglected or overdone. It all betrayed culture and generosity. A glance told what a loss had been Adora's.

"I know what you are thinking about, Craig," she murmured as she caught him looking in admiration. "No wonder I miss him. He gave me all this because he loved me. I'll never leave it—for anything or anybody. Here his memory will always be fresh and, somehow, I know he will try to help me."

Suddenly the girl leaned over the broad low mantel. An exclamation of pain followed. "Look, Walter, his glasses! The other night he was reading to me. I remember his raising his arms and laying them there."

She kissed them gently. "How can I put them away—for the last time?"

She wanted to be alone. We knew it. Craig shook hands with

her gently. I was too full of emotion to do anything but keep silent. That was best. Sometimes it conveys more than words. We left the room quietly. But before we had closed the hall door we heard sobs—the blessing of tears.

It must have been several weeks later, when the clicking of steam in the radiators, the falling of white flakes from the dull gray skies and the newspaper headlines about the shortage of anthracite impelled Kennedy to gather Southern hotel literature. Winter had come and as yet spring seemed far behind.

"Good heavens, Craig, those pictures of open verandas, sunshades, bathing suits!" I dug my hands into my pockets. I had been feeling that uncomfortable chill along the spine that one has with the coming of a cold. "Br-r! How can you look at them?"

Kennedy looked at me. "What you need is a ticket to the sunny South. I'm going to get the tickets. I leave it to you to arrange with the *Star* Syndicate to cover that aviation meet down at Fort Myers and take a little vacation at the same time. Be ready to leave to-night."

"Palm Beach first," nodded Craig as we boarded the train, "and no cases or copy to think about for a week."

I was skimming over some stuff about the aviation test to be held in Florida when an item caught my attention. "Harper is going to fly the De Haviland again, Craig," I informed.

"So? I don't suppose you read the society notes." He put his finger on an item. "The list of guests at the Royal Poinciana includes Adora Gaines and her mother."

"Is that so? We'll see her then. I suppose she went there hoping the change of scene would make her more able to bear up. It would be mighty fine down there, if that aviation meet on the other side of the state doesn't bring back memories."

When we called on Adora the morning after we arrived, we found that she had gone to the bathing beach with some friends. Craig and I strolled around by the beach to see her.

What was my surprise to find Reggie Harper among the

party. It was easy to see that Harper was doing his best to attract Adora and make her forget. But his mere presence must have been a constant reminder.

We strolled along the white sand while Adora took a dip. Out on the float we could see Harper with her again. Craig paused to watch as Adora stood up on the float, slim and straight in her plain black bathing suit. Some one was counting, "One! Two! Three!" They dove off together. There was scarcely a splash as Adora's body slipped into the water. A few seconds and she rose to the surface. They were off to the buoy.

Like a water creature herself she made her course direct for the mark. I could almost see the easy smile on her face. Harper reached the buoy about the same time. But returning to the float Adora was several strokes ahead.

Out of the water she drew herself, up the steps of the ladder. She accepted the scattering applause naturally. She had always been a swimmer. It came to her easily. Harper seemed to enjoy his defeat, too. But I wondered at Adora. The excitement of the contest over, she almost seemed to forget him. He was no more than any of the others.

Even back on the sand Harper did not take this indifference as well as he had taken the defeat. He was inclined to frown and sulk. I fancied even he concealed now a hostility to Craig, perhaps to me, too. But Adora's attitude made her entirely oblivious to Harper's ill temper.

I had been telling Adora how suddenly Craig and I had decided on our trip. Harper interrupted, sitting down on the beach with us. "You'll let me take you out on my yacht this afternoon, Adora?" he asked. "A number of your friends will be aboard."

"Not to-day, Reggie, thank you. I can't."

"May I ask why?" he asked, smothering vexation.

Adora herself seemed puzzled for a minute, then finally explained with a little nervous laugh, "I can't tell you. You wouldn't understand."

Harper was silent and perplexed. A party down the beach called to him. He excused himself to Adora, nodded coldly to us.

I fancied I saw a look of relief flit over her face as he went down the beach. She caught me watching her. "Walter," she confessed, "his attentions annoy me. When we are alone he has talked about Henry to me, oh, so sympathetically. But somehow I feel the sympathy doesn't ring true. I don't know. I try to be polite to him and as kind as I can, and distant. But he doesn't leave me alone. Do you know, he has sent me a message in some way nearly every day since the—er—accident? I am just a little bit weary of him. I thought perhaps by beating him in that race around the buoy I might make him angry. But it seemed to have the opposite effect. Then if I'm interested in anyone else he gets offended." She looked out over the sea. "He's so infernally chesty, too, about holding the world's record for altitude—35,525 feet, wasn't it?"

Kennedy nodded but neither of us said anything. Finally Adora drew her knees up and clasped her hands about them. She looked up at Kennedy. "Craig," she said slowly, in half a whisper with a far away look in her eyes, "do you suppose Reggie Harper had anything against Henry and Wally? He won't let me talk of that meet at all...."

Craig shrugged. "Who was his passenger that time?" I asked. "I've forgotten."

"Steele Porter," she replied.

"Oh, yes, that electrical engineer."

"They're having some kind of meet or test or something in a few days at Fort Myers," she continued. "I don't know much about it, didn't want to know. But I hear there is something they believe the Germans have discovered, some invention or other, about bringing down airplanes. Reggie is to fly, they tell me, and Steele Porter will be there. Do you know anything about it?"

Kennedy disclaimed any knowledge and I saw that it was my cue also to change the subject.

Harper left the following day, Adora toward the end of the

week to visit some friends at Pinehurst. That left us free to journey over to Fort Myers where I could write my story which was my own only legitimate excuse for being down in Florida at that time at all.

My story in the *Star* attracted considerable attention. It was one of those things illustrated by pictures that really did not illustrate the subject of the story yet caught the eye and went with the heading: "Mystery Ray Wrecks Enemy Planes."

I may as well give briefly a bit of what I wrote, here, for what it may be worth:

> Have German scientists discovered a way to disable airplanes? [my story began].
>
> This problem has been worrying the English and especially the French general staff. Now it is worrying American flying men and has been the subject of long investigation in secret at Fort Myers, including tests the results of which are being carefully guarded.
>
> For some time it has been whispered that some secret means discovered by Germans have caused damage to airplanes in flight. This is believed to le the explanation of nearly thirty forced landings made by French airplanes on German territory in the last eight months.
>
> Wireless experts are advancing the theory that by some wireless ray, known only to the Germans, the magnetos of the engines of airplanes are put out of action.
>
> Another group of wireless experts advanced the theory that rays which affect certain metals used in vital parts of the airplane are directed on it by reflecting mirrors. As Germany confiscates all machines making forced landings on her territory, it has so far been impossible to find out under what circumstances the airplane engines have been damaged.
>
> It is common gossip about the flying station here that there is a former German flier from whom the Government has come into possession of new and amazing secrets about a mystery ray that wrecks planes flying over Germany and that, after being held in New York some time, this German airplane expert

finally obtained the ear of our authorities, whereupon these tests were undertaken with the utmost possible caution and privacy.

I had a story, but I had mighty little fact. Among others I had the statement of a pioneer in wireless who had conducted wide researches into the transmission of power through the air who expressed the opinion that "it might be possible by strong oscillations to excite surgings in the metal of an airplane so that sparks might occur at wrong times and thus stop the engines."

Another scientist wrote for me a statement that "investigators were working on a means by which they might send in the form of oscillations through the air a force which on coming in contact with a metal would generate heat. If this force could be concentrated and made sufficiently powerful the metal of the airplane could be melted and the machine brought down, provided it could be directed along a certain path in the same way as the beam of a searchlight is directed."

Kennedy helped me a great deal in the phrasing of my article, but as far as he was himself concerned maintained a very non-committal attitude. He would not deny the possibility; nor yet would he affirm his belief in the existence of such phenomena. He vexed me a great deal as scientists usually do when they will not let their imaginations run riot to make an instructive news feature.

My own opinion was, of course, of no value in the face of the experts in aeronautics and wireless that I quoted. There was one incident that leaked out which impressed me, though why, or what its implications might be, I did not venture to guess. It had not so much to do with this mythical or mystical ray as with the thoughts that now were surging through my superheated brain as if some force were projecting them. Steele Porter, flying in a small air-boat, fell in the waters of the Gulf. Porter also, to me, stuck absolutely to the explanation that it had been an accident.

Back again in New York after the quiet winter in the Carolinas and Florida, Adora Gaines, now that the first bitter shock was over, sought desperately, often despairingly, to find again some part of the happiness she had lost.

"Craig," I reported one night, "guess whom I saw to-day?"

"Who was it?" he asked.

"Steele Porter. You know he lives in Westbury. He gave me the low down on most of the Wheatley Hills folks."

"Well, what am I supposed to ask? About Adora Gaines?"

I nodded. "Adora seems to be taking her place in society again—about as well as anyone could hope after her loss—goes in for charities, has taken up some of her old friends, quite the thing, the most intelligent, most substantially fixed and, I gather, the most moral."

"Has she any particular friend?" asked Craig quickly.

"Many would like to be, according to Porter. Wally Knight is one of the most attentive, he says. I asked him about Reggie Harper. He says he was a visitor, too, then he smiled a peculiar smile when he said Wheatley Hills was a community of sisterly love and the Gaines house was the shrine where they all worshiped. I gather that it is all in their heads; Adora looks on them all as brothers; nothing more."

Kennedy went into a brown study. "Nothing very strange in all that... Everybody knew that Wally Knight could hardly wait to get home from college that June two years ago. It seems quite natural for him to try to win her again." Craig paused. "Only he doesn't come up to Henry Gaines."

"All I know is what Porter told me. Knight gets the choicest flowers, the latest books, almost before the ink is dry. She doesn't go out much where there are many people, keeps quiet. But the young folks flock to her. She understands them so well, those who have troubles, you know."

Kennedy looked away reflectively.

"Dreaming over her, too, Craig?" I rallied.

"Yes. That confession lets me out. You know I wouldn't wear my heart on my sleeve even to you. Yes, I am dreaming of her—because I want that little girl to be happy—because I loved

Henry Gaines—and because I have known her since she was almost a baby."

I felt an intense sorrow for Adora. I sympathized with her, but I believed that she would be misguided if she ever sought happiness with either Reggie Harper or Wallace Knight. They were not the type of Henry Gaines, not her type.

The next thing I observed, as the spring advanced into summer, was a conflict between Wally Knight and Harper. Up to the time of the altitude meet in October they had been very good friends. In fact, I had heard that they had even gone into perfecting an invention together. Now, with Adora, there had been noticeable a growing coolness between them which finally broke into open hostility, I knew it was over Adora. Outwardly it as over the ownership of a patent taken out on their joint invention, a claim on the part of each as to work done and hence for a greater proportionate share in the invention.

It did not come to the actual point of court action, but there was considerable gossip about it and it interested both Craig and myself when we learned that the dispute was over ownership of a new turbine super-charger, or engine oxygen booster.

They had worked on and perfected the thing, hiring at times the expert assistance of Porter, in an effort to make it possible to establish the absolute limit for airplanes in altitude. That Wally Knight had given up flying after the accident did not prevent him from keeping his interest in aviation in general. In fact, I gathered that he had an even keener interest in this oxygen booster than before, although I think that if it had ever come to a matter of testimony in court Harper would have been able to show more work done on the perfection of the thing before the *Star* contest of the previous fall.

The booster, I may say, was now designed and built specifically for extreme altitude operation. It was rated to feed sea level atmospheric pressure air to an engine at a height of 35,000 feet which was a great deal more than the rating of the supercharger used in the contest. It was a small contrivance mounted just back of the propeller blade of the plane on the front end of the Liberty motor. It was operated from the red-hot exhaust from the airplane motor which ordinarily goes to waste. It weighed about a hundred and forty pounds, which might have been considered a handicap in altitude flying but for the fact that at 35,000 feet its operation would increase the power of the motor by at least two hundred and eighty horsepower.

Looking into it, I found that the atmospheric pressure at 35,000 feet is about one-fourth and the density about one-third that at sea level. The temperature is 58 degrees below zero, Fahrenheit. To supply the airplane engine its normal air at sea level pressure, the supercharger was designed to compress about 2,200 cubic feet of atmosphere a minute. The supercharger was rated at thirty-three thousand revolutions a minute, the outer end of the blade of the thing traveling 1,800 feet a second, almost as fast as an army bullet. Ordinarily 21,000 feet altitude was considered the ceiling, because of rarefied air. Not only would this invention carry a plane easily above that, but it would enable heavy bombing planes to attain altitudes nearly three times what they ordinarily could reach. It was important, for, in war, the plane which can hover over the other is usually the victor.

At any rate the dispute between the joint inventors, or rather adaptors, of the supercharger had begun to wax hot at the close of the summer, as their suit for Adora's favor grew keener.

It was a situation fraught with discomfort if not danger, at least to Adora, still gloriously oblivious to it, and I was delighted when, early in September, I heard that Harper had been given a most flattering commission in the air service at the great new British Singapore station. I was pleased, the more so when I also heard that an attorney, a mutual friend of the two, had brought the rivals together on one point at least and that Wally Knight, now engrossed in some financing which his banking house handled for the British government, had agreed to relinquish any claim to the supercharger in favor of Harper. I felt that it was fortunate. It was magnanimous, I felt, on Wally's part, too. Yet when I thought of the heat of the contest for Adora, I could not help having a feeling that Singapore was a long way off, that it looked as if Harper were running away from a fight.

Thus it came about that before I realized it, a year had passed from the tragedy of the flying field. Without a thought of it, with Craig I accepted a week-end invitation to visit the Ingrahams out in Westbury.

Our ride out took us through Wheatley Hills. The brilliant colors of the autumn foliage by the side of the road and on the arching trees above us challenged the grim white season to come.

"I never go through this part of the country, Craig, without thinking of the tragedy at Belmont Park," I remarked. "Do you remember that ride back with her to Westbury? I expected Adora to collapse any moment. She never complained; there was not a tear in her eyes; only that fixed stare. Her heart was broken."

We peered through a white-pine hedge as we rolled past the Gaines estate on the country road.

"Do I remember? I shall never forget Adora Gaines that day. Here's the driveway. Let's turn in and see her."

A quick twist of the wheel and we nosed up the white shell road to the charming place set in a locust grove. The sight that greeted us as we stopped was one to make me think.

Sitting on the lower step of the wide porch, in the warmth of the sunshine, bending over the face of a little boy asleep, Adora smiled up at us as we approached, with a quick move of her finger toward her lips.

She waved toward some chairs on the porch. "Do you mind waiting? He was so tired and I took him on my lap. I sang a little song to him and he fell asleep. I don't like to disturb him." She looked down at the child, then raised a pair of the saddest eyes I ever saw. Her soul was in those eyes.

"Whose child is it?" I whispered.

"My housekeeper's. Isn't he a wonderful little chap?"

The boy stirred restlessly even at the whispers and Adora was quiet again.

For several minutes her eyes had that fixed stare at the distant violet lights in the sky to the west.

"I just adore little boys. They've named him Henry."

A sigh escaped her. I studied her profile, eager to see how her grief had affected her. A trifle thinner, more subdued in manner, she seemed like some rare thing purified in the fire of sorrow.

It was then that I noticed Craig looking at another car just around the turn in the driveway. It was a snappy roadster.

"Were you going for a ride?" asked Craig. "We just stopped for a moment to see how you were and—"

The door from the living room of the house opened. Wallace Knight paused for a moment and I rather imagined our presence did not fit in with his plans, for I caught a shade of annoyance which quickly gave place to his usual easy debonair manner as he strode forward to greet us.

"How are you, Kennedy? Jameson, mighty good to see you! What do you think of Adora? I promised to take her for a ride—left the office in charge of incompetents, and came out here. Just before I arrive, this kid falls asleep on her lap and he must not be disturbed. He's tired. So am I. It's a long nap. She won't go until he finishes it. Can't you give him a pinch—just a little one?"

We laughed at his impatience. Adora smiled gently, too. "Wally's so kind—but this baby has privileges. I think that is the trouble. He's envious." She leaned over and kissed the child lightly, then smiled at Knight, teasingly.

"I should say he had privileges! Adora, you have the advantage. This boy gets for nothing what I am afraid to take."

A big St. Bernard bounded around the corner of the house and before she could stop him poked his cold wet muzzle between her and the child's face.

The boy was wide awake, ready for a romp with the dog. He wriggled off her lap and she followed him with a wistful glance. She said nothing, but the plaintive look meant as much as words, as if she had said, "I love children and Henry's son would have meant so much to me!"

Wally Knight was uncomfortable. I knew that he was very much in love. He hated to see her in this mood. He knew she was unhappy and this particular unhappiness pained him. He had been quietly urging Adora to marry him at the end of the year. He loved her and wanted all of her—even her memories.

"Well," he exclaimed to Craig, "that's the first time that dog ever did anything to please me."

"How's that?"

"He's chased that blooming kid away.... Now my two rivals can beat it together."

I wondered whether there was something cryptic in that last remark.

Adora smiled quietly. "Wally, you shouldn't say that. You are just a big selfish boy."

"The baby is just a little selfish boy, too!"

"Besides," she went on, "I love that dog. He was nothing but a pup, all legs and head, when Henry brought him home to me."

Knight again by an effort suppressed his annoyance.

"Well, Walter, we must be going, or we'll be late at the Ingrahams'," put in Craig. "Knight has had enough interruptions."

"Oh, are you staying with the Ingrahams?"

"Yes, we'll see you again, Adora, Good-by. Good-by, Knight."

We bowed our way back to the car.

I was thoughtful. It is painful to see a splendid woman with all the attributes for perfect motherhood denied that privilege by the sudden passing of one she loved.

"It looks to me, Craig, as if Adora hopes still to gain in the love of Wally Knight some of the happiness she lost when Henry Gaines died."

"I hope she gets it," was his only comment.

Sunday morning at the Ingrahams found the other guests headed for the links. Kennedy preferred a ride in the glorious country and I agreed with Craig.

It was a perfect day for a canter and Craig and I were enjoying ours to the utmost.

"Walter, did you ever see anything more beautiful than the play of the muscles of this mare I'm riding? Perfect co-ordination. She's a beauty." Craig straightened up in the saddle and looked down at her admiringly.

"She's showing off for you!" I retorted. "Now, this horse of mine has nothing to be ashamed of, either. Look at his sleek coat!"

I couldn't help leaning forward and giving his side a soft pat. Evidently he interpreted it as a wish to go forward quickly. I was quite unprepared for the sudden break and grabbed the reins tensely.

It was rather disconcerting to hear a girl's laugh. I thought it sounded familiar, and when my horse settled down to good behavior, I swung about. I could hear Craig exchanging greetings with some one who had come down a lane. It was Adora and Wally Knight.

As I rode up, Adora dismounted lightly, holding the reins in her hand. She shook her crop at me admonishingly.

"You can't ride them and love them at the same time. You'll come a cropper if you do. That horse of yours isn't a tabby by the fireside."

Wallace laughed easily, but I thought it was induced by the belief in his own superlative qualities. He knew he was handsome that morning. He felt happy because Adora had almost consented to set the day for their wedding.

As for Adora, she was beautiful. In her trim black habit, her little tricorne fitting snugly about her pretty face, she was a picture. To me there is nothing more beautiful than a handsome woman on a splendid horse.

"Don't you love these country roads?" she was asking. "Some are just bridle paths; no wider. You should go up that lane— nothing but maples—a glorious yellow shower."

"We were going by your place to make a call," nodded Kennedy. "This is better, however."

"It's wonderful," I put in, meaning her.

"Yes," she agreed, thinking only of the circumstances. "It's exhilarating. I used to ride a lot with Henry. He loved horses— and rode well, too; sat his saddle like an Arab."

Again I saw that slight frown on Knight's face. If Adora would only stop those reminiscences! They made him ill at ease.

"Wally, you have much to be thankful for. You are physically fit. You can do everything."

"Shall we ride on?" Knight urged, changing the subject.

Adora had been watching him earnestly. "Everything," she repeated, her eyes far away. Her voice fell into wistful cadences. "Do you remember, Wallace, the time he went to be examined by the insurance doctor?... Henry just laughed. He said he didn't believe anything he heard and only half of what he saw. Don't you remember? Weren't you at the house that night when he came home and told me?"

Knight was about to reply when his horse shied at some falling leaves and started down the road.

"Good-by, Craig and Walter! I'm off, too! Come around soon. I must catch Wally, now. His horse is faster than mine!"

A light leap into the saddle and she was off, galloping down the quiet lane in the direction in which we had just come.

We turned up the lane of maples.

At last we came out on the main road with its dirt border and rode along it, past the pretty little stone church in Westbury. It was where Adora and Henry had been married. I remembered it well. It was one of those spots a writer always keeps in mind. If ever I write a movie story, I had often told myself, I would have a wedding take place in this church. It was a "location."

My mind ran on—about weddings. I supposed Wally Knight was dreaming of leading Adora to the altar of this pretty little stone church....

Everything, it seemed, built up my sympathy for Adora. Yet,

I often asked myself why it was that I felt that intense dislike for Wallace Knight. I had nothing personally against him. If I had asked myself frankly, I am afraid I would have had to admit it was merely that he rubbed me the wrong way. There are some men so confident of their own superlative adequacy that they do not even need outright hostility or even downright superciliousness to antagonize you. To me he was like Dr. Fell:

> "The reason why I cannot tell,
> But this I know and know full well,
> I do not like you, Dr. Fell."

The day had been a busy day. After a few hands of bridge Craig and I decided to retire.

"It seems strange," remarked Kennedy to the Ingrahams, "but the amount of energy expended in play seems to me to have a more tiring effect than what must be a greater amount of energy expended in the labor and hazards of solving a crime. I suppose the elements of mystery and danger fool one."

My room had been darkened some time when I waked suddenly to the realization that I was hearing something quite unusual. Through the open windows the sound came again. It was the siren blowing weirdly in the night. I could hear the roar of the motors of the fire apparatus. In the direction of the turnpike I could see a glare in the sky, getting more vivid by the minute. I called Craig.

He jumped up, peered out of the window. "Get dressed," he decided. "Let's go."

Through the house we heard others. We hustled into our clothes. A fire in the country is an event. Everybody goes.

There was a general exodus of cars from Rolls-Royces to flivvers. We were first to swing past the lodge. "It's the Gaines house," shouted the lodgekeeper. "Central just told me."

The way Craig covered that road would have done credit to the advertisements of the stock car he was driving. He got more out of the engine than I had ever believed possible.

Turning up the private road we had a clear view of the fire. The flames were now licking up through the roof, it seemed from every side. Nothing could possibly save it.

"I hope everybody is out." Craig let the car roll off the road on the lawn, jumped out among the growing crowd of firemen and residents. "Where's Adora Gaines?" he shouted.

"No one's seen her. Wally Knight was among the first to get here," answered one. "He's gone in to find her. Neither has come out!"

Everything was confusion. One stream of water was already on the house; another line of hose almost laid. A ladder had been run up to the roof and a volunteer was hacking at the shingles in an effort to open a way to pour a stream in on the furnace of the attic. More cars were arriving every minute.

On the lawn the servants had gathered each with a little bundle of treasures picked up in a hasty flight. The housekeeper with clasped hands was calling for her mistress. Little Henry was sobbing, frightened, clinging to his mother's skirt.

Craig strode through them all, amid the smoke and stifle and falling embers, up on the porch. He flung open the door. Just as he did Wally Knight staggered out with Adora almost overcome in his arms. His own strength was nearly gone as he choked and panted.

"Take her, Craig; I'm all in."

Kennedy lifted her as Knight almost fell in my own arms. Adora's life had been saved. Everybody was willing now. The chief difficulty Craig had was keeping them back so that she could be restored. They fell back and she sat there wide-eyed, staring broken-hearted at the destruction of the link that had bound her life so closely still with Henry Gaines.

Again it seemed the question, "Why?" came to her lips. Even her loving memories must be destroyed.

Wally Knight came over to Adora and stood silently by her. He was splendid, I must admit, standing there, his dark eyes shining with excitement, his hair hanging damp over his forehead, his clothes scorched. The crowd regarded him with a certain awe. Adora heard him and looked up.

"Wally, how can I thank you? But for you I would still be in there." She shuddered and hid her face in her hands. "It was awful when I thought no one could come to help me."

He waited until she was quiet. Somehow, to me, he seemed too self-controlled, too deliberate. But I considered. That very quality of his was what made him such a successful aviator.

Adora was facing a sudden emotional crisis. She knew just as well as if Wally had spoken what was the manner in which he expected her to thank him. She read the question in his ardent eyes. She looked from his eyes to the burning house. Everything that belonged to Henry was being destroyed—everything but her thoughts. The world did not expect her to stop living. Evidently God had not intended it. Had she not been rescued by the very man who was urging her to mate with him?

Just then the roof fell in with a crash. In spite of the heroic work of the firemen the house had been doomed. Adora saw the sparks and embers, the dust and smoke filling the air about the house. It was a strange likeness to her own life. Henry's death had been the crash of her own romance; this fire was the carrying heavenward of the dust and embers of her beautiful memories. She must go on. Henry would understand. It was the severing of last cords, material cords.

A light touch on her shoulder caused her to turn and look up. It was Wally Knight. He was waiting for her answer.

I had been standing near. But I withdrew. It was Adora's and Wally's moment. But Wally had forgotten the crowd, the fire. He saw only the woman he wanted.

"Adora…you asked me how you could thank me. Please give me the life I have saved. I love you. I want you. Will you?"

The fire blazed as fires do with redoubled fury. The light shone on Adora's face. A twinge of pain flitted over her beautiful features. Her eyes closed as if in communion with another soul, opened slowly, with a smile. "Yes," she murmured.

"Soon?" asked Knight, his arm about her.

She nodded.

"Wednesday—at the little church?"

Another twinge as of pain and another smile. "Yes!"

Wally lifted her to her feet gently and kissed her. At the moment motherly Mrs. Porter claimed Adora.

"Adora stays with me to-night," she bustled. "A fire and an engagement are enough for any girl in one night. You'll come with me, dear?"

Adora gave her hand to the older woman with a quiet nod. The older woman's arm slipped about her. But as she was going to the car I noticed the girl's face was turned wistfully toward the burning building, not toward Wally Knight.

Monday and Tuesday, Kennedy was restless, almost morbid. I was very busy myself on the *Star* and did not see much of him.

Came at last the afternoon of the wedding.

"I am thinking Adora's second wedding day will not be as bright as the first," I observed. "It looks like rain."

"Maybe it will hold off until after the ceremony. We'll have to hurry," remarked Kennedy, who had come into cur apartment in a great bustle, late.

The sun was hidden and there was a chill in the air that to me did not suggest orange blossoms. I tried to throw the feeling off. In spite of his haste, Kennedy was moody, overwrought.

I could not forget the happy face of the little bride in white of not so long ago when she came down the aisle with Henry Gaines. What must be her thoughts at this ceremony? One thing I knew. What Adora felt was her duty she would do thoroughly and truly. She would make a faithful wife to Wallace Knight.

It seemed that a myriad of cars were drawn up on every road and far down the roads about the pretty little stone church in Westbury. As we drove up we had to wait a long time before we were even able to enter the church. Many people, tradesmen and servants, were standing outside waiting for a glimpse of the bride.

Inside, the assemblage was one of wealth and fashion. Beautiful girls and beautiful gowns vied in the display of charm. It was an eager, sympathetic group of friends, too. Everybody loved Adora Gaines, wished her years of unbroken happiness. Everybody came who knew her.

The usher led us to seats. I gazed at the altar banked with beautiful palms, ferns, and masses of white dahlias. Soon the little church was overflowing its capacity. The ribbon and flower-decked aisle was cleared for the bride and her party.

From the side of the church, back near a door leading out to the pulpit, came the groom and his best man. Wallace Knight was not the sort of man to be eclipsed even by a bride. He was handsome, proud of himself, proud of having won Adora. The world was his and he was satisfied with it.

The music played on softly. There was a ripple of conversation, an animated moving of heads, a whisper, "Here comes the bride!"

She was beautiful. Adora was a symphony in gray, shimmering gray satin, with rare old lace sleeves and lace panel, ending in a slight train, a large gray velvet picture hat softened with its graceful, fluttering plumes, and a flower muff of purple pansies. She was wonderful, queenly.

Wallace smiled as he watched her coming up the aisle. He was so happy he could hardly wait to carry her off in the little roadster on the start of the wedding trip. He could see himself and Adora visiting all the quaint, unusual places on the continent, picking up treasures here and there to be brought back to their new home.

At the altar they met. A smile of possession was on Wally's face. Adora's gaze was in his direction, but seemed to me to be searching through him—beyond him.

The rector began the service. I could see Adora's lashes fluttering nervously over her beautiful eyes. The excitement of the moment had darkened them. They seemed black, so intense were her glances.

"If any man knows any reason why this couple should not be joined in holy wedlock, let him stand forth and speak—or forever hold his peace!"

My heart almost missed a beat. Kennedy stood forth in the aisle, hand raised.

"Just a moment—please!"

All heads turned. A murmur ran over the startled throng. I think some in the gathering would have liked to have had Craig put out immediately. Nothing like this had ever taken place in that conservative little church before. The dignified dowager in the seat ahead of me turned. "The man must be crazy I Can't you—get him out?"

The rector stood very quiet—listening. He had asked the question, invited it, even though it was a form. He must listen.

Dazed, I watched them all. Everyone was agitated and waiting. What did Craig know? Something he must have found out this forenoon, when he had seemed to me so dilatory about leaving the city, starting for Westbury. Now I recalled how he had told me he was waiting for someone to get back from a trip. It must be. He knew something—and was forced to tell it.

I saw Adora's mother turn white-faced from the pew nearest the wedding party. Her hands were outstretched toward Adora and there was a beseeching look in her glance toward Craig as if she would say: "Spare my little girl! She has had enough to bear!"

Craig saw it. He paused only a fraction of a second as if sweeping away a last scruple. Craig had a message to deliver and he was going to the bitter end.

Impressively he stretched forth his right hand. At first I did not appreciate the direction in which his forefinger pointed.

"A year ago on yonder flying field that was not an accident!... That was murder!"

It seemed that a wild light leaped in Adora's eyes. She stiffened, listening tensely for the rest. Every murmur in that edifice ceased. The ticking of a clock could have been heard. Her mother paused suddenly, too, about to speak.

"Be careful!" the rector found voice to interrupt. "This is an awful accusation at such a time, in such a place!"

Craig was resolute. Adora's face now wore a ghostly pallor. But she was quiet. I saw she was not going to collapse. The nerves of this frail girl were of steel. Her eyes seemed to say, "Go on! Let me hear the worst! I can stand it!"

The smile had long since died on the face of Wallace Knight. At the first interruption he had turned on Craig, taken a step forward. Their eyes had met. He had seen not a flinch in the cold steel-gray of Craig's. Wallace Knight had seemed to freeze. The half formed words, "Fling him out!" had died on his lips.

Craig turned toward Adora. "I'm sorry, Adora," was all he said.

She started to speak, then changed her mind. It was as if she would have said, "Craig, why didn't you let me know before? This is not the place to tell such a thing." She had checked it because intuitively she must have felt that there was some reason why it was necessary, why it must be done then, before it was too late.

"I know… This is a frightful thing I am doing." Craig paused, speaking slowly as if answering the question he read in her face. "But it would be a far more frightful thing if I did not do it. How can I face myself through life, how can I face my God—knowing what I now know—and having remained silent?"

He paused again.

"It was only this forenoon, late, that the medical man in the Great Western returned from the insurance convention on the coast. It was only this forenoon, late, that I received from his files and from his lips the true story of what it was he told Henry Gaines. And it was only this forenoon that I learned from him what I suspected, that you, Wallace Knight, within a few days after the examination of Henry Gaines, applied for insurance in the same company, for examination by the same doctor, and guardedly questioned him, a flying man yourself, as to what would happen to you, granted that the test showed you had certain physical and physiological deficiencies—which you already knew Henry Gaines had!"

Craig caught the eye of Doctor Nesmith, seemed speaking through him to us.

"A normal heart would have adjusted itself up to the fifteen thousand feet, whatever it was, or higher, with the apparatus used in that altitude flight. There is, in high altitudes, more and more rapid respiration because there is less and less oxygen to the cubic foot of air. It puts an added strain on the heart. All the apparatus, the oxygen, and so on will not overcome that.

"Henry Gaines's heart could not pump fast enough. And in such a case much would have depended on the length of time taken and the rapidity of the ascent, for adjustment of heart and lungs. That ascent, as I remember it, was rapid, very rapid. His heart was not able to adjust itself.

"Doctor Macgregor, the insurance doctor, had told Henry Gaines that his heart was all right—but not able to stand sudden strains. He might live to his threescore and ten and beyond. But there were some things of which he must be careful.... Doubtless he never considered sitting still in an airplane among the violent exercises—"

"It's all a lie!" Now Wally Knight found words to sneer. "He wants her himself... Let me get at him!"

Two ushers, friends of both Wally Knight and Adora, held him back.

Kennedy resumed slowly. "It was Henry Gaines himself—Adora—with the report of the insurance doctor—who unwittingly gave you the idea, Knight," pursued Craig relentlessly. "There was just one thing that Henry Gaines could not stand—rarefied air, lack of air, less than or more than normal sea level air pressure."

Kennedy turned to Adora. "Wallace Knight knew it, knew it when he set to work, as his dearest friend, to persuade Henry Gaines to agree to fly with him as passenger in the contest in which he said he hoped for the altitude honors of the flying world against the expert Harper."

Craig swung about, towering. "Like men of your class, Knight, you can be fearless, play the hero—as you did at the fire—to gain and to keep that for which you had murdered. That does not excuse; that merely explains. And I know, too, the reason for and source of Harper's appointment. It came as your work in the international banking firm with which you are connected. You removed one possible, one powerful rival, one who might have surmised your dastardly trick, too.

"Clever criminals to-day resort to the refinements of modern scientific poisons—synthetic murder, as it were. By their very refinements they leave circumstantial evidence against themselves. The successful murderer is still one who strikes in the dark—and flees, unseen—elemental murder. You, Knight, are elemental. You wanted this woman with an elemental passion. And you took an elemental way to get her—with an element—air."

As Kennedy's words seared into his mind, it seemed that Wallace paled and cringed.

Kennedy took a step forward as if to take him into custody.

"You took Henry Gaines up, with murder in your heart.... Knight, you did not swoop down for a doctor. You swooped down for the widow!"

WATER

"**WHAT A DELIGHTFUL** relief, Craig, to get out of the sordid city, back again in a community where it's not all what you have, but what you are!"

The big closed car of our hostess had met us at the new Princeton station, which in my day would have been well on the way to the Junction. It was on the urgent invitation of Mrs. Paxton Whitehead that we were coming back to Old Nassau.

"Only," Craig smiled as the car turned on Stockton Street to the left, "I apprehend you would prefer turning here to the right—Nassau Street, the campus. Prospect. You cannot say it is not wholly what you have, here in this new Princeton that has grown up in the last twenty years."

We glimpsed wonderful estates.

"Both ways!" I insisted. "Town and gown. What you are. Only that makes it more difficult!"

The Whitehead place, the "Thickets," in the waning light of the afternoon sun was a place of beauty. On the top of a knoll, overlooking the beautiful grounds and beyond the sweep of the valley with the great Pennsylvania trunk line threading through, it stood with a simplicity that matched the quiet dignity of its owner.

The white paint of its shingles caught and seemed bathed in the translucent lavender lights that made it a thing of glory. The shadows from its white-pillared porch stretched out and merged with the heavy shining green of the shrubbery. Groups of pines

146

and cedars, sturdy but now bare old oaks and maples suggested the nooks and shady retreats when days were warm. The stately elms that bordered the winding drive did not suggest what only age can bestow. They left no room for dispute.

The lawn made me recall a remark of an acquaintance I once made who claimed distant relationship in old Warwickshire. I had admired the green lawns there, just as I was admiring now the sweep of velvet at the Thickets. And I had asked how they ever made such lawns.

"Well, you see," was my answer, "we plow it up, prepare it, plant it—and then we take good care of it for two or three hundred years."

It was a rambling house, the kind that seemed to love the old hill and cling to it. With its dark green shingled roof, its quaint green shutters, the big brick chimneys made me almost see the pleasures about the big fireplaces in these snappy days. It was more than a house; it was a home.

Swinging now up the winding drive, we could see the varied interests of the family. There were the modern chicken house and run, next the dog kennels with their share of noisy pups, greenhouses, and an aviary. Farther down, a little lake, or rather a series of little lakes with rustic bridges, a Japanese garden, the finest tennis courts, and a swimming pool the equal of which I had never seen in the East, even a nine-hole golf course completed the picture. With the huge garage and stable, a sizable guest house, everything from the lodge to the Thickets itself portrayed the quality of the owner.

Mrs. Paxton Whitehead, comely and gifted matron, glided over the waxed and polished oaken floor of her big reception hall with the ease and grace of movement that betrayed a training foreign to that of the loose-hipped jazz walk of the flapper of to-day. Only by many hours in an old-fashioned finishing school, practiced alone afterward with the surreptitious use of a cup of water on the head, was that elegant grace acquired. It meant work. The strain on the debutante mind of that day was that it might never be acquired. Few are born graceful, but all can jazz.

In her musical, well-modulated voice, she said evenly to the butler: "Lights, Luther, in my study. You may go downstairs afterward. I'll not need you for some time."

Yet I fancied there was a tenseness in her speech that indicated emotion in restraint, a color in her cheeks that betrayed excitement repressed, and a simplicity and directness in her manner that told plainly she meant business. She was silent until we could hear Luther's rubber heels padding along at the other end of the long hall.

In the study, with a nod of her gracious head indicating seats, she turned to Kennedy with a quizzical smile and a glint of humor out of her steel blue eyes.

"Will you catch a robber—a smart one—for me?"

Leaning slightly forward, animation and vitality expressed in every feature, she looked scarcely older than twenty-five, thought I knew she must be nearer forty.

"I don't mean to beg the question," returned Kennedy. "But I can answer that better after he is caught. Have you been robbed?"

"No. But four of my most intimate friends have been—and I suppose my turn will come soon."

I was startled by the certainty with which she said it.

Yet it was all unknown to me. "It hasn't become news yet, has it?"

"No"—shaking her head vigorously—"and I don't want it to become news. None of my friends do—certainly not yet."

"How were your friends robbed? Did the thieves make a big haul? When did these robberies occur?"

An expressive gesture of two up-raised slender white hands seemed to ask Kennedy to check the flood of questions and allow her to tell her story in her own measured way.

"No, these robberies have not been safe robberies in the dead of night, breaking and entering, nor even robberies from rooms left unguarded, nor hold-ups, I think you call them. The jewels have been missed by people themselves—at our parties—where everybody is around. And we do not know whether it is done by one of the servants or one of the guests!" The last accusation, cautious though it was, seemed to cost her something even to utter.

"Have there been large dances and receptions, or smaller teas and dinner parties?" asked Craig, thoroughly interested in his inquiry.

"One was a dinner dance at the Van Vlecks' old mansion. A débutante niece was the inspiration of the dance, and only the most exclusive, impeccable people received cards to that. The Van Vlecks are extremely fastidious as to whom Betty is to know.

"Why, Mr. Kennedy, I was there, and I saw no one for whom I would not have indorsed a note for thousands, if you could imagine such a thing. The soundest financially and morally. Yet, Mrs. Montague lost her famous black pear-shaped pearl, one of the most valuable of its kind."

"Was it snipped from a platinum chain?" I broke in, trying to reconstruct what might have happened, then adding as the most impossible situation I could imagine, "Or picked from its setting in a pendant or brooch?"

"No, unclasped simply from a lavalliere. But we have had cases where extremely valuable jewels have been clipped, as you suggested. Mrs. Montague was wearing it. There were thirty guests at that dinner dance—and numerous servants, of course."

It was with a satisfied straightening of the shoulders that Mrs. Whitehead looked at us. There was a certain distinction even in this affair, she felt. Out of her even tenor of life where comforts, luxuries, all things beautiful and cultural abounded, she had been able to pass along to Craig a crime, an unusual crime, for him to solve.

"Tell me, please, about some of the other cases," prompted Craig.

"Well, the Baldwins gave a house party over at their Lakewood estate, just a few intimate friends. There a wonderful diamond was missing from a guest. She told the hostess quietly. None of us want the scandal to get about—but we are not enjoying losing our treasures, either. All the robberies have been single jewels, by the way, always of the greatest value. Diamonds and pearls seem to be preferred. Strange to say, no necklaces or large pieces have disappeared."

"I can appreciate your feelings to the utmost, Mrs. Whitehead. It seems as if the wave of crime were seeping up into the highest strata of society from the lowest."

With a nervous laugh she returned: "Yes, it's epidemic; it's catching. But we must catch the thief." She paused a moment, considering. "I feel a sort of pride in American society, you know, and this season we have some people close to us from England—people who see only the dearth of years and tradition back of American culture and, I fear, would not hesitate to note our crudities. All the losers have been patriotic.

"They have kept quiet because of this innate feeling we have of putting our best foot forward. It cannot be denied we reflect to a great degree the growth and moral tone of our nation. As the strength and worthiness of its ruling, controlling classes, so the strength and worthiness of a nation." Her head was lifted proudly. Eagerly she would defend America and its system, with the same dignity and pride as might any English duchess.

Craig was thoughtful. "I see to what you are leading. You want these thefts stopped, Mrs. Whitehead, not so much for the recovery of the jewels, valuable though they are, as for the honor of American society."

She was every inch the grande dame, beautiful, dignified, kind, and human. "Exactly," she agreed. "You must find out, Mr. Kennedy, who is taking them—but it must be done under cover, with no brass band. This problem requires infinite tact. Society is scandalized by it. And we must protect society."

"Why do you seem to think you will be robbed soon?" inquired Craig keenly.

"I am giving an afternoon tea dance for some of the members

of the Junior League, and have invited all the people who were at the Van Vlecks' dinner dance. Will you help me protect my guests and possibly myself?"

"Mrs. Whitehead, this is mysterious. Certainly I shall do my best to help you find your thief. By the way, may I ask you for your list of guests? It will help me materially at the tea," suggested Craig.

"I hate to do it—but here it is. I thought you would ask for it, first. Many of them you know personally. That is the reason I have appealed to you. You are one of us," she added simply.

Kennedy glanced at, made quick mental note of the list, and returned it to Mrs. Whitehead.

"I feel," he said, rising, "with your permission, that I may be excused while I make some discreet inquiries?"

She nodded, and we left her until later in the evening, everything on the place at our disposal.

"I know the Montagues, Walter, friends of my mother," remarked Kennedy as we rolled out down the driveway from the Thickets in one of the Whitehead chummy roadsters. "I'm going over to see them. They might have some bit of gossip that Mrs. Whitehead hasn't mentioned, perhaps doesn't know."

We found ourselves ushered into one of the many exquisite old homes of the delightful little town, out Mercer Street way, past the old water tower that I had almost fallen off as a freshman, painting the class numerals.

Rare prints, beautiful bronzes, and tapestries, shelf upon shelf of books lined the walls.

I always had a weakness for the old town, more especially since it was more than a college town. It had what neither the city nor even a little village has. Cities too often are centers of aliens with a fringe of Americans. Princeton was a center of learning with a fringe of culture.

"Craig Kennedy! I am glad to see you! Wherever did you come from? When did you get down?" It was Stella Montague herself. She had one of those rich, resonant voices, a smile that showed a perfect row of whitest teeth, a personality that charmed and held. "When I see you I always think of the good times we had together as children down at the old Cape May. Changed, hasn't it? You rescued me from dire punishments many times with your ingenious excuses!" She laughed reminiscently.

"Now, you're getting everybody else out of trouble, too." There was a reflective wrinkle on her brow, of a sudden. She was thinking of her lost jewel, I knew.

"Oh, Jameson and I just ran down for a few days—the hockey team is very promising this year, and that new rink, and everything, you know. Besides, if the faculty should ever give me a call, I'd like to know just what sort of atmosphere I was likely to drop into, too. Though heaven knows what I'd do for a diversion from my chemistry. No crimes in an atmosphere like this, I'm sure. I just had to call, for old times' sake, to see if everything is going all right. How's Easton?"

"Oh, all roofed and sheathed and plated with copper, busy as ever. He's entertaining some Chileans in New York to-night. Wonderful property, I believe. They mine with a steam shovel, or a hoe, down there. No crimes. You just had to call. Indeed!" She laughed a bit seriously, however.

"Do you know, that reminds me." She lowered her voice. "I've lost mother's wonderful black pearl!" She regarded him with an anxious, almost hurt look.

"No! On the street? How?"

"If I tell you, you won't mention it? None of us are doing so. I lost it at the Van Vlecks' dinner dance last week."

"When did you notice the loss?" asked Craig.

"When I was dancing with Howard Thornton. It must have been unclasped from my lavalliere."

"What did Thornton say?"

"Oh, he was frightfully annoyed. I told him to keep quiet about it, that I might find it on the floor or in the dressing room. You see there had been other cases, quite similar. But it was gone, irretrievably gone, I'm afraid now."

I knew Howard Thornton. He was the only fellow I had ever even suspected of violating the honor system in the exams. I had nothing on him, however. I just did not like him.

"Has he asked since about it?" I questioned.

"No, he hasn't. But I suppose it is because the other losses have rubbed the edge off my mystery."

"But how could it have been done?" queried Craig.

"I don't know. People brushed me during the dancing, of course, but Howard is a good dancer, and there were no noticeable collisions," she added with an emphasis. "It's just a plain unclasping of a catch, a platinum catch, and I never saw it, even felt it. Some one is clever. But who can it be?"

"Other losses," repeated Kennedy. "Who else?"

"Oh, another friend of mine had an emerald necklace. Hanging on a pendant was the largest emerald of all, a perfect stone. Why, you know Sally Carroll. Of course. Well, it was she. Two nights before my loss, at a musicale at the Marquards', she noticed the little pendant was suddenly gone from her necklace. During the short intermissions people had visited back and forth among the chairs in the ballroom. It must have been—er—lost, then.

"It's incredible, I know, almost unbelievable, how it is done. If it was only once, you might think it was an accident, carelessness, or something. But to happen at almost every affair. Now, don't tell, please. Valiant Mrs. Whitehead has shouldered the responsibility of solving it. It's disgusting, she says, to think that in our ranks we may be harboring a—a thief—a person with warped morals. You've met her, have you not? You would adore her."

Kennedy admitted nothing even to Stella Montague. We chatted a few moments more, then I found that he was turning the car around the triangle over toward Sally Carroll's ancestral home.

"This makes me think of senior year," he exclaimed. "Bareheaded, how many times I have walked down this old lane to the Carroll house! An invitation to Sally's to Sunday night tea was an event. When I sat listening in those days to her father. Doctor Carroll, a gentleman of the old school, traveled, open-minded, a raconteur of humor and ability, I rather decided I would be like him as I grew old, Walter."

Dr. Carroll had died only two years before, and Sally had gone abroad for a long visit to her sister, Lady Leinster, who lived in England most of the time, but was now sojourning in America for a season.

The Carroll house would have charmed, fascinated a lover of the Colonial times and manners. Not so large a house as the others we had visited that day, it had something the others lacked—age and a history. Large for the period in which it was built, it had been carefully preserved by the Carroll family. They looked on it reverently.

Big oak and chestnut beams, weathered and time-stained, sustained the weight of the building. In the room where we waited for Sally Carroll was a fireplace to delight the heart. Modern heating apparatus was the only thing that jarred in that ensemble of Colonial architecture and furnishings. There was no fire in the huge open space of the hearth, only the old-fashioned andirons, kettles and brushes. A five-foot log was resting on the andirons.

I stood up, and my curiosity led me over to it. Stepping over the protecting rail, I looked up the chimney. There above me shining brilliantly now was a bright star. I was enthusiastic. Kennedy smiled at my discomfiture as at that moment Sally Carroll appeared.

"Mr. Jameson is thinking of writing some of this modern literature," laughed Craig. "He's preparing as a chimney sweep. Only he just saw a star up the big chimney. It may deter him, I hope."

Out her little hand came as I stepped back over the rail into the room. "I just love it, too. When I was a child, and things went wrong with me, I used to come into this room as the darkness settled, and if there was no fire, take my little stool, place it in that chimney corner and just enjoy my morbidity. Then common sense would tap me on the chin at last, and I would look up—up to the stars, and recover my peace of mind. You can't look at the stars through even a chimney and have morbid, ugly, misshapen thoughts."

"I never thought you had any other than beautiful thoughts, Sally," rallied Craig. "Your father's heritage passed on to you."

She took Craig's arm lightly. "Wasn't he a wonderful man, Craig? But I am afraid I didn't live up to his theories or your ideal of me, not a few days ago, anyhow. I was angry—and hurt."

"How?" asked Craig simply.

I fancied what was coming. I regarded Sally Carroll with interest. Petite, beautiful golden hair massed in a crown to add height, a delicate, clear complexion, a broad, smooth, intelligent brow, blue eyes that sparkled with humor and vivacity, a mouth that showed tenderness above a chin that denoted strength, she seemed scarcely more than a child, yet she was just past thirty. I recalled her with two huge St. Bernards, exact counterparts, "Whig" and "Clio." It was easy to see she claimed Craig as an old friend and true.

"You mustn't tell. But my emerald in the pendant to the necklace of emeralds mother gave me when she passed away was stolen. Think of it. Just clipped off, it must have been. I don't know how. Only, it's gone. I'm terribly distressed about it. Father bought that necklace for mother on their honeymoon in France. It was a rarely beautiful thing, had a history, too, and the loss of the pendant is irreparable."

"Where were you, Sally?" asked Craig sympathetically.

"At the Marquards'. They had a musicale. Jacques Thibaud played, and I was so interested in his technique, his varied program, I never saw or felt any one take the pendant. Music makes me forget everything; you know that."

Craig nodded. "Were you sitting near any one?"

"Oh, yes. Victor Bartley was sitting with me. He is crazy over the violin, too. You know him, fussy little man, always wanting to help everybody. Father used to say he needed more help himself, and didn't know it, than any of our friends. I didn't mention it to Victor. He would have had everybody down looking for it, including the servants.

"Then the Hon. Mr. Thurston was there—one of my sister's intimate friends—with his wife. I couldn't let them know that something else had been taken. I let Mrs. Marquard know quietly as soon as I could. She felt upset over it. But it isn't the first robbery of the sort. I had to bear it like the others. It's the mysteriousness of the thing that is so disturbing, too. I am completely at sea about it. I don't believe poor old Victor would have taken it, if he had picked it up on the floor in a room alone."

"What are you going to do?" asked Craig. "Anything?"

"I am going to get you to help me, if Mrs. Whitehead approves and doesn't solve the mystery herself at her tea dance tomorrow. Why, dear old Mrs. Ashton, a friend of father's, his chess and miniature friend, mutual hobbies, you know, lost a beautiful diamond at a morning meeting of their private Current Events Club several days ago. It was on a platinum pendant attached to a silk ribbon about the neck—and it happened to be the last gift Mr. Ashton gave her. She hasn't been out since, she feels so badly about it."

"Do you mean young Richard Ashton's grandmother?" I put in eagerly.

"Yes; do you know Dick? He is a bright boy and the chief jewel of his grandmother. His parents are dead, and when he's not up in the city he lives with his grandmother and the servants in that huge place of hers a few miles out of town. Delightful people, everybody thinks."

The conversation lingered about the missing jewels until we felt impelled to take our leave. "Come down and see me again, soon, before you leave, Craig. I may need your help." She included me in the invitation, and I went away feeling quite charmed.

"Craig," I exclaimed, "these people all take it wonderfully.

Thoroughbreds and game. I really believe they would keep silent forever rather than betray this thing that might look to an outsider like a weakness, especially to their English friends and relatives. I didn't know we had so many Spartans!"

"Do you know Dick Ashton well?" shot over Craig at the wheel.

"Sure do. Everybody on the *Star* knows Dick Ashton. He is a special writer. I'll say a future in the newspaper game lies golden before him. His millions that he's going to get don't distract him from his work. He has more application than the youngest cub reporter hustling his meals and clothes on a morgue assignment. Full of pep. And I imagine he often does a good turn to some of the other fellows, the way his popularity has grown."

"I'd like to see him, if he is in town, as I suspect he is," ventured Craig.

"Let's turn in here at the Nassau Club, then," I suggested. "I'll call him up, and if he is in town ask him to meet us."

I found that Dick was in fact in town, had not yet gone out to his grandmother's, and we waited at the club for him to drop around.

It was mighty good to be sitting there in that old place so full of Princeton memories, watching the older men, grads, visitors, faculty members, and three or four of the undergraduates, light-hearted chaps making friend-ships that would last as Craig's and mine had through all the years. Something of the same spirit gripped Craig. "Great to be back, Walter, great, isn't it?"

Just then Richard Ashton came in. Everybody knew him, had a greeting for him.

"Well, Jameson, what are you doing down here? Glad to see you, Kennedy. Now come over to Ivy with me. No, can't go to your club. Sorry. Have an appointment. There's a good fellow, both of you."

It was as we were walking across the campus to Prospect that Craig mentioned his interest in the robberies in the seclusion of McCosh walk.

"How did you know of them?" A puzzled, pained look over-spread Dick's face. "We have a feeling down here to keep it quiet—sort of 'for the honor of the family,' you know. The news hasn't become public yet, has it?" He asked it looking at us anxiously.

"No," Craig assured him. "But I know many of the people here, and a friend of yours invited me to look into the mystery for her."

"Who? Norma Whitehead?" guessed Dick shrewdly.

Kennedy nodded. "Know anything about it?"

Dick did not answer immediately. I felt that I knew why. As a "newspaper detective" he was reluctant to confess failure. "Yes," he admitted at length. "I have worked quietly on it. But I don't know any more now than I did when I began. Whoever is doing it is clever, I'll say.

"You know, of course, my grandmother lost a diamond. She was sitting on an end seat at the affair. It would be difficult to fasten suspicion on any one, really. People were passing her in the aisle, but no one occupied the chair next to her. She had been saving it for Mrs. Mackenzie, who couldn't possibly get there until the last minute."

"What about the people there?" asked Craig.

"Pretty much the same group of people in our set—reliable to the nth degree," Dick returned, now warming up as he came to what he had been doing. "You see, my grandmother was terribly shocked when she first discovered her loss. But she kept silent about it except for telling the officers of the current events club.

"She had invited Mrs. Gainesborough, a friend of Mrs. Whitehead and Lady Leinster to luncheon. Another jewel gone. It was impossible to tell. What would these people think of us? I don't see it, quite, myself. But then the rest of us do; so I must. Well, anyway, that's how grandmother felt. Why, Mrs. Gaines-borough, they tell us, is rather close even to the royal family.

"In these democratic days in England friendships are formed with the commoners, I understand, that prove lasting and valued.

Anyhow, this Mrs. Gainesborough was to take her little boy to our place. She is a widow. And grandmother expected some other guests. She had to appear calm and unruffled in spite of her loss. And she did. But after that luncheon she almost collapsed."

"You say you have worked on the case?" quizzed Craig. "What have you done? Do you mind telling?"

"No. I interviewed the servants. I did it quietly, of course, in a way that couldn't excite suspicion of what I was after. Nothing I missed as far as back stairs gossip was concerned. I couldn't talk, but I made them talk. They thought I was writing up something wonderful in the papers about society. I saw them all, all," he added, proud of his thoroughness and enterprise.

"Well, what did you find?" smiled Craig.

"Nothing, I tell you. Nothing. Hang it, Kennedy, after all that palavering, it suddenly dawned on me that I was up the wrong tree. They were all different servants, in each house, that I was talking to. They could never organize, even, as extensively as that. There isn't any blood brotherhood of crooks among servants!"

We parted from Dick Ashton after a very pleasant reunion at the club, but with mighty slim new information, except that we had seemed to eliminate the servant question.

We stayed at the Thickets that night. In the morning we happened around at the Golf Club, the real one, not the Whitehead private course. It was not so much for a game as to get the gossip.

I found, however, that there was little talk, even to Kennedy, of the thing that was uppermost in all minds. But it was underneath, nevertheless, in an undercurrent.

They were discussing the market quietly. Bartley, it seemed, had suffered some serious losses in oil. One of our classmates, who engaged in the real estate game in the town, informed me that Victor must be sadly hit this season, but was hanging on without a murmur. Then there was Thornton, too. It seemed he, too, had been squeezed in the market by the failure of Standard

Oil to take up, as had been predicted, some chemical company. So the gossip ranged on.

At the club that morning, too, I saw Dick Ashton and Thurston, M.P. Ashton was cultivating him, and Thurston was conniving at the cultivation, for it meant a series of syndicated interviews. Somehow I could not shake off the idea that Thurston was here putting something over. What was it?

One thing was assured. Society was scandalized by the robberies. Rather a large contract, too, for Craig, I thought. "You must find out who is taking the jewels—but it must be done under cover, with no brass band."

It was a vista of color that opened before us as we sauntered through the arched doorway of Mrs. Whitehead's drawing-room in the afternoon.

From that formal room we could see a most charming living room opening into a combined solarium and conservatory. The gowns of the pretty girls vied with the flowers in brightness and freshness.

We were early. Only Peggy Whitehead, a pretty girl of about eighteen, with three or four other girl friends, was there besides Mrs. Whitehead. Our hostess had arranged it so. Besides, she wished to talk with us over the guests she expected and what we should do if we should discover the thief.

"I feel sure we shall," she asserted. "Things either end or begin at my parties. I am responsible for more romances, I think, than any other hostess in this vicinity. I believe my conservatory has been the silent witness of more genuine cases of love at first sight and betrothals than any other in New Jersey. I just love it for that.

"I am never so happy as when I see two young friends of mine starting out in life together, happy. Oh, if we Americans could only realize the importance and sacredness of marriage, how much everything depends on it, the future of our race and the country!

"Do you know, it almost seems there is hardly a family among my friends around here that hasn't a Norma Whitehead in it?

They name their babies after me, bless them, all on account of my conservatory. And these babies are a joy to me. I always feel so disgusted at small families. I rather think there was never a baby born that God couldn't find a place for it if its parents only both hustled. The most patriotic thing a wife can do is to present healthy children to the nation.

"However, I think the other guests will be arriving soon, Mr. Kennedy. It might be well to stand near me so that you can hear the names of the people as the butler calls them. Many of them you know, of course. But there will be some strangers. When my guests have arrived, the young folks will go to the ballroom for the dancing."

Peggy Whitehead and her young friends, including Betty Van Vleck, received with Mrs. Paxton Whitehead. What pretty girls they were, simply and beautifully gowned for the afternoon dance. I quite lost my head over them, and I could imagine the havoc they would spread among susceptible hearts on the campus.

"Mr. Victor Bartley," the butler called.

I looked eagerly, and saw a little man, in his early fifties, entering. He tried to do everything so correctly. His formality was amazing. Looking neither to the right nor the left, eyes only on the receiving line and his hostess, he entered.

But how changed when he had greeted Mrs. Whitehead! Then his volubility was unrestrained. It had not even distant relationship to the brook. It was a veritable Niagara, a torrent of words. Mrs. Whitehead was clever, passed him along to her daughter. His interest in these buds was no less apparent. His thin, wrinkled face was in a constant state of animation, wrinkles shifting faster than a line formation in a snappy football game, as fast as I hoped the team might be next year against Yale. It was with good-natured tolerance that the young girls accepted his banal gallantries and turned him to the newer guests.

Mr. Bartley now devoted himself to the others. Just before his arrival a pompous, dignified woman had entered. We didn't know her, but heard her announced as Mrs. Reginald Blossom. Victor Bartley hurried over to her and was soon going strong again.

Mrs. Blossom was wearing an exquisite pendant of diamonds and emeralds, small but with large, valuable stones. Evidently it was the subject of conversation. What was my amazement when I saw Victor Bartley lift it up quietly and look at it with admiration. Was that a furtive look in his eye around the room, too?

I glanced at Craig. He was watching Bartley, also, fascinated. Evidently it was perfectly proper, however. Mrs. Blossom laughed at some witticism of his, tapping him lightly on the arm, and turned to greet some other friends. But we were watching him almost continuously, and he was keeping in close attendance in the wake of Mrs. Blossom.

Just then "Mr. Howard Thornton" was announced. Thornton was a type of masculinity most popular with girls of a certain type. Tall, with regular features, black hair slicked smoothly back from his forehead, big dark eyes, he strode into the room with the bearing of a Caesar performing with all three parts of gall. He could not more have sought to focus attention if he had been the chemical company and Standard Oil both.

Thornton was power, and he was willing to use all of it for the ladies. The rest of the afternoon I saw him developing his muscles sliding chairs under ladies whose embonpoint suggested the actual desirability of using their own muscles. And as for the buds! He seemed to like dancing with Peggy Whitehead, and as she had been trained to be a perfect hostess by a perfectly trained mother, she was too polite and considerate to do other than accept his attentions when there was no obvious excuse.

Also I noticed Peggy wore a bracelet of strands of pearls and one large pearl dangling from the strand nearest her hand. In fact, as I looked them all over, I was struck with wonder at the bravado, if you might call it so, with which they still wore their jewels.

"Walter, I've been watching you." It was Craig whispering

aside to me. "The way you are taking in these ladies and their jewels is alarming. You'll be seized as a suspect!"

"Craig! Are you here, too?" Sally Carroll breezed by with Mrs. Gainesborough and her young son.

Introductions followed and Craig quite won the heart of the little fellow.

"Mrs. Gainesborough, I can think only of Little Lord Fauntelroy, one of the best loved child characters in American fiction," inclined Craig.

It seemed to please his mother, who was rather of a nervous, high-strung temperament.

"He is just as good as he looks, too. I am going to have him educated in America, you know. I am waiting only to place him in the lower forms of a school that prepares for Princeton because its honor system appeals to me. My husband had many interests in America, and, you know, too, he"—here she took a delicate little lace handkerchief and dabbed her eyes gently—"had that fine English sense of honor. I want it developed in his son. At the same time I want Merton to know his America perfectly. He must." She turned quietly, and I firmly believe she was weeping at the memories suggested by the turn of the conversation.

Mrs. Whitehead joined us for a moment as the little boy and his mother were claimed by the Hon. Mr. Thurston, M.P.

"This is like the Pilgrims' Society transplanted from London," drawled Kennedy.

Mrs. Whitehead seemed delighted. "And, oh, Mr. Kennedy, I came over to tell you. Please don't permit Mrs. Gainesborough to have the least suspicion that we are harboring an undesirable. I just happened to think of it. She must not even suspect. What would she think of our American society and our institutions? I feel sure she has come over to make a study of them. Herself an Englishwoman of breeding and high social position, she may even have been commissioned by some one high in authority to make this exhaustive study. Please!" Mrs. Whitehead left us with a quick motion of her finger to her lips.

A moment later Craig, encountering her again, was asking about a young chap, Billy Sewall. "Oh, Billy! You don't know him? I think he is all right. Paxton says the Sewalls are living far beyond their means. It may be. I don't know. I have never seen anything other than uprightness. They pay their bills and club dues. They are above reproach, that way."

"Oh, there is something else. What has Thornton been doing lately?"

Norma Whitehead looked over at her daughter before answering. She was sitting on the edge of a big high-backed Philippine chair in the sun room. What a fascinating picture she made! Golden curls that could not be restrained clustered about her face. Her hair was arranged low in back, her slender white arms were resting on the edge of the broad supports of the chair. The folds of her bright blue dress fell gracefully over her small and slender ankles.

Thornton was standing by Peggy Whitehead, on the side where the bracelet was clasping her arm. He leaned over suddenly, put his hand down by the bracelet, and suddenly strolled off in the direction of the ballroom with Peggy. Our hostess looked frightened at Craig, and he at both of us. She did not answer his question.

"Mr. Kennedy," she said, "let me get near Peggy."

Taking his arm, she strolled where the young people were dancing. Strains of music from a trio, violin, cello, and harp, came softly through the door in a dreamy, enticing waltz.

"Just once around, Mr. Kennedy. I don't want anything suspicious."

Norma Whitehead danced with all the grace of the generation that passed out when fools rushed in with hesitation where angels were forced to trot. They danced by Peggy and Thornton. Her mother asked Craig to dance slowly. He did. She looked sharply at Peggy's arm. There was the bracelet, yet, and the pendant. Then she whispered, "All right, now, Mr. Kennedy. Please take me back."

While they were dancing, I decided to investigate among the servants. I found Dick Ashton ahead of me on the same mission. He could not get the idea out of his head.

"All afternoon I've been watching them carefully, Walter," he said aside. "They have apparently confined all their activities to the domestic duty of service. Not one thing suspicious has taken place. They have not unnecessarily touched any of the people. In fact, I haven't seen any servant very close to a single guest."

I, too, was ready to eliminate the servants.

It was just at this interval that something very interesting happened for the titillation of the aesthetic palate. Mrs. Montague had arrived a little late, bringing with her an unexpected guest. I recognized her immediately. The gloriously beautiful Vienna diva, Laura Sheriza, had made a hasty visit to Stella Montague.

Not singing that night at the Metropolitan, she had come down to the Montagues' to renew a friendship begun in Europe before the world war. Mrs. Montague had worked indefatigably among her many friends to secure the singer a chance before American music lovers, and had succeeded. Fame, fortune, and wonderful friendships had come to the young singer. But of the many new friends, Stella Montague was first.

"Norma, dear," she imparted to Mrs. Whitehead, "Mme. Sheriza has consented to sing. A real treat is in store for us. If you don't mind, I'll accompany her, myself."

"Stella! How wonderful you are—to share this delight. I'll go to the ballroom. The acoustics and the air are best there. It will be only a few minutes before I am ready."

Servants bustled about. Everybody was on the *qui vive*. In an incredibly short time all were assembled in the ball room.

Victor Bartley and Mrs. Blossom were sitting together. Howard Thornton, Peggy Whitehead, and Betty Van Vleck were in the seats just behind Mrs. Blossom.

I looked around for the others we had been watching. Billy Sewall was sitting with a little girl who, I learned afterward, had no jewels to her name, in the corner, making desperate love, his heart in his eyes.

Suddenly a rich, vibrating voice addressed us. "I am going to sing a song the wanderer sings when he is away from his fatherland, his home. It is little known, but the melody of it has crept to my heart and sustains me when I long for my own mountains."

A smile to Mrs. Montague and the singer began.

Next to Mrs. Blossom, on the side opposite the attentive Bartley, was the Hon. Mr. Thurston, M.P., and his wife, visibly affected by the singer's little impromptu speech. They were away from Merrie England. It was their homeland, the old country, and it stirred memories. There they were, clasping each other's hands in sympathy.

The sweetness of the ballad found its way to the hearts of all of us in the room. At some time every one in that room had roamed far away from home—so far it would take weeks to get back. To the rich sweet voice that sent quivers of delight over me, I listened raptly. For a minute I forgot to watch. I shut my eyes and floated with the singer on those wonderful waves of melody. Down to the very end. Heart-sickness, home-sickness was vibrant until the singer suddenly and thrillingly realized that the hills may be different, the rivers not the same—but the same God reigns over all and cares—cares!

One could have heard a pin drop, the silence was so intense. It lasted several seconds. Then there was a vigorous hand-clapping for an encore.

With a happy little laugh at the genuine appreciation, Mme. Sheriza leaned over and whispered to Mrs. Montague. The next was the Berceuse from Jocelyn, beautifully rendered. With smiling bows, blowing kisses to those around, *madame* seemed to be an exponent of harmony in graceful movement as well as music.

At the end of the improvised concert, Norma Whitehead asked her friends and guests to adjourn to the dining room, which, with the glass-enclosed breakfast room, made a little wing of the rambling house itself. Here tea was to be served.

Craig and I stayed in the neighborhood of Thornton and Bartley. As the Hon. Mr. Thurston, M.P., and Mrs. Thurston, were leaving with Mrs. Blossom, the Honorable M.P. was enthusiastically greeted by Mrs. Gainesborough.

Gently pressing her eyes with her handkerchief, she murmured through her tears, "I could see the old park, the little stream I knew—and my husband—what a voice to bring such memories back to people! I could love her!"

The press was rather urgent to get to the refreshments. The young people had been dancing. Sweets could still be taken by them in considerable amounts without the nightmare of another inch in girth or a pound more on those fatal scales. Hurrying to get through, the older guests were carried along to the same goal. Our little group seemed to break up suddenly, just melt away.

"We might as well go with the others," Craig nodded to me.

I saw that he had stooped to pick up a handkerchief lying on the floor. It was Mrs. Gainesborough's bit of dainty lace which she used so effectively. She was quite Victorian in her manner. To her the ideal feminine charm was still to be pale and interesting.

"Shall we go over to her now?" I suggested.

Craig caught a glimpse of Norma Whitehead approaching, white as a ghost.

"Mr. Kennedy! Can you believe it? There's another jewel gone—the Blossom diamond!"

"You mean," I queried excitedly, "the one I saw Bartley touch when he was looking at that pendant of Mrs. Blossom?"

"The whole pendant is gone! The setting is small. The diamond is the thing. She has just told me, Mr. Kennedy. Help me to solve this last—please. I feel terribly about it, happening in my house."

"I'll do my best," he said simply.

There was an assurance in his manner and voice that thrilled her and puzzled me. What had Craig observed this afternoon that he was keeping back from me?

Mrs. Whitehead was moving among her guests with less vivacity, but game and proud. I think no one knew except Mrs. Blossom, the hostess, and ourselves.

If that thief were to be caught, if the diamond were to be restored to its rightful owner, something would have to be done, and done quickly. Many would be leaving shortly after tea.

Most of the guests as we entered the dining room were standing or seated in little groups still talking of the wonderful Sheriza and partaking of the refreshments.

I heard a child cry. The cry ended in a yell, a genuine "holler" of temper—then miserable blubbering sobbing.

It was little Merton Gainesborough, jumping up and down screaming with a temper which is always perfectly unaccounted for in the best trained children. They will do it at most inauspicious moments. In fact, as I have often observed, children are no improvement on grown folks.

His mother tried to comfort him. And of course everybody wanted to help, which served only to complicate things the more. I thought a little woodshed treatment or a nice slipper would have been the thing. But buttered toast, little cakes, ices, and candies, all were requisitioned and thrust forward as bait to ensnare quiet and peace by the debutantes fluttering about.

Mrs. Gainesborough was thoroughly depressed at her little son's behavior.

I was vexed at the diversion from the main business in hand. Dick Ashton, near me, had somehow, I suspected from Mrs. Blossom herself, been apprised of her loss. Aside Dick and I agreed that suspicion certainly must roost on the officious little Victor Bartley.

"Don't you think, Craig," I whispered, plucking him aside, now that there was this diversion, "you might invite Bartley to the men's dressing room, search him, frisk him? If he refuses, there, clout the little shrimp on his teapot dome! He's so damned oily—he is oil—run to salt water!"

Kennedy nodded a negative scowl to wait.

There is nothing more exasperating than for a child to kick up a rumpus when one is trying to show him off. Poor little Mrs. Gainesborough could only sputter. She seemed for the nonce speechless. A great deal of her English dignity slid off her shoulders mighty fast. Even pompous Mrs. Blossom forgot her loss and was the mother trying to soothe a wayward child.

"There! There, dear!" expostulated Mrs. Gainesborough. "We'll go. Right away!" She murmured it, head down, with lips set with apparent vexation.

"That's it. He's tired, the little dear," Mrs. Blossom explained to those around her.

Big tears were running down the little lad's cheeks and his face was not as clean as it might have been. Mrs. Gainesborough fumbled for her own handkerchief, did not find it, leaned over and taking the child's handkerchief from his pocket, wiped away his tears. There were tears of mortification in her own eyes as she hastily wiped them and her face before she put the handkerchief back in Merton's pocket. Everybody was so sympathetic and kindly toward the little fellow that his grief was beginning to be a bit assuaged. She looked up, relief written now all over her face.

"Mrs. Whitehead," she now smiled resignedly, "I fear I must be leaving. Merton is so tired. Could I have my wraps brought down?"

"Of course, my dear. So sorry you feel that you must leave us so soon. But you know best about Merton. Jenkins, will you get the maid to hand you Mrs. Gainesborough's and Merton's wraps, please! You may leave them in the reception room, and let us know when they are ready. Then you may summon her car."

If any of the servants could possibly be suspected, it might have been Jenkins, I thought. He had the freedom of the house, as it were, had superintended arranging the ballroom for the music. But I hadn't seen him near Mrs. Blossom until now, that I recalled.

"Tea, Mr. Kennedy?" It was Peggy Whitehead giving the invitation with smiling graciousness.

Her mother was busy trying to make Mrs. Gainsborough feel at ease over the interruption, and also trying to engross the attention of the child, to divert him from a recurrence of his troubles, whatever they had been. Besides, she was secretly anxious to speed the parting guest, lest she should by any mischance learn of the latest *faux pas.*

"Thank you, yes. Miss Whitehead. And I think Mr. Jameson will have some, too."

I looked at Craig in astonishment. Were his senses wool-gathering? How could Craig take time for tea when there was a jewel robber, one of the cleverest I had ever heard of, to be caught, and at once?

"Sugar? Cream?" Peggy asked.

"No, thank you. Just lemon. A whole lemon, please—and a knife."

Peggy looked incredulous. But she thought it was a joke, and her youth pardoned and indulged it. Those near by who had heard, smiled, supposing Craig was going to do some little trick for the benefit of the still sniveling child.

Craig smiled at the boy, smiled harder, made a funny face. The tears were drier, now. Merton kept looking at Craig, solemn but interested and amused. His attention was not allowed to wander. Each face Craig made was funnier than the preceding.

The maid laid the lemon and knife before him.

"Mr. Kennedy, are you going to use the whole lemon, or shall I have it sliced for you?" Mrs. Whitehead asked it, a little perturbed at Craig's behavior before some of her guests.

"I want it all, please. Let me cut it myself."

He held the lemon up so that Master Merton could see it. The boy watched wondering what he was about to witness. His mouth was open. He was fascinated.

With a flourish of the knife, a tightening of his cuffs and sleeves of his coat, Craig deliberately sliced the lemon, slowly, making a mess of it. The juice was running all over. The girls were giggling; there were suppressed snickers from the young fellows.

I wondered. Was Craig going to do a trick, produce the missing Blossom diamond from the lemon, like a magician on the stage?

Mrs. Whitehead was nervous. Was Kennedy falling down in catching the thief by his absorbing efforts to interest Merton? Would these people never go?

Craig was slowly cutting the lemon, still. He put a few drops on his tongue from one piece. Mrs. Whitehead gasped. There was a titter of amusement in back of me at Craig's manners.

Merton, watching Craig, came a step closer. Craig smiled invitingly. The boy's mouth began to water. The smell of the lemon was beginning to work. He was drooling. Down his chin from the corners of his mouth the saliva was running at the sight of the lemon.

At the end of the reception hall I could make out Jenkins approaching. Merton moved still nearer, drooling, as Kennedy smiled an invitation to share the lemon with him.

"Not tears this time, is it, son? Your mouth waters for this lemon. Let me—"

He reached over, unbuttoned the pocket, and pulled out Merton's handkerchief. He shook out the handkerchief to wipe Merton's lips.

The Blossom diamond clattered to the parquet floor.

Craig reach down quickly and picked it up.

"Why, bless me, it's a diamond—of the first water!" he exclaimed, seeming to hang on that word water. "You are shedding them?"

Then he looked fixedly at Mrs. Gainesborough. I had fully expected that weepy lady to collapse. Instead, she seized Merton's hand roughly and started suddenly toward the door. Merton set up the wail again.

Craig seized her wrist.

"Not so fast, I beg you."

For a moment their eyes met. Neither wavered. "Mrs. Gainesborough—really, I should say, Roszika Ginsberg—internationally famous, if I recall the old Victoria, for your sleight of hand stunts on the stage, years before the war. The hand is quicker than the eye!"

Sally Carroll stood aghast between Kennedy and me. The shock was something as if Vesuvius had been found guilty of surreptitiously freezing ice cream.

Craig smiled down at Sally's shocked upturned face. "I think you told me of the Ashton robbery, first, at the Current Events Club? That cut the suspects into half right there. It was a woman, then, not a man."

He turned again on Roszika. She no longer looked into his eyes brazenly.

"Presto! The diamond—in the mouth—then to the weepy lace handkerchief, unsuspected. But I had that weepy handkerchief. I saw that it was dropped by you. You could not talk while the diamond was in your mouth. It interfered with that wonderful acquired broad 'a.' You are a quick thinker. The vaudeville gave you that; what nature did not in the first place. You pinched this 'stall' kid, Merton, and made him cry, ostentatiously cry.

"It would make an excuse, too, for a hasty getaway, now that you had the diamond. His handkerchief wiped his tears, then your own eyes, and your lips. And back into his pocket, buttoned over carefully—with the Blossom diamond. Merton didn't know, even, that it was there. But I did. The lemon detected it. Water was the excuse to conceal it. Water was the means of discovering it! Mrs. Blossom, permit me. If any of you others miss anything, I would advise holding this lady and an immediate search of her effects."

EARTH

"**MEADOWBROOK FARM IS** rightfully mine! I am the daughter of the rightful heir. And I am the only living heir of my uncle Jasper, who holds it. It was my grand-father's and my great-grandfather's, on my mother's side, before that. It is mine. Is there no justice, Mr. Kennedy, in the earth?"

Ruth Sanford Saxton's big brown eyes seemed almost black in the intensity of her feeling as she leaned forward on the hassock on which she was sitting. Tears of passionate disappointment were perilously near the surface.

"Have you ever seen your uncle Jasper?" asked Craig.

"Only once. My natural curiosity took me down there with some friends. I left them in the car in the lane and knocked at the door alone. I waited a long time and then the door was opened by a wizened, bent old man.

"I was frightened and for a moment I thought he was, too. He had to hold on to the door to steady himself. Hate and fear were in his face as he saw me. He put up the shaking fingers of his other hand as if to shut me from his eyes. 'Uncle Jasper,' I said, 'this is Ruth Saxton.' At that his claw-like fingers reached and pushed me away. His voice was so cracked he could hardly speak. 'Go 'way! Go 'way! Don't look at me!' he gasped. 'Sammy's eyes and Mary's face! My God!' He slammed the door in my face, locked it, and I could hear him running, actually running, away from me down the hall. That is all I have seen of my precious relative and the ancestral farm," the girl added bitterly.

Kennedy and I had met Ruth Sanford Saxton at a club luncheon some days before, a club composed of well-known New York women who were trying to give young genius an opportunity on the stage, in opera and concert engagements. I felt that there was a future for Ruth Sanford Saxton. Her beauty would carry her far; big brown eyes, limpid and melting one minute, gay and impish the next.

"But why should he be afraid to see your mother's and your father's face?" I asked with curiosity.

"That is what I want to know! It may be only a woman's intuition, but I think strange things happened down there that no one knows anything about. And I—" the girl hesitated, "I have no money to find out with, now. Some day, maybe, when my ship comes in—"

Craig was thoughtfully studying the earnest face of the girl. She had that something which is born in an actress, feeling, charm, personality. From a drawer of a little desk she took two yellowed photographs.

"My mother and father," she said simply to Craig. "You see, I am very like my mother there—only I have my father's big brown eyes.

"You know, my mother died when I was a baby, under particularly harrowing circumstances. My grandmother raised me and we had a terrible struggle to make ends meet. Then when success began to come, I lost her, too. I feel bitter toward my uncle. The thing I can never forgive is his callousness to my mother's wants before her death."

"What made Jasper Saxton act that way?" prompted Craig.

"Mr. Kennedy, it is a strange story." She settled back on the hassock. "My grandfather, Eli Saxton, was an old Scrooge of a man. Hard times for other people had made him rich, in a way. He built up an old Scrooge fortune by oppression and sharp dealing—small dealing, small fortune. He had been dead twenty years, but from the tales my grandmother told me I wonder yet if he is able to rest in his grave." Ruth seemed very much ashamed of her father's people and hesitated.

"Go on, please," assured Craig. "I'm interested."

"Well, in the hard times of 1893, he took away the big Meadowbrook Farm from my mother's family, the Sanfords. They had owned it for generations. Then through sickness and death of my other grandfather, the Sanfords sank lower and lower socially. They lived in a little house, not much more than a shanty, across the railroad.

"But grandmother and her daughter, Mary, my mother, though they were terrifically poor, struggled on. Mother had to work, too. Poverty forced her into some situations that caused unfounded gossip. Finally she had to go out as a household servant to the rich families in the neighborhood. It was hard. Mother had lots of pride and was really a beautiful girl as you can see. But work and worry and poor clothes made her look like a slattern.

"At last their finances were in such a condition that my mother, much against every instinct, was forced to take a position as the servant in the great house of her own ancestors at Meadowbrook."

Ruth lowered her eyes. Tears were gathering in them again.

"There the two sons of old Eli Saxton saw much of her. Both fell in love with her, but in different ways. My father, Samuel Saxton, the elder, was evidently a quixotic sort of man, with a twist to right the wrongs that the Saxtons had committed. He married my mother secretly."

Craig nodded and smiled encouragingly.

"The marriage was kept a secret successfully until one day the Saxtons' servant did not appear in the Saxton kitchen. In the shanty I was born that day. It seemed after my birth that misfortune came alike to both Sanfords and Saxtons.

"Just about a week later, when the news was being gossiped about the country, my grandfather made my father confess the marriage. In his apoplectic wrath he cut him off, disowned him.

Uncle Jasper was in a secret jealous rage, too, at the way things had gone. He had lost out with my mother, for whom he had been scheming. To the public, his open righteous wrath—if righteous it was—was made to seem like Jacob over Esau, and birthrights, and messes of pottage, and all that.

"That same night," Ruth continued, "my father was killed. Along the railroad that ran through the valley of the meadow from which the farm took its name, my father's mangled body was found. It had been tossed many feet. He must have been crossing the track from the shanty where his young wife and baby were. He had been struck by the train. The head was never identified, but the body was, completely. They assembled it as best they could for burial and it lies interred in the Saxton plot. The shock killed my grandfather, old Eli Saxton.

"It was awful, Mr. Kennedy, this tragedy. It made my mother delirious. She got up too soon from her bed and that night she wandered out of the little house into the darkness. When my grandmother found her, she was near the Saxton house, in the meadow, demented. She never recovered from the shock."

Ruth's big eyes gazed distantly out of the window as if peering into the past. Her lips trembled as she went on.

"You see, now Uncle Jasper was sole heir. He refused to recognize me as a Saxton. Then a few nights later my mother in her madness disappeared again. She had resumed her wandering over the Saxton meadows, for some reason, out of her head, I guess."

The girl left the room and returned with a package which she handled almost reverently. "Mother's shoes," she murmured.

The wrappings fell off and in Ruth's lap were Mary Saxton's shoes, preserved by her own mother, Ruth's grandmother. They had been torn by briers; the marks of red mud were still incrusted on them, uncleaned, just as they were after the wandering in the delirium.

With eyes fixed on the mute evidence through all these years of her mother's suffering, Ruth continued softly. "Mother went at last to the old Saxton house, which was still her home, in her upset mind. She denounced Jasper for disinheriting me. He only laughed at her. Finally, with a wild cry she fled from him, up the stairs, through the halls, up to the cupola from which she threw herself in her deilrium to her death.

"Ever since then, on wild nights, people say they have seen the spirit of Mary Sanford in the tower. Everybody thinks the place is haunted. But Uncle Jasper lives on in it, hanging on grimly to the little ill-earned fortune, never increasing it by much, never diminishing it by ever so little, a crabbed old man who never married, for there was none who would marry him.

"I have heard that servants came and went in the old house at first. But none stayed long. Finally none would come. Uncle Jasper didn't seek to encourage them, then, to come. Gradually the old house up Saxton Lane, off the high road, has become the house of a hermit.

"Grandmother moved to New York with me, a tiny baby. Some charitable relatives helped provide for us. Now I am fighting life alone, Mr. Kennedy. But it is hard to be kept out of what is really mine!"

Ruth confessed that when the play in which she had her first important part had looked like a success, she had dreamed of saving money until some day she might buy back Meadowbrook. She had heard of her uncle Jasper's intent to sell now and it made her eyes flash with indignation when she mentioned it. But they had withdrawn the play. It had gone the way of so many productions of real merit that season. Her dreams had gone glimmering. There was no fortune, no pot of gold at the very beginning of stardom.

"Spring is here!" exclaimed Craig one bright morning later in the week. "How would you like to take a ride down Jersey way, Walter? Wouldn't you like to get out into the country a day like this?"

The night before Craig had talked to Ruth Saxton over the telephone, but I had not heard the conversation, nor did I think of it at the moment. The idea seemed good; I needed a change, so I took the day off with him. I must admit that on the way down through the state that morning in his speedy roadster, Craig's enthusiasm for country life was a bit infectious. A country club on the road proved an added argument. By the time we reached New Brunswick I was wavering.

Down the hill, over the bridge into the quaint town, on a street not very wide, one receives the impression of a hustling, much-alive little city, with trolley cars, taxi-cabs, banks, good hotels, and a state university to add distinction.

It was then that Craig confessed a desire to look over the old Saxton farm. "Ruth Saxton says it is a splendid investment and that it's on the market at a ridiculously low figure, if you can get on the right side of that peculiar old Uncle Jasper of hers."

We stopped to make inquiries as to the road to the Saxton farm. What amused me at once was the way people spoke of Meadowbrook Farm—with bated breath, a catch in the voice, an almost awed inflection, even an incredulity at our assuming a desire to go to the old place. They regarded us with interest and city-wise superiority at our suggesting it.

"Why, man alive," said one, "no one would spend a night in that place, no one around here, not for a thousand dollars. It has the haunts!"

Kennedy thanked the volunteer for the information, but we went on. Gradually I was getting an angle on what I came to think of as the secret of the Saxtons.

Jasper Saxton was prematurely old. His was a strange countenance, too, with a protruding forehead, pinkish and shiny, surmounted and crowned with snow white, thin hair which showed a pink scalp peeping through on the top where nature had been least kindly. He wore his hair long and was not particularly neat about it. Now, in the sunshine and the breeze, wisps and strands of it lifted gingerly from his brow and back of his neck and waved like tiny flags of truce to halt relentless time in its further ravages.

In spite of his age, the man had not acquired poise or ease of manner. His fluttering hands were constantly and unconsciously smoothing the small flat top of the little wooden gate post, as if to give him confidence, an added strength, as he stood and looked at us under heavy, bushy, grizzled eyebrows.

His eyes were a faded blue and afflicted with tear ducts that refused to function fast enough in the March winds. His cheeks were sunken and his chin pointed, narrow. His ears were tiny, mostly flat and close to the head. They were peculiar, too. The middle extruded, as it were, reddened and hairy, beyond the outer edges, and gave one the impression that the whole ear had been turned inside out. A long scraggly neck with a prominent, thrusting, active Adam's apple completed the weird physiognomy.

The clothes which hung upon this strange specimen were of a sort more useful than ornamental, made for him when his girth was a bit greater and his shoulders square instead of round. And when he talked it was hard to understand him. Shrunken gums caused a shifting and dropping of false teeth.

"Ye say, d'ye, ye wanter look at the farm?" he inquired, still sizing us up shrewdly.

"Yes, Mr. Saxton," ingratiated Craig. "I would like to look around. I'd like to see the house first, then the land."

"Going in for psychic research?" I remonstrated.

Craig shook his head thoughtfully as he scanned the broad acres of the farm. "I don't think I'd want the house. Probably I'd tear it down. What a site on that knoll overlooking the meadow! I would build there. The brook—I'd leave that as it is, winding through the sweep of open space. What a glorious quiet here!"

"But, you, of all things, what do you want of a house in this out of the way country? What's wrong with the city?"

"Tired of the city; fed up on the city; that's all. I want rest— and exercise. I want health—and quiet."

"Then this is your place," drawled old Jasper Saxton, who had been listening and watching Kennedy keenly, paying little attention to me. He straightened slightly and opened the gate for us to enter. "I ain't put it in the hands o' none o' them agents. One o' them offered me a little money down. But the rest was to remain on mortgage. I seen his game. He was a goin' ter cut it up into little lots an' pay me that there mortgage as he sold 'em. Sharpers! I don't wanter see the old place sold on the install-ment plan. I'd like to sell it to someone'd keep it whole, pay for it whole. I'm gittin' ter be an old man, and the winters up here don't agree with me like they use ter. I'm thinkin' of locatin' down in Floridy, somewhars south."

Things might have looked better and more salable for a coat of paint. Also one could see no signs of the recent presence of a carpenter. The house was just dull and uninteresting. It lacked, to me, that decrepit picturesqueness of houses haunted and neglected. This house was haunted and prosaic. I thought of it as built of frame, with clapboards, rather than as being romantic and eerie. Perhaps it was because I was looking at it rather as a story than as an investment.

The front door opened on a rather wide central hall, with rooms on either side, four of them, and a broad staircase to the second floor. Rambling from the main floor was an extension in the rear, with an extension to the extension, back of that. Surmounting this house was a cupola on one corner.

There were four rooms also on the second floor, opening from the hall. And everywhere inside the house was dust, gray dust, thick dust, feathery dust. It betrayed one thing: the lack of a woman in the household. The furniture, too, was fair, far from modern, yet not old enough to be of any value from the point of view of a collector.

Downstairs we noted that there were no telephone or electric lights; upstairs no modem bathroom. Jasper Saxton had lived alone so long that his wants were few and simple. Two parlors, unused, a dining room with closed and broken shutters, a huge kitchen made up the first floor. The kitchen and extensions showed evidences of most use.

Upstairs, to the big front room to the right, dimly lighted from small-paned windows, all a dull drab, Jasper Saxton led us.

"I've never been in it since father died. It's all right, y'know, but it's just the way I feel about it. It's the largest room up here, too. The hall is cut off from the others."

It had a commanding view of the meadow and the knoll beyond. Jasper did not enter, however, just stood by the door. Was he, too, a believer in the haunted house idea? None should have known better. Besides, none of these bedrooms so far looked as if they were used. Everything was too dust-grimed and dust-covered.

The old man must have known intuitively of what I was thinking. "I never come upstairs at night—to sleep. Downstairs I sleep, mostly in a big chair. I'm troubled with asthma, bad. I eat, sleep, and live downstairs in that kitchen facing the woods."

He tried to make out that it was a humorous idea, this using only one room when there were so many. At least that was the only funny thing I could see in it. But the slipping of his teeth in his whistle-like mirth was all the humor I could extract from it.

He seemed to avoid entering the rooms at all, just hung on the knobs of the doors and extolled their wonderful qualities as to size, light, and air. Even a dead chimney swallow, long since nothing but feathers and bone, did not interest him in the other front room. This room was smaller. Something was cut off it.

"What's up these stairs?" asked Craig, opening a door next it in the hall. "Oh, the cupola. Do you use that for anything?"

"No, no. I never use it for anything. I never go up."

Kennedy looked at the old man rather keenly as he murmured his hasty answer. Here was a strange personality. What was it, fear or laziness? Apparently there was everything at hand, with a little care, to make him contented and comfortable.

Downstairs again to go out and look over the place, Jasper stopped in the kitchen for his hat. It was a queer old thing, a little circular crown with a plain band that settled down on his head like a turban. Made of black, it gave him a look almost of a gnome.

Preceded by Jasper we started to look over the barns, the stable with a pretty sound old horse in it, a box wagon, a buggy, a plow, a harrow in a shed, a corn crib built on four piles surmounted by inverted dishpans, chicken house, a pig pen. We paused by the old well, looking out over the meadow. Tall and lean, Craig stood with a glow of pleasure on his strong face as he turned his back on what was sordid of man and looked forth on what was glorious of nature.

As he spoke of rest and health and quiet, and of what a site was the knoll across the meadow, Jasper Saxton listened keenly. Kennedy asked about boundaries, landmarks, acreage, title. Old Jasper excused himself to go back to the house to get some ancient deeds, papers that would settle forever the confines of Meadowbrook Farm and the ownership.

Leaning on his stick, Craig waved his arm. "Out there, Walter, with a saddle horse, two Great Danes I have just bought, work to do on the farm, getting close to the old earth from which we sprang, I feel I'd get away from crime. There's too much of it in the world."

As I looked at him more closely, he showed plainly the lines of care and overwork on his face.

Old Jasper had returned with the documents and was listening intently.

"It isn't the house that means anything to me," went on Craig. "But over there on that grassy knoll, the other side of that little grove of buttonwoods, is an ideal place for a rambling type of house. I can see it now, protected by the trees from the north winds in the rear, the sloping hillside merging into the meadows by the river in front. What a place to dream and ponder—and write!"

"Yes, they'd call my stuff 'Ravings from the Raritan.'"

Old Jasper had been listening patiently, a great deal more patiently than I had, as Kennedy rambled on about his ideas of

what should be done with the farm by himself as country gentleman. I did not understand the reversal of the usual process. But
this was, as a matter of fact, Kennedy's sales talk to the seller.

"And ye'll build out there, maybe tear down the house, keep
the meadowland, not cut the old place up in little building lots
and sell it to these here city people?" drawled Jasper. "Well,
p'r'aps ye're right. It's not much of a house, not in these days.
And if ye were to fix it up, ye'd still have an old house. And then
ye might divide and sell to pay for the improvements. But ye
would not want to sell if these new little boxes of houses was
goin' ter spoil yer view from the knoll, now would ye?"

Kennedy smiled. "Most certainly not."

"And ye'll pay my price, agree not to divide the property, say,
for twenty years?"

Kennedy nodded.

"Then p'raps ye'll drive me back to the city with yer in that
fine car o' yourn and we can see my lawyer, old Ezra Throop,
and draw up the papers, maybe pay a little to bind the bargain?"

Kennedy nodded again.

"I'm a-thinking maybe I'll buy me one of these here flivvers,
now," commented old Jasper, hanging on to his brimless hat as
the car whizzed back to town. "Kin I get one second handed?
Do they cost much? Do ye think it's any trick to make the durn
things go?"

At the lawyer's Kennedy arranged for a search of the title to
the place and a guarantee. It was stipulated also in the contract
that everything must be left as it was, the furniture, all but old
Jasper's personal effects in the creepy old house.

Though bad luck had pursued the Sanfords and the Saxtons
in the ill-omened mansion, it was a gloriously beautiful April
day that Kennedy took possession. The buds were peeping out
here and there on the trees, the delicate green tips of leaves
giving promise of beauty to come.

Craig did not bring much out there with him to the old house.

"I'm going to wait, Walter," he said, "until I get my plans for the other house."

"I noticed," I returned, "you were very particular in stipulating that everything must be left as it was. I'm sure it's good enough for this place until you build on the knoll."

But I had not much heart in it. To tell the truth I was worried over Craig's buying of that house. I had often wondered why a man of his engaging personality had never married. There had been plenty of girls I knew who had been deeply interested in him, had he but returned the interest. I wondered whether Ruth Saxton had anything to do with it. She was pretty enough to please any man, and talented, too.

Apparently Craig's mind was not traveling along my road at the time. "I've had a couple of rooms downstairs in the front cleaned out. We'll sleep in one of them to-night. There are two old couches there and I think we'll be more comfortable than upstairs in those musty bedrooms. Jasper Saxton will never be mayor of spotless town."

"What about the dogs?" I asked.

"Give them the run of the place at night. They will keep intruders away, or at least notify us of their presence."

The dogs were two beautiful Great Danes who had romped their ponderous way already into our hearts. I loved to watch them. They were scarcely more than out of their puppy days yet, but their blooded qualities were manifesting themselves. Nothing escaped their watchful eyes and ears. Their voices were formidable. Every stranger warranted suspicion. None got by until we had given the word. We felt very safe—from material intruders.

We had dinner at a hotel in town and while we were there Jasper Saxton joined us. The sale of the property seemed to have made him a bit remorseful, already, in spite of his new acquisition, a second-hand flivver, in which he was deeply interested and awed.

"You don't mind if I go up with ye a little while to-night?"

Kennedy nodded and after dinner we went out to the Saxton house. The old man seemed reluctant to leave, but now, even after the papers were signed, sealed, and delivered, he showed no hesitation in talking about the haunts of the house. Still he was leery at the mere suggestion of going upstairs after dark.

It was just damp and cold enough to make the warm glow from a couple of logs in the fireplace feel snug. Jasper acted as if he never could get warm. Even as late as it was in the spring when the farmers in the vicinity were undertaking their spring plowing, he stood with his back to the fire and would suddenly turn and stretch his two thin, pasty white hands over the blaze and rub them.

"Why didn't you mention some of this before?" I asked bluntly as Craig smiled.

"I wanted to sell," confessed Jasper frankly. "Now, Mr. Kennedy can't believe the old house has strange things a happening into it—and maybe it is my imagination," he added, shaking his head.

"Well, there will be a chance to find out soon enough," put in Craig. "When do the haunts start work? Will you stay and play with them?"

The invitation failed to please. Jasper's interest in Craig's plans for the Saxton farm vanished. He mumbled under his breath some unintelligible apology and left to go back to his room in town.

Kennedy and I sat and talked late over the good times we would have in that farm. We were planning a tennis court and even a little golf course, though not of nine holes. It was well on to midnight when we retired.

We had to make our own beds that night. Each of us had one of those couches that were popular about thirty or forty years ago, green leather and lightest of oak frames. The springs were stiff and the leather covering tufted tightly and fastened with little leather-covered buttons. Even with blankets, they were uncompromising. I rolled and tossed on those hard biscuit-like protuberances.

I could hear the clock in the hall striking twelve. Again at the half hour it reminded me was still awake.

"What's the matter with you, Walter? The haunts getting you?" Craig called unsympathetically.

I counted sheep. I got up and ate some crackers and drank some water. Nothing made me sleep. By this time, however, I knew Kennedy was in the land of dreams.

Suddenly I heard a noise. Tap, tap, tap! It must be in the house. The dogs were quiet.

"Craig!" I called softly.

No answer.

Tap, tap, tap!

So lightly it came that I felt that only hands capable of working invisibly could ever hope to have a touch as light as that.

Craig was still sleeping soundly. On second thoughts I did not want to wake him. I might be imagining things. I wished it would stop. Tap, tap, tap! I got up softly and steeled myself to go into the kitchen. Everything was all right. I couldn't hear it there. Tiptoeing back into the dark, unfamiliar yet with the positions of the furniture, I stumbled and fell over a chair as I heard overhead the unmistakable noise of soft feet, ghostly feet.

"Craig! Did you hear that?"

"I hear you!"

"No, I mean that noise just then. There!"

"I don't know. Let's look."

On the table was an old-fashioned oil lamp, with a plain square iron base and a glass oil bowl. I felt indeed that we had skipped back thirty years when Craig lighted it.

We started to look for the noise. As we entered the lower hall it seemed louder, coming from upstairs.

"I'll say old Jasper Saxton showed good judgment when he

refused to use those upstairs rooms—if he had to listen to those taps, all night. That's someone moving, above!"

Craig was silent. As we were ascending the steps to the second floor, noiselessly, a sudden draught seemed to strike us. The lamp went out in Craig's hands. We were in total darkness.

I felt as if old Eli Saxton's bony hand was at my throat. I might even have sworn I saw the ghostly filaments of Mary Saxton fleeing before me.

Tap, tap, tap! It came now, a crunching sound.

"Whatever it is," I tried to whisper nervously, "it sounds as if it had been either to a graveyard or a butcher. Bones! I don't like hunting noises like that in the dark—in this house!"

"Keep quiet! Whatever it is, we want to see it."

"I don't know whether I do or not. Jasper didn't. If it's what people say it is, if it's a ghost, I want it to stay invisible."

Outside one of the pups howled, dismally, in which he was joined by the other. They were too old to miss their mother, knew us too well to be lonesome, I thought.

By this time Craig had another light. As it flashed up there was a sharp hollow sound as of knocking on wood. Or was it of something small that had dropped suddenly and rolled? I glanced about, fearful of being pelletted with ghostly missiles.

"It's up above!" Craig whispered.

We went on until we came to the cupola door. We could find nothing. But the sounds were still plain.

Tap, tap, tap!

"It's in the cupola!" I exclaimed. "You don't suppose it's Mary Sanford—getting ready to jump again?"

By this time Craig was up there. Suddenly I heard him laughing, immoderately.

"Come up!" he called.

I climbed after him. Anyone on the high road seeing our wavering forms in the light must have thought the cupola haunted. Standing, holding the light in one hand, Craig pointed with the index finger of the other, to a hole in the ceiling.

"There's the ghost!"

My foot crunched shells of black walnuts, hickory nuts on the floor.

"Squirrels! The thing you heard drop was a walnut. It rolled away, the squirrel after it. See, they can make a jump from the branches of that old tree—and in this window."

I had a feeling of disappointment in spite of the certain satisfaction that it was nothing supernatural. I followed Craig down and now indeed I was soon sleeping, tired.

Yet it haunted my dreams. The strange rappings, those rappings, were explained. But what was the secret of the Sanford-Saxton place? What was it that loosed Jasper's tongue about the house, talking much, but saying little?

The following day was Craig's first full day in actual possession of old Meadowbrook Farm.

We rose early. How strange this old place was! To realize the conveniences of electricity and gas and plumbing one must live in a house without them. We took our cold tubs in a cold tub, an old wooden tub that leaked through the sides all over the kitchen. The result was that the kitchen had to have a mopping, too. We built a wood fire in the old range and managed to get a little breakfast. It was funny while the experience lasted and was new. I shall never forget that first meal in the farmhouse.

We fed the dogs, the horse, the chickens, and the rest of the live things about the place.

All that day we had to stay on the farm. Craig was expecting an architect and a landscape gardener whom he knew, and also a man who was to help with the chores.

In the shed of the farmyard the old plowshare seemed to catch Craig's eye.

"It's been a long time since I walked back of one of those things," he remarked meditatively. "That will be great exercise."

Craig looked in the direction of the meadow. My heart sank. There were a good many acres. It would be some exercise.

"You don't mean to tell me that you're thinking of plowing in those meadows to-day?" I asked. Country life to me was country clubs; I was used to a putter, not a plow.

Still Craig took the old horse and hitched him up to the old-fashioned plow. Then he started off in the direction of the meadow. I followed.

Here we were dressed in sport tweeds, out to do our spring plowing! I felt more like swinging a driver than a whip. Along the meadow ran a public road too. Some of the wiseacre farmers in the neighborhood must have enjoyed the sight of us in our unusual attire for work in the fields. The only things we lacked in their estimation must have been silk hats and gloves.

"Well, here goes, Walter! Once around the meadow!"

With a chirrup to the horse, we started around the meadow. Craig plowed deeply and thoroughly, taking his time to do it carefully. Close to the wire boundary fence he worked as he came back after once around the other sides, smiling at the people who went by.

The soil in that part of the country is very peculiar, of a dark red color. It is called red shale and is the discouragement of every neat farmer's wife on a rainy day. It tracks in and stays tracked.

Craig was almost completing his first lap, singing as he bent to it, now and then stopping to joke with me. Up the road, coming in from the direction of the highway to town was what looked like a car. As it came nearer I could make out that it was Jasper Saxton in his second-hand flivver, rattling along, "I-think-I-can-do-it. I-think-I-can-do-it!"

"Here comes that old pest again," I let Craig know.

"That's queer. He told me he was going to start on his trip to-day in that can. He must have changed his mind. I wonder what he wants now."

Looking down the road where it swept up the knoll and was pretty soft and squashy I smiled involuntarily. The old flivver was swinging from side to side, and bumping. It was as if a ship pitched and rolled, both at once. How old Jasper's teeth must have rattled: "I-think-I-can, I-think-I-can—I-know-I-can-n-n't!"

He got out of the stalled bus and as he came nearer he waved his scrawny hand. Nearer still I saw that he was smiling, a smile that was most uncanny. His teeth had dropped and the smile lost itself in the cavity between teeth and gums. I thought, if Alice had only been there she might have solved the mystery of the Cheshire cat.

"Purty hard work ye're doin', Mr. Kennedy," he called, still smiling that ghastly smile without teeth.

"I don't mind it, Mr. Saxton. It keeps my hands busy. I feel I'm doing something really worth while, at last!"

"Yeh. I s'pose it's all the way ye looks at it. Ye want to begin it. I'm glad to be able to stop it. He! he! he!" He laughed a ridiculous laugh. If there were derision in it, it would be hard to determine whether it was objective or subjective.

Craig plowed on quietly to finish his once around.

"What ye goin' ter do with it? Plant it?" Inquisitively.

"Perhaps so. I haven't decided yet just what it will be. I want to get some advice from a soil specialist."

"Yeh? Labor's purty scarce hereabouts, and purty high. Ye can't get a good man fer love nor money. And the prices ye gets ain't so good any more. Acres and acres of potatoes rotted hereabouts last year. It didn't pay to dig 'em."

Kennedy paused as he finished his once around, looked back contemplatively over the roll and sweep of meadow and field. It was pretty big. Evidently, too, he was thinking of that last remark.

He turned again to the old horse, "I think, after all," he said with a sudden decision, "I'll plow up only about an acre or so, right here at the corner by the barns."

Saxton's face seemed to become more natural. He had his teeth back in sub-normal. He stood silently with me a long time as Kennedy went once around what he judged to be a good acre, then twice. Finally the old codger sloughed back over the uneven ground, with a curt good-by, to his flivver. It started down. Gravity was with it, not against it. "I-think-I-can-do-it; I-think-I-can-do-it." Only once did he look back. Then he nearly ran into a tree.

Kennedy plowed the acre or so and called it a day.

The second day of our stay at the farm was another of those spring days when it is a joy to live but how irksome to work. The golf links called; every glimpse of good road was an invitation to step on the gas, to go, one didn't care where, but just step on the gas and go.

This morning Craig dressed for work. I looked at him in amazement, a bit peeved.

"What's the matter, Walter? Does the ghost of work frighten you?"

I hated the very word work. "Craig, you're a hog—a hog for work! Look at us. We're thin enough. We don't need that kind of work."

"Oh, come along with me. Be a sport."

For some reason, to me inexplicable, perverse, Kennedy had changed his mind. He decided to plow much more than that acre in the corner of the meadow. He had gone back to his first idea. Round the great meadow he started again. Occasionally he would stop, break up a clod of earth with his foot, or examine the character of the soil.

"You're getting mighty particular in your amateur farming," I exclaimed.

I watched him, amused, interested in spite of myself. Round and round the great meadow we went, taking turns back of the plowshare. Each time we did it a shorter time by a few minutes was required. Craig would straighten up frequently and look over the plowed ground with satisfaction. I'll say it was plowed well. Spring though it was, I mopped moisture off my brow. I felt it trickling down my back. I felt like an advertisement for

Omicron Oil for all aches. Kennedy was caroling a ribald ditty
we had heard "over there" during the war:

> "Big brother Bill
> Is removing a hill
> With the aid of a shovel and gin!"

We were smoking and resting when a neighbor rolled by in an
old farm wagon on his way home from town. He was a shrewd
native and looked askance at our city farming.

"How's things comin' along? I seen old Saxton back a piece
on the road. He was swearin' a blue streak over puttin' a new tire
on his gas wagon. I expect he might be comin' down to see ye."

"I thought he was going away on a trip," I returned.

"We thought so, too. But it is purty hard to pull up stakes on
short notice and clear out when it's home yer leavin'."

He clucked to his old mare and passed on. Sure enough, soon
we had another visit from the recent owner.

"Changed yer mind?" he inquired.

"About what?" Craig asked.

"About yer plowing up the field." He smiled at us indulgently
as if he thought we were mythical characters of old from the
pages of a fairy tale book, set to work emptying rivers with a
spoon in order to win some fair princess held in durance by a
wicked fairy or a cruel giant.

Jasper leaned against the fence, legs crossed, an elbow on the
post, his hand cupped to hold his wizened face. Out over the
meadows he looked.

"Some job ye got before ye, boys. It looks easy now. But
weedin' and harrowin' and dry spells 'long about the end of July
are troublesome visitors to pester ye." He cackled dryly. Kennedy
looked at him silently, nodded and smiled and completed the
furrow.

Once again he went around in the ever decreasing oblong.
Slowly, slowly but constantly he was plowing. By nightfall he

had completed perhaps a score of furrows about the meadow in addition to the acre or so plowed in the corner by the barns.

As he drove the old horse back to the barnyard, turning him over to be fed and made comfortable by the man we had hired, his eyes swept the neatly furrowed paths the plowshare had left. "It's work, Walter, but it's worth it!"

I did not feel his enthusiasm. I felt if it were to be plowing every day, I'd put in a fictitious hurry call from the *Star*. I was bored to death at this first manifestation of eccentricity on the part of Kennedy. Back to the soil meant nothing in my life.

The third day was much like the other two. We plowed all morning, ate our lunch, and started the afternoon's plowing. I was tired looking at dirt. I hated red shale with a bitter hatred. I saw red at the very idea of the growth of the soil.

But things went a little faster. For that I was thankful. The furrows were quite a bit shorter in length and I had the satisfaction of seeing a new one started much more often.

That day we had no visit from Jasper Saxton. I thought perhaps he was tired watching us make such industrious fools of ourselves.

But late in the afternoon we had an interruption. It was a real-estate agent from town who had driven out. He was anxious to buy the place. He had been told by neighbors our freshly plowed meadows showed promising soil. I wondered if they were becoming envious. He hinted that he had a client who wanted to farm for a living, a dirt farmer, not for exercise. He told the old story of the gentleman farmer who asked his guests whether they would have milk or champagne. "It costs the same!"

At last he came around to the purpose of his visit. "Will you sell this place, neighbor?"

"I just bought it," was Craig's wisely naive answer.

"Oh, that's all right," came the airy reply. "If you don't care to sell it that way, I'll help you make a pile of money out of it another way. I'll let you make a reasonable profit, something pretty fair on the turnover of your money."

"No. I don't want to sell."

"It would make a good development," persisted the agent. "The railroad right past it and all that. With my influence I could get a station located there. We'd run a parked avenue right up from it to the knoll. Tell you what I'll do, neighbor. I'll make a dicker with you, pay you a fair cash advance, let you in on the profits of selling the lots as a bonus. You can name your figure, your advance, your cut-in. I'll consider them—if they're within reason, leave me a chance for a profit, a chance to live under them. In a few years we'd both be on easy street, sitting on the top of the world, pretty—you with this land, me with my selling organization and experience."

Craig listened patiently to the very end. "Not a chance, sir," he returned flatly. "You see, when I bought it, it was restricted. I can't cut it up for twenty years."

"I'll take a chance on getting that restriction removed by old Saxton," persisted the agent. "I know how I can get around his sentimental reasons. Come on. Make a dicker. Here's my check." He had pulled out a check book and a fountain pen, resting them on a brief case he carried. "I'll make an advance on the contract—five thousand, say—name it!"

"No!" Kennedy was curt. "I'll not sell!"

The agent gone, his persuasive arguments and his valuable time wasted, Kennedy turned back to his plow horse.

"Gee!"

He turned the horse's head at last to the barn again and as I looked at the meadows for the last time that day, I felt that the poor animal and myself had earned our dinners. I was never made for a farmer.

If I had kept a diary those days it would have read something like this:

"Got up. Bathed. Breakfasted, Plowed. Lunched, Plowed. Dined. Bathed. Went to bed. Slept."

I was reaching the end of my patience. To show how I felt about this plowing, I kicked the old plowshare maliciously as

I went by it. I was childish, I know, but it gave me some satisfaction.

The end of the fourth day of plowing found us with many of
the acres of the meadow ready for planting.

"Are you going to rest any before you start to plant, Craig?" I
asked desperately.

I looked at my blistered palms and felt the tired, sore spots
over my shoulders, all over my back. The furrows were going
quickly, now, compared to the start. Every oblong was decreasing in size fast. Each day Craig was getting nearer and nearer
to completing the task he had set himself to do.

But after these days of grinding, monotonous work I was
ready to go on strike. I swore at the mere mention of the plow.
The old horse had been presented with a new set of shoes; his
harness had been patched up pretty by the hired man. The plowshare had been braced and strengthened. But nothing had been
done for me.

Craig was just as zealous, just as painstaking. Each lump of
dirt, each clod was broken patiently and serenely.

"I'm going to call up the 'Follies' if you persist in this cussed
hobby!" I exclaimed. "Right down there, I'll build a platform.
And I'll have the show transported to the banks of the Raritan.
We'll have a sylvan frolic, end it with a Jersey lightning party,
hitch all the girls to the plowshare and drive them around the
last furrow!"

Kennedy smiled indulgently at my weak attempt at humor—
and kept on plowing.

It was somewhat after lunch time when plowing was in order
for the afternoon performance that we saw old Jasper Saxton
stop again. He had driven by nearly every day. So had the rest
of the countryside. Our industry was quoted far and wide. I was
looking even for a special writer from the *Star* to come down to
see if I had gone insane, what institution they expected to place
me in. I was never known to have worked so hard in my life. I
really believe I felt personally acquainted with every horse hair

in old Dapple's tail. I had found myself counting them, counting furrows, counting anything.

Jasper sidled over toward us. "By golly! I'd like to have had
men working for me the way the two of ye work!" He turned to
Craig at length and asked sort of casually, "Be ye goin' ter finish
the whole durned meadows?"

Craig nodded. "Yes, I guess so."

"Then what will ye do? What will yer next exercise be? Will
yer tear down the old house yourself, maybe?"

"Maybe." Kennedy shrugged.

I smiled, but to me the old man's inquisitiveness and interest
were only natural. Probably he was thinking if he had showed
the same ambition as we were exhibiting the last few days he
would have had money enough to keep his old home and go to
Florida, too.

Kennedy looked at the old man's face sharply. "I thought you
were going away, Mr. Saxton."

Jasper Saxton seemed ill at ease. His manner diverted me for
the moment from the plowing. "It takes longer to get things
settled up than I thought. I'll be goin' in a few days, now." As I
regarded him now more closely, I noticed he was even whiter,
thinner than when we had first seen him hanging over the fence
the day Craig started negotiations for the old Meadowbrook
Farm.

Then, too, I noticed he was constantly expectorating. That was
a new habit I hadn't seen before. What was the matter with the
old codger? Was he getting home-sick? There was no evidence
of banter in his tone today. It was grieved, peevish.

Looking over the meadows he remarked slowly, "I calc'late
another day an' ye'll be finished with this meadow." He was
looking away, his eyes squinted up shrewdly, deep crows' feet
about them.

"Just about—one more day." Craig said it slowly to the
haggard-faced old man.

Jasper Saxton turned to go away, without even a good-by. He
plodded over to his flivver.

"Durned fool! Durned fool! Durned fool!" I heard him muttering under his breath. I wondered was it Kennedy he meant, or himself?

I was tired that night, tired and hopeful. Only one more day and that plowing would be over, anyhow. I had been glad to hear Craig admit it when old Saxton had asked him. I wanted to go to bed early and be fresh for the morrow's work.

But Craig was alert, active, full of nervous energy. He could not even sit still in any chair for long. By this time we had all the rooms on the first floor cleaned. He roamed the length of the house and back again.

It was getting late. "I'm going to bed, Craig."

"Not yet, Walter, please. I feel like talking, like having company. Stay up with me."

I marveled at his stamina. There must be some good in plowing for him. Was the strength coming to him out of Mother Earth direct? The physical exercise of the days past could not dull that mind nor still that nervous energy. I sat back resting in the one big comfortable rocking chair, silent. Craig was pacing quietly back and forth in the room. It was getting late, near midnight.

Suddenly I was aware in my half drowse that there was a noise outside.

"What's that?" I startled. "Did you hear it?"

Bedlam had now broken loose with the dogs. They were barking furiously, deep, low, long barks. Now they were sharp, snappy barks that indicated the sight of their quarry.

Craig had thrust a gun in my hand. We dashed out of the house, never stopping for hats or coats. Ahead we plunged in the blackness over to where the sounds of the dogs indicated trouble. In the darkness I could make out someone running desperately, stumbling over the furrows. Who was it?

"Go back—go back—I tell ye!" We were still too far away to recognize either the voice or the form. We ran. Now I could see it was a man, that he was getting winded. Blindly stumbling, he had used up all his strength.

Out of the darkness, out of the plowed meadow came a voice, imploring. "Call off them dogs, Kennedy!"

Craig called. "Down, Raffles! Here, Sherlock!" The dogs obeyed, crouched. As we came up to the man, he sank to the ground, exhausted. There, before us, was Saxton, haggard, winded, all in.

"What's the matter, old man?" asked Kennedy. "Did you leave anything here?"

Saxton's head dropped low on his breast. He was silent. I looked on, amazed at this inexplicable thing that seemed unfolding before me. He put out his trembling hand furtively, as if grasping for some support. Then with an effort he raised his eyes to Craig's face. The whiteness, the pallor stood out in the circle of light from my flash.

Kennedy leaned over and raised the tottering old man to his feet, still weak, quivering with fear. His face wore a hunted, haunted look. Kennedy half dragged, half led him toward the barnyard and house.

"Kennedy!" old Jasper Saxton peered forward, wringing the words from his chattering teeth. "Every day you are getting closer and closer to the middle of that meadow!"

Then there was a silence in the darkness, a silence charged with tragedy, with crime.

"You know—and you know I know!"

Another pause.

"Kennedy—it's in the earth!"

In the shadow of the shed he turned trembling, shuddering, away from the meadow. I kept the dogs quiet. A train, the midnight "Owl," whistled shrilly. The old man jumped as if he had been on the track, chattering.

"That night," his voice had sunk to little more than a hoarse whisper, "that night, I met my brother Samuel on his way to the Sanford shack, across the railroad. We quarreled, over Mary Sanford, the baby, the estate. In the heat of it I shot Samuel— with the derringer of the old man! There was his body, at my feet! It would be found in the morning. The whistle of the train! I dragged the body to the railroad track, laid it across the track.

"But what I had hoped did not happen. The head was severed, tossed forty feet or more from the body. And in that head was gaping that bloody bullet wound! I buried the head—in the meadow, somewhere in the middle!"

A stifled groan escaped the trembling lips of the old man. "Out there, in the meadow, you will find my shovel. I was going to try and dig it up. I dropped the shovel when the dogs heard me."

Kennedy dragged him on into the house. There in the kitchen he sank into a chair, his chair, quaking. Outside the dogs were at the door. He shuddered again, apprehensively, as he thought of their burly forms, interrupting him, pursuing him.

"That night—no one saw me!"

"No one?"

Kennedy was toying with a pair of worn woman's slippers he had drawn from a package in the old secretary in the front room. I recognized them. They were the slippers of her mother that Ruth Sanford Saxton had once shown us. On them was incrusted thick yet the red shale of the meadow.

"No one?" Craig repeated. He paused a moment. "It drove some one insane!"

"I know! I know! I know! The memory of it has driven me insane, too!" In the half dark, his coat off now, his while hair whiter than ever, he started forward from the chair, his arms raised in agony to heaven. "My life has been hell! Sam has been paid—paid in full! Everywhere I looked I saw them. Every voice sounded their voices. They were with me all the time. I couldn't stand it any longer—at my heels, at my elbows, pointing fingers at me in my sleep! I couldn't get any comfort in the house I stole from their child. I sold it, to lose them. And in selling it, they have found me—come closer to me than ever! Oh, my God! Have more mercy than I showed!"

"Though they did not know how well they builded," pursued

Craig relentlessly, "those people who said this house was haunted were right. It was haunted, Jasper Saxton, haunted by Mary Sanford's spirit. She knew—and it had driven her insane—to her death!"

Jasper Saxton was shaking, staring, drinking in each word with a quiver.

"And, now, what are you going to do with me, Kennedy? To-morrow—" He paused as if what would happen to-morrow were too terrible even to think.

"No statute of limitations runs against this crime of yours, Jasper Saxton!" Kennedy's voice had a hard impersonal ring in it, more menacing than anger. "The spirits of Samuel Saxton and Mary Sanford haunt justice. There is no change of venue for that case!" Kennedy stopped. "You can make a will that shall do justice to the baby Ruth. All else is between you and your God!"

Craig dropped the shoes on the deal table. Jasper jumped at the clatter.

"It's not what I am going to do with you, Jasper Saxton. It's not what the law is going to do with you. It's what you are going to do with yourself!"

"My—God!"

The old man rose, tottered toward the front room. "K— Kennedy, is there a pen—and ink—and paper—in that there secretary of father's?"

"Yes."

Five—ten minutes passed in the creaking old kitchen.

Suddenly the silence was broken by a shot in the parlor. I followed Craig in.

Jasper Saxton lay across the hearth. On the secretary lay a hasty, trembling scrawl, leaving all to Ruth. On the floor, beside the body, was the old derringer with which he had killed his brother Samuel.

"In the end," muttered Kennedy, "he was his brother's keeper. Dust to dust, ashes to ashes, earth to earth!"

FIRE

"**OPERATOR, I HAD** the Follies box office. You cut me off.… Some one calling me?… Gamble's Funeral Parlors?… What! Oh—hang it!—Leslie, that you?… Trying to get me?… Well, you are a joy killer!"

Kennedy turned from the telephone a moment later. "Mrs. Oakley Asche is dead and her physician refuses to sign the death certificate. Doctor Leslie—you remember him, the medical examiner?—is up there and wants me."

"Mrs. Oakley Asche?" I repeated. I was thinking of the vanity of the rich old lady. Several months before she had startled the readers of society news by marrying the Broadway health culturist, Professor Gaston Asche.

Craig smiled. "Must have been well into her sixties to get the name of the million-dollar gray flapper."

At Gamble's Doctor Leslie met us and his face wore an expression of perplexity.

"Kennedy," he explained, "it began when Doctor Davids expressed a doubt that it was a natural death. You know it almost never happens in a poisoning case that the attending physician has an inkling of what is going on.

"Davids's hesitation about filling in the certificate aroused the health authorities. They called in the police. That's how I got here. But I can't find anything wrong, except that there must have been arterio-sclerosis, high blood pressure and all that; nothing else, however—yet."

"Davids—Davids," I repeated. "I could swear I have heard that name and Mrs. Asche's—and not in the capacity of her physician."

"Very likely you have; Doctor Oakley Davids is her nephew," returned Leslie, adding reflectively, "he would also have been her heir if she had not married this Asche. That's what makes me go slow. I see in it the possible foundation for a will contest— 'undue influence' on the part of Asche at a time when it might be that Mrs. Asche was mentally incompetent."

"Davids is really a specialist in cancer treatment by X-rays," interposed Kennedy.

Leslie nodded.

"Tell me something of the history of the case," continued Craig, as we walked down a somber corridor.

"Well, I understand that this afternoon she had a sort of stroke, in her boudoir. Her face was covered with some beauty clay or other at the time. Her maid thought it was apoplexy. Maybe it was. She called Doctor Davids. Mrs. Asche was unconscious when he arrived soon after—and died a few moments later, before he was able to do anything for her, without regaining consciousness."

"But how does it come the body is here? I understood that the old Oakley house was one of those remodeled in the old Chelsea district, with a private park shared by the houses fronting it, and all that."

Leslie shook his head. "I don't know how it came about that her body got here so soon. Some mix-up between the Health Department, the police and her husband, I imagine. Anyhow, it's here and the police are here, I'm here, and now you're here. It's up to us."

Unconsciously one treads softly in the presence of the dead. The room was dimly lighted by one shaded electric bulb. The draught from a ventilator made the draperies about the crypt move uncannily.

It seemed impossible to think that Mrs. Oakley Asche was

dead. Even in death appeared her love of the beautiful, the exquisite. Her hands folded, she looked like one asleep. There was certainly no evidence of violence, of fear, of terror, of emaciation, or, now, of suffering. I looked at the woman and marveled.

Kennedy's own first glance brought an exclamation to his lips. "Leslie, that woman past sixty looks like the Sleeping Beauty waiting for the Prince to waken her with a kiss!" He stood before her a moment contemplating the form now in deep shadow.

"But counterfeit youth doesn't fool Death," observed Leslie sagely.

No lines or wrinkles were noticeable on her pretty face, only the waxen pallor of death. Her face, a delicate oval with perfectly bow-shaped lips, long black lashes, sweeping over her upper cheeks, eyebrows arched gracefully above her closed eyes, suggested the work of the masters in their portraits of noble ladies many years ago. Her hair was curly and tinged with gray and seemed to be more than most young persons have in these days. It had been brushed lightly from her face and rippled softly over her ears. Of medium height and daintily slender, she made a wonderful picture.

"Only the wealthy can do it," considered Kennedy, as he bent over her examining. "Time and money are represented here. Many visits to the masseuse, the hair dresser, the figure expert, were needed to produce this woman before us."

He was now bending more closely over the body searching for some mark or evidence of violence. There were none apparently any more obvious to him than to Leslie, as he knelt between the dim-shaded light and the beautiful body, the body now in his own shadow.

We had been followed into the crypt by the policeman detailed to watch. Flaherty stood quietly back of us. There was nothing said or done that he did not observe, yet he acted as if he did not relish his job.

Suddenly Craig stepped back, over to the wall switch and turned off even the dim light. I could not imagine what the darkness was for, here, until I heard the policeman muttering thickly to himself, "Look! Holy Saints! She shines! Her lips—her face!"

Then, indeed, I did look, and in astonishment. It was a fact. Her lips, her whole face, her hands, all of her seemed to glow. It was too much for Flaherty. He drew toward the door, still whispering hoarsely: "I feel like I'd like to beat it! It's the corpse light, I'm tellin' ye!"

"I fancied I saw a faint glow in the darkness of the shadow," now observed Craig, straightening up, by way of explanation of his weird discovery.

Leslie was silent, assuring himself that it was no optical illusion. As for me I was speechless. A corpse that shone, not with an aura, which would have been startling enough to me, but with a light, faint, delicate, evanescent, but of its own making, as it were! If the gray flapper of the much-written-about million had risen on that catafalque or whatever it was, had pointed a finger at me and spoken, I could not have been more awed. Faint, delicate, evanescent though it was, it was to me like a fiery accusation of—what?

I am neither scientist nor criminologist. I felt like following Flaherty. But I stood rooted to the spot.

Protesting voices outside broke the spell.

"It's all right, I tell you. She is Miss Millard." I could not recognize the voice of the man speaking.

"See what she wants, Walter," asked Kennedy.

I opened the door with alacrity and saw our frightened Flaherty, now recovered far enough to argue with some one.

"I'm the undertaker. Miss Millard wants to see Mrs. Asche, too. She always patronized the Millard Beauty Shop. She feels that she would like to do the things for Mrs. Asche this last time that she did so often for her when she was living."

Behind me I caught Leslie whispering to Craig. "Davids told me about her, that Mrs. Asche often went for treatment to the Millard Beauty Shop, run by this Irrita Millard, on the first floor of the building where Asche had his health-culture gym and

institute on the roof. I couldn't quite make out what was back
of it… some innuendo, though. Gaston Asche and this Irrita,
he said, were very friendly. It seemed to weigh on his mind—
this pretty girl in the beauty parlor, Irrita Millard, and Gaston
Asche. I believe he meant to imply that Asche was using her
in some way."

"It's all right," called Craig. "Let her come in."

"All right, Mr. Kennedy, if you says so—and she wants to,"
Flaherty stood in the doorway where he could make a quick exit
and at the same time do his duty of watching us all.

Irrita Millard stepped into the room. The light had been on
just long enough for her to locate the position of the body.

Again Craig switched it off.

"Oh-h! It must have—" The girl suddenly stopped.

Again the lights came up quickly. "Must have what?"
demanded Kennedy quickly.

Irrita seemed suddenly to regain her self-possession. She
seemed annoyed. "I must have been dreaming," she muttered.
"I thought I saw her face glowing in the darkness and I was so
frightened I hardly know what I did say."

Irrita was exceptionally beautiful and young. She possessed
unusual limpid brown eyes and golden hair which had never
been bobbed. It was high up on her head in the prevailing mode
that Paris was then trying so industriously to reestablish in this
country. She was slender, not very tall, carried herself with a dash
and verve that would compel attention.

"I came to do the last few things for Mrs. Asche—Mr.
Kennedy," she began.

Kennedy regarded her silently. But it did not seem to ruffle
the composure she had regained.

"May I?" she pleaded.

"I'm afraid, Miss Millard," he replied slowly, "that will have
to be postponed. But I can promise you I will let you know the
moment it is possible. Where can I find you?"

"At my shop, or call the apartment on Fifty-ninth Street. My maid will tell you."

"The shop? Where?"

"In the Broadway-Forty-fifth Street Building."

"Oh! Where Professor Asche has his institute?"

Craig watched her face. There was not the quiver of a muscle. She was a good actress.

"Let me see," he pursued. "Isn't Doctor Davids in that physicians' building on Fifty-ninth Street?"

"I believe he is." She nodded with a look of naive questioning that said, "What can that matter?"

"I will let you know the earliest moment I can. You will be ready?"

"At any moment. She was always so gentle and kind to me, seemed to appreciate all my efforts."

Kennedy bowed Irrita out into the corridor. Then, between them, Kennedy and Leslie, after Irrita had left, arranged for an autopsy to be held in Leslie's laboratory.

"And in this matter," added Craig, "I am your deputy? I shall need official status."

Leslie hastened to assure him.

It was then I saw what Kennedy was contemplating. He was bent on a visit, a surprise visit, immediately, to Mrs. Oakley Asche's house in the old Chelsea district.

The old Oakley house was distinctive. In front of it was the park with its well-kept little lawn and ancient trees, with clumps of dense shrubbery, a constant invitation to the eyes of the dwellers surrounding it, a bit of country in the city within sound of the elevated railroads.

It was a house that betrayed its owner. Just as she had preserved the body, so she had preserved the house to set off and add distinction to herself. It was different from the other houses. Here a personality had lived. It also had taken on a new youth, like its owner.

The house conformed to the main lines of the old-fashioned red brick houses, with their monotonous high stoops now eliminated. In place was a beautifully arched window with soft lights shining through the draperies. The entrance had been transformed into the still older English basement. At the door were two antique lanterns. Rare old tiles, imported, were on the floor and the walls were paneled in softly aged oak. The lights with their batik covers, the unhemmed pink taffeta curtains, the soft blue and ivory of the furniture and upholstery breathed exquisite youth.

I looked out at the park again before I followed Craig into the interior. The shadows of the trees seemed to be engaged in a game of chase with the slenderer shadows of the high iron fence, as if in a desire to efface them with their more expanded surface. The breeze was constantly moving the trees and it seemed a never ending struggle with the fence shadows holding their own in steady defiance. In the center of each side of the park fence was a high grilled gate, four in all. Only the owners of four of the houses on the square held the keys to these gates.

Inside, where there were no oak panels in the walls, there were mirrors. I could imagine the handsome Mrs. Oakley Asche as she flitted about glimpsing herself, complacent at the pretty picture she made.

It was not without some difficulty that we got in. But Kennedy was a diplomat. He found that the maid, Marie, who came to the door, loved her mistress passionately. In his best phrasing, he told her he had come to make inquiries about the death of her mistress, showed Doctor Leslie's credentials, and in a moment had Marie won.

To his inquiry Marie replied by leading the way up to the second floor. "Here is her boudoir, Doctor. The adjoining room is her bedroom.

Marie smiled as she saw my look of astonishment. The boudoir was bizarre, indeed. What with white columns wrapped in boa-constrictor skins, one electric light shining from a rattler's mouth, as he coiled, stuffed, ready to strike, another shining from and through fossil resin of claret red, lights of innumerable odd conceptions, the bookcase surmounted with a mummy head under glass, rugs made up of skins of all the pets for sixty years, it was characteristic.

"Mrs. Asche always did things unusual, y'know," explained Marie to Craig as he questioned her, leading on.

"How? What do you mean?"

"You asked about her papers, did you not? Well here they are—some of them."

She bent over a stuffed Irish terrier and putting her hand about the dog's neck, pressed a concealed button. Immediately a little box dropped to the floor from the body. It seemed to amuse Marie to catch my surprise.

"She said that Mike was the most faithful guardian she ever had while he was alive—and she gave him the job after he was dead. Rather good, eh?"

Kennedy took the opportunity to run through the papers. Everything was in order, apparently untouched. Each little group of papers was in an envelope or neatly folded. Some of the envelopes were still sealed, intact. There were several bunches of keys. Craig looked at them all. One bunch he examined more curiously than the others. I saw that little reflective frown come between his eyes as he regarded minutely one key that was tagged. Then he dropped them all slowly back in their places without a word.

"May I see her creams and lotions which she used at home to preserve that marvelous complexion of hers?" asked Craig next.

"Through that door," Marie pointed to the bedroom.

We entered. It might have been the room of a little girl, all yellow maple with sea-green silk hanging.

"Over on the dressing table," indicated Marie, "there is her beauty clay—something she mixed herself. I have hated to shut it up. It was the last thing she touched, you know. Her creams are there, too, everything she used afterward."

Craig went over and looked carefully, smelling the clay, then laying it back in the jar on the glass-topped table. "Did she use much of this, Marie?"

"Glory be!" The girl threw up her hands with an air that suggested an endless stream of creams and lotions. "I don't believe there was ever a new cream or clay or powder that was put on the market that she didn't get. She tried them all—everything."

"Do you think they did any good?" I ventured, skeptically.

"Something did," Marie answered, briefly. "She was three times as old as I am and I declare I looked older than she did. But I used to be afraid of accidents, sir—I did. I used to say she would poison herself or get hurt. But with some women, it's anything to keep looking young!"

Craig behind me, had been examining the clay carefully again. Now he dipped his finger into the jar. Marie brought him several empty bottles which he rinsed, then took in them specimens of the clay and of the creams and other toilet articles Marie said she used most.

He was looking about the room curiously. Marie saw his glance resting on a big old-fashioned maple chest of drawers. On the top, with the lid still loose, was her jewel box.

"That's where she put the jewels she used for the time being—took them off at night, stuck them up there."

Kennedy took a step over and examined them on the dresser. As we surrounded the little table we shut off the direct rays of the softly shaded light. No lights glared in Mrs. Asche's house. I saw Craig lean over with interest.

"Mon dieu! Just fancy! I never noticed that before!" I heard Marie exclaim.

In the darkness the diamond necklace, the rings, the brooch, all these jewels of Mrs. Asche glowed!

"Marie, the police must hold these," decided Kennedy, promptly. "I will give you a receipt, be personally responsible.

Don't mention it until some one else does. Can you keep a secret?"

"Indeed, I can. Doctor. I didn't work with the pretty corespondent in that last big Vandam divorce case for three years without learning that!"

The doorbell downstairs rang.

"Marie, get us out of here quickly," nodded Craig. "I'd rather not be seen in Mrs. Asche's rooms—yet."

Down the winding flight of stairs we hurried after Marie into a charming library. We had just got in when we heard a deep voice and the servant's greeting to Doctor Davids. Davids did not know any one was there and was talking with a certain freedom to another man with him.

"Something strange, Welburn—mighty strange, to me. She was always going to remember me and I hear this new will cuts me off without a cent. Why, she used to urge me to go into things, said she would back me financially, often told me she had taken care of me in her will. Now I learn she has left everything to him. I am sore—and worried, too."

A polished, well-modulated voice replied. "I think we can do something about it, Doctor."

"Evidently Welburn is retained as his attorney," whispered Craig to me behind his hand. "Clever lawyer; mixed up with half the will contests for a generation."

It was apparent that Oakley Davids was preparing a bitter lawsuit over the will to Gaston Asche.

A tall, handsome chap now followed the deep voice and we saw Davids himself in the doorway. I had never seen him, but he struck me as a typical society physician, very much of a ladies' man. He paused for a moment, his eyes roving from me to Kennedy, whom he evidently had met.

"Hello, Kennedy!" he exclaimed. "Beat us up here?" Underneath that deep polished voice and easy manner I fancied he was nervous and ill at ease. "Find out anything?"

"Haven't had a chance yet. Have you told everything you can about the case to Doctor Leslie? Is there anything more?"

"Not a thing that I haven't told him or the health authorities—except that I am determined to have my rights. I feel that my aunt desired me to have the Oakley money. She wasn't a woman to say a thing and then go back on it. There is something mighty like undue influence, coercion, on a sick woman. I have brought my attorney up here to look things over, perhaps talk with Asche. If he won't talk, I'm going to fight."

"Well, fight then I My wife knew what she was doing. She had been throwing bones to you long enough. She thought it was about time you did something for yourself!"

Gaston Asche had let himself in downstairs quietly with his pass key and had mounted the first flight, unheard in the reverberation of David's deep voice. He now stood in the doorway of the library, hands gripped on the portieres on each side of him. He was almost white with anger and the muscles of his face twitched.

"It's a nice thing, a considerate thing, to come into a man's house, to berate him while he is away attending to things that sudden bereavement make necessary. By the way—this is my house, now. She wanted me to have it after I advised her how to fix it over for its effect on her physical and mental health. And she was my wife." He faced us all with indignation and I must say I felt the lash of it.

"Yes, your wife! She was my aunt; you might say raised me. I was running all about this place, and my mother before me, years before my aunt ever heard of an Asche!"

"Haven't you any appreciation of a man's sorrow?" There was a note of scorn in it. "I came home to be with the things she loved—and I walk into—you—and an insulting row. Fine comfort!"

"Well, who carted her away from the place she loved best? Is that love? You got her, somehow, into a public funeral parlor. I suppose you want to hurry her right along!"

"You dog! Up to your old tricks, with that fog-horn voice of yours. Well, you can't talk me down. She told me enough about you."

"I doubt it." There was a fine edge to the towering scorn that Davids, on his part, worked himself into. "I doubt if you were with her long enough for her to take you into her confidence. You're too busy with that physique trying to fascinate Broadway flappers, organizing beauty contests—Advertising pays!"

"Davids!" Asche seemed to hold himself in leash only by realizing that the rest of us were there. "I know what you insinuate. It's your own jealousy, jealous of your aunt's fortune, jealous of me of my success, everything. Say, Davids, you were a pretty constant visitor to Irrita Millard, were you not?" he retorted.

"Well, there's nothing criminal in that, is there?"

"No, and there's nothing criminal in my meeting her occasionally in the same building where we are both rather good tenants. I suppose, to suit you, I ought to move out of the building where I've been for over five years? Or maybe if I see her on Broadway, I ought to run across Longacre Square and come up by Seventh Avenue to my own gymnasium, eh?—especially when my wife used to bring her up herself to see me!

"You want to see me, talk with Asche, eh? If I won't talk, you're going to fight. Well, you can get out and be quick about it. My attorney will talk to you, Littlefield, see? I thought you'd retain Mr. Welburn. Well, my attorney will talk to yours. Gentlemen, good night! By the way, Mr. Kennedy—may I ask you to remain a few moments?"

Davids and Welburn withdrew, I felt, second best in this first encounter. I felt that Asche seemed to tower over them in his righteous indignation and interrupted sorrow. Was he also a poser? As for Davids, I was not greatly impressed. Somehow or other men who impress the ladies never impress me. I often wonder at the fair creatures' judgment. However, there are some things past finding out.

Asche calmed down now as quickly as he flared. We talked several minutes as Kennedy explained his position in the case.

"I told Doctor Leslie I welcomed him in the case," remarked Asche, pacing the library. "And I tell you, Kennedy, I welcome you. Of course, my theory has been that it was an accident. By that I mean something in the course of nature. No one, not even a remarkable woman, in search of the fountain of eternal youth, will ever find it."

He paused in his pacing.

"But, sometimes, now, especially after that visit, I am forced to wonder. Could my wife's nephew and physician, in some way, perhaps under cover of some one close to her—you understand, some one close to her because of this hobby of beautification— could he have hastened her death, hoping perhaps in some way to throw it all on me, at least force me to a settlement? Mind you, I make no accusation that anyone close to her may have been more than an innocent tool."

I saw there was no concealment now in the bitter implication thrown by Asche. He had come out into the open.

"Another thing, Mr. Kennedy, you know this man—an X-ray specialist—eh?"

"And you mean by that?"

"I don't know what I mean, sir. Only I seem to have heard that X-rays are not the safest things in the world unless they are in the hands of one mighty well skilled. He seems to have been at the top of his profession—in that respect."

Kennedy talked for several moments, made an appointment for the following day, then excused himself. I knew he was anxious to get to Leslie and the autopsy and to his own laboratory, where he might study this beauty clay and the glowing diamonds.

As for me I knew I had a good story for the *Star*. But I could not finish it. How did Mrs. Asche die? Was it an accident, an outgrowth of her own inordinate pursuit of beauty? What really had killed old Mrs. Asche?

The entire next day was spent by Kennedy and Leslie over the autopsy. Not until evening did I see Craig, at his own laboratory at the university. Even then he was silent as to his findings with Leslie, his own study of the beauty clay and what had made the diamonds shine with a fire in the dark.

"I'm going to see Irrita to-night," he announced.

"Does she expect you?"

"No. I'd rather she didn't. I thought something might happen while we were there that might suggest a clue."

Irrita received us amiably enough in her tiny apartment, but there was a restraint about her that boded no ease in getting information from her.

"You see, it's this way, Irrita," and Craig fell so easily into the slight familiarity that it seemed rather to flatter her. "I feel that Mrs. Asche made a friend of you, even more, a confidante."

"But that doesn't signify that I'll make a confidante of you." She tossed her head and watched him, lips just a little bit curled in a knowing smile.

"No. I only feel sorry for that poor little woman and thought you might be a little sorry, too—that you might want to help me."

"How can I help you? Aren't all men self-sufficient? At least we've been told to believe that. Now that we're no longer cling-ing vines, I suppose we aren't so popular."

"You are clever at changing the subject, Irrita. I admit woman is a fascinating topic to discuss. But what I want is a little infor-mation. Has it come to your knowledge that Mrs. Asche was on bad terms with any one related to her?"

Irrita seemed to have to think before she answered. "As to relatives, she didn't have many. Her doctor and her husband are the only ones I ever met. She never discussed either with me."

Craig was watching her with rapt attention. "You are your own best ad for your business, Irrita. Charm and intellect."

"Yes?" She said it with a lift of the brow. "Most men praise a woman's intellect to her when they want to use her for something. What's the idea?"

"I've told you. I thought you would be woman enough to stand by another of your sex who has met a fatal misfortune, to right a wrong, if wrong has been done."

"I think I would—if wrong has been done. Ask me some questions, and if I can answer them I'll tell you no lies." Her accent was on the "can answer" and I felt it would not get us much.

The door bell burred. I watched her as she waited for her maid to answer it. She was beautiful, yet unconsciously I did not like her. Perhaps she was "too modern." Still, I must admit she was striking in an evening gown covered with sparkling blue sequins, her white shoulders and fair hair radiant. She was excited. Her pupils were dilated until her eyes were almost black.

"Dr. Oakley Davids," announced the maid.

"All right." Irrita turned to us tantalizingly. "It's a good thing I didn't say I hadn't met him!"

"I've a surprise for you, Rit!" he called from outside.

"Splendid, Doctor. I have some guests here—Mr. Kennedy and Mr. Jameson."

Davids seemed annoyed as he entered. He looked at Irrita inquiringly, as if wondering how much she had been forced to tell.

"Well, Irrita, we'll be going now, if you had an engagement." Craig held her hand a moment longer than was necessary, I thought, and with a trifle more interest than I liked. In an undertone he added, "At least I have found out enough to make me jealous."

With a quick little nervous motion she brushed her forehead, then suddenly faced Craig. "And I have found out enough to make me mad!"

Davids took a step toward the door with an air as of one who would make a farewell brief.

Outside, Craig observed to me, "Oakley Davids is in love with her—I wonder if anyone else is in love?"

It was the following morning that Craig and I were crossing Longacre Square when we heard a familiar voice in the crowd.

"Did you get the information you wanted, Mr. Kennedy?"

We turned to look into the smiling face of Irrita Millard.

"Do you still feel mad, Irrita?" countered Craig.

"I'm over it." She laughed again. "Ask Mr. Asche. He will tell you I am very agreeable this morning."

Then I saw it was Gaston Asche, a few feet away, unlocking a roadster.

"Not only agreeable, Irrita, but very beautiful," returned Craig, and it seemed to please Irrita.

Asche heard it and was annoyed. At the seeming good terms between Craig and Irrita his hospitality of the other night vanished completely into sullenness.

"Come, Irrita," he called, brusquely. "I have many things to attend to." Then to us he explained, "I am taking Miss Millard to see about the flowers and other things she was kind enough to order." He stepped on his starter.

I wondered if it were meant to cut short the chat with us. I thought Irrita would have liked to wait.

They left us at the curb and I turned to Craig. "What is that girl's game? She puzzles me."

Craig merely shrugged.

About the middle of the afternoon Kennedy and Leslie completed their autopsy. It was not many moments before Craig had Asche on the wire and the funeral was fixed by Asche for noon of the following day.

Next day Kennedy telephoned to Irrita. "I promised you, Irrita, that I would let you know as soon as I could. If you will go up to Gamble's, you may perform the last offices of beautification for Mrs. Asche. Tell me when you can be there, so that I can see that you have no difficulty."

"I'll go right away, just as soon as I can get a few things together."

At Gamble's we did not have to wait long for her. Irrita came with a little handbag filled with the accessories of her profession. At once she proceeded to lay them out.

"Not with those, Irrita," cautioned Kennedy. She looked at him, startled, but said nothing. "I have some of her own things that she used at home. First I want you to use this beauty clay."

"Beauty clay—on a dead woman?" the girl exclaimed.

Kennedy nodded. "Yes, and when it is removed I want you to use this powder, her own, as well as this lip stick, and other things. Er—Marie has sent them over."

"Well, this is the strangest thing! I'll do it. I suppose you have some mere man's reason!"

In an incredibly short time the girl had finished. The face of the dead woman had taken on a new beauty. The cheeks glowed with an artificial color of health. The hair had been arranged a little more elaborately. In spite of the artificiality it seemed the beautification of the vain old lady.

As she worked, Irrita now and then talked. I noticed that she referred always to it as the "accident." Through it all Irrita seemed to show a quite sincere emotion over Mrs. Asche. But I still wondered if it were genuine. Did she know something she was concealing?

Irrita had scarcely finished and we had taken leave of her when Kennedy telephoned to Doctor Davids.

"I called up. Doctor, to let you know that Mr. Asche has decided to hold the funeral services at noon to-morrow. I thought you would like to know."

I could almost hear the resonant voice in reply, a bit angry, somewhat blustering.

"It's very kind to let me know! I'll surely be there—if for no other reason than to have one real member of her family present at the public funeral parlor. She's the first in the family to be buried like that! By the way, has everything been attended to? Did you let Miss Millard help? She told me you refused her offer."

"Miss Millard assisted," replied Craig, briefly.

"Another thing, Kennedy. I don't like the way you hound that poor girl. She was just a friend and adviser, had nothing to do with the case, whatever it is. It's an outrage to drag her into the mess.... How's that?... Well, all I have to say is that detection of crime does not consist in dragging the name of an innocent girl into the thing!"

As Kennedy repeated it to me I wondered if Irrita did know something that he was afraid she might tell. One thing was now sufficiently evident. Both Gaston Asche and Oakley Davids were "rushing" Irrita.

I shall not even describe the simple services in the Gamble Funeral Church on the forenoon of the third day after the strange death of Mrs. Asche. There were two incidents, however, which I cannot possibly pass by.

The service had proceeded to the prayer when over our bowed heads the lights suddenly winked out. It was then that I noticed that Craig, who had been next to me, was not in his seat. The prayer proceeded to the end. Then, as we raised our heads, I saw again that strange, mysterious, awesome glow on the face and hands of the body in the rich casket, banked with overpowering lilies. It was a shock, even to me.

I heard an audible gasp from some one. Then the lights came up as suddenly as they had darkened. I watched them all, Asche, Davids, Irrita. There was not a quiver. Were they all good actors? Or had it been an accident? What did that impassiveness mean?

Then a second time. It was when the relatives were asked to take the final parting look that Doctor Davids and Gaston Asche met. They were the only relatives present. Irrita Millard rose with the men. I fancy she feared a clash and thought her presence might avert it.

Asche went first and tried to make way for Irrita next. But Doctor Davids insisted on being second. Leaning over, he quickly took Irrita by the arm. With a challenge in his eyes he accompanied her to the bier. Asche was furious. Doctor Davids was ready even for a clash, only for the place and the occasion. For once Irrita was frightened.

She turned down the aisle, trembling. Her face was white with emotion. As she reached us, she almost gasped: "Please, Craig, take me home! I don't know what to do—which way to turn."

It had been a dramatic encounter, this of Doctor Davids and Gaston Asche at the funeral under the eyes of the detectives. Yet, was it anything more than a deep-seated rivalry for Irrita? It seemed to frighten her—for the first time in her life—the elemental passions of these men—to shake her in her confidence that a girl is the equal to any situation in the world.

To me it seemed now that Irrita was turning to Craig—from both of them. She had called him "Craig," by his first name, as he had called hers. Was she falling in love with Kennedy? It worried me, as it always did when I saw a girl scheming to fascinate my friend. Craig was only human. Was it a game on her part?

I saw that the anger of Asche against Kennedy now was bitter and genuine. Davids made no concealment of his jealousy, either. Was it to involve Kennedy, pull the wool over his eyes? Then there was the type of Irrita. She alienated me, at least, by the smartness of her modernism.

I did not see Kennedy much during the rest of the day, nor in the evening. When I came into our apartment I found him seated before our piano, slowly running his fingers through what I thought was a curious selection. It was the "Glowworm."

He did not stop when I entered, nor did he say a word. I dropped into a chair. Ordinarily I would have enjoyed it, for I like it. But now I would have given anything for a glimpse into his mind. Of what was Craig thinking? He was putting a sadness into the touch.

Suddenly he broke off, wheeled around, jumped up. "It's after midnight!" he exclaimed. "Why didn't I think of this before?

Come, Walter, slip your automatic into your pocket. Hurry. I'm going over to the laboratory."

I never question Craig's sudden flashes of induction. I followed him.

In the campus he left the paved walk, where the sand grains made our steps audible, and took to the grass.

We had got not more than a hundred feet from the building where his laboratory was when I could have sworn that I saw a shadow skulking out and into the shrubbery a few feet from the entrance. Kennedy must have seen something, too. He flashed his pocket electric bull's eye. But the beam of light was swallowed up in the darkness at the distance. There was nothing, nothing but the crackling of a dry twig. It must have been under a foot.

"I was right!" he muttered.

Then I knew what his induction had been. The skulking shadow had confirmed it—an effort to break into the laboratory. We separated, gave chase, but, though we had not frustrated the attempt, the intruder had made good the escape.

In the hall, now, we could see that some one had indeed got in. Inside, I hurried over to a steel cabinet where I recalled I had seen Craig place the jewels and the beauty clay.

It was open. I looked in. They were not there! I turned to Craig with a startled gaze. He was regarding the open cabinet calmly.

"Do you think I would leave a hundred thousand dollars' worth of diamonds, for which I am personally responsible, here, in a mere fireproof safe?" he asked. "No. They are in the safe at headquarters. The samples of beauty clay are there, too."

He busied himself looking for evidences of identification, but I could tell by his expression that the intruder had been clever and had left none.

As we closed everything up again, he said, thoughtfully, to me, "I want you, Walter, to get a story into the afternoon paper, the first edition, something as if announced by the police that they believe it is a poisoning case and have a clue to where the poison was obtained, by whom, and are just about to locate where it is hidden—you see, I'm building—first the glimpse of that glowing face to Irrita, then at the funeral to all, now this story."

I had the story published. But for the whole day the friendship between Craig and Irrita worried me. Nor was I reassured when Craig told me, about six o'clock, that we had a dinner engagement with her. The only crumb of comfort I had was that they were not alone.

By dint of dining and dancing the evening wore away until it became pretty late.

It was not until it was far too late for anything except dancing and dining that I began to see the direction of Kennedy's purpose.

"Irrita," he said, leaning toward her, his voice low, "are you game to learn whether there really was anything wrong in the death of Mrs. Asche?"

She met his gaze squarely; a little shiver seemed to run over her as she looked away momentarily, then quickly back again with clear eyes. "Yes!"

"Then come with me now to Oakley Square."

Though I did not understand it, I fancied I began to see the direction of Kennedy's building. He must have calmly calculated to start one of the two, either Davids or Asche, to do something to cover up guilt, if indeed either of them were guilty. Or was it aimed at an unknown?

At any rate, now I had an added worry. If, indeed, it were either of them, would the demonstration of that fact, the shock, clinch matters between Craig and this girl?

It was with small joy that I accompanied Craig and Irrita to the private park that night.

As I have said, there were four grilled gates to the park. Each owner about it had a key to the park, Craig had somehow got the key to the south gate.

It was dark, and he posted me in the shadows to watch some-

where between the north gate and the east gate. Just inside the
north gate, facing the Oakley house, Craig had placed carefully
a small wooden box with holes in the sides and a loose cover.

And now I spent a most uncomfortable hour. To me Irrita was
baffling. Yet she was plainly showing a deep interest in Craig.
I wondered. Why was there always a girl to keep me in anxiety
over Craig? Every time I thought of her I could have kidnapped
her. I had been cautioned to keep quiet, yet I had to listen to their
sentimental conversation as I crouched in the shadow.

I was eager for action. Somehow I felt it would be solved
that night whether it was an accident or a crime. Again and
again raced through my mind the query whether Irrita was not
using Kennedy to get information to shield some one. At least
to-night he had been careful to give her no chance to commu-
nicate. I listened.

"Irrita, you were very ready to talk about women the night
I came up to see you with Jameson. You seemed fired with the
idea of women and their wrongs."

"That was different, Craig. I didn't know you quite so well.
The better a woman knows a man, the less she likes to discuss
women with him. In her mind there is no desire for the plural.
It is always singular. Woman means herself."

Craig laughed. I swore under my breath, muttering, "It has
reached the first name stage; next it will be pet names!" I lost
their voices. But I still crouched at my post, waiting.

They must have retraced their steps on the lawn.

"Irrita, you are really in love with love. You can't be in love
with any man."

"You men are all alike. You can't see anything unless it is
fastened to the end of your nose. As a crime detector, you may
be all right. We'll see. As a love detector, you are—terrible." A
low, tantalizing laugh followed.

I couldn't make her out. Was she suggesting a proposal to
Craig? If I had been in Kennedy's place and she hadn't been such
a modem, efficient young creature, I would have kissed her and

taken the wrath that followed as an index that she liked it and was trying to hide the evidence of it.

"So—I am in love with love." She repeated it dreamily. I fidgeted nervously where Craig had stationed me. I could not desert the post, nor even speak. How I longed to break up this tête-à-tête before it was too late.

Footsteps, stealthy footsteps, on the street!

I was not the only one who heard them. The voices of Craig and Irrita were hushed. They must have stood as quietly as I. I scarcely breathed.

The click of the key in the grilled gate!

I started forward.

"Wait!" a whisper from Kennedy, who had silently, Indian-like, crept up within a few feet of me. "Not yet! He might get away in the dark! Watch!"

The gate creaked on rusty hinges. There was a noise as of something wooden falling over on the flagstones.

Suddenly, rising from the ground, streaks of veritable fire zigzagged through the air in graceful arcs—weird, startling, as if alive! One—two—three—four—five—I counted them. They did not die away.

"What is it?"

"West Indian fireflies," he whispered back, "the most brilliant fireflies in the world—primeval fire! Pyrophorus—the fire carrier! Click beetles, cucujos, of the West Indies. There are ninety or a hundred species in tropical America. The natives of the tropical islands sometimes keep them in small cages for illumination—even make use of them for personal adornment."

One of the fire-bearers, more brilliant than the rest, was circling the face of the intruder. Viciously, with a quick, angry motion, he struck at it, killed it.

But in this weird light of nature three of us, unseen, had seen Gaston Asche!

Quickly he turned toward the corner of the garden park

where the shrubbery was dense. By the sounds, he must have been digging. We waited, silent.

In a few moments his hasty feet crunched the gravel path. Irrita, Kennedy, and I now strolled from the other end of the park, apparently.

"Good evening, Asche."

Asche turned to Irrita, ignoring Kennedy. "May I ask you to take a little walk with me, please?" He indicated the other end of the garden. "I have something very important to tell you."

"Just a moment, Asche," interrupted Kennedy. "Give me that key in your left-hand pocket. There was a key in your wife's effects, tagged. It had just a trace of wax on it. I knew some one had made an impression of that key, that some day he would use it. Hand it over!"

A firefly flitted about the face of the man. It was literally ashen.

"Hand it over!" Craig took a step forward.

Asche fumbled in his pocket.

"Thank you."

Then Craig reached for a little lead casket under Asche's right arm. I saw now that he held his automatic in his own right.

"Don't move!"

Asche froze.

"Walter, take this gat. Cover him."

On the ground, gingerly, Craig opened the casket. It contained a bottle with a liquid in it, and something in the liquid. Craig spilled some of it; it was water.

Then with his knife he poked it, cut a bit of what was in the water. As he withdrew the knife into the air something on it glowed and flamed, like a glowworm. From it arose curling luminous fumes.

Irrita gasped. "Months ago, Gaston," she blurted out, "you told her that the fountain of youth was in the elements, in what you called the mother of all elements, radium, that she might attain youth that way. And to me you said, 'No—it is bunk—besides, it is dangerous. Don't use it!'"

"This is not radium or radium salts!" he shot back superciliously.

"No," Kennedy smiled quietly. "I have the whole story. Mrs. Asche came to you, a health specialist, to find a way to renew her youth. You persuaded her it was not in glands, not even in physical culture, that it was nothing she needed but elemental life and fire—radium!

"You married her. You were playing on her elemental love of beauty and youth. You planned not to kill her—but to let her kill herself through her vanity. Radium, internally, may be compared to the sapper and miner whose tunnels blow up the trenches. Externally it is like an overhead bombardment of high explosive shells.

"There was the beauty clay into which she put the radium salts for radium rubs, perhaps radioactive water and food under your suggestion, infinitesimal amounts, of course. She was to be killed by high blood pressure created, induced, increased by the constant surrounding of radioactivity.

"I knew there were radium salts somewhere, knew it as soon as I saw the phosphorescent jewels. But could there be enough radium to kill, without burning, without leaving its traces? What about the glowing face and body?

"You were not content with the slowness of radium. It did not go fast enough. Radium salts are expensive, too. You turned to phosphorus, a deadly poison, hoping it would in some way be confounded, if it were ever observed, with the radium she obtained at your suggestion. No, this is not radium in the lead casket. You are right. It is phosphorus. There was phosphorus in that beauty clay!"

Kennedy paused. Asche made no move to escape the automatic which I held close to him.

"I felt that some one had hidden the poison somewhere. Here! I was sure of it. The key told me. I knew of the phosphorus in the beauty clay. I isolated it. You knew it, too—feared that I knew. It was anything to destroy it, destroy the evidence, my laboratory, if necessary.

"I was sure of my case. But you never can tell what juries, grand juries as well as trial juries, or judges, from the magistrates up to the judges of appeals, may do.

"The fireflies—cold light, light without heat, like the law—have revealed to me—to Mr. Jameson—to the girl for whose love I have brought—"

"Love?" interrupted Irrita. "In love with love?" She laughed as she repeated Craig's own words. "Mr. Kennedy, you have flattered yourself!"

"No, Irrita. I know you, have read you better than you know. You were afraid that I suspected Oakley Davids—and you were really in love with him, feared for him, wanted to watch what I did, to save him! Asche, I thought of this thing, this poetic justice—primeval fire—to catch you in the light of the fireflies with this leaden casket of elemental fire!— Walk? You'll take a little walk with *me*, around to headquarters! That key opened the gates of hell fire for you, Asche!"

SMELL

"**EVERY CRIME DEPENDS** for its solution on one of the five senses—touch, taste, sight, feeling, or smell."

Craig Kennedy, tall and spare, leaned back in the big leather club chair, with an indolent smile on his lips. No one at that moment would have thought that his active mind was engrossed on an unusually gruesome murder mystery.

Yet I knew that he had spent many hours on a case for the prohibition director and that now, for relief, he had asked me to meet him in the exclusive All Night Club which carried on its roster some of the keenest men in the big city, men of high standing in the financial world, internationally famous artists, writers, and playwrights.

No vacuous mediocrity ever gained entrance to that huge lounging room. To be a habitue of the All Night Club meant that one must have appealed as a mighty fine fellow to practically the entire membership list. This was a club where the name of a new member was not decided on by any committee of three or five. It must be unanimously approved.

Craig had been asked to join some months ago, and to his reflected glory I felt I owed my admittance. It was a good thing for us. It meant a convenient place for us to meet any hour of the night, centrally located, and if one cared for the society of others, there was always some congenial soul hanging about the place.

Planned by one of the best known architects, built under conditions fostered by wealth and brains, there was nothing lacking so far as beauty and comfort were concerned. The rooms were large and lofty, furnished simply with the things that men know other men need and like, and not with the things a feminized world thinks men ought to like and need.

Kennedy was a popular member. To many, his startling, unusual profession gave a kick after the grueling competitive stress of the day's work. There was always a crowd near Kennedy, and this night was no different from others.

It had been a hot day. Many of the men were temporary bachelors, detained in the city by business responsibilities while their families were away. Among them were faces I saw frequently in the *Star*—people who were doing things of interest in the world. There was Chalmers Chandler, the famous playwright who had made a half million in royalties from his latest play. Larry Halpin, the middle-aged importer, reputed wealthy, retired, but whose activities in the way of pleasure drove him all over the country. There was Clarke, the banker and broker, whose fortune was long, but mercy scant when he had the market rigged right. There were others, a never-ending succession of them, coming and going. It was the uncertainty and surprise at the appearance of prominent men which was the chief charm of the club.

It had not been long with our little group of four or five in a corner before the discussion turned to crime and its detection. There is just enough devil in all of us to like to listen to such tales. The news of the world is, therefore, full of crime, because crime interests human beings.

"Oh, I say, Kennedy, you can't mean that!" There was good-natured raillery in his laugh as young Hewitt stood up, smoothed his fine mop of blond hair thoughtfully, and took a step or two nearer from the chair where he had been sitting apart. "No, Kennedy, That stuff about the five senses will not go here, with us. Now, for example, that Cronk case, which I understand you are interested in, dismisses that statement as too broad."

Craig half turned intently on Hewitt. He had been left half a million and had run it up to four times that in a couple of years.

Hewitt was not one to be disregarded. His was an unusual grasp of the practical things of life and he merited the attention the older men of the club gave him at times.

"I am willing to wager with any of you," persisted Kennedy, "that when the Cronk case is solved it will be found that one of the senses is at the bottom of it."

"Now, Kennedy, when it comes to vision, for instance, most of us have seen something that wasn't just on the level. But that is hardly what could be called detection through one of the senses. It is sight, of course. But that's too broad, too obvious. We'd do nothing at all if we didn't have eyes and ears, tongues, noses, hands and feet, and so on." It was Larry Halpin who spoke. Larry was a popular man about town and the club.

"You're right, Larry, as far as you go. What most of us think we see is only half, or less. We supply a good deal mentally for many a thing we see. Probably we give to deeds the impelling thoughts that would have prompted us to commit the same acts. We don't see straight. Very few do. That is the trouble with so much of our direct testimony. If I were on a jury and a man's life depended on such direct evidence alone, I would hold out for a long time. The right kind of circumstantial evidence is the best evidence."

Kennedy had been drawing with a pencil on a piece of paper, two lines, with flanges of arrows at each end, turned inward on one line, outward on the other:

"Which is the longer line?" he asked.

"Why, this one, of course." Larry had put his finger on the line with the arrow heads turned inward.

Kennedy laughed. "Each line is exactly an inch. It's the arrow heads fool the eye. Now how far off, about, will these two lines meet?"

He had drawn two lines, one intersected by a series of short cross lines on a right-hand diagonal, the other with a diagonal to the left:

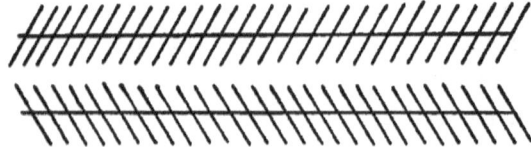

"About out here," indicated Hewitt on the table top.

Kennedy laughed again. "Never—unless you are one of the twelve men in the world who understand the Einstein theory and know where parallel lines meet. These lines are parallel. It's the cross lines fool you. So you don't want to be too sure of even your senses in this "Cronk case, either. Maybe the cross lines will fool you!"

A deep booming laugh from Chalmers Chandler. He was a lovable type, cultured, a traveler all over the world, well read, observing. His plays were popular because they hurt no one, but appealed to the ideals of struggling humans. "Isn't that the case of Hinman's chauffeur you're talking about?" he asked as he sauntered across the floor.

"Yes. The papers are full of it," I explained. "It's mighty queer because there seem to be no clues. The police don't seem to have a thing, yet. If they have, they're mighty reticent."

"Well, who did it, do you think? Hijackers? That is my impression," added Chandler. "How does that strike you, Kennedy? Don't you think these hijackers are responsible for most of the bootleg crimes nowadays?"

"Chalmers, I haven't figured that out, about hijackers, yet. But I think I'm on the way. When I find out, I'll tell."

"You can't pump anything out of Kennedy that way," I

cautioned. "He'll talk when he gets something to talk about. Why, he refuses even to discuss this case with me. Usually he takes me into his confidence, at least to a degree. So far he has seemed to me to avoid it in this case. I'd like the story. So would the *Star*. Yet here we are at the club having this ridiculous argument. It's all interesting, and all that. I don't mean ridiculous in that sense. But I would prefer, when there is some one to catch, to be out catching him."

It may have sounded a little more pointed than I had intended. However, Kennedy took it in good part, smiled again. "Very well. Why not do it? You have all your five senses—the compleat angler for criminals. Go to it. I'm sure the director would thank you,"

The laugh was on me. "You're invited to try out some of those five senses, I take it, Jameson," laughed Larry Halpin, provokingly.

I subsided. Kennedy's offer was one that is always calculated to floor a critic in a mystery case.

Chandler was leaning back in an introspective attitude. Passing his hand slowly over his face, he remarked, thoughtfully, "It's drama—this Cronk case. There's drama in it, somewhere. Some one is going to make a name for himself with a hijacker drama. I would like to do it."

"The great American drama," added Hewitt, mischievously. "Hijackers vs. Bootleggers. Quite American, I'll say."

"What are the facts of the case—and what case is it?" A newcomer had joined us. It was General Tams, whose reminiscences of two wars were the delight of the club.

"Why, this Cronk case," I took it upon myself to answer.

"What did he do? I haven't heard a thing about it. My boat just docked to-day. It must be interesting or you fellows wouldn't all be discussing it."

"It is interesting," returned Chandler. "At least, we're interested. Cronk was Hinman's—Percy Hinman's—chauffeur, and Kennedy had just informed us that every crime depends on one of the five senses for its solution. I should think that was enough to get us interested."

"Well," drawled the general, "it seems to me a great many crimes could be brought under the sense of touch. I have been touched so often that it's a crime. What did this Cronk do?"

"That's just it, General. We don't know just what he did. He seemed such a harmless, inoffensive sort of fellow, attended to his own affairs, apparently had no enemies. It wasn't what he did. It was what others did."

Kennedy nodded tolerantly at my assumption of knowing anything about the case. Again I subsided, determined to let the others do the telling, instructing Tams.

"But what was it and when did they find out about it?" insisted the general with some asperity.

"Last night they found Hinman's car, a big blue Packard sedan, upholstered in whipcord, abandoned on a lonely Long Island road down Smithtown way. It was empty, too. But from what we hear, it couldn't have been empty when Cronk started out with it."

"No, it was not, Chandler. It had some of that one thousand cases unloaded at Nissequogue from that German tanker that steamed up Long Island sound last Saturday night, lightering off stuff by appointment at various places all along the shore."

"Now, Kennedy," bantered Chandler, "there might be something to your theory as to taste. Suppose there's some poor devil hasn't had a taste of anything for a long time, dry as a camel's tonsils. There might have been a crime committed."

"Yes, I was talking this evening to one of the Hinman girls— Gladys," informed young Hewitt. "They feel terribly about the whole affair. In spite of the notoriety it will bring them, though, they have acknowledged frankly the ownership of the stolen contraband stuff. They are going to make a fight to bring the criminal to justice. Gladys says her father feels responsible in a way for Cronk. If he hadn't sent Cronk out for the stuff, she says, it wouldn't have happened."

"But," suggested Tams, feeling out the facts of the case, "Cronk might have stolen the stuff, sold out his boss, Hinman, fled with a pocketful of money by this time."

"They found his body!" Kennedy cut in, slowly.

"Where? Near the car, as if there had been a fight? Was the car out of commission, too?"

"No; nothing as simple as that," I intervened. "They found his body in the cellar of the old fish-glue factory down there, along the road, not so very far away. He must have been murdered before he was taken there."

"Hijackers, I tell you, General," reiterated Chandler. "Don't you say? Nothing under the sun but those criminals. Picture that poor devil of a driver shooting along the dark road with the stuff piled in the back of the sedan, probably scared to death, scared at the possible appearance of revenuers, more scared of the very men who got him." Chandler was peering backward in thought, trying imaginatively to fill out the gaps.

"All right, Chandler, but will you tell me how the case of that poor chauffeur of the blue sedan full of rare wines and liqueurs smuggled in, who was killed on a lonely Long Island road and whose body was hidden, has anything to do with the senses, any more than with the circulation of blood?" It was Timothy Dodd, an old recluse as far as anything involving the ladies was concerned, but upon whom many men's clubs depended for his generosity of support. His was a mixture of sound reasoning and curious hobbies.

I nodded in accord with him this once. I was a little put out at what had seemed to me Kennedy's dilatory; and lackadaisical method about this murder. Once or twice I had suspected he was getting tired of hunting criminals in the hot weather. Besides, I was jealous for his reputation in the hands of these keen kidders of the club. And always before, an unusual mystery like this would get under his skin. He would never seem to rest until it was solved. Why should he lie down now?

"That's it—a fact, not a theory," I chimed in. "Some one killed

Cronk and hid his body in that place, of all places, apparently just because it was most convenient."

"You don't suppose, putting a little horse sense into this mystery," queried Timothy Dodd, "that anyone from that German tanker, knowing the value, could have stolen back the goods?"

"Not likely," I considered. "The stuff was delivered to some Italian bootleggers working in harmony with the tanker on shore. There were five of them. Their headquarters for the time were in an old deserted bungalow down close to the beach. That's where Cronk was to pick up the stuff for Hinman, and did."

I was busy building up a story as pretty as if I had been writing it. "Now suppose one of them had a hand in it. They'd have driven off the car, most likely. As it was, they might have gone on undiscovered, except for the attention called by this abandoned car, if a motorcycle state trooper on duty out near Smithtown hadn't seen a high-powered motor car speed into the main road from a little-traveled side road, after he had been called in on the case. His suspicions were aroused and he decided to investigate the few shacks along the beach near the end of that road. You know reports of rum running soon spread. Those who hate liquor hate so intensely that their ears are always open, and those who love it and have the money—well, I needn't say anything more. They say enough."

"I see. Ears and tongues!" exclaimed Hewitt. "Is that what you're driving at? What about Kennedy's theory and taste, though? From all accounts of this choice collection of wines and cordials, it must have been extra fine, worth a king's ransom, to have so many people after it. Some sense they displayed, in a way, after all, then!" Hewitt's sally was greeted with a laugh.

"That's right about rumor," agreed Kennedy, thoughtfully. "The gossip was that many bottles of fine wines and cordials had been taken ashore at Nissequogue from this German boat, along with a thousand or more cases of other, common, stuff, stored in one of those shacks. The revenuers got a tip from the gossip, whatever the motorcycle man may or may not have suspected."

"Yes," agreed Larry Halpin. "I heard something about that raid along the beach, too. They got the men, all right. And I, for one, wouldn't be surprised to hear that the same men who acted to deliver to Cronk his carload, as agents, were the ones who followed him up and got it away from him again as hijackers."

Kennedy nodded politely, then went on with the facts. "When they organized the raid on the shacks, there were six men, all told—two revenuers, two state troopers, and two special county officers. When they approached the beach they saw five men sitting on a sand pile in front of the suspected shack. In all they got over a hundred cases of stuff that hadn't yet been removed. But not a smell of the choice wines and cordials from France and Italy and Spain. If they had had a thousand cases in addition to that stuff of Hinman's, they must have been working fast to move all but a hundred cases before the following forenoon, down there."

"Did they put up much of a fight?" asked Chandler, always with a sense for the melodramatic.

"No. The raiders didn't give them a chance," returned Craig. "One of the men pulled a gat, but the troopers were expecting that and winged him in the forearm. He dropped it and they closed in. They got this chap so suddenly it took the breath away from the others. I don't believe they knew whether they were captured or surrendered. They've been questioned at Riverhead, but have shut up like clams."

"Is that the whole gang or just a part of it, do you think?" inquired Tams.

Kennedy shrugged. "I believe there are a couple of Eagle boats cruising up and down the Sound now. But they haven't got the tanker, yet. Also they've tripled the number of revenue men on shore. It's hard to tell whether it will do much good. They just move from the south shore to the north shore of the island. You've got to keep the boats away from both shores."

"I see," nodded Chandler, always coining phrases. "Rum-runners and hijackers are the root of all evil."

"The thing that seems so ridiculous to me," I put in, "is where the murderer or the murderers hid the body. It seems to me that that old fish-glue factory was about as poor a place as they could have selected. There were much better places that were passed up. A hundred yards nearer, and away in from the road, is an old clay pit. There's a pool of water now at the bottom of the clay pit. The body could have been dropped in and would likely never have been found. Occasionally the glue factory is used and it just happened that they had determined to open it up the day after poor Cronk was dragged there and thrown in the cellar. But that old clay pit, and the kiln, even, further along a few feet from the glue factory, either would have been a safer place to hide a body. Then it would have been just a case of an abandoned car found on a road."

By this time the earnest voices in our corner of the lounge were arouseing curiosity, to say nothing of the personnel of the party. Besides, General Tams was back. Previous to prohibition, like many of the other members of the club. Tams stocked up his locker in his room for the future dry spell. Our legal talent had worked out a way for the All Night Club to be a legitimate oasis. There was no lawbreaking, but occasionally the corks popped in spite of the Eighteenth Amendment.

Men came straggling over to our corner to join us, and when one fellow left, there was always another to take his place, perhaps two. Secretly, too, I knew these men would have liked nothing better than to make Kennedy out a theorist. I think men look at the detective profession much as women look on the stage and spiritualism. With very few exceptions, women think they would have made either great actresses or great mediums, if they had had half a chance. Every man feels he could give the greatest detective points if he would only take the trouble to get down to it. Here was a chance to get down to it.

"I'll tell you what we can do," breezed Chandler. "Theoretically we'll solve this case, sitting right here in the club. We can put our wits to work—not our senses. What about it, Kennedy? Then when we have it all logically constructed, I'll dress it up, put the old hokum in it, shove in the gags, and we've got a Broadway-success!"

I never knew whether to take Chandler seriously or not. He was standing, with a sort of dramatic flourish, as he spoke: "Now, gentlemen, you are looking at a play similar to the 'Yellow Jacket,' a few years back. Your own imagination must do the work. Six club members in search of a plot, or something. There sits a fine-looking detective." He bowed deeply to Kennedy with the mock dignity of an announcer. "And his newspaper friend." He bowed toward me. "Murder, a fiendish, horrible, brutal murder has been committed. A man's body has been found in a fish-glue factory, some yards up the road from a blue Packard sedan, empty, empty as a hijacker's heart. Just visualize it. Where would you start?"

There was a pause. "You might have the senses come on the stage, Chalmers, one by one; make it allegorical," suggested Larry Halpin, maintaining an utterly serious face, to the amusement of the others. "Put every sense on the witness stand—or perhaps in the prisoner's dock. Bring 'em on, handcuffed; try 'em, convict 'em, sentence 'em, hang 'em!"

"No, no, Larry. Don't make a joke out of it," interposed Clarke. "I'm for good old deduction. Where would a detective be if he forgot and left his deduction locked up in the vault until morning with a time lock on it? That chauffeur's car was full of good cheer. Its selling price is high. What is more natural than to deduce that we must look for some one dispensing cheer? Look in the social register, go over the list of our friends, many of them living on Long Island, see what names haven't been giving parties lately, but have just sent out invitations. There's your man! Deduct! Find out where the cheer was needed. There you will find the murderer!"

"By jingo! I sent out invitations to a clam bake next week," exclaimed Hewitt. "Where'll I get my alibi? I'll have to hold you up, Clarke, and hijack one from you!"

"No, Clarke," cut in Dodd, "it's not who's going to give parties. It's who has been giving them. Whose cellar is depleted, must be stocked up, at any cost?"

"Exit plot number one," returned Kennedy, quietly. "Clarke, your deduction theory is non-alcoholic. It won't hold water. It is water."

Hewitt broke into the discussion again. "Do it by scientific evidence. This detective is a scientist. Science works better than the senses."

"I haven't said the senses were in conflict with science," amplified Kennedy.

"Gentlemen, catch a criminal for Chalmers," remonstrated Halpin. "Do it spectacularly. He wants to make another fortune. Make it a one-act play."

Larry tiptoed, holding his arm as if he were dragging a body and clamping his nose tightly with the thumb and first finger of the other hand.

"I have it! Smell the shoes of all the Long Islanders. The ones that smell of fish glue will be those of the murderer! The nose has it!"

"Just a moment," remonstrated Hewitt. "Has anybody advanced the theory that there's a woman in it? It's the case in almost every crime. Why, it's the rule. *Cherchez la femme!*"

Dodd scowled even at the mention of the sex. Chandler nodded with interest. "Had you thought about a woman, Kennedy?" he asked. "Or is it too much for the sense theory? We've got to have a woman lead in this play, you know."

Kennedy replied, slowly: "I always think of a woman in every case. There is a woman in the Cronk case."

"Cronk's woman?"

"No. Cronk was a married man, devoted to his family. No, not Cronk's girl. I'm afraid you'll have to fall back on one of my senses."

"The thing I have been thinking about," hastened Dodd, changing the subject, "is what became of the thousand cases.

They certainly weren't ever in Hinman's blue sedan—and you tell us they captured only about a hundred, from the Italian bootleggers. Somebody got away with the others. Who was it? How?"

Kennedy took a moment to answer. "I have been out on Long Island all day, or nearly so. I think I have been on every road that had anything to do with this rum-running episode and poor Cronk. That stuff you were wondering about, Dodd, was loaded on two trucks. The trucks were held up along the turnpike by a bunch of fake revenue officers. The drivers tried to bribe them. They took the money—then the hijackers took the stuff—and the trucks, too."

"The same that held up Hinman's chauffeur?" asked Larry Halpin, quickly.

Kennedy shrugged.

"Who told you that?" I asked, eagerly, seeing now a story. "How did you find it?"

"A woman" returned Kennedy, with a smile at Chandler. "An Italian woman, who knew one of the men arrested. She heard I was interested in the case. She was afraid her lover would be held for the murder of Cronk, as well as for bootlegging. She told what the prisoners refused to tell."

"Didn't I tell you?" exclaimed Chandler. "Didn't I say, General, the murderers would be hijackers? That Italian woman puts drama in it. I'm beginning to get it. If we're going to get it right, we've got to have some conflict in the story, conflict of two women over one man, conflict of two men over one woman—something."

"There," smiled Hewitt, "the murder's being solved—and not a sense in it, Kennedy."

"I quite agree with you."

Craig's subtlety did not go over their heads.

"But, Kennedy," remonstrated Chandler, "there's some sense in my putting a woman in this play—even if the woman in the case didn't show any sense—which I doubt."

"Bah!" This from Dodd, disgruntled.

"About this Italian woman," cut in Halpin, eager to help the playwright out. "She spoke for the bootleggers, not the hijackers, did she not? She—they didn't know the hijackers, did they?"

"That I am not at liberty to say. I turned her statement over to the proper authorities for what it was worth."

"Those men shouldn't be held for murder if they didn't do it," considered Hewitt.

"They're not, as far as I know," returned Kennedy.

"Just a moment, gentlemen," interrupted Chandler. "I want this play finished by you before you leave. You have left it up to these hijackers, without putting it on any one of them. Did they all do it—or was it done by one man?" He had turned to Craig.

It was thinly veiled that, under pretext of the play, Chandler was quizzing Kennedy. I wondered how Kennedy was going to take it, how he would turn it off. Instead, he met it.

"Cronk was killed by one man. A terrific blow on the back of the head, a fractured skull, concussion of the brain, finished him. Probably he never knew what struck him. Yes, probably there were others involved in the hold-up of the trucks. But Cronk and the murderer were alone, miles away from it, when that deed was done. That is how I sense it to have been." Kennedy dwelt on the word.

"You said you were at the glue factory where they found the body. What kind of place is it? I think it might make a good set for my play. There ought to be realism enough in it to get over, quite the popular touch. Holds of ships, rooms of fallen ladies, glue factories, they're sure to claim the attention of the public of to-day."

Kennedy smiled at Chandler. "Well, it is lonesome enough, for one thing. Just a dirt road leading to it, with a footpath on one side made by the laborers and a ditch on the other toward the clay pit. The factory is really almost on the beach, just out of reach of the highest apogee tide. One smells it before one comes in sight of it. The laborers are not of the highest class. How could they be and work with a stench like that in their nostrils all day long? It smells within and it smells without. Most nauseating place I was ever in—and the cellar is the foulest place of all. Outside the building are bins to hold the fish not used immediately. Not used immediately may mean several days, and decomposition of fish waits on no man.

"Rubbish, scraps of dead fish in all stages of decay, old overalls, a general mess of filth, was the hiding place into which the body had been dragged, not just thrown. But a complaint had been made of the stench. The owners had been ordered by the county health authorities to clean up. Thus poor Cronk's body was spared that indignity for a longer time. But it was bad enough. There were no trees on this side of the road and the direct rays of the sun made it hot and putrid. Do you know, I felt so covered with slime and stench that I had to take a dip in the Sound to rid myself of the feeling."

"But did you find anything else?" It was asked almost simultaneously by Larry Halpin and young Hewitt.

Craig shrugged again and avoided answering. But I felt he must have something, else he would not have been now so apparently inactive.

"What about the clay pit?" asked General Tams, more interested in the terrain than the odors.

"It was strange, just as Jameson says, to leave a body in a cellar, such a cellar, just because it was a cellar, and a little easier, perhaps, to get to than the pit. I was looking over the surrounding land in the hope of finding something more. It's true, the body would probably never have been found if he had flung it into the pit."

"Who was with you, may I ask?" put in Clarke. "Were you alone?"

Kennedy shook his head. "The sheriff and a deputy. They were unusually obliging, and wide awake, too. The eyes of those men and their memories for cars are remarkable. I said something about it. You see, since the last murder out there of an enforcement officer the city papers say things have quieted down and that the rum runners have gone elsewhere. It's only that the runners are more careful. And the law enforcers are keener, too. They notice every car on the road, day or night, can tell you more about the make and trim of a car than a Broadway salesman. They know they never can tell nowadays how soon they may be asked questions or called to identify some particular car. And they've got a regular net of a secret organization, citizens who are good and tired of the antics of desperado rum runners and hijackers tearing up and down the roads, shooting up at night, a menace to every innocent automobile driver after dark."

Chandler fidgeted, a bit vexed at the turn of the conversation away from the drama as he saw it. Kennedy eyed him with a twinkle. "Aren't you satisfied with how your play is coming on?"

"No, I'm not. With all you fellows around, with your keen minds, I ought to get a little more imagination out of this crowd than I am getting. That woman ought to do more, much more. Hang the facts! Are you going to spoil a good story for the want of a few facts?"

"But you all crabbed your own game. I suggested the unusual, the senses, and immediately you reject it, because it is a new idea to you. Perhaps it's too obvious. You can't seem to use the very senses God gave you. And if you don't, will you tell me what else you've got that is any better? I'm afraid you may have to make up your last act as you think the case should be solved. That's the trouble with you playwrights. You can't see how to use what you've got already. Then you go off and make up something and alibi yourselves by calling it realism and shouting that fiction is truer than fact. Now, if you want a real mystery melodrama, I tell you again you can have it without moving from this corner. Only use one of the five senses. Count 'em—five!"

"But things in real life end so prosaically," returned Chandler, with artistic asperity. "I want a kick at the end, something that will send 'em home happy—and talking—so their friends will buy tickets to the show. That's the only advertising that counts."

"It's a case of the hijackers stealing all the kick," laughed Larry Halpin.

It was a remark that seemed to start other trains of thought. Kennedy caught it.

"I'll tell you what I'll do," resumed Kennedy. "Upstairs, in my locker, in the room, I have some rare old cordials, probably like some of those stolen from Hinman's sedan. I'll blow the crowd. Maybe a shot of that cordial will stimulate the sluggish imagination and we can get a better play for Chalmers. Maybe the kick in the cordial will make up for the kick the hijackers stole, as Larry suggests."

General Tams began expatiating on the merits of some of the stuff in his own locker, in comparison with Craig's.

"George," beckoned Kennedy to the boy, "get me a bottle of that French cordial I have upstairs." Craig selected a key on his ring, gave it to George as he whispered some directions. George bowed and departed eagerly. On an errand like this there was always a tip.

"There is a little history connected with this cordial," Craig leaned back lazily in his chair, slowly puffing at his cigarette, eyes upturned to the ceiling. "Years ago, before prohibition came along, I happened to be able to give a helping hand to a mighty fine Frenchman who was quite troubled over the loss of some trade secret which had been in his family for over two centuries. I located the chap who had stolen the key to it, here in America, and he was very grateful to me. He sent me these cordials from his own cellar when he heard the country was going dry. I have some here, the rest at home."

"Golly!" It was Hewitt's exclamation. "Think of having a whole sedan full of liqueurs stolen! Awful to think about—when you haven't had a charitable Frenchman in your past. I feel sorry for Hinman."

"Back to the Cronk case," exclaimed Clarke. "Well, you'll have a drink of genuine B.P. cordial, anyhow, soon, even if we

didn't solve the mystery of Hinman's chauffeur to the satisfaction of Chandler."

George's beaming face appeared. "This bottle, Mr. Kennedy,
makes me think of the old days. It was always good, but this is
so much better, now, because it is harder to get."

"You said a mouthful, George," nodded Hewitt to the boy,
who was a favorite of the club.

Halpin looked at the bottle narrowly. "This is like the stuff I
used to import before prohibition. Much of it passed through
my hands. I used to take some wonderful orders from this club
alone. With the coming of dry times a big source of income
dried up, too. Well, I was due to retire, anyhow, getting along
in years, not many more years to play, if I was ever to do any
playing."

Carefully George opened the bottle, almost reverently. Its
aroma, heavy and sweet, seemed to permeate the air about
us with a delightful reminiscent odor of other days. Into the
little thin cordial glasses the yellow liquid was poured, shining,
smooth, heavy like a scrap of old-gold velvet.

"This is a chartreuse," I observed, catching sight of the label.
"No fake about that."

"But you'd be surprised how much of it is faked," Halpin
pursued. "I found that out even in my business years ago. I
learned to tell the difference."

"How do they fake it?" asked Hewitt.

"In the making. The best is distilled. You see, the makers of
a cordial macerate various aromatic substances, such as seeds,
leaves, roots, and barks of trees or plants with strong spirit and
subsequently distill the infusion, generally in the presence of
the whole or at least a part of the solid matter. Then they age
it," Kennedy was speaking contemplatively. "This is distilled,
and old, too."

"Of what do they make this? Can you tell?"

"What's the information for, Hewitt," asked Halpin. "Do you
like this so much?"

"I sure do. Perhaps I like things better not quite so sweet. But you see I don't know much about drinking or drinks. I've been very busy," the young man added.

"Well, my bootlegger can help you out if you want to buy any cordials. Vermouth, benedictine, chartreuse, curaçoa, kirsch, absinthe—he handles them all. Very secretive he is, but he manages to get me all I need. And you know the saying, Hewitt. When a man is willing to share his bootlegger with you he really cares for you!"

"It beats the devil," Clarke nodded, "how the stuff creeps in. No dearth of it anywhere. Crimes increase as the demand for it hangs on."

Hewitt was thanking Larry, but looking at Clarke out of the corner of his eye. One doesn't like to make a date for a bootlegger when one's prospective father-in-law is near—or perhaps one does with some other than Clarke. Halpin's offer was ignored, at any rate for the time.

Chandler was still engrossed with his notes, scribbling over what he had written. Nothing seemed to suit him. It amused Craig.

Again the little glasses were filled.

"Excellent!" Clarke exclaimed.

"Marvelous!" admitted Chandler, bowing appreciatively.

"Fine!" added Larry, sipping slowly at his glass and seeming to roll each sip about in his mouth.

Kennedy held up his glass. Through the amber-colored liqueur the light filtered and glistened like the rays of the morning sun, golden, translucent in its sheen.

"Ah, it's not the taste alone; it's the bouquet," remarked Kennedy with the enthusiasm of the connoisseur. "That is not a drink. That is a perfume—fit for an empress. Most exquisite. Its age makes a drop of it priceless, nowadays."

"Do you know, Kennedy," hastened Chandler, "I've seen some of it an exquisite green. This is yellow, golden, beautiful. What's the difference?"

"One difference is the percentage of alcohol. The green is about fifty-seven, the yellow forty-three. But it also is caused by the varying nature and quantity of the flavoring matters employed. This was made in France years ago. But since 1904, all the best chartreuse is made in Spain, I believe. It was during that year that the Carthusian monks, makers of the genuine Chartreuse, left France because of the Associations Law." It was Larry Halpin who answered, the facts of the business on the tip of his tongue, as of old.

"Oh, if I could only get a setting like this in my drama. The glamour of real chartreuse in dry days, good friends awaiting the coming in by some secret channels of their liqueurs, and end with a raid and a fight—and the murderer!" Chandler could not get his play out of his mind. The liqueur seemed only to increase his imaginative longing. "Then, there's another one, I used to like, Crème Yvette, wasn't it? Distilled violets! Ah, what a drink when one has a bedroom farce to finish!"

I was watching Kennedy's face. It seemed, as Chandler spoke, as if his nostrils dilated. I wondered at Kennedy for being even a bit suggestible.

"In the old days it was more appealing to me," resumed Kennedy, "this matter of drinking liqueurs. These rare cordials need an element to get the most out of them, that is æsthetic, elevating, calming. Now all the art of these things has gone for the drinker of to-day. Where before one could see the simply clad monks at work in the fields, in the distillery, busy to distraction, with pride and confidence in their ability, absorbed in their tasks, realizing that with the money obtained from the sales of their secret beverage they could carry on their beloved benevolences especially in the neighboring villages about their monastery. It was they who built the churches, the schools, the hospitals and orphanages, and maintained them."

In a rapt, almost detached voice Kennedy continued. "In the present time when drinking most cordials, one feels and knows he is a lawbreaker. Most of what one gets now one should not have, by all that is legal. Bootleg has made it so plebeian, common, ordinary, low. There is nothing much that is aesthetic about it any more. It is just drinking, drinking for the effect. Even when one feels the warm glow stealing down the throat, the senses charmed, quieted by the fragrance and taste, one cannot forget the evil conditions. We do not feel assured that the patient monks distilled it. We are wondering: Oh, this is something synthetic. Tastes like it; but not the same. Is it that it lacks the perfect bouquet, the spirit of the makers?"

"Great guns, Kennedy! Give me another glass!" General Tarns ejaculated it earnestly. "How soon again may I know I'll have the real thing? If you talk that way much more I'll clean forget the Cronk case. Just let me feel that warm glow stealing down my throat that you so gloriously described. Kennedy, you should have been a cordial salesman!"

There was a laugh at the general's enthusiasm, for he had a reputation as a conscientious two-handed drinker. I noticed, too, that when Craig had finished speaking everyone took a sip with renewed fervor and appreciation.

George had come up quietly beside Kennedy's chair. Not for the world would he have interrupted. He just stood there with his finger on the chair, drinking it in, waiting for Craig to finish. Then he bowed, leaned over, and whispered some message to Kennedy. Of its purport we could get no inkling from the faces of either. Kennedy's was motionless, expressionless. Only there was a stiffened restraint for a moment, a mute hesitation, until Tams spoke.

"I hope it wasn't to tell you your last bottle of Otard was broken," joshed Tams.

Kennedy merely smiled and the smile flitted politely. He sipped at his cordial slowly, lightly. He raised the glass to his lips again, closed his eyes, and swallowed slowly. I don't know why we watched him so closely. In some way was conveyed to us a surcharge of feeling in that little group. I couldn't tell whether it was the effect of that forty-three-per-cent cordial, or some static, electric, mental force emanating from Kennedy. I felt it, we all felt it as we sipped slowly.

Suddenly Kennedy opened his eyes and spoke. "They have captured both the hijacker trucks, the trucks the hijackers stole with the stuff loaded on them—and the men that drove them off from the rum runners."

Somehow was conveyed the impression that Kennedy had not told all.

"Caught the hijackers themselves!" exclaimed Chandler, excitedly. "Where did they get them?"

"Oh, on a little farm back of Laurel Hill Cemetery. I expected they'd locate them—but sooner." Kennedy was speaking in a slow, matter-of-fact tone.

"Well, did the senses do it, make the arrest?" asked Larry Halpin, with a wink to us.

"Can it, Larry!" adjured Chandler, his interest fired at once. "I'm going to stick along with Kennedy to-night, so to speak. I believe if I have enough patience and he doesn't run off the track with this new and very interesting theory of the senses, I'll get the finale of the play before I leave him, some way or other."

Kennedy looked at Chandler with a glint of humor.

"That means. Chandler," I put in, too, "that if you for a moment think you're going to get a play out of it, I'll stick, also, and get my story!"

"I know why I'm going to stick," chuckled the general, his eyes significantly on the dwindling bottle.

"For the same reason that I have," added Larry. "For the sake of the cordial—and old times' sake."

Kennedy held up the bottle reflectively. "I must admit I'm glad you're not the last bottle I have. The general's regard for me can be satisfied. I expect to be assured of his friendship for some time to come."

Up in the light Craig held the bottle. He filled the glasses of those who cared for more. Then he took it, held it gently to his nostrils.

"Ah!" It was long drawn out. "Some perfume! Just smell that bouquet, that aroma."

Everybody sniffed, paused, held for a second the delight of the intake of breath through the nostrils. There were renewed murmurs of approval. They rhapsodized over the aroma.

"How about it, Larry? Like it?" asked Craig. "Do you ever get anything like that that's synthetic?"

Larry Halpin raised his hand protestingly. "I love it. But my regard depends on my taste and other things. I? I can't smell a thing. It's congenital with me. I like the stuff, love it—but I can't smell it." He smiled deprecatingly at us as if nature had cheated him in bestowing gifts upon him.

I felt a sense of sympathetic curiosity.

"H'm!" Kennedy considered. "So!" He paused a full minute. "Can't smell a thing." Again he paused, as if running back over something in his mind. "Larry Halpin, retired, once importer of wines and cordials. People thought you got wealthy out of it, Larry. They didn't realize how prohibition had knocked out your income. But I know now how you secretly adjusted yourself to it, how, as head of a syndicate, you organized an underground rum-running system of importation of the stuff from Quebec. Then the rum fleet knocked that."

Larry Halpin stood a little apart from the rest of us. Unconsciously we had dropped away from him as Kennedy focused attention on him. Defiantly he glared at Kennedy.

"When you start something, Kennedy, be sure you can go through with it and finish it—or there's likely to be an awful come-back. You'll have to back up those insinuations. You can't convict a man just because he can't smell."

"I'm not worrying about any come-back, Halpin. The deputy out in Suffolk identifies your Sunbeam, seen on the same road where they later found the blue Packard sedan, not long before the time this murder must have taken place. They've noticed it about taking an active interest in what's doing at the ports on both shores of the island. That was a bit suspicious, considering the profits you made importing wines and liquors before prohibition."

"The rum fleet means nothing to me, Kennedy. I've never bought a case from them," growled Halpin.

"Probably," agreed Craig. "You smuggle it in from Canada. But these rum runners from Rum Row were cutting into your border bootleg profits frightfully. It had to be stopped. I have the facts from your agents. There's no honor among rum runners. A syndicate was formed, and you were at the head of it, to organize the hijackers."

Halpin took a step forward as if to controvert it, but Kennedy raised his hand. "Just a moment, Larry. Hear me out. Besides, Percy Hinman had been one of your chief customers, in fact carried with him many other customers, here in this club, in the Rock Club out on Long Island, and others. When the German system was tried, of bringing the stuff by an old tanker to these shores and lightering it in, Percy Hinman canceled a large order. So did others. They could get it cheaper, delivered almost at their doors.

"It must be broken up, if the Quebec ring was to survive. One way was to tip off the revenue men, ashore and on the boats. If they did not get them, then the hijackers, to seize the stuff. So, in effect, you turned hijacker, promoted hijacking. It was up to them to get the trucks. But there was Cronk in Hinman's car. It would never do to let him get through your line. Some one must stop Cronk. You did it. But Cronk knew you. Therefore he must be put out of the way. You did that, too."

Chandler was leaning forward in his chair, his play forgotten in the daze of surprise and horror that one of his club mates should be charged with the brutal crime.

"The very idea of the fish-glue factory touched your fancy as being repellant, keeping folks, prying folks, away. Only a man without a sense of smell would have gone in that place and overturned the refuse as you did when you concealed poor Cronk's body. The workmen themselves, used to inhaling the stuff every day, wondered how the murderer could have done it. It seemed to have been done so deliberately and thoroughly. Why, it would have turned any other man's stomach not accustomed to it to do what you did. So! You're the man without a sense of smell! Well—you're wanted!"

General Tams, playing nervously with his thin-stemmed glass, twirling it again and again, was muttering: "Thought they'd take Kennedy into camp, eh? The five senses! Then the sense of smell was the solution, after all!"

Kennedy still met the defiant stare of Halpin. "It's no use. You'd know it if you knew what I know. It's the message George brought me from headquarters. They've found the Sunbeam— and Hinman's stolen cordials with it!"

Larry Halpin seemed now to wilt back into the leather chair behind him, his hands before a colorless face. He seemed to shrink.

"Sorry, men," cried Kennedy, brusquely. "Sorry to have this happen here. But it's the only place I was sure to meet him this evening. George, you may tell that Central Office man to step in—the fellow that brought the message. He can take you downtown, Larry, with the bracelets, if you pull any rough stuff."

Chandler was fondling the almost empty cordial bottle, as if getting ready to introduce it as a prop in his stage set.

"By the way, Chalmers," smiled Kennedy, "George is not merely careless. He is stupid. That bottle he brought wasn't the cordial I wanted, not the one I told him."

Chandler shrugged. "But you caught your man just the same."

Kennedy nodded. It wasn't worth arguing.

"That's not the point. Chandler, to me," I jumped in. "He proved his case—that crime detection depends on the senses— or the lack of them!"

"Yes, by golly!" broke in Tams, in his jovial voice. "Yes! Convicted him on the sense of smell—and he couldn't smell a damned thing!"

SIGHT

"**LET ME GET** you off, Craig. You're too busy just now with that counterfeit case and all the other cases. I know a politician in the office of the commissioner of jurors. I'll have it fixed."

Kennedy's brow was knitted in a deep frown as he held in his hand a paper that is unwelcome to millions of us—a jury notice. This summons was returnable in General Sessions, Part IV, in the old Criminal Courts Building down on Centre Street, with the Tombs back of it and the famous Bridge of Sighs between the two. I knew it was Judge McLean sitting and that there were only criminal cases tried in this court. Kennedy noted the time and place, folded up the unwelcome paper, and placed it carefully in his pocket.

"No, Walter," he replied, slowly. "It's every man's duty to serve on jury. Especially is it mine and for men like me. No, I'm going to serve."

Thus it was that the following Monday morning at nine thirty, having nothing better to do, I accompanied Kennedy down to that brick-and-stone structure which to a newspaperman is a ceaseless story factory, the Criminal Courts Building.

Avoiding the elevators at this hour, we passed on up the wide stairs under the rotunda to Part IV, through the crowds, friends of the court, friends of the prisoners, friends of somebody in particular and of everybody in general, professional bondsmen, alleged fixers of this, that, and the other, lawyers, witnesses, policemen, detectives, court attendants, the idle public, the worried public.

They always make me think of my friend Goldstein, the lawyer, who told me, "Yes, Mr. Jameson, it is all very well to know the law—but it is much better to know the judge." As I pass through the carbolic odor of sanctity that overhangs justice in the Criminal Courts Building I am always wondering each time how much closer the great city is getting to that high ideal of justice.

I knew McLean. But I would never have attempted to presume on that personal acquaintanceship in behalf of Kennedy, nor would Craig have allowed it, even had he been disposed to accept my offer to get him off. There are other ways far more effective than by wrongfully trespassing on the friendship of the judge.

It happened also that I knew the doorman in Part IV. It turned out to be Pat McCarthy, a captain in a rock-bound political district downtown. He took Kennedy's notice, glanced at it, waved toward the rapidly filling benches where some scowled and fidgeted, crumpling folded newspapers, others read newspapers, and still others gazed curiously about, regardless of their newspapers. I have noticed that in the morning in court everybody appears with a newspaper. Perhaps it is as a badge of some special fitness, proof of literacy, although I am sure that our newspapers are now mostly for the illiterate, half-tone readers.

Kennedy passed in, and I was about to follow him when out of the corner of my eye I caught a resigned look on McCarthy's face as he wagged his head resignedly. I paused, glanced at him inquiringly. Evidently he had not noticed that I was with Kennedy. He seemed to assume that I had come to court to report the trial.

"Do yez know who thot mon is?" McCarthy jerked his head toward the disappearing figure of Kennedy. "He's that scientific detective, Craig Kennedy. I get the Kennedy, all right; but where did he get the Craig, huh? Now why do they dhraw a mon like

thot, I'm askin' ye? What's gointer happen when this here labor-
a-tory detective gets up against facts, real evidence as we have it
down here? I'm askin' ye. Oh, I forgot, Mr. Jameson, beggin' yer
pardon. He's a frind of youm. Well now, just the same, I shtick
to it." He wagged his head sagely as if he foresaw trouble looming for the austere goddess of justice. "We'll see!"

I made no comment beyond returning his friendly smile, went
on in, made my way to sit down with Kennedy on the bench
outside the rail. But I was mentally determined, if Kennedy was
accepted on the case, to take a seat in the back and get the ear
of McCarthy. At least there would be some recompense for the
hours in the big, dingy, yellow, oak-paneled court room.

Slowly the minutes dragged. The clerk and the other attendants of the inner circle appeared. The time came when at the
signal all in the court rose as the majesty of the law strode in
and took his dignified position on the bench. McLean was a big
man, physically, mentally, and in soul, with a shock of whitening
iron-gray hair and a florid face, by contrast, a man who, when
not on the bench, was most at home out on his wonderful estate
on the heather hills of Shinnecock.

Then came the reading of names of the panel, the answers,
"Here!" "Present!" from the unfortunate victims of the mill of
justice whose prospective duty it was to become those cogs in
the jury machine which is the hereditary palladium of our rights
as free men. Came next the time when those with excuses were
allowed to present them, when they matched wits with the keen
judge as to whether they were deaf, ill, all but in the grave, or so
busy that the business of the nation would be ruined by their
absence—excuses that show the profound resourcefulness and
inventive ingenuity of the human mind. Kennedy did not take
his place in this line, but it seemed to me that nearly half the
panel did. Very few got away with it.

At last that wrangle was over. The clerk rose, read a name.

"Craig Kennedy!"

He stood looking over the faces in the court room a moment,

waiting, daring the culprit not to answer, at a penalty of not less than two hundred and fifty dollars. Kennedy rose. The man waved with a lordly gesture toward the twelve vacant seats in the jury box. Kennedy stalked over toward them, was about to sit down.

"Sit here, sir." It was emotionless, impersonal, this grinding of the wheels of that thing we call justice. He had indicated seat No. 1. Kennedy changed, sat down.

There was a movement about the long table at one side as attorneys conferred.

The clerk was asking Kennedy's name, his address, his brief pedigree for this purpose. Judge McLean was as oblivious as if he were blind justice. But he was far from blind. He was employing every minute, listening, signing papers, pausing to emphasize with his gold pencil some point to the officer who brought them.

"What is your occupation, Mr. Kennedy?"

"Professor of science and crime at the university."

For once the court room was stilled. The assistant district attorney and two with him conferred. The attorneys for the defense conferred. It was not until then that I realized what indeed it was that I had heard upon the opening of the case. "People of New York against Thomas Brainen."

This was the Crowe case! Susanna Crowe, a wealthy old lady, an invalid, was alleged to have been poisoned. Her nephew, Thomas Brainen, an attorney, and a slick one, was alleged to have first influenced her to make a new will, mainly in his favor. Then, one Saturday night last August, she had died. A suspicion had arisen that her demise had been hastened. It had grown into the covert assertion that she had been poisoned. There had been an autopsy by the medical adviser to the district attorney. The exact findings I did not know. They, of course, had not been made public. But the implication, when a week later the grand jury handed up an indictment against Brainen, was that there had been discovered evidences of poison. Somehow it had leaked to the newspapers that the poison in this case had been good, efficient, sudden cyanide. That, in brief, was all that I knew.

I had been cudgeling my recollection to recall that much, mechanically watching the two groups of attorneys, waiting for the examination and perhaps challenge for cause, or, in Craig's case perhaps a peremptory challenge, when suddenly I heard another name called.

"Henry McCord."

The man in front of me rose. Then I woke up. They had accepted Kennedy.

This was to be a famous murder case. Kennedy was sitting in No. 1 chair. Barring the unexpected, Kennedy would be foreman of that jury. This was a story for the *Star*—Craig Kennedy on a jury, this jury, the Brainen jury!

My place was not on these benches outside the rail. I should be in there at that table just before and one side of the clerk of the court with the other newspaper men and women of the various morning and evening journals, the city news and other associations. But our man from the *Star*, Lindsey, was there. No, my original idea was best. I got up, moved back quietly. McCarthy's scowl changed to a smile as I sat down in one of the few remaining seats back by the door and him.

"What'd I tell ye?" he whispered back of his hand. "This ain't right! What's them attorneys thinkin' about? I'm an old man, an old hand at this business. It ain't right! I tell ye there's gointer be fireworks! This is a court. This ain't no college nor no Sunday supplement!"

McCord was excused after a lengthy and bitter clash. It was on a Scotch reluctance to commit himself on whether he would convict on circumstantial evidence. I thought of Kennedy's contention that, after all, the only really reliable evidence is the right kind of circumstantial evidence. Then it began to dawn on me that that presaged the course of the case, that it was a case built up largely on circumstantial evidence.

It came to the recess for lunch and still there were only five men in the box. The afternoon moved faster than usual, though. The New York courts were clogged and Judge McLean was not disposed toward red tape that would clog his court. By night, when all the challenges were worn out by both sides, the box was filled by the acceptance of a draftsman, Wanger.

The judge turned, bowing in his official robes toward the jury. He made his little speech.

"And if Mr. Kennedy will agree to restrain his imagination," he beamed, "I will designate him as foreman of this jury. Court is adjourned until ten o'clock tomorrow morning!"

It was late, well into the dinner hour, as Craig and I left. I was uncomfortable. I think I would rather have been with Judge McLean. On technicalities, like discussing a case with a juror, under such circumstances, Kennedy is inclined to stand so straight that he leans backward. However, we managed to exist and I did not forfeit his friendship.

Some murder mysteries are just ordinary, lacking that stimulating quality which is so necessary if Kennedy were to take up the case. Otherwise he would have been overwhelmed by the mere volume of his professional business. Always there must be a touch of the unusual to arouse Craig to activity. A pitiful twist to it, unusual characters involved, or what seems an immovable impossibility in the solution, will lure Kennedy.

"For once," he smiled grimly, "I am concerned with a case not because I want to be but because I have to be. It is a solemn duty. But in this case, Walter, I think I shall be rewarded. I believe it has the elements that satisfy me."

I wanted to ask a leading question, why this Susanna Crowe murder case suddenly loomed important in his mind. But I did not dare. "The papers haven't played it up—much," was all I could say, colorlessly. "The attitude seems to have been: Another old lady possibly put out of the way for somebody's benefit. It's not exactly sordid—and it isn't just what you'd call exciting. It lacks romance, human interest, I guess, seems dull."

"There was nothing dull about Susanna Crowe—and nothing

dull about her death." Kennedy said it with a finality that did not encourage me. He might as well have added, "And that's that!"

I had been with Craig at many murder trials, but never when he had acted in this capacity. It was a novel situation for me and I was prepared to derive all the satisfaction I could out of it. In the crowded courtroom, as it filtered about that Kennedy was the scientific detective, it had seemed to me to be the feeling that they expected a speedy and sure conviction. Tom Brainen's path to Sing Sing and the electric chair seemed to them to be made straight and sure by Kennedy's presence among the jurors.

The next day I was early on the job. I did not want to have to rely on McCarthy to save me space beside himself. The prisoner was brought in, the indictment read, and the trial was on. Now there were no empty benches in Part IV.

There was even a thrill in the ordinary tiresome procedure of presenting the facts of the case at length, in that calm, even manner which to the public stresses no act or fact as more important and more incriminating than any other.

Yet, even so, one could see that the accretions were as a mountain of circumstantial evidence built up against the man who was being tried for his life.

Tom Brainen was clever enough lawyer himself to see the impending gravity of his position. And he showed it physically in spite of his debonaire acting. His confinement before the trial had paled his face, robbed it of some qualities of his assertive assurance, tamed him, so to speak. Yet that fire smoldered. It was there, as if banked.

Susanna Crowe had been of the type that clung to her open barouche and team of horses. She would have nothing to do with motors, even now. They, like subways and busses, were things of the devil, to destroy and maim. She entertained rarely and sparely, was of simple tastes. Her wants had made no serious inroads on her fortune. Under her frugality and that of her bankers it had grown until it was computed in seven figures.

There was nothing for Susanna Crowe to worry about in her

future. While she was an invalid, she might live for years with no other pain than a growing gradual weakness. The suicide theory must be cast aside.

But she had been found poisoned. At first the servants had been suspected. But there was lack of motive. Their alibis were perfect. They were here merely as witnesses to establish various things.

Thus naturally suspicion had dwindled down to those who might have profited financially in her death. Who would be disappointed in the reading of the will—and who would profit? She had had few near of kin. One by one they had been eliminated, leaving only Brainen. Brainen had a reputation, too, not exactly disreputable, but such that people smiled at the mention of Brainen's legal advice. As an attorney he was of a type increasingly common in these days, sharp and slick. It was better to have Brainen working with you than against you. And as fact and suspicion developed, Brainen had been accused, held, indicted.

I shall make no attempt to give the trial in detail or to present the evidence except in a general way. The servants were called, for example, but not much of importance was developed in that way. However, the eccentricities of the victim were brought to light and her relations with her relatives brought out for judicial eyes as the backstairs and kitchen viewed things.

The state at this stage of the case was banking its strength on the recent will Susanna Crowe had made. Here was the motive. Next came the facts of the case, the autopsy, the finding of the poison—cyanide—in the body, proof of the crime.

"Doctor Norton!"

Now one felt the tenseness in the court room. It is strange how the calling of a name in a case as it is being built up can cause a tenseness where indifference has existed before.

Doctor Norton was a well-known astronomer at one of the universities in the city whose gentleness and industry were bywords to most of the students who studied under him. The man hesitated in his walk to the witness chair. His feet seemed reluctant to carry him from the unobtrusiveness of his place with the others in the colorless background of the court. It seemed that one whose time had been spent in the solitude of study-ing the heavens revolted at this crowded courtroom, this sea of faces. His hands trembled before him as though he would like to push aside gently this distressing experience through which he must pass.

Doctor Norton went through the formalities of being sworn in, took his oath solemnly, and waited to be questioned.

Followed a succession of perfunctory queries leading up to the points to be developed.

"Doctor Norton," began the assistant district attorney, in a casual tone, "just how are you related to the deceased?"

"By marriage. I am not a blood relation. My wife is a niece of Susanna Crowe."

"Was your wife on friendly terms with her aunt?"

"Always until recently, when there was a slight coolness. One would hardly have called it an estrangement because neither my wife nor myself would allow it to assume such proportions. We realized the age of her aunt, her natural peculiarities that would increase with her infirmities, and we made allowances. We humored and mollified her on all occasions."

Doctor Norton's voice gained a little in strength as he went on with his answers, but his nervousness was apparent. Even Judge McLean smiled kindly on his evident gaucherie on the witness stand. The district attorney let his answers run without cutting them short. They were not accustomed to the scholar in the witness box.

"Did you ever hear Susanna Crowe discuss her intended distribution of her money after her death?"

Doctor Norton's lips opened and closed, emitting no sounds. He seemed overcome with sorrow. With compassion he looked in the direction of Brainen, sitting so tensely in his chair, flanked by counsel and an assistant. He turned to the judge as to a friend.

"Your honor, I can't stand this. I know nothing about this murder—and I don't want to say a thing that will in any way help to jeopardize a fellow man. I..." His voice trailed off.

The judge looked at him kindly. "Just tell the truth, the whole truth, as you know it. Answer the questions the best you can. If what you know convicts, that is up to the prisoner at the bar. He should have thought of those things before."

The district attorney framed his question again. "Is the will placed in evidence the only will with which you are familiar?"

Doctor Norton's white face turned tremulously toward the prosecutor. "There was a will before this last one was found, and my wife had been the principal heir. Her aunt had appreciated her many kindnesses to her, her hours devoted to her when she had been seriously ill. But of late there had been this coldness, not so much interest shown in my wife."

The district attorney nodded, glanced at the jury as if to emphasize the restraint of Norton in refusing to mention that Jack Brainen was the chief beneficiary of the second will. He turned again to the witness. "The new will. Were you present when it was read?"

"Yes. It was read the day after Susanna Crowe was buried. All the relatives were asked to gather at the office of the attorney of her banker. Those who could get there attended, and it was a surprise to most of us when we heard that Mrs. Norton was left only a few hundred dollars by her aunt."

"Had you heard anything about a new will before that reading in the office of the attorney for the banker?"

Doctor Norton smiled wanly. "I suppose the family is like most other families. The members know what is transpiring, at least they think they know. There were rumors and indications that things were not as harmonious as before." He finished regretfully. It seemed he thought the murder was enough unpleasant publicity. It didn't at least warrant all the family bickerings being exposed at the same time.

"What do you mean—rumors and indications?" insisted the prosecutor.

The opposing attorney was on his feet in an instant with an objection that rumors and indications were incomplete, immaterial, irrelevant. There was an argument over it. Doctor Norton coughed slightly, took his handkerchief and wiped his lips with a vigor that was in contrast with his tremulous condition before. It was apparent he did not want to testify against Brainen. He wished to get out of it, welcomed even this faint hope of doing so.

After an acrimonious discussion over the question as it was framed a second time, the judge overruled the counsel for Brainen. He wanted the jury to get the whole story and this man's manner of telling his story was such that he had to be treated differently. With an admonition to confine himself to what he personally saw, heard, and knew, the witness was allowed to go on.

"I meant that several times my wife and I had called on Susanna Crowe, a friendly call. Her eyes were bad and Mrs. Norton would read to her. But her last visits to her aunt were decidedly a trial to my good-hearted wife. Now all her kindly ministrations were refused ungraciously and the last two visits she wasn't even seen."

"Was any one else present at these times beside yourself?"

"During all these visits Mr. Brainen was about the house," the astronomer answered, reluctantly. "It seemed as if my wife was not to be allowed with her aunt, alone. There was no way of offsetting this influence. Then we heard through other relatives of a now will to make Thomas Brainen the chief beneficiary."

Questions followed as to what relatives had made these statements about the new will, and the prosecutor was back again, skirting the subject of "rumors and indications."

Doctor Norton continued, after one carefully framed answer: "That, at least, is how it looked to me. Those things I know. But of the murder, if it was murder, I knew nothing." He looked over at his vacated chair wistfully. It was easy to tell that he was not at home in courts.

I could not avoid reflecting how different Brainen's attitude would have been if the situation were reversed. Nor could I understand the almost crushed, hopeless spirit that Brainen could not seem to conceal, try as he would. It was unlike the man whose reputation as a slick attorney was almost national. Was it that he was trying to counteract that unsavory fame? Was an appearance of docile hopelessness calculated to gain a little sympathy, a little leniency from that jury?

"When and where did you see the accused on the day of the murder?" Again there was silence, reluctance, and the question had to be repeated.

"I had hoped," answered Norton, resigned to telling now—"I had hoped to intervene in my wife's behalf. The Saturday noon before the evening of Susanna Crowe's death, we thought we would go to see her. We took a taxi, my wife and I, When we reached the house we saw Mr. Brainen entering just ahead of us. It would be a useless call, we knew. We didn't even get out of the taxi—simply turned and left the place. I went to the observatory and my wife went home."

Doctor Norton's tortoise-shell spectacles were the object of his constant solicitude. In his nervousness he took them off repeatedly. Fingering them awhile, he would replace them in a halting, half-absent manner. His life was surely the life of books, of the observatory, and the skies above him. Other questions tending to throw the onus on Brainen were met by disclaimers from him, or so it seemed.

"Where were you the night of the murder, Doctor Norton?" asked the prosecuting attorney, now a bit testy at the failure of the witness to co-operate as he had hoped in building up his case.

A smile spread over the man's face. Now it seemed he could talk about something he knew, something with which he was familiar.

"In my observatory. I had been busy every minute finishing my map of the moon." He said it quietly, confidently, with a touch of pride in his specialty.

"Were you alone?"

"No. One of my brightest pupils was with me, Alma LaSalle, a student of whom I am proud."

"May I ask exactly what was the map on which you were working?"

At last the district attorney had discovered a subject on which Doctor Norton was not only willing, but eager, to talk. He could talk more about maps and the moon than he could about murders.

"I was completing mapping the mountains of the moon," replied the astronomer, slowly. "You see, I have published several text books on my work, and with Miss LaSalle's help I was completing another. These text books of mine are used a great deal in the universities and my study on the subject has made me somewhat of an authority on the mountains of the moon. Miss LaSalle and I had made many drawings within the weeks previous to that time. I have brought them along, among them that on which I was working the night of the murder." He turned unconsciously toward the table of the prosecution.

The district attorney picked up a sheet of paper. "I hand you this and ask you if you can identify it."

Norton fumbled clumsily with the drawing as it was passed to him by the prosecutor. Again his glasses needed straightening. Now he was away from talking about his beloved subject, in some way back again to this case, and his old nervousness, his indecision, his absent-mindedness came back again. He seemed to lose his realization at moments of just where he was—a fitting example of the absent-minded scholar.

He laid the paper on his knees, leaned forward in his chair, hands clasped nervously, and looked intently about him. "If you care, Miss LaSalle, who was in the observatory that Saturday night of the poisoning, is here, too." His glance seemed to turn instinctively toward the faces in the vicinity of the chair which he had vacated to step up to the witness box.

Kennedy, as foreman, was watching him closely as he had watched all the witnesses. I, too, followed the doctor's glance to where two women were sitting together. One was a woman in her forties, the other a younger girl, apparently not much past twenty. I took the younger to be Miss LaSalle and I was right. As Doctor Norton mentioned her name she smiled toward the district attorney, bowed her head slightly, seemed to acquiesce in the facts as Doctor Norton had presented them.

"Is that drawing the one which you were working on the night of the murder?" The district attorney asked it kindly, getting back to the subject.

Doctor Norton picked up the paper, fumbling the edges of it, showing painfully his utter unhappiness over his ordeal.

"Yer know wot I think? That old guy b'longs in a nurs'ry! Some moider case! A germ detective on the jury—and a bug for a witness! Wot with mountains on the moon, I'll be gointer lunch and eatin' mountains o' green cheese!"

I shook my head to silence McCarthy as I watched the thin white hands of Doctor Norton, almost like the paper itself. Finally, after a nervous fluttering about the edges of the drawing paper, he managed to calm his nerves enough so that he could pass it over as a result of his work on the night that Susanna Crowe was murdered.

That done, his face lighted up with pleasure, and I think that if this more serious and distasteful business had not been on hand we would have been rewarded by a dissertation on the mountains of the moon that would have aroused McCarthy's humor. The map had been painstakingly done. It might provoke humor in the uninitiated. It is a human failing to laugh at what we do not understand. Those hands might fumble and fuss with nervousness in a court, but I thought how accurate and steady they must be to accomplish this task—to set down those things that ordinary people can't see.

"I ask that this be marked in evidence," concluded the prosecutor, whereupon it was, and also handed to Kennedy and the jury for their inspection and edification.

"Doctor Norton," began the district attorney again, "had you ever witnessed any friction between Susanna Crowe and Thomas Brainen?"

"Oh," he answered, easily, "wherever there is money there is friction. Where there are two strong-willed people there will be conflicts. Aunt Susanna used to quarrel. When she had nothing else to quarrel about she would make up a good fight with some one. She had reached the stage where she needed a certain amount of emotion and attention to exist. When she didn't get it naturally, she manufactured it. She would have nervous spells, periods of depression when she imagined every hand against her. It was a sort of inferiority complex, I think. We would call in doctors, and when the spells began to cost money she would recover quickly."

There was an audible titter in the court room. Even the quiet scholar could prove himself a gentle humorist. The thing that impressed me was the clever avoidance of the doctor. He had told the truth, evidently. But his reluctance to testify against Brainen had caused him to make light of the quarrels.

"Did you ever hear Thomas Brainen quarrel with his aunt?" The district attorney was not going to let him slip away so easily.

"On one occasion. That was over some investment he had advised. He told her she would regret it. Then another investment he had made turned out profitably, and a few days later she sent for him and there was a fine reconciliation. After that we were out of her good graces entirely."

"Have you ever heard any other quarrels or threats against Susanna Crowe?" persisted the prosecutor.

"No, I have never heard any other threats."

"Do you know of anyone who might have a feeling of hate toward her."

"No person I know harbored such a feeling as far as I am able to judge. Of course I know nothing about her business."

"Do you know anything about the financial relations that existed between Susanna Crowe and Thomas Brainen? Did he owe her any money?"

"I have heard of some loans, yes. But how much I can't say."

Doctor Norton again found the question distasteful. Yet he had to tell the truth and I could see that the prosecutor was leading him on to help really convict the accused. Even by his faltering testimony Brainen had quarreled with the dead woman; the will was all in his favor; he owed her money. It was damning in its implications.

"One more question, Doctor. Had Thomas Brainen the freedom of the house?"

That question, too, carried a kick. A long time be thought of it. It was as if he had been asked, "Would it be possible, from the freedom allowed him, for him to administer poison in her food or drink?" He was pressed. He must answer. "Yes," he admitted, finally, "he had the freedom of the house. He could go anywhere without suspicion."

So it progressed. It was evident to us all that by the very reluctance of his testimony there was growing a feeling against Brainen such as he sought to avoid. My impression was that he could have said much if he had wanted to say it. But all this was dragged out of him.

"That will do. Doctor Norton. You're excused."

The relieved look that swept over the scientist's face was good to see. But how that questioning had weakened him! As he went to his seat he had to put out his hands to the chairs for support, the revulsion of feeling was so great. Finally a court attendant assisted him to the chair beside his wife. He sat down, his glasses now off and in one hand for several minutes, the other hand over his eyes as if to shut out all unpleasant memories through which he had just passed.

It was McCarthy who roused me from watching Doctor

Norton. "Now, if they'll put the man in the moon on the shtand, we'll get some real evidence!"

Mrs. Norton's story was quite different in character. It passed without comment. She had come home from her aunt's nervous and ill at ease. Toward evening a bad headache had developed which made it impossible for her to sit up. About the time of the excitement of discovering the murdered woman, a doctor had been called in attendance on Mrs. Norton. The call from Susanna Crowe's home had been answered by the doctor himself. He had decided not to let Mrs. Norton know anything of the tragedy until the next morning.

In her testimony along similar lines to that of her husband, disclosing the unpleasant family relations, Mrs. Norton was businesslike, efficient, answered briefly and briskly, made a splendid witness.

There was a conference between the prosecutors and it was evidently decided not to call Alma LaSalle. Enough irrelevant testimony had been given already by the servants in the house. The case proceeded by calling a couple of expert toxicologists on the matter of cyanide found in the organs of the dead woman.

Step by step the prosecution built up its structure of circumstantial evidence against Brainen, until finally it closed with what was admittedly a strong presumption. Not the least important part in this structure in the minds of any jury, I began to realize, was the impression left by the reluctant, considerate testimony of Doctor Norton.

It was not until the third day of the trial, which, at that, was proceeding with more than ordinary speed, that the defense opened. It was a carefully planned defense, attacking the credibility of witnesses, going deep into the credibility of the testimony, drawing diametrically opposite conclusions from whatever before had seemed damaging. Yet it was not hard, as one thought about it, to put one's finger on the weak spot of the defense. Shatter as it would at the foundations of the prosecution, it was floundering when it came to offering any alternative theory. Rather it offered so many alternative conclusions that it weakened its own case. Granted that the evidence was insufficient to convict Brainen, who, then was guilty? The very multiplicity of negative arguments weakened the defense. The district attorney had built up a plausible case. There was nothing plausible offered in its place. But there were many things half-plausible.

It was under such circumstances that the story of the accused himself was to swing the tide. At least he could go on the stand and show that, no matter if it were not known who else was guilty, at least he was not guilty.

Thus finally came the time when Brainen took the stand in his own defense. The wretched man stood up, tall and slim, with a face which at a more favorable time and under other conditions would have been prepossessing. It had been his stock in trade as a clever rather than a good lawyer. Now it was lined with care and worry. I wondered at the apparent slump in his former brisk, pert manner. Was it that he realized his own poor fighting chance?

He told a simple, straightforward story, harping on his complete ignorance of the deed, passing lightly over the impossibility of its commission by him to the points where it seemed the deed had not been hung on him. It was a clever defense, but not impressive. We waited expectantly for the cross-examination of Brainen.

Slowly the district attorney rose, then suddenly swung about on him as he shot out, "When did you see your Aunt Susanna Crowe alive last?"

Brainen was expecting it, answered promptly. "That Saturday I had luncheon with her, stayed about an hour afterward to give her some advice on investments she was contemplating. She seemed unusually affectionate, for her; asked me to come back in the evening to talk over automobiles. I had prevailed upon her to give up her carriage and get a modem car of some good make. I think she would have done so if she had lived."

"When the maid found your aunt's body, the maid did not know you were in the house. Why was that?"

"I usually let myself in. I had a key. So did some others. It was always my habit to go directly to my aunt's room. She was usually there after dinner. But this night dinner was exceptionally late for some reason. It was already dark. I waited up there for her to join me, when I heard the maid down in the dining room scream for help.

"Naturally, I rushed down. Aunt Susanna had fallen from her chair and was lying on the floor, very quiet. The maid was screaming, and when she saw me enter from upstairs she lost her head and accused me. It was a maid, by the way, who had always sought to curry favor with Mrs. Norton. The first chance she had to prove herself a deliberate enemy of mine she took—and this is the result. She has made the mere fact of my presence in that house, unknown to my aunt, brand me a murderer. I came to see her with only a brief-case full of automobile circulars."

There was a latitude accorded Brainen also in his answers, as if it were the least that could be done for one in jeopardy for his life. His manner and tone were quiet. There was a silence in the court room, a dramatic silence that concealed more emotion than tears or shouting ever betray.

But public opinion was not with the man. He has used his profession too often to outwit the law—not to aid it. There was no reliance now on his statements, and as he looked about him and smiled a bitter smile he must have realized it. I looked at Brainen's face. It was a study. Clever lawyer that he was, he knew only too well that a net was being spread by another clever lawyer to catch him.

"I had won enough on a deal to pay my debt also," he replied to another question touching their financial dealings. "She knew it. Aunt Susanna was money crazy and exact. What she had made through me did not affect in her mind in the least the fact that I owed her that money. I was ready to pay it that very day. I was not broke." There was a bitterness in his tone.

"Why didn't you go into the dining room the night your aunt was poisoned? Did you know or expect the maid would find what she found?"

His pale face flushed at the insinuation as he leaned forward with a flash of his old spirit. "I didn't go into the dining room because my aunt would have made me eat. I didn't care to eat. So I stayed in her room upstairs. That was my only reason."

"Did you have any quarrel with your aunt the day she was poisoned?" came the next insinuation from the prosecutor.

He was ready for that, too, primed. "I wouldn't say it was a quarrel. I got excited at lunch time over the cars. Aunt Susanna and I were much alike. When I am deeply in earnest I am likely to get excited. So did she. I was arguing with her over the various makes of automobiles, the first cost and the unkeep. She wanted the cheapest. I said only the rich could afford the cheapest. She always posed as being so poor. My argument was that a poor car will break a poor man. I suppose the maid heard our excited voices, jumped to her own conclusions again."

I was trying to analyze the man. Were his hopes for evading justice sinking fast? He had the look of a wounded animal, unable to put up the fight he could in health, but with his back to a wall and prepared to fight to the last. I began to pity the man. He had a certain brilliance which, if it had not been diverted from the right road, would have taken him far. This once had he strayed too far from the beaten path and had the jungle of crime overwhelmed him?

Brainen's testimony for his defense in, it seemed that all the witnesses had been called. Their cross-examination and recall was now over. Masterly summing up by his own attorney for the defense and by the state followed.

As the district attorney closed, and when all the legal tricks had been resorted to, I felt unconsciously that it looked mighty black for Tom Brainen, stripped of all the legal verbiage. The evidence had all seemed against the man. I could see his attorney trying to cheer him. He might, for all I knew, even have been encouraging him with the prospect of another trial if this one went against him. Subtly I felt that the presence of Kennedy on that jury had turned out to be a blow, they felt, for the defense. Perhaps they feared that his acute mind might supply any deficiency they had claimed in the wonderful structure of evidence against Brainen. Brainen was feeling he was not as clever as he had supposed.

The judge charged the jury. My own impression was that there was scant hope for the accused in that speech which made clear the rules governing circumstantial evidence. The jury filed out of the court room.

Those vacant seats after a murder trial always give me a thrill. I can imagine what the sight of them must be to the man whose life depends on the conclusion the men who occupied those chairs must reach. At that time imagination must be a curse. But then there is always the inference that a murderer cannot be very imaginative. The very act of killing precludes it. The dreams, nightmares of ages to come would deter him. He feels, but does not dream. The murders of insanity are different. Tom Brainen seemed as sane as anybody.

Even McCarthy felt the drama of the moment. It subdued him. Of those who remained in the court room, some were reading newspapers, others talking in low tones, apprehensively looking toward the door through which the jurors had filed. Doctor Norton and his wife, most of the other witnesses, remained in their seats. None but the judge had left the room. That would come later after the jury was out for hours wrangling and it might look like a disagreement.

The Nortons were talking quietly, the doctor bored and looking weary, wishing it was all over so that he could go to the peace and quiet of his observatory.

Suddenly Mrs. Norton leaned over, touched his arm excitedly, whispered, and pointed to the door that led to the jury room. Naturally my gaze turned in that direction, too. I almost gasped with surprise. McCarthy unconsciously put out his hand, whispered, "Look!"

There stood Kennedy in the doorway. At first I thought the evidence had been so plain that the jurors had been able to agree after an absence of only fifteen minutes or so.

"That's a quare bit of actin', I'm tellin' ye," muttered McCarthy. He was so surprised he had forgotten to take his hand from my arm. "I never saw the likes of this before. That's wot the judge gets for puttin' a book detective in as foreman of the jury!" Amazement, disgust were written on his face, yet underneath was a current of amusement. He seemed to feel that he knew more of court routine than Kennedy, that he could have put him wise not to make such a blunder as this.

Then the rest of the jurors entered quietly, taking their places. The judge was summoned from his chambers.

I grant that I was excited. What decision had been reached? Papers were laid aside. Attention was strained. The reporters were ready for the jury's verdict. Everybody was tense. The time had been so short that almost everybody in that court room knew what the verdict would be. Kennedy, as foreman, rose to address the judge.

"Your Honor, may the jury recall one of the witnesses and ask a question?"

What a reprieve! I do not know how Tom Brainen felt about it, but I know how I as only a casual witness reacted. I was spinning after that sudden let down in suspense.

Tom Brainen had been resting his head on his hand, his elbow on the arm of the chair. At Kennedy's question his elbow slipped; his face would have fallen forward only for the wonderful self-control the man revealed. He moistened his lips and nodded to his attorney when the latter flashed him an encouraging smile.

I think Judge McLean was astounded, too. But in his most formal manner he answered, "It can be done only with the consent of the court and of the attorneys on both sides."

The prosecutor looked at the counsel for the defendant. Neither wanted to allow the question asked. But on the other hand, if either refused it would not look well for his case.

This was almost unprecedented. "It is allowable for the jury to ask to have any part of the testimony read to it," suggested the judge.

That did not seem to satisfy. From Kennedy's face one could get no idea of the question. Its very passivity concealed whether the question was for or against Brainen. Everyone in the court room was on his toes.

For once opposing counsel agreed. It was with curiosity. What was Kennedy up to? Each hoped the question in some way would help his side of the case.

A moment the judge had it under advisement. Then he granted the request. The granting was much to the disgust of McCarthy, who, never having heard of such a thing done before, thought it was wrong. "Humorin' that glass-bottle detective again!" he exclaimed, peevishly. I smiled at his sarcastic adjective and thought of the quiet chuckle of pleasure Kennedy would derive from it later when I told him.

"I would like to ask Doctor Norton a question."

Doctor Norton started slightly, as if he had not heard aright. Was his tranquillity to be disturbed again?

"Oh, why do people do things to get me in these predicaments?" he whispered sorrowfully to his wife. She only smiled gently and helped him to the witness stand. His nervousness was appealing. But he had been recalled as a witness. There was no way to get out of it. He sat peering at Kennedy, wondering what he wanted to know now.

"Your frind mighta called on some other geezer," commented McCarthy. "He ought to leave thot mon to his mountains!"

"Better wait until you hear the question," I advised. "Maybe no one else can answer it."

Above the slight whispering could be heard the sound of

the gavel. The judge demanded silence. In that silence Kennedy spoke, slowly:

"When did you last observe the moon. Doctor Norton?"

There was a revulsion from sheer overstrain. The man hesitated pitifully, aware of his own weakness in this atmosphere, but unable to help himself. Sitting there mumbling, as if trying to recollect, his eyes were staring about as if trying to find the simple answer in the air about him. There was sympathy on all faces. Such sensitive people should not have to face these abominable situations.

It was the prosecuting attorney who came to the doctor's rescue. "Your honor, I object! That is a matter of record. The witness has already answered that question."

Kennedy had handed to an attendant a paper containing the question and the paper had been handed to the witness. At once the other lawyer was on his feet. He did not know what it was all about, but if the district attorney objected, he was for it. He was a man who could give seven reasons, too.

The judge sustained the objection as Norton held the paper in his hand, feeling nervously about its edges, but with eyes staring in the direction of Kennedy.

Slowly again the jury passed out, closing the little door behind them. It was an exciting interlude. What did it protend?

Again Doctor Norton walked feebly to his chair, gasping with relief as he regained his wife's presence. Again the heartbreaking wait began. This time so many heads did not bend over newspapers. More were intently watching the door. Tom Brainen was watching it too, row, with flashes of excitement gleaming in his dark eyes. Even the Nortons were anxious. I saw Mrs. Norton gently encouraging her husband and talking earnestly with Miss LaSalle, as if trying to convince him that his testimony was not the sole thing that would send Tom Brainen to the chair, but Tom Brainen's own actions.

It is tragic how long a minute seems when death hangs. I was intensely anxious to hear how that jury decided. I tried to interest myself in the crowd about me. But the only faces that drew my attention were those of Brainen and Doctor Norton. Even McCarthy's Celtic humor fell flat. Either his jokes were not up to standard or I was not attune to laughter. I looked at my watch. Scarcely ten minutes had passed. It seemed like ten hours.

Suddenly I heard a slight commotion, like a shuffling of feet. It came from the direction of the jury room. Again the door opened.

Kennedy entered the jury box, the rest following with serious faces that betrayed nothing. Only poor Tom Brainen gripped his chair a little harder. The judge was summoned. Was this to be another question, or had a verdict been reached? The jurors did not seat themselves, just stood, waiting for the judge. It seemed as if everybody was taking so much time; things were working too deliberately.

Finally the judge entered. That increased the tension. He stood, justice personified in his black robe. Slowly he asked, "Have you reached a verdict?" The words sounded ominous.

"Yes, Your Honor." Craig as foreman, answered, in a clear voice. He stopped.

Now that we were certain we were going to hear what we could scarcely wait to hear a minute ago, we could almost wish to postpone it. Would that verdict be the means of hurling Tom Brainen into the other world by way of the electric chair? It seemed as if there was nothing else to expect.

I think the judge was giving Tom Brainen a chance to get a grip on his reserve strength, for he had seen him falter slightly at the answer of Kennedy. He was so slow asking what that verdict was. He even looked the jurors over calmly. I wonder if those solemn-faced men, judges of courts that determine the life of man or woman, are ever tempted to indulge in a wager with themselves? Do they try to outguess the outcome before they ask?

"What is the verdict?" If the idea a moment ago had been ominous to me, this was a death knell, I felt, to one man's hope.

"Not guilty!"

Could I believe my ears? Had I heard correctly? Where under the heavens did they hear any evidence that could lead them to that decision?

"Well, I'll be damned!" came from the flabbergasted McCarthy.

The face of the accused man lighted with hope. But he looked about him as if to ascertain whether the other people had heard the same as he. He was leaning forward in his seat, mouth agape, as if to drink in for his famished soul the next words of Kennedy, for he was plainly about to speak again.

I could not help but admire Kennedy in his new role. He, too, had the sense of dramatic values. He was doling out his words slowly and carefully. It seemed as if that crowded court room might be the harp of life and Kennedy was touching each string slowly, lightly, to get the most expression.

"And, Your Honor, this jury charges the witness on the stand, Doctor Norton, with perjury!"

There was consternation in the room. Mrs. Norton was screaming with anger. Doctor Norton had all but collapsed in his chair, and Alma LaSalle was trying to help them both. Tom Brainen, I think, was the coolest man in the court. He seemed to take good news and bad news with equal self-control.

"Doctor Norton's eyesight must have failed him, without a doubt, just before the murder. Few know it even yet. That carefully framed, plausible alibi he gave, of being in the observatory, is no good. He couldn't have drawn a map if he wanted to. Those drawnings of the mountains of the moon were done by the borrowed eyes of his star student, a girl so engrossed in her work, her hobby, she would likely never have noticed the absence of the professor from the observatory for an hour or even more that night."

Kennedy paused. No one, not even the judge, interrupted as he resumed. "With failing eyesight, it was more than ever necessary that his wife inherit that fortune as in the original

will. He needed it to live. Possession of poison was not proved
on Brainen. Yet Brainen must be convicted, to save himself I
Draw your own conclusions as to motive. Members of this jury
have asked me to move for the indictment of Doctor Norton
for the murder of Susanna Crowe!"

"But this court cannot indict. A grand jury must do that."

"I quite understand that. Your Honor. I so told my fellow
jurymen. But we can present the facts before you."

A moment the judge considered what Kennedy had said.
Then he turned suddenly toward Norton. "I hold you, Norton,
for the grand jury!" he said, quickly.

An officer stepped over as Norton stared about, with all but
sightless eyes, eyes that saw the electrodes fastened to his head
and legs in the electric chair.

Together Kennedy and I were leaving the Criminal Courts
Building down the long wide flight of steps under the pillars
to Centre Street. I was still keyed up with the drama I had just
witnessed.

"Tell me, Craig, how did you get it? That was terrific, that
scene in the court. I must go down to the *Star*, see that it is
written right."

Kennedy smiled. "That map as passed elaborately to the jury
bore the initials and lettering of Alma LaSalle. It wasn't *his* map.
It was on a special drawing paper with the embossed stamp of
the manufacturer. You all have eyes. But only one in a thousand
really sees. You're not looking with your eyes. You assumed he
could see, because you could see. But that man was blind, nearly
blind. He was as a blind man reading Braille when he fingered
so carefully that drawing paper for the embossed marks. Besides,
when he entered court each day he was almost the only man
who never carried a newspaper. I knew then it was an alibi, that
carefully framed story of being in the observatory that night.
That was enough. One thing led to another. Look back at it. You
will see his attitude under all. He must convict Brainen, to save
himself and get the fortune for his wife. My first hint came when
he testified he saw—and he could not see! The rest was easy."

TASTE

"**EVEN THE MURDER** of Marguerite Moller was aesthetic. Everything but her actual dying was aesthetic."

Doctor Seaman, from the homicide bureau of the office of the district attorney in New York, was like a demon of discord in our own aesthetic surroundings. Kennedy and I were on the colonnade of a pink stucco bungalow in the island of Nassau, rented for a month along with a quiet, efficient Chinese servant, Chan.

About us were vines and brilliant flowers, and, as if nature wanted to humor us still more, the sunset cast a rosy glow of beauty about us. In the Bahamas life is worth the living. There was a sensuous tranquillity. How could one be morbid with the colors of energy, hopefulness, and life enveloping and inspiring one? Yet here was Doctor Seaman, to my mind the foremost specialist in the grewsome in America.

I was toying with a bell on the table near my wicker chair. Inadvertently—at least I thought so—I tinkled it. A moment and Chan padded in. There was ice tinkling musically in a bowl, fresh limes in another azure bowl, and something in a bottle.

Never a word had been said. The laugh was on me. I disclaimed it vainly.

"He saw the desire in thine eyes, Walter," chuckled Craig.

"Well, it might have been there. I was thinking a little cheer might make the doctor forget his mission and spare us."

"I wish I could. But I can't. There is only one man I know to whom to go for help, and, by a fortunate chance, he is on the island." Doctor Seaman bowed toward Kennedy. His face was earnest and troubled. "My reputation depends on this case."

Perhaps it stirred a qualm of conscience within Kennedy. As for me, I was annoyed. I had come on this trip not only for a change, but for a story. Kennedy had perfected an improvement on an electro-magnetic gun, a flashless, smokeless, noiseless gun that would rain steel bullets out so fast that it was as if a knife were cutting through the air. He had set the thing up on a bluff on this opposite side of the island from the great New Colonial Hotel and here we were operating now and then on some luxuriant semi-tropical foliage, testing the device out.

"Fortified with this, we might hear you out, Doctor," suggested Kennedy, shaking his glass enough to elicit music from the ice. "How did the little actress die?"

"Poisoned!"

"What?" I exclaimed.

Kennedy turned to me. "Did you know her, Walter?"

"I certainly did—a wonderful woman. She's the one gave me that famous interview, 'Marriage Clips the Wings.' Oh, it was a shame that girl ever married. She had Bernhardt's voice and sense of pathos, the living, exultant spirit of youth and grace of gesture of Duse. When she married Walton Wright the stage lost a shining star—a real jewel."

"It was for her jewels," interrupted Doctor Seaman, quietly, "that she was murdered."

"Her collection of diamonds?" I inquired, quickly.

"Exactly. They have been stolen—all gone except those with flaws."

"I have seen them. There was a fortune in that collection. Most of them came from South Africa. In the old days, to know Moller one had to bestow a diamond, at least. There were many rivals—and many diamonds. Every admirer tried to excel the others. Hence the collection."

"How do you know so much, Walter? Did you contribute?" asked Kennedy.

"Do cub reporters buy diamonds?" I paused a moment. "She liked publicity. I could have been her press agent. Only I prefer traveling with you, Craig." I knew that would get him.

"What became of her husband?" asked Kennedy, with a smile.

I knew what prompted that question. He might be a suspect. "She divorced him. Wright was a steel millionaire. He has married since, a nice little woman who could never emote in the least—and I doubt if she'd be able to tell a brilliant from a real sparkler."

"Was he jealous of his first wife? I mean, did he ever try to see her afterward?"

"Yes. Moller wasn't up-to-date; she was ahead of it," cut in Doctor Seaman. "What was a husband, more or less, if she might add to her collection and indulge her whims?"

"But, Craig, Moller was a genius," I remonstrated. "Brains, beauty and beaux—she had them all. And she used them all to the limit. She could paint, she could sing, she could act."

Again Doctor Seaman interrupted. "I've been over her papers. She had a most unusual intellect for a woman. Also she indulged in many fads. I couldn't begin to explain some of them logically, because I have never happened to get that way, myself. She went in for aestheticism with a vengeance. She looked on life as rhythm, harmony, was always trying to get attune with nature, and all that. It is for us ordinary folks to understand it in music and color. But she lived it. All her activities must co-ordinate with her acute sense of harmony. There was rhythm in her food, in the very taste of things. Nothing must jar about her. She seemed to glide through life as easily, as beautifully, as that cloud touched by gold in the sea of lavender lights above us."

Kennedy looked at Doctor Seaman quizzically. "Whence the inspiration. Doctor? From Moller, or the Bahama sunset—or the glass?"

Doctor Seaman merely smiled.

"Moller was an inspiration to many." I was ready to rise in her defense. "She was an art patron, as well as a *bonne vivante*. We shouldn't speak of her lightly. She has done much in the world besides collecting the most perfect diamonds."

"Was she beautiful?" inquired Craig.

"Here's her picture." Doctor Seaman took a photograph from his pocket. "A very recent photograph, I believe. Time could not dull that beauty."

Moller was truly wonderful in that tinted portrait. Great blue eyes looked out at one, searching, it seemed, after we had heard her attributes, for the beauty, the joys of this world, not seeing the dross, the crude, the ugly. Golden-brown locks that seemed wind-stirred even in the inanimate picture crowned a face of perfect contour, oval, but with a well-chiseled chin. Her lips appeared tremulous with emotion, as if, having found the beauty, her soul was ready to acclaim it with her sweet voice. A slender, swan-like throat that curved to her slim, fair shoulders with the lines to stir the heart of an artist, she was grace and beauty, harmony itself.

"You say the woman was poisoned?" asked Craig.

"All the evidences of it," returned Doctor Seaman.

"What poison was used?" pursued Kennedy.

"Strychnine. We know that."

Kennedy leaned back, silent for a few moments. "You say it was strychnine—and she was an epicurean. That's strange. There is nothing denoting exquisite taste in strychnine. Why, Doctor, you know that drug is intensely bitter—one of the most bitter known to science. Even an ordinarily intelligent woman would refuse food or drink with strychnine in it, for the bitterness alone. This bitterness is so marked that one part of it gives a decided taste in as much as seventy thousand parts of water. It is a bitterness that is very persistent, too, clinging tenaciously to the tongue, and is removed only with difficulty. Are you sure it was strychnine?" Kennedy asked it incredulously.

"Positive, from its reactions on the body. Some people in death assume an aspect of placidity when suffering has ceased, but beautiful Marguerite Moller was terrible to look at. The muscles of her limbs had taken on an extreme rigidity. Neither her arms nor her legs could be bent back to a proper position for dressing for burial. Her eyes were open, staring, the pupils widely dilated. She had died alone—no hand even to wipe the foam from her lips. Her beautiful face was distorted in agony and her mouth was twisted into a ghastly, grinning expression."

Kennedy raised an admonishing hand. "Those are the symptoms, undoubtedly. But how distressing to introduce them here. Seaman, I'm resting. This case would appeal to me if I were in the States. But why chase me here? I don't believe I'll take it up." It was said with an alarming sound of finality of decision in his voice.

But I was interested, twofold. I knew the lovely woman— and what a story must be back of it. Then, too, Doctor Seaman seemed to want to confide in me. I was not at all flattered into imagining he thought me a great detective or scientist. I knew why. Holding on to me, he might get Kennedy's help in the end. But I was curious, and asked, "Just how was the poison given?"

"That is the queer part of it. In spite of its bitterness, it was taken as a drink—in a highball. On a stand beside an easy chair were all the makings—two glasses, the decanter, and the siphon of vichy. Both glasses were empty, except the dregs. These we examined. One was all right. The other still contained a trace of the poison. The whisky in the decanter was pure, too. Someone slipped the poison into her glass."

Kennedy was lying out straight now, eyes closed, apparently unaware of our conversation.

"It's quite self-evident," I considered, "that the person who took the diamonds poisoned the drink. But it must have been some one with whom she was extremely friendly in order to inveigle her in such a manner in her own beautiful home. It was her boast that only congenial, harmonious people entered her abode. She felt discordant natures and refused such friendships. Something unusual and unexpected must have happened."

"Something very unusual did take place," replied Seaman,

with an evident avidity to talk. "Many people laughed at Moller and her theories, but at least she had ideas. Her head was no vacuum. On a long table in the same room where we found her lying dead were several rows of tiny glasses. Each glass was about the size of a cordial glass. And all were numbered. In each was some liquid. On the table were countless notes concerning the exhibit. After repeated tests we found out that all the contents of the glasses were harmless. It had been an experiment she had been carrying on with some intimate concerning the harmony of tastes. The first glass was of an extremely sour liquid and all the other glasses were slightly less sour in rotation until they actually became sweet to the taste. To be able to appreciate those gradations one must have an acute sense of taste. Evidently Moller and her friend had. Their notes showed they were working together to find a 'nectar fit for the gods.'"

Doctor Seaman seemed to be regarding the warble of a bird in a tree. "They reasoned out the idea in the same way as the chromatic scale in music. The union of perfectly adjusted tones makes harmony in music. The union of perfectly adjusted liquids would produce a harmony in taste—a delightful drink. And on that idea Moller had been working."

"There is something in that, I think," Kennedy interrupted, unexpectedly. "The blending of colors makes a delightful harmonious unity, just as the blending of notes makes a harmonious, sweet chord."

It was a new idea to me. But I had to admit that it sounded reasonable, to a certain extent. Then I wondered if in some way these liquids might have caused her death. But no. Doctor Seaman had already told us positively that they had all been tested and found innocuous. Somehow I couldn't remove the idea from my head that a combination of them might have produced the unexpected results. I made the point. The categorical answer was that there had been a theft—and there was strychnine in the glass. That was the poisoning. My theory was out.

"Who found her?" I questioned next.

"Her maid. We have held her as a witness. She said that the night her mistress was poisoned was her night off. She left in the early afternoon and at that time Marguerite Moller was alone and well. When she came back the next morning to resume her duties she opened the door as usual. She was astonished to see the lights still on in many of the rooms. All the shades had been drawn. When she came to Moller's little informal studio, she was shocked to find her mistress lying on the floor—dead.

"She called to her—and when she did not receive an answer she lost her head completely and ran screaming from the room for help. That inadvertently helped us. There was no mixing up of things and disturbing positive clues. The manager of the apartment, knowing of the valuable collection of diamonds that belonged to the actress, took charge, allowed admittance to no one but the police and the doctor."

"Were there any recent scandals in Moller's life that the police have unearthed, still unknown to the public?" I asked.

"No. Moller seemed to be behaving herself. She had friends, purely platonic, I believe. Anyone with the charm and beauty of that woman could have hosts of companions, if she so desired. In fact, the maid insists that except for her peculiar passionate love for her diamonds which she weighed and studied and gloated over for hours at a time, her heart seemed to have cooled to mere man. She spent her time with her music, her art, her treasures, and her theories. She lived a peculiar life and died a more peculiar death."

"Well, have you any idea about these purely platonic friends? It seems to me that if it weren't love they were after in the case of such a beautiful woman, it might be the treasure. Almost everybody is after something these days," I added, with a touch of cynicism.

"We have looked up those who seemed most intimate. It was the maid who helped us out so splendidly there. She had met many of Moller's friends. One man in particular her mistress seemed to fancy. She appreciated his talents, unusual talents."

"Who was that?"

"Oh, he called himself Alfred Raver. But if the man contemplated doing such a thing as this crime, you can rest assured that Alfred Raver is a simple alias. You see, the reason why the maid told especially of him was that so many of his hobbies and theories coincided with those of the murdered woman. He, too, was aesthetic in his likes and dislikes."

"How did she meet him?" I asked. "How did you find out?"

Kennedy laughed quietly in his silence, at my insatiable curiosity. In spite of my admiration and love for Kennedy, his gentle way of poking fun at me always provoked me. I couldn't help it. I felt hot and uncomfortable about the ears.

"Just for that, Craig," I exclaimed, "since you have turned down Doctor Seaman, I'm going to stick along with him on this case. Those who laugh last laugh best. I'm determined to see him through this."

Dr. Seaman seemed to take it as a cue to keep on talking about the case to me—at Kennedy.

"As to your question, Jameson," he remarked, unperturbed, "from what I can gather, Alfred Raver was a society bootlegger. He qualified in all aspects for such a job. He was suave, handsome, secretive, with abundant intelligence and resourcefulness. He never disappointed a customer. But he was clever. Information about him is almost as hazy as some character in ancient history. I have been able to deduce his qualities only from the mass of hearsay evidence! nothing about his friends and manner of living. He was more than a bootlegger. His taste was remarkable. No vintage fooled him. Good 'old' Scotch fabricated synthetically on the high seas was never found in any of his consignments to wealthy patrons. In fact, his taste sounds like a fable or a fairy tale."

Kennedy moved restlessly on his wicker *chaise longue*. I knew he was interested in spite of himself.

"And to clinch matters, so far as suspicion has fastened on

this Alfred Raver, the maid informs us that he was to call on Marguerite Moller that night," Doctor Seaman added.

"Well, Doctor, if you had a suspicion as healthy as that, why didn't you send for me, instead of coming all the way to the Bahamas after me? Much can happen back there in New York while you are away." Kennedy suddenly sat up and questioned.

"From information—maybe you would call it rather hazy—gleaned from some of Raver's wealthy patrons along the boot-legging line who would talk, it is suspected he had come down here to winter under cover, perhaps on a boat in some of these coves and bays in the Bahamas. So, you see, Kennedy, the chased and the chaser have sought you out in your retreat. It looks very much as if you were predestined to help us in this emergency."

"Are there other suspects?" I asked.

"Several friends. But they don't qualify like Raver. You see none but an eccentric genius could have committed this murder The murderer must have had certain talents, and none of the other suspects possess them. Moller would never have given them the chance. Raver had a peculiar bent toward art, drama, poetry, and music. It was easy for such a man to ingrati-ate himself with such a woman. The acquaintance was formed because of his skill in providing the requisite stimulants to her exclusive palate. What more natural than to drift from a discus-sion of such a sensitized taste to Moller's theory of harmony in all existing things? Finding that much in common, it must have been easy for kindred spirits to commune."

"What sort of looking chap is he?"

"Handsome, they say. He possesses a magnetic personality, I believe, has an uncanny attraction for and toward the ladies. If we only had it, many ladies' names might be found on his list of wet patrons. Only for his superlative charms, Marguerite Moller would never have fallen for him to the extent of showing him her valuable diamonds, or at least giving him some inkling where she concealed them and providing him with an opportunity to do away with her."

"I suppose," I suggested, "while he is hiding down here, he will be trying to locate some more of his stock in trade for the people back in the States? You might be able to get him that way." I put this suggestion timidly to Dr. Seaman. For once Kennedy was quiet.

"If Alfred Raver is the man we really think he is, he has used many an alias in his lifetime. Some things we do know of his record. He has been a tea-taster, a famous one. In pre-prohibition times he was a wine salesman. He is known as a gambler. As nearly as I can estimate him, his life has been such that to safeguard himself, he has depended on senses that are keen and keyed up. He is an erratic, an erotic adventurer in all that is at once artistic and sensuous." The doctor turned toward Kennedy as if that picture at least ought to be a last appeal to his interest.

Puffing lazily at his pipe, Kennedy explained his seeming lack of interest in taking up such an extraordinary case. "You know, Doctor, I had this chance to come down here and be quiet for a month. But it was for something more than rest that I came. Otherwise I might occasionally be celebrating freedom over at the New Colonial across the island. We are quiet in this little cove, and I have a splendid chance to work here unobserved."

"What are you doing down here, then, may I ask?" inquired Doctor Seaman, rather surprised. "I thought there was only one reason why people from the States visited Nassau."

Kennedy shifted his pipe. "I have an electro-magnetic gun, not exactly an invention of my own; but I am perfecting it. It pours out steel bullets like a sheet of steel disk, as it revolves through any arc you set. It is mighty interesting, and entirely different. That is why I am enjoying it here. Walter and I are mighty happy, with the resting at night, golfing and sailing in the daytime, when we're not at work. I want to finish my work before I go back. And if I let any other work interfere, my reason for coming down here will be nullified."

As I listened. I refrained from saying that Kennedy really was not interested in anything particularly except that gun. As to golfing and sailing, I might have added that I was the one who indulged alone in these diversions. Still, I decided that the time on my hands that Kennedy did not require my help I would turn over to Doctor Seaman. I really meant to take up the case seriously, as an experiment.

"Have you any other clues, Doctor, besides those you have told us about?" I asked, eager to get down to work on the case.

"I have several things—photographs of the room as the body was lying when it was found, the box of candy I found near the glasses, and the decanter." Doctor Seaman was opening a small package he had laid on a chair with his hat when he entered.

Once again Kennedy showed animation. "What kind of candies?"

Doctor Seaman displayed a temptingly arranged box of chocolates and bonbons from the top layer of which only five or six had been taken. "We tested two pieces. They were all right. One a dog ate. The guinea pigs finished the other—and all are still living."

Kennedy picked out a chocolate and smelled it carefully. "Doesn't smell wrong." Gingerly he tasted a bit. Then he moved his tongue and lips as he tasted. "No strychnine in this. I would have detected it. The candies seem to be all right."

For a moment he thought, leaning over to the stand by his side and sipping his drink contemplatively. It seemed to give him an idea. "Summon Chan, Walter."

The Chinaman glided in. "Bring me that bottle of extra-fine Scotch that was sent to me this morning." Chan bowed his way out.

As we waited, Kennedy broke off small bits of the chocolate and insisted on the Doctor and myself tasting them.

"Craig, I could wait just as well, and buy a box for myself. I would feel more comfortable."

But he insisted, and when Craig, usually so polite and thoughtful of other people's feelings, insisted again, I partook. He must be convinced that the candy was safe or he would not have had us taste even a small bit of it. He must have a reason. For the life of me I could not figure it out. But to show my good will I bit into the little piece. It was sweet, not as sweet, however, as some I have eaten.

Chan entered with a tray. "Walter," remarked Kennedy as Chan set it down before him, "this Scotch was given to me by the governor to-day. It is special, old, has come out of private stock. No chance for tampering with labels, cutting, faking age."

I was anticipating it with pleasure and no anxiety. No beautiful lady had just died after drinking that. Glasses were brought, the charged water and ice. Kennedy measured and mixed and passed to us. When he had served himself we raised our glasses silently to one of those toasts that may mean anything under the sun, and took a drink.

I was heartily disappointed. Of all the tasteless, inane, spiritless highballs, that one took the prize. This was nothing but alcoholic; and alcohol is tasteless to me, has none of the refinement of its many popular potable forms.

I looked at Doctor Seaman. Well-bred boredom and mild surprise shone in his face, but he was too polite to say anything. I was not.

Kennedy leaned back, the picture of a satisfied host, an inquiring smile playing about his lips.

"What are you trying to put over on us, Craig?" I demanded. "Get out your best. We're ready for it after that."

"How? What?" he exclaimed, rising. "What's the matter with you, Walter? Something doesn't suit you, perhaps?"

"Well, if you don't know, you have been stung. A joke has been put across on you. There is no taste to that stuff."

"How is it with you, Doctor?" He turned.

"I am afraid I shall have to agree with Jameson's statement," he added, with a touch of droll humor.

I was completely floored when I saw Kennedy slap his knee with satisfaction, turn again to us with a beaming countenance.

"I've got it—at least a part of it. I know how it was done. Some clever personage, that poisoner of yours!"

Naturally enough, now we were excited, too. Gone was my disappointment over Kennedy's refreshments. I wanted to know what he had been up to.

"Give me another of those candies, Doctor. I'll analyze it, prove to you that it has gymnema in it." By this time Kennedy was helping himself to a fat one.

"Gymnema!" Doctor Seaman said it in an uncertain voice. "I never thought of that."

"Gymnema!" I repeated. "What's that?"

"Gymnema sylvestre, a drug derived from the leaves of a plant found in India. It is non-poisonous, but destroys taste. The poisoner knew strychnine was quick and efficient—but bitter. Moller would detect it in her drink. Circumvent that by chocolates touched off with gymnema sylvestre. She would taste no bitterness, have no suspicion."

When Doctor Seaman rose to leave us that night a full moon was rivaling in beauty the glowing sunset of the earlier evening. Across the water, as I stood by the balustrade, was a shifting iridescent path of light. That beaming path was a call to me from beauty. All about us the stucco houses and buildings seen through the strange foliage had a silvery whiteness that was entrancing. Shadows only accentuate beauty.

"Craig, I don't feel like going to sleep. I'm off for a stroll with the doctor. Come along." It was asked dubiously. I felt sure of a negative answer, and I was not disappointed.

"Not to-night, Walter, I want to get up early in the morning. Just a little more to do on that gun."

"Well, I'm going with Doctor Seaman." Our visitor seemed delighted that I took a little interest, though I knew he was troubled over Kennedy's indifference. "Come, Doctor, let us stroll along the waterfront. Maybe if we try hard enough we can look something like a pair of thirsty pirates from Rum Row, make a deal to go into the business, or something. We might hear something of this Alfred Raver, whatever his new alias may be. Anyhow, that old moon seems to call me."

How can I describe those roads, those sights? There is nothing in all the world quite like Nassau with its gumbo-limbo trees and its grotesque silk-cottons. No other sands seem so golden in the daytime, so silvery in the moonlight. No other air seems so pure, so fresh, virginal, untainted by human breath.

The only real rivals of the sunset are the flowers, was thinking, as I poked along the road and noticed a poinsettia tree, small but full of blossoms brightening its gray boughs, how futile, yet still beautiful, are the tiny homesick plants one sees in the florists' up north. There was a witchery about the place.

As we strolled on to that part of Nassau where gossip of visiting yachts could be heard from garrulous colored natives, I wondered at the many beautiful boats. It truly is a yachtsman's paradise in the Bahamas, and Nassau is the favorite resort.

Since my stay there, I had made friends with an old colored man, Joel Doxsee, whose wife bore the euphonious name of Dixey Doxsee, having come herself from Virginia. Joel's business in life was doing odd jobs for all the visitors who happened ashore from the yachts. He knew where the fishing was, where the fishing supplies could be got, knew practically the entire activities of the waterside.

I had told Doctor Seaman of him and, late as it was, decided to look him up. He had told me where his small thatched cabin was located, and we wandered in that direction.

It proved to be a tumble-down and decrepit cabin, but there was a suggestion of romance about it and its surroundings. Banana trees and cocoanut trees sheltered it and the bougainvillea shed purple rain on the walls upon which it had clung so long.

As we neared it, the weak but sweet toned voice of the old man was singing a queer, monotonous dirge—something that had been handed down from the past by his parents. It was a touch of Africa in the Bahamas. His parents had been slaves left at Nassau as unprofitable freight while our Civil War was being fought. Some of the older negroes had learned and remembered snatches of their mother tongue—but most was forgotten. We stood and listened, captivated by the moonlight, the melody, and the man.

"Ah!" murmured Doctor Seaman. "There is harmony!"

When the last note died away I called, softly, "Joel!"

"Yes, sir!"

"I just dropped over to have a talk with you."

"Very good, sir. Glad to see you, sir, any time, sir."

Seaman had expected Southern darky dialect. He was not prepared for an almost cockney accent. A smile greeted him as my friend and we took the proffered seats, some old stenciled cases that here, too, betrayed the ruling industry of the island now.

"Why the music? Do you sing like that every night?" I asked the old darky, kindly.

"I'd be scornful to—only when I am moody for it," he answered, solemnly, sure of the sound of the words if not their precise meaning.

"You like harmony?" I pursued.

Suddenly his eyes opened wide with joy, as if the remark had recalled to him a vision he still saw, a delightful vision. His arms, brown and thin, waved with a sort of tremulous pathetic rhythm. "My music is so little. But, ah! I heard music to-day!"

"You heard music? Over at the hotel?"

A pressure of the lips, a closing of the eyes, and he shook his head. "No, sir." He opened his eyes, "On a boat, Mr. Jameson. A fiddle it was."

I looked across at Doctor Seaman curiously. On our walk down just now he had told me another fact about the man on his mind. He had come across a portfolio of music in Moller's studio, music arranged for a violin, and it was marked with the name of Alfred Raver. That chance remark by Joel was no direct evidence. Only this thing under the mystic night skies seemed more than a mere coincidence. Were we at last on the trail of our eccentric, erotic genius?

The doctor knew of what I was thinking. He was thinking of the music scroll, too. "Jameson," he remarked, aside, "that music was never played by an amateur. Only some one proficient could play it. It required technique, skill, months, years of practice."

"This man has all of that," put in Joel. Whatever those words meant, they meant melody to him, and this man had it, he knew.

"What kind of boat is he on, Joel?" I asked. "I love music, the violin, too."

"A yawl, down in the cove, not far from your place."

"So?" I wanted to question the old man, yet I did not wish to give him an inkling. "How did you meet him?"

A secretive smile was my answer—and that smile could mean only one thing—something to do with booze for the States.

"I see, Joel. You can get something else than music on board that yawl. Is that it?"

Again that smile of white ivory against black skin, no confirmation and no denial.

"What's the name of the boat, Joel?"

"The *Vagrant,* Mr. Jameson." Joel was a bit confidential. My name sounded like a familiar brand to him. "Now don't you get Mr. Greason into any trouble, sir. My tongue would stick to the roof of my mouth, sir, if you did."

"Don't worry," I reassured. "Is he alone on the boat, Joel?"

"No, another man, Mr. Norcross, his friend. I think it's he knows more about sailing, sir, than the violin. It sounds so."

I had expected, when I asked the question, that the answer would be about a girl on the boat. However, I could see that a sailing master, under the circumstances, was more essential.

Dixey came home from some racket in a cabin down the line and Joel became reticent. It was not long before the doctor and I were retracing our steps. I was insisting upon the doctor returning to our bungalow, so we could start out early in the morning on a catboat that was available to me to scrape up an acquaintance with this Greason if it were possible.

So it was that the next morning we were out early, sailing about the cove. There was just enough breeze to make sailing a dream instead of a drudgery.

It was just as Joel had informed us. There was a yawl, a beautiful boat, about eighty feet over all, white, against whose sides the morning sun glistened as the brass gleamed.

We tacked across her bow, came about. We could hear the notes of a violin, sweet, plaintive. As the player in the cabin finished we applauded. A man appeared in the cabin doorway, saw us, waved a hand good-naturedly in our direction as we edged closer, then disappeared again down the companionway.

"So that is where they are, Doctor!" I remarked, with suppressed excitement, as we wore away. "Did you see that little motor tender, almost a cedar speed boat, off the davits, out on the end of a boat boom? It looked to me as if they were about to go ashore for supplies or something. Let's get back to the docks."

My surmise was right, but they must have taken their time, as we were not only in our slower cat back at the public docks, but had been hanging around an hour, it seemed, when we saw the tender of the *Vagrant* coming up to the landing stage.

Greason looked at us and smiled as he caught sight of us at the top of the runway. I casually returned the greeting. I knew that on boats it is easy to make acquaintances. Ordinarily I would have thought nothing of it. But just now I was delighted. I wanted to talk to Greason.

Greason was a blond, rather handsome, with a certain charming ruthlessness often mistaken for manhood. I liked his chuckle. It was boyish. A flapper would have called him adorable, simply for his shoulders, his narrow hips, those laughing blue eyes, and that chuckle. In the old days he might have been a swashbuckling knight. Now it was hard to tell. It was up to me to find out.

I was elated at the way things were going my way. For once I was going out over my depth alone in the realm of detection, without the assistance of Kennedy. And I seemed to be succeeding. I was rather ashamed of my elation, but I couldn't help it. Kennedy had guyed me so often that I had made up my mind to show him, just once. Kennedy wasn't interested in a thing except that confounded gun. Well, I wouldn't tell him of my discovery until I had everything clinched.

Greason was the sort of person known as a good mixer. He had that easy way with him, an ability to make you think for the time being that you are the most interesting person in the world to him. He was a subtle flatterer, it is true, but most of us like it. All one had to do was to observe the readiness of laborers and visitors alike on the docks to speak to him, help him.

"Where are you chaps staying?" he asked, in his hearty, breezy way, when I had engineered ourselves alone together. "Over at the New Colonial?"

"No; we have a bungalow for a month. Are you living on your boat?"

"This time. I don't always. We're very comfortable. I have a friend with me who likes it. He doesn't care for hotels and excitement much." He smiled his fascinating smile. "I like a little life."

"Well, I have a friend up at the bungalow, the same way." We had been talking long enough to become confidential. "It's pretty quiet. I wish you could manage to come up and take dinner with us. I'm spoiling for a regular party."

"Glad to. Thanks." There was no visible evidence of suspicion yet. I was watching carefully for that.

"Can't you bring your violin?"

"We'll see. Where are you?"

"It's up there." I pointed out the place along the shore. "Let's make it for to-night."

"All right. I'll be up."

He was off, claimed by others. His popularity was a certainty about here. I wondered why. Then I began taking myself to task. I had nothing on this man. He might be just a handsome, debonaire man of the world, an accomplished violinist. Probably there were many more also who could play a violin in Nassau. Just because some violin music was found in Moller's studio and Alfred Raver could play did not make Greason a poisoner, even though Raver was known to be hiding here under another alias.

I determined to make an exhaustive inquiry. Before the doctor and I rejoined Kennedy we had as complete a picture of the man as is possible of a stranger in a strange country. Everywhere it was the same. The man was liked. Apparently he was well known. People spoke of him as a frequent visitor. He seemed wealthy, able to indulge in all the pleasant things of life. He tipped royally. Through it all I obtained a glimpse of the man's unusual qualities. Some spoke of the delightful dinners, the exquisite cuisine, on the *Vagrant*. There were suggestions of art, of talent with colors. There seemed an endless variety in this man's interests. The more I inquired the more convincing became the impression that we were at last on the right trail.

"It might be well for us to get back, prepare Kennedy, give Chan a chance," suggested Doctor Seaman.

I realized the good sense in his suggestion, and we turned toward the bungalow, pausing only at the shops, loading ourselves with treasures for the kitchen. I think we had more delicacies in our arms than Craig and I had indulged in during the entire visit.

"What's the idea?" demanded Kennedy, in mild surprise.

"Just this, Craig. I'm not sure, but I think I'm on the way toward catching that exotic genius!"

Kennedy looked toward Doctor Seaman for confirmation.

"I believe Greason is the man. You should hear the gossip about him. People have heard wonderful music coming from the yawl. We heard it. He is handsome, attractive. His dinners and parties are famous and he is spoken of as an art patron, too." Doctor Seaman was an able defender of my enthusiasm.

"What are you going to do about it?" Kennedy asked it with a certain gleam of interest.

Chan had caught sight of the delicacies. The prospect of an elaborate dinner filled his soul with delight. He was smiling ecstatically. Some cooks are so proud of their skill that nothing pleases them more than the opportunity to show it off.

"I've invited him up to dinner."

"Some fast worker, Walter! Hear of the crime one night—and catch the criminal the next. I have a rival. How are you going to crash him?"

"I thought that would come to me during the dinner to-night. I want you to look him over, Craig, see if you don't agree with me—and help me take him in."

Kennedy's face lighted with the joy of battle, the war of wits. "Good!" he exclaimed. "We'll trap him!"

I was wondering whether there was subtle sarcasm in that, when Dr. Seaman interrupted. "How did the gun come along to-day? Make any headway?"

"I think I overcame the trouble this morning. A little more work on it this afternoon and I'll have it for the finishing touches to-morrow. I'll feel more like taking an interest in this case when that gun is off my mind."

I really felt Kennedy meant it. I was more relieved at Kennedy's remark about trapping Greason at dinner, if he meant it. It sounded easy—but how was it to be done? No one realized it better than I. I had gone so far, but it was about as far as I felt competent to go. I couldn't just ask Greason, "Are you guilty? Say yes!"

During the rest of the afternoon I was as busy over my dinner as a bride at the first dinner party for the in-law family after the honeymoon. I wanted the choicest food, the best wine. I wanted the table just right. If there was to be a proper denouement for my esthetic poisoner, I wanted it at an aesthetic meal in an aesthetic environment.

I really didn't know I was so accomplished in planning a meal, and I surprised Craig into grunts of amusement as he sauntered in at last, greasy and dirty from his work. I was arranging flowers for the table, with the able assistance of Doctor Seaman. Hands that could perform an autopsy actually seemed palsied into awkwardness when they came in contact with flower stems.

I confined my attention to the table. I am afraid that if we had interfered with Chan's part of the work the dinner would have been a failure. We let the kitchen alone.

Finally things were arranged to suit me. I had poked around in the pantry for the choicest china the little place afforded— some Scandinavian pottery with its bold and brilliant decorations in violets, reds, and greens. I ignored Chan's objections. He was evidently thinking of the owner's interests. I insisted on its use. A colored glass set almost the equal in beauty of color to any glass turned out by the Venetian glass blowers of old, purple as the tints of the skies at home in the autumn, were in harmony with the flowers of the china. Perfect clusters of purple grapes openly flirting with yellow tints of bananas against which they rested delighted the eye. Even Kennedy bestowed an honest compliment on our efforts. We had everything ready, waiting for the guest and the hoped-for exposé.

Out on the colonnade we waited. That dinner might be delicious, the decorations harmonious, but I was atingle with excitement. Not every day did I have the chance to bag a poisoner through my own efforts. I was keen to show off before Craig.

Suddenly Chan announced the arrival of Greason.

It was no effort at all to entertain Greason. His travels about the casinos and sporting resorts of the Continent had given him a fund of anecdotes that would interest any group, and he told them in an inimitable manner.

As we entered the dining room, almost *al fresco*, glassed over, with vines trailing over the overhead glass, I expected to hear Greason make some remark about the artistic effects we had achieved on the room and on the table. I watched him eagerly, anticipating from his artistic reputation an expression of pleasure, some exclamation of delight. My spirits fell very low indeed when he took his place calmly, apparently oblivious to all the effects I had worked so hard to create for the benefit of his aesthetic personality. I was plainly discouraged, if not disconcerted.

But a glance at Kennedy straightened my back. If ever a man wanted to laugh at another, it was Kennedy at me. Yet there was a spirit of commiseration over my disappointment, too.

Greason's only remark relating even remotely to the appointments was, "No ladies here, to-night?" I think he was amazed at our fussing over a stag.

My most tempting viands disappeared with no more approval than any hungry man living on the water would show a well-cooked, well-balanced meal. I had hoped to make him betray his exquisite love for the beautiful—and I had failed.

I began to wonder again. Was this Greason cleverer than I suspected? Was it I who was the bonehead? Had he imagined, after entering, that things were not aboveboard, as he had thought, and was he trying to conceal and disguise his real self? He would make it seem that he knew nothing of art, that the beautiful in life had no visible effect on him. Against that smoke screen I was unprepared.

I looked desperately at Doctor Seaman. He hadn't an idea in his head to lead the conversation in the channels we desired, without betraying it flatly. I smothered my pride and looked appealing at Kennedy. Craig suppressed a smile in my direction as if he would have delighted to say: "It's your case, Walter. Handle it!" He was gaining much pleasure watching me with my recalcitrant suspect.

I breathed an inward sigh of relief at last. Craig was coming to my rescue. It was toward the end of the dinner. He had taken his glass of Rhine wine and looked at it closely, sipped it. "Do you know, Greason, no one can fool me on this. I've bought a lot of it. But I don't know how to take it back, unless I take it back inside of me."

Greason looked at him thoughtfully, said nothing, smiled.

"I have tasted wines all over the world," continued Kennedy, slowly, fishing, "and can almost recognize any vintage. It is a great gift in these days of poor wines and high prices."

"I am something of a connoisseur myself." At last Greason was biting. "Not much that has been faked gets by me. When we get back home, look me up. I was fortunate to lay in a stock before prohibition."

"It's strange, isn't it, how people are born with those various gifts?" asked Doctor Seaman. "As a doctor it has always inter- ested me. Some never forget a face. Others have exaggerated memories for musical notes. It may happen with any sense and in many occupations. Back home I have a friend who is employed by one of the largest Fifth Avenue jewelry establish- ments. For what, do you suppose? He knows diamonds! Not an imperfect stone gets by his eyes!"

I was watching Greason carefully. He was strangely silent, and at the mention of diamonds I imagined I saw the first slight nervous fluttering of the eyelids.

"Well, there are many jobs like that. Every big perfumery house employs special men with a special sense of smell." It sounded like a tame remark after I made it, when I considered how worked up I felt playing this game of cat and mouse with Greason. Yet every minute I was afraid he would turn into some- thing else than a mouse.

Greason suddenly tried to change the subject to the violin. "I hope you fellows don't think I'm sour for not bringing the fiddle over, but I didn't want to bore you."

Again we were at an impasse. I yielded to Kennedy. Kennedy was quite ready. He sought to draw him out along musical lines. He mentioned the names of the most popular composers of the day, he talked of their most recent work, criticizing and compar- ing. Only the most fragmentary remarks now were made by Greason.

I realized the task was far beyond me. It was a Kennedy- sized job. Either this man was playing a role consummately or he was a dub of the first water. The only thing he seemed willing to enthuse over was the history of the Bahamas, now. That either appealed to an immature respect and awe for pirates and buccaneers of old, or it was another game. Was he simulating a boisterous love of adventure that was entirely foreign in his cultured mind?

Disappointment and defeat met me at every turn. Here was not my erotic lover of the beautiful. Art failed to stimulate his imagination. I could not get a reaction out of him on anything. He was perfectly well-bred, but dull on everything else but what he wished to discuss. I glanced in hopeless surrender at Craig.

Craig called Chan. "Get me some tea, Chan."

There was an understanding glance between Craig and the Chinaman. Two hours before I should have been horrified if anyone had suggested serving tea to Greason at dinner that night. Now I was so disgruntled over my failure that they could have served him cyanide without causing me to raise a hand.

"I just happened to think about this tea," Craig put in casually, by way of explanation. "It is a Formosa 1492, unexcelled, makes the most wonderful brew imaginable."

Kennedy was now busy making tea. I had qualified on so many perfectly lady-like jobs that afternoon that I expected next to be asked to pour. It was my party. I had to see it through.

But Kennedy completed the job with the efficient help of Chan. All the while Kennedy was telling us interesting facts he had learned about the many varieties of teas, the Oolong from Formosa, the Orange Pekoe, Pekoe Souchong from China, the green teas from India and Ceylon, and the brick tea for the use of Tibetans.

As the cups were passed, Greason himself seemed bored. At last he looked about him and observed that all had been served.

"There are so many grades," he murmured.

He leaned over the table, took up the sugar tongs, and dropped a lump of sugar into his cup.

There was silence.

As Greason held the cup to his lips and sipped, now delight-edly, we heard the put! put! put! put! of a motor boat.

From his seat Craig could look out over the cove or bay. So could I. A tender, the tender of the *Vagrant*, was slipping away from the yawl, headed across to the other side, perhaps out of the cove.

Suddenly Kennedy looked from the boat to the man sipping his sweetened tea so comfortably. He was taking it with evident relish.

Craig rose quickly. "Walter, I must stop that tender. It is getting away, to the other side."

Greason started to rise, but sank back in his chair. Kennedy had absently, methodically taken a small automatic from his side pocket.

"Come with us—go ahead!"

Kennedy hurried us up to the bluff where the gun had been set. Quickly he manipulated it. A moment and the long-arm steel knife of shot rained out over the water The man in the tender put on more speed. The rain of shot just followed him, circled, fell directly ahead. He stopped, shut off his engine. The hint was plain.

"Doctor, take charge of this gun. Let the man see you. That is all that is necessary. He won't start that engine till we get to him. Now for your boat, Walter."

Kennedy, with his gat in his pocket, made Greason walk down the bluff ahead to my cat, get in, seat himself forward.

A sullen, handsome, dark-haired man glared and swore at us from the tender, but he, too, was covered by Kennedy. I saw in the tender, hastily thrown, a violin in its case, music, magazines, some books, too, to while away quiet hours when the get-away was accomplished and the hiding was good. I wondered what Greason was thinking. He looked so sour and quiet. Were both of them waiting for a chance to tumble out and escape? We were watching them too closely as we turned back toward the yawl.

"I'm going to look through the *Vagrant*, Walter. Keep them covered."

In the main cabin he started in. Set in the woodwork was a chronometer. It was not long before Kennedy paused before it. Then I noticed what had caught his eye. The "XII" was not precisely at the top. He reached up, turned it to its proper vertical position. The chronometer screwed into the wood work. Counterclockwise Kennedy continued turning it thoughtfully. It came out.

Back of the chronometer was an empty space, a veritable hidden wall safe built in the mahogany.

Craig wheeled. He looked again from the empty wall safe toward Norcross. Then he stepped over quickly, felt Norcross, patting him over swiftly as one who sought something on the hip.

About his waist he found a lump. He reached in, pulled out a small chamois bag. By now my eyes were bulging, what with watching Craig and covering these two. Would Craig never open it? He was so deliberate. I could not wait.

Slowly Craig opened the bag on the table in the cabin. There were the diamonds of the dead actress, the amazing Moller!

"Norcross, I want you," repeated Kennedy. "I want you. You're the erratic genius we're looking for, the connoisseur of diamonds and, no doubt, of tea. I don't care for your friend, Greason, here. He's no taster—just a gambler, your stall, your foil. He puts sugar in his tea!"

TOUCH

"**FIND YOUR HUSBAND,** Mary? I wouldn't know where
to look."

"I know that, Walter. But I thought you might get Mr.
Kennedy interested. I need help desperately."

"So, 'Fat' Barr deserted you—ran away with another woman.
I'm so sorry to hear that. But why have you waited ten years,
Mary? He might be dead and buried by this time."

Mary Barr shook her head, did not answer immediately. Over
by the laboratory window, she was glancing anxiously at the
door, now and then, for Kennedy.

I noticed now the lines that time and many troubles had
drawn on her face. Of medium height, a trifle thin, she seemed
tired, weary of everything. Possibly her tiredness was more of
the spirit than of the body, but that made it worse. Yet she still
possessed that wonderful auburn hair. Her blue eyes had still
some of the old snap and fire in them. Her complexion was just
as milky white as ever. But there was a little droop at the corners
of the mouth. In the old days she was always smiling.

Kennedy swung breezily into the room. I saw Mary Barr brace
up. I knew she was calling on all her reserve force, smothering
pride, to meet this ordeal of baring her troubles to a stranger.

Craig stopped suddenly as he caught sight of his visitor. It
was only a moment, and the formality of introduction was over.
There stole over his face one of those slow smiles, the kind that
starts at the corners of the mouth and works up to the eyes. I

think that smile of Kennedy's might have been valuable enough to insure. It was an absolute asset in his profession. It inspired confidence, and that was the foundation of Kennedy's success.

A minute and I was starting to tell him as much of Mary's story as I knew. For I remembered her romance well. As a very young girl she had come to the *Star,* had been there when I joined the staff of reporters. Mary Baker, as she then was, had been one of the best operators in the telegraph room. During her time the favorable rating of other telegraphers in the wire room depended on their comparison with Mary Baker.

I recalled there had been some disappointment on the part of the staff of the *Star* of those days when Mary announced her forthcoming marriage to Jim Barr. Somehow we felt that, with her personality, Mary should have picked a richer plum off the matrimonial tree. But then, Barr was popular, apparently good-natured, and showed all the evidence of being head over heels in love with Mary. He was a telegrapher, too, and a mighty good one, an expert, and it was he who used to be called on to send the world series, the big football games—in fact, on any occasion where speed and accuracy and a pile of work demanded the top-notcher. Everybody knew him as "Fat" Barr, and liked him. He was a living example of the fallacy that "nobody likes a fat man." To Mary the name had been only a nickname, not an adjective.

I was in the midst of telling Craig about Mary Barr when he raised his hand. "If you don't mind, Walter, I would rather have Mrs. Barr tell her own story."

I nodded. Mary Barr fumbled with her bag for a moment, silent, as if considering just where to begin and what to tell. Then she looked up directly, frankly into Craig's eyes.

"Mr. Kennedy, if it weren't for my boy, my poor little crippled son, I wouldn't be here. 'Fat' Barr would never be disturbed for myself alone. But Buster Barr needs a father just now, if ever any boy did."

Kennedy nodded gravely. This was a case of mother need. My hopes ran high for his acceptance of Mary's case.

"It was a matter of a sudden bit of good fortune—and another woman," went on Mary, tremulously. "Jim and I always lived in a nice apartment, simple but in a good neighborhood. On the floor below us lived a couple by the name of Rice. They had no children and Frank Rice was a traveling man. You know what that meant. There was little work to do in that apartment below me. All Fanny Rice had to do was dress and make herself look pretty.

"I had a baby boy to take care of, the apartment, and meals to prepare for a man who believed in eating. I couldn't help knowing my neighbors. You don't need any introduction when there is a baby around. They speak to the baby and to you. That's how I met Fanny Rice.

"I was pleased over her interest in Buster. I didn't think about having a good-looking husband. Jim wasn't too heavy to be attractive, and he was jolly. Before I knew it Fanny Rice was up in my apartment a good deal of the time. And she didn't leave when Jim came home. Often that meant asking her to stay to dinner. I got tired of it, but Jim enjoyed her jokes and liveliness.

"Fanny was always beautifully dressed. I suppose it was a study in contrasts—hot damp curls clinging to my face and a smooth blonde marcelled wave on her. It's no wonder, I guess, he turned most of the time to Fanny. I didn't have the clothes, couldn't afford them and couldn't have worn them under the circumstances if I had had them.

"It was easy for Fanny. Jim started to stay out late nights, and then somehow Fanny's calls became less frequent. Just about this time an uncle of Jim's died and left him about fifteen thousand dollars. Then Fanny stopped calling on me and changed her tactics and went out to places with Jim openly. It was like a defiance to the world. That went on for a couple of weeks. Then they both disappeared, left New York.

"She went away a few days before Jim. But neither Frank Rice nor I have seen them since. That is, until about a month ago. I met Frank Rice. He told me he was sure they were in Texas, that he had heard of a fellow, through a friend, in some little jerkwater Texas town, known as Baiting Hollow. Fat was always talking about Texas. Got it from the movies, I guess. I thought that would be the place they'd travel to on account of Jim always wanting a ranch down there. It seems I was right."

"Where's this Frank Rice, now?" asked Kennedy.

"In New York, when he isn't on the road. He never tried to get a divorce—held off for spite. That wasn't my reason. I was thinking of my boy. If anything should ever happen to me before he grew up, the boy would have more chance if Jim had no other legal wife living."

Mary was glancing absently away. "It was an awful shock to me at first. But, like most things, time heals the wounds. You know it's the wrong one does that eats like a canker—not the wrongs that are done to one."

"You didn't try to locate Jim Barr when he first left you?" inquired Craig.

"No. I couldn't hunt him. I had to hunt work. The actual matter of living took most of my attention in those days—bread and butter, and a roof over my head and Buster's. I didn't have the money or time to hunt with, and I did have pride. If Jim could leave me for another woman—well, let him have her, I wouldn't be the one to beg him to come back.... Then, as the years went on, I wondered at my own apathy. Possibly there had been something wrong with my capacity for loving that I couldn't hold Jim. I gave him the benefit of the doubt in my argument with myself and left him alone. Before I was married I used to think what wasn't worth fighting for wasn't worth having. You see, Jim had sunk pretty low in my estimation."

Mary Barr leaned back a moment as if trying to gain strength to tell the rest, then began again. "Now I have come to my worst sorrow, Mr. Kennedy. It is over my boy. I can sink all my pride, all my self-respect, anything, if I can do him any good... A month ago he was as well as a boy could be, an active boy, intelligent.

"We just lived for each other. Of course Buster asked me where his father was, why he did not live with us. I told him the truth. Instinctively the little fellow resented his father's actions and, if that were possible, gave me more of his childish affection. Buster and I were pals.

"Then this accident occurred. Buster was out playing with some other children. An automobile, a reckless driver—that tells the story. They got him. No money. A jail sentence. But Buster hasn't walked since. There's something wrong with his spine. Another operation is necessary, one that can be performed only by the most skillful surgeons. His recovery from it is not assured, but there are hopes if he has it done that possibly in a year or so he'd be able to walk.

"Even after the operation it means that the child must be flat on his back for months. Buster is willing to do anything— the bravest little spirit in the bravest little body I ever knew." Tears were trickling down Mary's face, unashamed tears, over her boy's suffering. "But Buster has my hopefulness. It is the only thing that keeps us both going, just now. Mr. Kennedy, don't you think that boy's father should be made to help?"

"I do." Craig was emphatic. "And I'll help you find him. If you write, or if you start inquiries down in Texas through strangers, he may find out, pull up, and leave. Then you'd be no better off—worse, with the useless expense. You seem to feel that from Frank Rice you have a genuine clue?"

"Yes, I do. Frank is convinced. But he does not care."

"Could you go down to Texas with Walter and me?" asked Craig, with a slight hesitation.

"Why, yes. I could leave Buster in the hospital. I have money enough for that and to see me through the Texas trip. After that, though, I'm broke. I've had to spend so much of my savings on Buster since the accident."

Kennedy nodded, appreciating Mary's financial frankness, and I rather admired her for it.

"It was in this town of Baiting Hollow that Frank Rice last heard of Jim Barr," he repeated, thoughtfully.

"Yes; he had a ranch near it. He also heard he had taken another name, Butler, Henry Butler. When he told me about it first I thought he had got the information to fight back at Fanny. But he doesn't seem to care much about her, either, now. The only thing he said was, rather bitterly, 'Fanny broke me before she left; she'll break him!' They don't call him 'Fat' any more, I believe. He's no longer fat; just stocky. Possibly Fanny has started to worry him a little. I wasn't thinking of that so much, though, as that it might make it a bit more difficult to identify him. I'm glad you'll go with me, for if Jim has changed so, how will I hang it on him if he denies me and disowns Buster?"

Mary had a worried, apprehensive look. Kennedy just patted her arm lightly by way of encouragement. "Go home and get ready. Make the boy comfortable while you are away. I'll get the transportation and all that."

At once Kennedy and I hustled into making arrangements for this sudden trip. Between us it was easy. Buster was to stay at the hospital. And Craig was not too busy to plan a little surprise for the injured boy. He picked out a couple of armfuls of boy stories for the nurses to read to him, some joke books, some toys and puzzles suitable for a youngster who has to lie on his back all day while he is waiting for his mother to come home. It was a pleasure to select those things for Buster, pack them into the car, and drive up to the hospital with them.

It would have been hard to tell who was the happier, The boy or his mother. "Mr. Kennedy, I can't express my thanks! I wanted to do something like that, but I couldn't afford it." Mary turned her face away. It is hard to see another man, a stranger, doing for a child those thoughtful things the boy's father should have done.

As for Buster, it was difficult to describe the pleasure of the child. When one is strapped in bed, must lie on a little back that gets very tired from one's lying in the same position, the smiles are likely to be wan. Only the great luminous eyes showing the brave soul within responded. They were agleam with boyish pleasure. Over the pale white hand Mary's lay in an affectionate clasp. It was easy to see where the boy got his indomitable spirit and infinite patience. Mother and son had the same inspired features, the same hair, the same brave eyes. I made up my mind then that even if Buster received help from his father, I, for one, was going to remember that little lad who was putting up such a fight for his mother's happiness.

"Take good care of mother!"

It was said quite earnestly. In fact, his mother's welfare on this trip seemed to be his sole thought. His own loneliness was forgotten.

I often wonder why it is that such children are taken away from us, or, if they are allowed to remain, so often join the ranks of life's sufferers.

Now and then we find some human feeling in this sophisticated modern world. When I went down and told them back on the *Star* staff about Mary Barr and her boy, the *Star* agreed to finance the trip. It was an errand of mercy and a mark of respect to Mary. Her feelings were mixed over the trip. She appreciated the kindly intentions, but wouldn't take a cent herself.

"But, Walter," she exclaimed, "how good it is to know that all of the *Star* is backing Buster and me!"

As we passed the boundary of each state, she seemed elated. It meant that her trip was just that much nearer being completed.

We had found that the nearest sizable city to Baiting Hollow was Junction City. Accordingly we stopped there.

"Mary, you must stay here," decided Kennedy. "We'll get you a comfortable room in some hotel, and for the present your chief duty will be writing encouraging letters to Buster and lying low."

She understood. "I think that is a good idea, myself. If Jim

Barr saw me he would know that something was in the air. He might make a get-away."

"Yes; and he will be less likely to see you here than if you went on with us to Baiting Hollow." Kennedy stopped at Mary's serious look. "What is the matter?"

"Simply this. If I'm compelled to stay here many days, I'll have to get some work to do. I can't take any money from anyone for my maintenance—and I haven't very much myself."

Kennedy smiled indulgently at her discomfiture. "Well, Mary, if you had to get in debt to the *Star*, I'm sure they would take a note and let you renew it indefinitely until you could pay it. But I think, under the circumstances, the idea of a job is good. For a while there'll be nothing you can do but wait, and that is a mighty hard thing to do. You'd probably be less nervous working at something congenial than you'd be sitting around the hotel, wondering what in the world we are doing. I'll try to get you a temporary job somewhere as a telegraph operator before we go on to Baiting Hollow. How about that?"

Mary expressed her approval. I respected her quixotic independence. In these days such a spirit was unique.

By a fortunate chance it happened to be fair time in Junction City. The annual county fair was just about to open and we found that the local telegraph office at the railroad station was short-handed. It did not even take influence to place Mary. The district manager was only too glad to pick up an expert operator temporarily.

Accordingly we took the noon train for Baiting Hollow.

Baiting Hollow was not much of a place as to size, but the people seemed prosperous enough. Main Street could not boast of a large number of places of business, but there were enough stores and they looked prosperous. This was a money-making country. Still it was real country yet and the people were just plain folks, mostly old stock.

We sought out the only hotel the town boasted. Fortunately,

although it was small it was quite modern. The old one had been burned the year before. Kennedy and I engaged rooms.

I knew that Craig had made no definite plan of campaign. I felt that he was going to let conditions and circumstances guide him largely in this search.

It was not long before we were chatting with Peck, the clerk, an affable sort of chap with a Texas breeziness about him. Kennedy was making random inquiries, engaging Peck principally in harmless gossip concerning the region and the more important ranchers settled in it.

"Are there many cattle raisers in Baiting Hollow just now?" he asked. "I should think, with the county fair at Junction City, they would begin to come in."

"Oh, there's a lot of 'em. Some go in for hogs, others for cattle, and 'most all the ranches breed horses to some extent. We're a busy lot down here. Why, I suppose some of the men take more time off during this coming week than they do all the rest of the year. They go up to that fair every day to see what the other fellow is doing with his live stock. It's a great place to get information—and talk politics."

"And do many of them stop at the hotel?"

"Oh yes. A good many. There ought to be some of the ranchers coming in to-night with their families, or alone with their men. Most of the cattle to be exhibited have been sent to Junction City to the fair grounds already."

"Somehow I've always wanted to own a ranch," confided Kennedy. "I've read of them, and once during a college vacation I spent the summer on one. I wish I wasn't such a stranger. I might look over some of the big ones around here."

I suppressed a smile. The clerk nodded sympathetically. "Why don't you hang around here at the desk? There'll surely be some of the ranch owners here this afternoon. I'll be glad to make you acquainted. Hello, Tibbetts! Got time to meet a couple of strangers?"

The clerk was genial, and there was no doubt of his popularity among the patrons of the new hotel. A tall, lanky individual in a wide-rimmed hat, prosperous-looking, strode over with that gait acquired from constant sitting in the saddle. He shook hands heartily.

"Comin' to the fair at the Junction? I've some mighty fine cattle on show. Mustn't miss them." Tibbetts was as hearty in his words as in his handshake. He seemed interested just to talk cattle, with Kennedy ready to listen.

"Many of the folks around here exhibiting?" asked Kennedy, casually.

"Nigh all of them. But they'll have to go some, sir, to beat my white-faced beauties." Tibbetts added with pride. "They're the purtiest things you ever laid eyes on."

"I suppose this is a sort of halfway house between the ranches up country and the fair," I suggested, glancing about.

Tibbetts nodded. Kennedy seized upon my question. "Do all the men leave the ranches before the fair is over?"

The cattle man shook his head an emphatic yes. "Stranger, those men couldn't be held down this time o' year. It's almost a patriotic duty with them. All day before the stalls cocky cowboys will be showing off the good points of the cattle from their ranches. But the big day is the day after to-morrow. Then the boys have contests, mighty interesting, I should think, to you Easterners—roping cattle, riding horses, and breaking in peppy little pintos. We call it a rodeo. I don't know what you folks'd call it, but we think it's lots of fun. And how the boys enjoy it!"

"I should like to see one, and I shall. How do they train for those things, and when?" asked Kennedy, enthusiastically.

"On the ranches, and every day at their work. Our men are having a big time this afternoon getting ready for to-morrow. That's the opening. I'm on my way to get things started the first day at the fair. Such a combin' and brushin' up of ponies you never saw. And every last one of my men's tryin' to outdo the others in lookin' wild and woolly!"

"I'd like to see them. If you'd let me I would ride out," hazarded Craig.

"Would you? My folks are here at the hotel. This far. I'd kind of like to take another look at the boys myself. I'm a jealous rancher, at fair time. Dixie Ranch has had its colors up for more points than any other ranch these three years. And the boys are determined to win again. It's gointer to be hard this year. Down at Vic Lowndes's ranch they're bettin' heavy. Must have somethin' up their sleeve. Hen Butler's men are out to win, too. Oh, everybody's stirred up. More fussin' over winnin' than a hive of bees gettin' used to a new queen. Yes, sir, though the folks has got so far, I wouldn't mind takin' a look at the men getting ready for the rodeo again. I'll take you out to my ranch in my little car. She can travel."

Kennedy and I exchanged a glance at mention of Butler's name. He decided to take advantage of Tibbetts's offer. We got in the little car and Tibbetts made good. It could travel and he wasn't afraid to let it out.

"That's Lowndes's ranch," he pointed out, after riding what seemed half across a state, but in Texas was merely half across a county, "a pretty one. His father handed it down to him and I think Vic has even more cattle sense than the old man had, and he was smart enough. Lowndes is on one side of me and Butler is on the other. Both are fine, but Butler's not so old. Going strong for a youngster, though." Tibbetts laughed good-naturedly at his own humor. "Yes, sir. After we stop at Dixie I'll stop over at Butler's and see if he is home. He used to live in the East, years ago. He might like to get a little news from the East, first hand. You'll like him most everybody does. The boys on his ranch like him mighty well. They like him better than the missus," and he chuckled softly to himself.

I wondered what that chuckle might mean. Also I began to wonder whether "Fat" Barr's affinity had turned out a shrew. If so, possibly Frank Rice and Mary both had done the right thing. I thought of Mr. Kipling's lines: "Let him take her and keep her; it's hell for them both!"

Dixie Ranch was like many others, teeming with excitement, elemental. There was not much chance for culture or fine clothes, but wonderful opportunity to meet real men. With it all there was a sort of holiday feel in the air. Work had relaxed slightly— never altogether on a ranch.

Out in the yards we met many of the men. Tibbetts was a big cattle raiser, one of the largest in Texas, and employed many men. Even the ponies seemed to be on their mettle, beautiful beasts with fiery, impatient eyes, yet knowing the will of their masters. To-morrow was opening, but the big day was still to come after that at the fair. They were putting on finishing touches for that. It was a helter-skelter entertainment, almost like trying to watch all three rings in a circus. Wherever there was a man and a horse there one could see some unusual stunt, muscles of horse and rider working in perfect harmony to achieve it.

It was regretfully that I left Dixie Ranch. But there was a kick in the idea that Tibbetts put forward.

"Had enough of Dixie for one day?" he smiled. "You can come back here again. It's getting late. On the way around back to the Hollow I'd like to take you over to Butler's."

Kennedy had been quietly hinting at and promoting the idea. Now it came out as the spontaneous fruit of the hospitality of Tibbetts.

It was about five miles away, by detour, and it seemed as if that little car flew. I couldn't help thinking that if Tibbetts represented the drivers out here, they were much more particular over the lives of their cattle than over their own. Reckless though it seemed, nothing happened.

The Butler place looked newer than Dixie Ranch. The house was more modern, rather fussy in appearance. It made me think of those people who use the word "swell." With them elegance never means simplicity, no matter how elegant simplicity may be. It was just "swell."

It seemed quiet about the place. Only from the cattle yards came any evidence of life at all. Thence we heard voices and the lowing of cattle. Finally a man came forward to greet us. He was rather awkward and slender. I knew that wasn't Hen Butler.

"Mr. Butler's not here now, sir. He's over to Baiting Hollow, I allows. Somewhars. I don't know whar. Any word, Mr. Tibbetts?"

"No, no word, Duke. Just brought over a couple of friends to see the place... S'long, Duke!"

We were off again. "Calc'late we might as well be gettin' along back to that hotel. Might meet Butler over there to-night. Can't tell. The crowd goes to bed early. Have to. Everybody's up at four at least to get an early start for Junction City.... Y' see we loosen up after the prizes is awarded." He winked and poked Kennedy in the ribs with a long, slender, friendly finger and laughed loudly.

It was after nightfall when we reached the hotel. Tibbetts scanned the crowd carefully for his nearest two neighbors. Vic Lowndes we met and liked. But Butler hadn't showed up, at least not yet. He might have gone on direct to Junction City, I hazarded. But the clerk, Peck, insisted not, that he was somewhere in Baiting Hollow and would make the hotel his headquarters.

I was disappointed. But Kennedy was ready to make the best of it. "We know there is a Henry Butler," he observed. "We know where he lives when he's home. Even if we can't find him in Baiting Hollow to-night, we may do so to-morrow. And we know a man who knows both of us, now. That will remove suspicion from his mind, if he has any."

We met many people that night, but no Hen Butler. We heard enough about him and his men. They were known to be a determined lot, set on carrying home the most of the prizes. All evening we absorbed rodeo gossip, comparisons of the star lariat man of this ranch with the star of another—horses, cattle, men, all jumbled together in a medley of excited conversation.

One had to know as much about cattle and Texas to feel at home in this atmosphere as one had to know smart society and smart homes to feel at ease in exclusive social circles in New

York. Only, down here, there was this difference. In Baiting Hollow one spoke of horses and men familiarly in order to gain prestige for oneself. In New York one must be on terms of intimacy with matrons of the smart set. In Texas, men ruled society. In New York, women.

Craig called up Mary and told her what had happened. He was impatient, though not anxious. But I was so restless that I could scarcely sleep in the strange surroundings. Toward morning, when I might have put in a bit of sleep, it seemed to me as if all Texas was stirring in that hotel. There was a tremendous commotion, getting the people off, commands to animals, salutes to one another, a good natured bedlam. I got up and dressed, but not before Kennedy.

"How do you like cattle hours?" I asked.

"I just don't want to miss anything," he replied.

The upshot of it all was that we went to the fair with the others. It seemed as if all the county was there, and a couple of adjoining counties. There was something doing every minute and in the excitement we were separated from Tibbetts and did not meet Butler. But Kennedy had promised to meet Tibbetts at the hotel in Baiting Hollow that night and we were hoping Butler would be there then, too.

The little hotel was crowded when we arrived. We looked in at the dining room. It was full and everyone seemed to be talking at once, with much laughter. It was a mixed crowd, but amiable. Now and then a newcomer would saunter in, somebody who had won a prize, and there would be a cheer and a shout.

Over in one corner there seemed to be a crowd louder even than the rest. I wondered who they were and was wishing Tibbetts was here to let us in on who those various local celebrities were. Just then a booming voice shouted our names.

"Kennedy! Jameson! Right over here!" It was Tibbetts himself calling us. He and his party were seated next to the hilarious crowd.

Tibbetts had places for us in a moment. The hospitality to

strangers down here, if they made a favorable first impression, was amazing. Nothing was too good for us. It was delightful to meet such warm-hearted folks. I hated to be playing a game among them.

"Butler's here to-night," Tibbetts whispered. "Over in that corner. Celebratin'. He's happy to-night. His men carried off a good many prizes, but my cattle got most of the honors. Glory for Butler's men, but reputation and money for my ranch. That's how it sizes up. Next year we'll get everything. The boys are talking it up already. I'd like to have you meet Hen. He's kind o' lively now. You can overlook that. You can't blame a man for celebratin' once in a while." I looked over in the direction Tibbetts was looking. "Hey, Butler!"

Butler raised his hand and beckoned us over. It took only a few minutes to tell how we had missed him at his ranch the night before. Butler evidently felt it was up to him. His cordiality to friends of Tibbetts's rivaled the native-born Texan's. He was full of joy at the victory for the men of his ranch. It was the chief topic of conversation at his table.

Kennedy began by flattering him subtly, especially when Tibbetts was called away by a new arrival. I watched Craig working on Butler in spite of carrying on at the same time a most engrossing talk with the champion rope thrower of the day. I was thoroughly enjoying myself. These people, the majority of them, were honest and sincere. Living close to the earth and homely things, their ambitions and desires were simple and honest, too. It was the same with the women as with the men—those that we met during the day.

I could see that Butler was falling for Kennedy. Praise of the town of Baiting Hollow and the county by Kennedy was followed by an invitation for another visit to the Butler ranch. "Meet the people here," he urged. "Buy up a place somewhere near by and settle down among us. We'll be glad to have you with us."

"I'll consider it, Butler. I'd have to look around a little bit more, however. When I get my ranch it means quite a large investment. I want a good one. It won't do to step into a big thing like a ranch lightly. It takes thought and capital."

"Well, I wasn't always a rancher, either. But now that I am, I want to be one always." Butler declaimed it loudly and his men cheered him. "Don't you want to come out to my place to-night? I'll take you out with me after the fun is over here."

"I'd like to go," hesistated Craig. "But I have some important matters before I go to bed. I must go down to the railroad station. I have a couple of telegrams to file and I must make two or three long-distance calls."

"Get the stuff off, then I'll take you out in my car. The boys want to go home and have a little celebrating with those there, too. They're starting soon. I'll take you over to the station and then we'll skip out in my car."

Kennedy agreed. "I'll telephone here at the hotel in the booth in the lobby before we start. Walter, we'd better throw some things together, we might need to-night."

Outside and apart, Kennedy paused. "Now, Walter, if you want things to happen fast, you've got to help me make them move. I'm going to telephone Mary at her hotel. She expects a call from me after dinner. You can throw anything you want into a suit case. I don't think we'll need it. But your first job is a real one. You'll have something on your hands, all right. Before I reach the station, in about fifteen minutes, with Butler, I want you to get that operator away from the key, away from the station. Keep him away for half an hour if you can. You remember him as we came in from the train? They tell me his name is Rinehart, very faithful, always on the job."

"Well, what do you suppose I'm going to do with him? Grab him by his collar, lift him out of his chair before the key, and carry him off?"

"That's one way. But you're a resourceful reporter. I've seen you use ingenuity and tact on assignments for the *Star*."

Kennedy flattered me. I made up my mind then to get Rinehart away if I had to use force, but I began to see a better way, safer.

"I'll be back with Butler as soon as I telephone. We'll be at the telegraph office in probably fifteen or twenty minutes. Now get busy."

It was a dark night. The moon had not come up yet. The lights in the hotel and the mirth looked good to me. I would much rather have stayed. But I went along, turning over in my mind a half-formed scheme. Leaving the hotel, I avoided a group of young chaps, men off the various ranches, and sought the station. But that sky-larking crowd gave me an idea, too.

The station was not very large or pretentious, but it also was new. The railroad telegrapher occupied a little office in the front of the building, away from the waiting room. I sauntered into the station. It was deserted. There was more fun to-night up at Junction City or down at the hotel in fair time. Ordinarily, though, Baiting Hollow was much like other country towns. The station and incoming and outgoing trains afforded periodical village excitement.

I looked around. From the distant office I could hear the click! click! of the telegraph instrument. I looked through the grating. The operator was there, all right, taking messages.

Casually I sauntered outside the station again. It excited no suspicion. There was no one much to be excited. In fact it was still a quarter of an hour before the last train for Junction City would pass through.

Once outside, I walked slowly down the railroad track. I must have gone a couple of hundred yards when I stopped to look about. There was what I had been seeking—a shack for storing tools and repair paraphernalia. I looked in. There also was what I had hoped to find—a coil of wire.

I looked about me in every direction again and listened in the darkness. I seemed to be entirely alone. Now I could see my way to get that telegrapher, the faithful Rinehart, out of the station office. Those cattlemen had helped along my idea. This wire showed how to do it.

I threw off my coat, unwound a hundred feet or so from the coil. Telegraph wire is recalcitrant stuff to handle. Besides that, I was nervous. I expected any minute to have someone come along, find me up to some trick.

When I had unwound what I thought would be sufficient, it had been my idea to throw it high enough to catch on the telegraph wire overhead. I had not reckoned with that most cantankerous inanimate thing to handle a coil of wire. My hands were sore and my patience giving out. Every minute now meant success or failure for Kennedy's plan, whatever it was. The wire bent and twisted and squirmed in every direction, got tangled with things in the dark, did everything except what I wanted.

There was nothing else for me to do but to climb that nearest telegraph pole in the dark, with a loop of this unruly wire about my waist. I was glad there was no one in the daylight to guy me. But I was really exasperated at Kennedy. I was supposed to be a newspaperman, not an amateur lineman. I think my exasperation must have given me some agility. I managed to get up that pole until I found there were some insecure cleats fastened to it. With perspiration seeping from every pore and my hair falling into my eyes, it was some relief when I was able to grasp the cross-piece at the top of the pole.

I felt along from one insulator to another. To make sure I swung the wire over all of the wires, carefully looping it loosely on one so that an extra smart yank from below would free it from all, then I dropped it to the ground.

There were footsteps approaching. I almost held my breath. Would I be found out, now, in that ridiculous, monkey-on-a-stick perch on the top of a telegraph pole? What explanation could I give? Quite naturally, the passersby saw nothing. I had forgotten about the darkness. It seemed as if a thousand eyes penetrated it to see me—eyes that I could not see. Then I began to think, this was my scheme, not Kennedy's. In the blackness

Kennedy himself would not likely have seen me up there. And why be vexed at him? He had told me to get Rinehart away—he had said nothing about climbing a telegraph pole.

I slid down carefully. That was as bad as going up. A cleat gave under me, the lowest, and I went down like a greased pig the rest of the way. I was dirty and dusty and my hands were bleeding. But I did not mind that as I completed my job. The Baiting Hollow wire was grounded along with whatever others the pole carried. No message would go over it, now. And with my yarn already made up to tell Rinehart at the station, I knew that nothing would keep that conscientious telegrapher from flying out of his office the moment I sprang it.

With my handkerchief I mopped my face, managed to get some of the dirt and blood from my hands, straightened my hair a bit, and crushed my hat down on my head. Then I hurried back into the station.

There was no need for me to assume a part to fit with my story. I was made up for it. No one was standing in front of the station or in the waiting room, though there were some on the platform by this time. Thus I made sure that no one had observed me on my first visit and could spoil my second.

I hurried over to the telegraph window. There I heard Rinehart mumbling and swearing to himself, moving around. Then the little wicket door that opened from his room to the rest of the station opened hurriedly.

"Having trouble?" I inquired, eagerly.

Rinehart looked at me sharply. "How did you know that?" he demanded.

"I heard you swearing," I replied, hastily, with a smile.

"This is no laughing matter, sir! Trains go through here. The lives of passengers are in danger when anything goes wrong with the railroad telegraph lines." The little man was dead in earnest, as he should be, took his job seriously, personally.

"I know it," I hastened. "That is the reason I've run all the way back here to tell you. There's a bunch of fellows, men of Bar Ten ranch, skylarking down the line. They made me do an old-time tenderfoot dance. The idea's this. I heard one of 'em make a bet he could clip a telegraph wire at fifty paces in the dark if they'd let him spot it with his automobile searchlight."

"Did he?" inquired Rinehart breathlessly.

"I don't know. I beat it when they forgot me. But I heard shooting as I ran away. I was afraid they did. I came here. Did they?"

"Yes! That's it. Where was this, stranger?"

"Oh, about half a mile down the line." I waved in the opposite direction from where I had made my little plant.

Rinehart ran his fingers distractedly through his hair. "My Gawd! man, what shall I do? Number 247 goes through here soon, is due at 9:05. What if they are trying to send me any orders for her? How many of those devils did you say there were?" he asked, anxiously.

"About a dozen of them. I don't think they realize the seriousness of their offense. They have been to the fair and are all lit up like a church. I beat it as fast as I could to warn you, but it seems I was too late. I'm sorry."

Rinehart grabbed his hat. "All this devilment! I got to go out now and repair that break. And just now, at fair time, of all times, when traffic on the wire is heaviest—and a train due! Do you want to help me out, partner? Hang around this office a minute. If anybody comes to see about anything just explain where I've gone and what I'm doing. I'm not supposed to leave the damn place. But what's the use staying in it if the line is interrupted?"

The station door slammed and he disappeared in the darkness. For a few minutes I watched him walking down the track, followed him by the light of his oil lantern. I must confess I felt a sort of contrition for causing all this trouble. But when a vision of that pain-wracked little boy flashed through my mind, of the sorrowing, troubled mother, I fully (determined to finish this job successfully.

Now I felt safe to run back to the place where I had strung

the wire over the line. I slipped out and hurried up the track in the other direction. It was much easier to pull that wire off the others than it had been to get it over them. In an incredibly short time I was back again in the station.

The telegraph was ticking busily again. I had been a little worried for fear I might have done something to put the wire out of commission. Now I could hardly wait until Kennedy arrived with Butler. I was going to let Kennedy assume, then, the whole responsibility. He had instigated it and if there was any trouble over it he would have to get us both out of it.

Meanwhile I was going into the waiting room to wash my hands and make myself a little more presentable before the arrival of Kennedy and Butler. I felt better. Also I had a feeling of elation at my successful ruse. Rinehart was out of the way.

Soon I heard the honking of a horn. It was Kennedy and Butler, and Butler was impatient to be off. I watched the hilarity of Butler, I must confess, with a little scorn. I wondered, also, at Kennedy's plan. Now that I had the telegrapher out, what was he going to do? What was the purpose of my activity? My mind was conjecturing all sorts of things. Was he going to kidnap Butler on the train, force him back as far as Junction City to confront Mary? What had he done to identify Butler? Nothing. Was Butler indeed the right man? There was one thing certain. Mary would not be able to get down here to Baiting Hollow. There weren't any more trains. The only other train was the 9:05 to Junction City none *from* it. Well, I would know soon, for they were coming in.

"Hello, Jameson! All set?" called Butler, good-naturedly.

I noticed, as he stood there, that his clothes had a good deal more attention given them than many of the ranchers out here gave. That made me think he was Fat Barr, with his Eastern care of his clothes.

Kennedy looked at me with a question in his eyes. He found the answer in my returning glance. His face lighted hopefully. He said nothing but strolled over toward the telegraph office.

"This fellow's name is Rinehart, isn't it? I thought I heard Tibbetts call him that."

Butler nodded, then turned toward me. He was full of the coming celebration out of his ranch. "I don't believe you ever saw anything like it, Jameson. When those fellows get started to-night there'll be no stopping them. I hope you don't care about your sleep."

Somehow, celebrating over at Butler's seemed flat to me just now. I didn't want to go. I wanted only to know what Craig's game was and what further part I was to play in it.

"That's queer." Kennedy had returned, frowning and rather vexed. "Rinehart isn't here. Did you see him, Walter?"

"No; I wasn't looking for him. Not there? Maybe he'll be back light away. I thought they were not supposed to leave the place for any length of time."

"They're not." Butler confirmed my remark by shaking his head vigorously.

I looked at the station clock. It was almost nine. Well then, the train to Junction City would soon be pulling in and possibly a message would have to be sent. If Kennedy would only do something! Rinehart might be back any moment, change his mind, desperate to prevent any accident.

"Rinehart will be back," asserted Butler, confidently. "He'll be here before the 9:05 rolls in. He knows the rules of the office. No use worrying over that man's job."

Suddenly through the open grating of the missing telegrapher's room came the ticking, ticking of a message. I listened anxiously. Now we were up against it! What would we do if it were something that needed an answer and we couldn't answer? Over the wire we could hear ticking BH... BH... BH. It was the call for Baiting Hollow.

None of us said a word. Both Craig and I knew enough to know what that meant. I realized now that Butler knew. Would he betray his knowledge? His face was a study, stony, blank. If he knew, he was keeping all that to himself. If he were Fat Ban, I thought, what an actor he was!

Again we heard BH... BH... BH... Rinehart was still away. Kennedy stood startled, impassive, waiting. If that were his game, I would play it likewise. But I was on my toes with excitement suppressed. What was the message? What was the trouble? Might it, after all, be something inconsequential?

Suddenly, as if in despair at getting the operator, Rinehart, himself, the message began to come over the wire. One could have heard a pin drop in that room, save for the ticking of that instrument. It was not an ordinary silence. It was portentous, fraught with horror, breathing of calamity. I felt it and I knew Butler was feeling it, too. He couldn't keep his feet still. Yet, on second thought, I was forced to admit to myself that his nervousness implied no guilt. It might simply mean worry over Rinehart's absence, with a message coming in and no one to answer it.

Relentlessly the ticking continued.

"Has 247 gone through yet?"

I glanced at the clock. The minute hand showed one minute past nine. With bated breath I waited for the rest of the message.

"Freight wreck between Baiting Hollow and Junction City. For God's sake, hold 247. Answer. J.C."

We looked at each other solemnly. Craig and I knew the purport of the message. Did Butler know? He still seemed calm, unaffected. Something must be done to shake him.

"Good heavens, Walter! What shall we do? I can read—but I can't send!" Kennedy looked wildly at me.

Butler turned to me as if seeking what I was able to do. "I can't do either. What is it?" I managed to gasp.

I was desperate when Kennedy blurted it out. To think of having a thing like this happen the very time I pulled a trick on poor Rinehart!

Butler was pacing up and down the floor, worried and undecided. Suddenly he turned to both of us, hesitated, then started toward the instrument.

"Well, I used to send—a little bit," he managed to ejaculate, almost incoherent with pent-up emotion. "I'll answer if I can."

Ticking at the key, we heard Butler sending over the wire, "JC…JC…JC…."There was a pause, then an answer. Again he was at the key. "247 late. Will hold. B.H."

Suddenly Craig dashed out of the railroad station. Neither Butler nor I thought anything of that under the stress of this new circumstance. It might be something perhaps with regard to the approaching train 247.

Out on the platform, Butler and I were straining our eyes and ears, waiting nervously for the first signs of 247, Up and down, out on the tracks, even, we paced. I knew the train would stop. It had to stop. What if this time it didn't? All sorts of wild thoughts raced through my mind.

There she was!

At last, up the tracks we could see the headlight along the shiny rails, coming closer, around the bend. The shrill whistle cleft the night air. It must stop. That was the only thought in my mind.

The train slowed down with much fuss of air brakes and hissing of escaping steam. There was a thankfulness in my heart at the saving of lives.

Butler's arm was raised to catch the attention of the engineer. I was running, beckoning the conductor. We must warn these men of the danger.

Butler shouted.

He was abruptly interrupted. Kennedy had returned from the hotel across the street suddenly, and was standing relentlessly in his path.

"That will do, Butler! You'll come with me on 247. Mary's waiting for you at Junction City. Buster needs you—desperately!"

"Mary? Buster? Who's Mary?" Butler repeated it incredulously and a bit defiantly.

"Who's Mary? Who's Buster? Who are you—really? Come clean!"

"Hen Butler of Baiting Hollow. That's who I am. Everybody here knows me!" The man muttered it sullenly.

"Like the devil you are! You're Fat Barr. You sent the world series in 1914. There's no wreck on the line. Mary sent that message from Junction City, where she is working. It's a trap. You fell into it—and answered it. Mary just telephoned to me at the hotel she'd recognize that *touch* on the key among ten thousand!"

HEARING

"**YOU THINK YOU** have been cheated, Miss Neely, robbed of your share of the Gowdy money?" repeated Kennedy.

"Yes. When they read Uncle Jeremiah Gowdy's will, I found that my cousin, Jim Camp, was made the sole heir. And Uncle Jeremiah hated Jim Camp worse than he hated me—even after his favorite nephew, young Jerry Gowdy, died in France. I don't believe Uncle Jeremiah would have discriminated between Jim Camp and me. He disliked us both—but for different reasons."

"Why?" persisted Kennedy.

"Well, he hated me because I would grow up to be a woman. His life, he said, had been poisoned by a woman, so he hated us all. Jim Camp he called a slacker, a quitter, a coward."

"And of course," nodded Kennedy, "this Jim Camp whom you had never seen showed up to claim the fortune."

"Yes. Strange to say, Jim was at the funeral. He appeared just as silently as they say he once disappeared when he was cut off. Up to that time there was no suspicion by any of us of a new will. At least everyone thought the money would come naturally to Jim and to me, because of Young Jerry's death years ago. But after the funeral the will was read. You can imagine my surprise when I found that everything, even the house in Brooklyn, had been left to Jim Camp. I still can't think it is right."

"Is this will signed?" asked Craig. "Does it look all right?"

"Yes, it seems to be properly signed, and witnessed by Julia Crandall. You see, she was the nurse to Uncle Jeremiah when he died. I suppose they just had her because she happened to be there. The strange part of it is that Jim Camp fell madly in love with her. He gave her a whirlwind campaign, swept her off her feet, and before the week was out they were married. Julia Crandall is good-looking, spick and span, like most nurses. Probably that is one reason why Jim fell for her. I'd never seen Jim before, but he seems so careless of his appearance. I was quite charmed over her at first. She urged me to stay at the house, but I didn't. Now I'm glad I didn't. I feel I have a perfect right to half of that money—and I am going to contest the will."

Nan Neely paused. "You see, what makes it difficult for me is that twenty thousand dollars seems so little to most lawyers to fight over—I mean lawyers who are any good. And I have nothing. But ten thousand dollars would go a long way in getting me the right teachers for my voice. Oh, if I only had it!"

The girl might be naive. But there was nothing scheming or debasing about her. She merely expressed the yearning of an artistic temperament hampered by inexperience and lack of money.

"I can sing," she continued, eagerly. "I know it. But I have had no famous teachers, no chance. I don't want to go in as a chorus girl. Not many of our great artistes have been chorus girls. That seems to make a ragged voice. I want to study, be introduced to the musical world right."

Nan Neely's face might have been a model for divine inspiration. She had grayish-yellow eyes, large and well shaped, lashes black as night sweeping rosy cheeks that showed every evidence of the simple life. No paint was necessary for that blushing hue. A light-brown hair with Titian tints was made glowing from the afternoon sunshine sweeping over it through the window. There was character in her chin and mouth, but life's molding of these features had been determined by a buoyant, happy spirit which had eliminated all that was sad, grim, unlovely. I could see that Craig was favorably impressed with Nan, who was slender with the slenderness of youth, not that of emaciation which so many girls vouch for as style. There was no suggestion of boyishness; rather the delightful suggestion of fascinating womanhood.

"What was your uncle's reason for feeling so bitter toward you all?" retraced Kennedy.

"It's a long story. Perhaps I can tell you briefly. You see there were three of us, two nephews and a niece—young Jerry Gowdy, as everybody called him, who died, Jim Camp, and myself. Uncle Jeremiah always liked Jerry best. In fact, Jerry lived with him. I saw Uncle Jeremiah Gowdy several times, but he never asked me to visit him. He came West some time each year to see my mother. But when she died he lost interest entirely in me."

"What became of young Jerry?" I inquired. "I think you said he died in France."

She nodded. "Yes, he was killed in France, in the second battle of the Marne. Young Jerry was mighty fine most of the time and died making a most self-sacrificing rescue of a buddy who had been wounded. They brought both of the men in, but it was too late. Jerry had lost too much blood, and he died. Uncle Jeremiah never forgave Jim Camp for not entering the army. Young Jerry enlisted before the draft, but Jim Camp evaded the service, proved himself a slacker by taking advantage of some technicality in the draft."

"There was a will then?" inquired Craig.

"At that time the first will had been made. Everything was left to young Jerry, the whole twenty thousand, on condition that Jerry would sign a pledge not to drink. I didn't think anything of that. If Uncle Jeremiah loved young Jerry so much and wanted him to have his money, it was right that he should have it. But there was a decided antipathy, a hatred in his heart, toward Jim Camp. After young Jerry's death the bitterness grew and I know there was never a reconciliation. But here is a new Gowdy will, leaving everything to Jim Camp. I don't believe it is legal. I mean, there is something wrong somewhere. When it comes to settling up the estate now, I feel like fighting. I have as much right to my half as Jim has to his. Neither should have it all. And it means my whole future—my happiness."

In her eagerness the girl had leaned forward and her eyes were glowing with the fervor of battle and hope for a musical career.

"How did you come to go to Mr. Jameson on the *Star?*" inquired Craig.

She thought a moment. "A neighbor of ours out on the Coast was married to a man who seemed to be on the level. But she learned the facts. She wanted a divorce. Some one advised her to try her case in the newspapers. It made a good story and the papers printed all the facts she gave them. She got her divorce, and at the same time the people were with her. Mr. Kennedy, I decided to do likewise. I am a stranger here in this big city. I thought I could tell my story to the people through the *Star* and it would help. It has helped, only differently from the way I expected. It led me to Mr. Jameson, and he brought me up here to you for help."

"Where has Jim Camp been all these years?"

"No one knows just where he really has been. But we all know he hasn't been near his uncle, even during his last illness. In fact, as I said, after young Jerry went to France, Uncle Jeremiah publicly disowned Jim. He was just indifferent to me and I was too proud to annoy him by any unwanted attentions. Possibly he may have hated me more, but he kept it to himself. It was as if I'd never lived."

"But what does Jim Camp say he did after he was disinherited?" I could not help interrupting.

"Disappeared. He says he has been out on the Coast part of the time. But he never bothered us in Los Angeles."

"From Los Angeles, eh?" smiled Craig, glancing at her appreciatively. "Why not the movies?"

There was a defiant little flash in those grayish-yellow eyes. "Possibly if you had lived in Los Angeles as I have you wouldn't be such an enthusiast about the movies for a girl. I know girls raised there, as beautiful as any star. But they just simply will not try the movies. Those movie stars may twinkle from afar—but they lack luster among some of us natives of the movie center. I want to sing. I have the voice. And I want to sing—right."

"You say Jeremiah Gowdy hated women?" repeated Craig, thoughtfully.

I could not imagine him hating Nan Neely if he ever had a good look at her and talked to her.

Her answer was so positive that it made Craig chuckle softly with amusement. "Did he hate women? He hated us so much that he wouldn't look at us any more than he could help. Why, I have heard him say the Turks were the only ones who understood women. 'They cover them up, lock them up, watch them. They're all of the devil!'"

"Yes; but you say he visited your mother once a year. How did he feel toward her? Not that way, surely."

"N-no. She was his only surviving sister. That was one case where he hadn't allowed his heart to freeze. Until her death he saw her once a year. But he had no use for me, just the same. Mr. Kennedy, don't you think such a violent hatred of all women, good or bad, indicated a weakness, mentally, an incompetency of judgment?" Nan's big eyes were raised directly to Craig's.

Again Kennedy smiled. "A surprising lack of judgment." He paused. "But a broken heart might cause a bitterness so unreasoning that it might amount almost to an insanity. Sometimes, though, it isn't pure hatred, or even bitterness, really—only a mask that some wear through fear, fear of a repetition of blighted hopes and broken dreams."

Nan was silent over that. The romance of the idea stirred her sensitive soul. Perhaps she was thinking for the moment that maybe if she had been a trifle more persistent she might have broken through that wall of icy reserve barricading the way to her uncle's affections. But there was, on second thought, nothing in her memory of him that even seemed to show it. She remembered and almost cowered again at those malignant glances, the threatening upraised cane if she ever so much as stumbled in his way in her play as a child on his yearly visits to her mother's.

"No, Mr. Kennedy," she said, decisively, "he was crazy over women, in no way competent to make a fair will, even toward one of the sex."

Kennedy said nothing at that. A moment later he resumed. "Are you sure, quite sure, you have told me all you know—or suspect—about this Gowdy will and the persons involved in it?" He eyed her closely. "Isn't there something else?"

Nan seemed to react to it, not as if she were concealing anything, but as if she were reluctant for some other reason. "Yes," she began, slowly, "there is something. Only I didn't say anything about it because I know how men are, lawyers and detectives and all that. They want facts, not feelings. And I have a—well, a feeling, I guess you'd call it, maybe an intuition. I wouldn't have said anything about it if you hadn't asked the question and looked at me that way."

Kennedy nodded encouragingly. "Let me hear it. You might as well, now."

Nan was looking absently away. "Oh, it's only this. They say young Jerry and Jim looked a good deal alike. Young Jerry might have been a bit stouter than Jim in the old days, but then he was a couple of years older. Besides, Jim, too, may have taken on weight in more than five years. I don't know. I never saw anything but their pictures and heard people talk about them. You see, it's this, Mr. Kennedy. If I didn't know young Jerry was dead, how would I ever know Jim Camp when I met him? There's enough alike about them even in the old pictures." She lowered her voice.

"Just what do you mean by that, Nan?" insisted Craig.

"I—I don't know." Her voice was low and there was a sort of tremble in it as if she felt her thoughts were being torn from her without her consent. Then she raised her eyes, decided to make a clean sweep of it. "I'm not a bit sure this is Jim Camp, really... How do I know it is not—young Jerry?"

"Young Jerry?" Craig straightened up at that.

My mind was alert at it, too, eager to hear more of her feelings in the matter. I sensed in it a mighty sensational story for the *Star* about mistaken or concealed identities. Instantly its dramatic value loomed greater to me than its probability. My next impulse was to glean from her why she felt it, why there might be even a probability. If she were right, this was a far more interesting story than I had anticipated. That would have a kick in it.

"But, Nan," pursued Kennedy, evenly, "did you notice anything in the actions, the appearance of this Jim Camp to make you think it wasn't Jim Camp, but young Jerry?"

"Not exactly, except the slovenliness. But then that, may have been from the wild roving life he has led in the last few years. Or it may have been a pose. Maybe he isn't really slovenly. Julia Crandall is so—neat. Why did that appeal to him if he isn't that way himself? By opposites? I don't know."

"There's something else, isn't there?" asked Craig, with assurance.

"Y-yes. There is. I smelled his breath. He had been drinking the first time I met him. But in the old days, whatever they said about him, Jim Camp never drank. It was young Jerry did that. That was what rankled in the mind of Uncle Jeremiah. His favorite nephew would get drunk. But Jim, for whom he had no use, seemed to have too much sense for it. It was a galling thing to him."

"Does—er—Jim Camp drink since he married?" I asked.

"No. I don't think so. No, I have heard there has been a most wonderful change in Jim since his marriage. He may have learned to be wild and to drink since Uncle Jerry disowned him. But now Julia Crandall has him as docile as a lamb. He seems to think so much of her that he has curbed all that. And young Jerry had that reputation, too. He would go for weeks, leave it alone, then go back."

"H'm!" Kennedy was silent a few minutes as if debating

whether to take up the case for the girl or to go on with plans we had had for a vacation. Finally he spoke. "Nan, I'll take up the case for you. If there has been wrong done, I would like to see it made right. And we need good singers."

I was pleased, but could not help putting in my word. "Suppose it *is* young Jerry. Then you'll lose all, anyhow."

"No, not necessarily. There's this other will. We'll break both, break one on the other, like a couple of sticks. Anyhow, I've lost everything this way. I've got a chance if I can shake either will. None, if I don't. I have everything to gain; nothing to lose."

"Very true," I agreed, still raising questions in my own mind for which I wanted her answers. "But why would young Jerry do it?"

"Oh, there might be reasons. Maybe he didn't want to be known as wild all his life. Maybe he didn't believe he could ever keep the pledge and the money according to the first will. He might have been afraid to lose it. A chance may have come to him, over there. Better to have us think he was dead. He might have recovered, been invalided out of the service. He might have kept in touch in some way with the real Jim Camp. Or Jim Camp might have died. Then he might see a chance to make a come-back, as some one else. Young Jerry might have decided to become Jim Camp, wipe out his black-sheep name with good behavior under another name."

"And plant a will, forged, somehow?"

"Yes, maybe that. Then the unexpected may have happened— and he has fallen in love with Uncle Jeremiah's nurse. All the more he must make a come-back. Julia Crandall may have reformed him, one of those temporary spells. Maybe she reformed the wrong nephew!"

As I sat back and listened to her, some of the improbability seemed to vanish. It began to seem less chimerical. Why, the whole thing could have taken place, easily. No need even to wonder what had happened to the real Jim Camp who had evaded service. He might have been overcome in the keen struggle in the West, not fighting Indians on the prairies, but Indians of industry and finance.

"Now, Nan, let me tell you what I want you to do," began Kennedy to instruct, thoughtfully. "You have said that Julia Crandall, now your cousin's wife, asked you once to visit or stay in the house with her a short time. Please accept that invitation. It will give me a chance to study this Jim Camp. Humble yourself for your rights. Act as if you thought ten thousand dollars… wasn't worth fighting for and you had given up all idea of contesting the will."

The girl nodded. "I can do that. I love to act—act and sing. When shall I begin to be friendly?"

"Right away. Call up Jim Camp. Tell him you have about decided to go back to California in a few days and thought you would like to go back at least good friends with your nearest relatives. Make him think that you have no quarrel now. If you do it right, it will pretty likely bring about an invitation from Julia to visit them. If they ask you, make your stay as agreeable and protracted as possible. It may be that things will break so that it will be short."

Nan's face flushed with eagerness. "If there is anything phony about this Jim Camp, do you think I'll be safe?"

"That, Nan, is what I want to arrange with you. Your cousin must know that you sing. I want you to bring it about so that they'll consent to a musicale, or some quiet evening party for you, before you go, something to speed the parting guest. You must play your cards well."

"But how will a musicale help me to protect myself?" she inquired timidly, puzzled.

"The musicale will not help you. But the sooner you can arrange it, the sooner I can be sure of this new will. It will be a means of my getting in the house to see you. Mr. Jameson and I can pose as musical friends, or some thing, in conference with you for the future. To make things seem more plausible you might confide in Julia that you may soon have some good news to tell her. She will suspect only one thing, a romance, and will probably encourage my coming to visit you."

Nan smiled, and a few moments later left us in a great deal happier frame of mind than she had been in when first she was referred to me down at the *Star* office. At least there was a plan, although she had not the vaguest idea of what Kennedy purposed. Nor did I.

I tried to figure out the difficulty over the Gowdy will myself after Nan Neely's departure. There was no use talking to Kennedy. He would confide nothing, yet. But to me, as I thought over what Nan had said, there was something mighty fishy about this Jim Camp. I had tried so often to solve things in my own way as a surprise for Kennedy that, in spite of my lack of success, I was ready to try again. This time I felt I could almost figure it out already, but I determined at the first opportunity to make sure before I made Craig in any degree the partner of my thoughts.

I felt the force of Nan's feeling. Was this really Jim Camp, after all? I had heard Craig ask Nan if she had seen anything different in Jim Camp from what she expected. That must have been his idea, too. But if it weren't Jim Camp, who would he be? The most likely thing, then, was that he was the man Jim Camp so closely resembled, young Jerry Gowdy. But it was supposed that young Jerry had been killed in France. At least, as I found out later in the day, there was a little white marker in a cemetery in France with "Jeremiah Gowdy" written on it. He couldn't be dead and here, too. Who, then, was the man in the grave? Some unknown soldier? And had young Jerry been willing to let things go so that he could drop out over there, wipe out his past?

The more I looked into it, the more I was convinced that Jim Camp was none other than young Jerry, posing as his own cousin. His drinking had been evidence of his real identity. Rumors of his general lack of manners, his slovenliness, seemed to confirm it. That would be only a cover.

Along in the afternoon Nan called up. "It worked, Mr.

Kennedy," she exclaimed in excitement. "When they thought I was going back to Los Angeles without causing any trouble for them, their hospitality was amazing. I am leaving my hotel now to go to the Gowdy house. I'll explain your visit right away. You're a friend of mine from back home. I'll let you know when I can have the musicale."

Kennedy went out, but, since he did not ask me to accompany him, I decided he was doing a little sleuthing and took the opportunity to do some on my own. I sought to hunt up the past friends of Jim Camp's in the city, some of the boarding houses he had frequented. I found that there had been such a chap, but that was about all. He had been swallowed up completely. All that people knew was that they had heard he had gone West. I began to wonder what was really the significance, perhaps hidden to them, in "gone West."

That evening I found Craig with a number of bundles in our quarters. He was not disposed to confide what had been his intentions in his shopping tour, nor did I question him. All I could think of was what an elusive chap this Jim Camp had been, evading everybody for years, then seeming to be right on hand the moment his uncle was dead—not only on hand, but married, reformed, heir to twenty thousand dollars. It seemed like a fairy tale to me.

Nan Neely dropped in to see us in the laboratory the next forenoon. She was apparently delighted at her reception at the Gowdy house.

"I'm going to have my party much sooner than I expected," she imparted.

"When?" asked Kennedy.

"To-night. Will you be ready? Good! I find that Julia has social ambitions in a small way and the prospect of this small legacy for Jim paves the way financially for her to indulge them."

"How did you get her to consent to it so soon?"

"Two reasons. I think they want to get rid of me, ship me east of Suez, and by flattery, too. I mentioned that I was going home after I had a chance to say farewell to some friends here. Then after she heard me sing, Julia was ready for the musicale idea. She has suggested only just a few of our most intimate friends. Of course you and Mr. Jameson come under that."

"May I have something to say about the program you arrange for to-night?" queried Craig. "I would advise you to keep the evening decidedly informal. For reasons that I can explain better when I see you there I would suggest a very patriotic program, something pertaining to the World War and the A.E.F."

"Fine!" exclaimed Nan. "When I select my songs I can sing something in the early part of the evening that will satisfy their simple operatic demands, some aria that will indicate the range and quality of my voice, and my ability to keep the tones pure. I want you to hear it, yourself. Then for encores I can sing some of the popular patriotic songs and we'll end up by singing the things our boys liked during their stay in France."

"That's splendid. Let gentle hints fall that you intend to make it a patriotic evening, perhaps even that you may have as an intermission to the music some games that you have played before and enjoyed. I can tell you about the games when I get there. You can say you think such an evening would be a nice bit of sentiment for the memory of the hero of the family."

There was vivacity, animation in Nan Neely as she planned with Craig. Her career meant everything to her. Here, she felt, was a legitimate chance to help herself on her way, in some manner to advance toward a fair division of the legacy.

It turned out to be one of those cool, snappy evenings in October when living is a joy. I was glad that weather caused no postponement of the affair. Already I had surmised the kind of thing it was to be—a little music, some better than ordinary, some popular songs, perhaps refreshments of a simple nature, with the surprise act, I hoped, sandwiched in somewhere in some manner. I was curious and a little peeved. I had not been taken wholly into their confidence. I felt that the next time I played the good Samaritan to a pretty girl I would make sure I was not entirely eliminated if I had to have it in writing.

"I have laid your clothes all out for you, Walter," informed Craig as we went up to our apartment after an early dinner. "They're on your bed."

It was said innocently enough, but the act was unusual. "Since when have you been playing valet to me?" I asked, in some doubt whether I was to be laughed at or with. "I deserve it. But it's an unprecedented kindness."

On my bed I discovered a most unusual array of apparel— not a thing that I had expected to find. My evening clothes, everything I usually wore to an entertainment in the evening, were still reposing in closet and drawers. And here was this stuff, this O.D.

"Theirs not to reason why." Since my association with Craig those seemed to be general orders.

Gingerly I picked up these clothes. I knew they were not mine, yet they seemed to be about my size. Here was a captain's uniform and insignia. Had he been rifling one of these Army and Navy stores? Not being quite fully acquainted with the program, I did not hurry dressing. In fact, I had not started when the door opened and Craig walked in—officially.

Could I believe my eyes? Kennedy was saluting me. But somehow it didn't seem just right. In fact, nothing seemed just right. Feebly my memory was stirring back to the days when those olive-drab ranks of men went stepping blithely by to entrain for camp or transport. But none of them looked just like Craig. His eyes gleamed with mischief.

"What's the matter? What's wrong with this picture?"

"Wh-at's wrong? Why—everything's wrong. It's a patriotic party, I suppose. But those clothes! You think it's a burlesque? You have on a lieutenant's suit, but, great guns! man, you're wearing cuff leggin's with it! Oh, boy! your Sam Browne belt is looped through the wrong shoulder. And when you came in you saluted with the left hand—and such a salute! Say, if a real soldier ever saw you he would give you the bum's rush."

"Never mind me. Get into your own togs. I hope you are right."

Now I began to see Kennedy's strategy. He expected to trap this alleged Jim Camp. If it were really young Jerry Gowdy returned and reformed, he would surely betray his familiarity with the American forces abroad when he surveyed Kennedy. He could not help it. His very amusement and knowledge, even though he said nothing, would amount to a betrayal.

I returned to an inspection of my own clothes with added zest. What was in my prize package? It was not long before I had on my captain's uniform. But with it I was expected to wear a private's cap, and on my arm the service chevrons had been inverted. The only thing I liked about the ensemble was my officer's boots. They made my feet look as nifty as ever.

"Stick me jes' as deep as yoh wanto, but do don't fasten that on *me*," I objected as Craig approached with a bayonet in a case to fasten to my felt. "I'm a *captain!*"

"We may need it," he said, merely, going ahead fastening.

"Say, you don't think the party's going to get rough, do you?" I inquired.

"You never can tell. I may need to use it."

We were a couple of strange gentlemen starting out for an evening's fun. It was a very good thing, I felt, that we could go in the car. If we had walked a block under the lights, with all the ex-service men there were in New York, we would have been mobbed.

I began to feel a thrill of excitement over the adventure itself, however, as we drove up to the Gowdy house. It was a very old frame house, the kind one sees often in the older parts of Brooklyn. The boards were laid on vertically and the joinings seemed to be covered with strips of moulding to make them weather-proof. It was two stories high and had no basement. There was a little attic under the gabled roof and an extension seemed to have been added to the rear. A little side entrance led to the rooms in the rear. It was like an ugly duckling among the three-story-and-basement brownstone houses surrounding it.

Evidently Julia was reckless with lighting. Every room seemed lighted. I was glad the street was dark as we parked our car, locked it, and left it some distance up from the house. Craig rang the bell, and I was pleased when the door was opened by Nan herself.

But such a Nan—the sweetest little buddy of them all. She was attired as an ambulance driver and correctly.

"I hope you can sing," she imparted under her voice. "You'll have to help me out with the war songs. Jim says flatly he can't sing and nobody's going to make a fool of him." She glanced skeptically at us as she said it.

There was a suspicion racing through my mind, also. Just why wouldn't Jim Camp sing those songs the boys sang during the war? Was it that he feared to show that he knew them too well? I wondered if that was what Kennedy was thinking, also.

Nan was a lively little hostess. "We're just plain folks here, so make yourselves at home. I'll call Julia and Jim." Then she whispered. "If they seem very curious concerning you, Mr. Kennedy, play the part. I have let them think as they please about us." She impulsively pulled Craig nearer. "My heart is out in Los Angeles. An old friend is waiting for me!"

With a laugh she turned quickly and led us into the living room. "Julia, this is Mr. Kennedy—and Mr. Jameson."

I saw Jim Camp look up at us with interest. He seemed to be observing us both carefully. I held my breath with suspense. Except for the usual acknowledgments in meeting strangers he was decidedly reticent. If he had noticed anything wrong with our uniforms, he carefully kept it to himself. I began to think this man called Jim Camp must really be young Jerry Gowdy and that he was indeed a clever man. He was able to keep his thoughts to himself, and in these days when so many people talk themselves into jails and out of friendships, few are blessed with the cleverness of silence.

Right away Kennedy's attack through the sense of sight had failed, at least so far.

There was nothing very arresting in the appearance of Julia except that she possessed to an unusual extent that practical gentleness acquired in hospital training. To men of a certain type, particularly that exemplified in Jim Camp, a practical yet feeling wife is like an anchor. It holds him safe.

Her hair was dark, much of it, too, and fastened in graceful coils at the back of her head. She had a rather pale face lighted with brilliant dark eyes. Her other features kept her from being handsome. It was easily seen, too, that hers was the stronger will. Jim Camp seemed to feel that doing her bidding was the height of bliss. I watched them as a bachelor with interest and amusement.

Evidently old Jeremiah Gowdy had not believed much in improvements, but had clung to the old things. The room was heated by an old Baltimore heater, antiquated, but still glowing through the little isinglass windows. Over it was a dirty-white marble mantel. There was a nondescript Brussels carpet on the floor and a fancy suit of furniture, walnut, and overstuffed. The room was lighted dimly by gas, old-fashioned gas, modernized very lately by one Welsbach burner. But Nan seemed at ease. Apparently the inconveniences and incongruities failed to disturb her brightness.

A few other guests, friends of Julia, arrived, and I was glad to note that none of them seemed to have seen service overseas. I knew they hadn't, because they took our uniforms to be bona fide.

Somewhere Nan had found a pianist capable of accompanying her. When all the guests were assembled and chatting perfunctorily, Nan stood before us. "We're going to have a real old-time soldier night for my friends." She nodded toward us. "But not for worlds would I disappoint you about my singing.

I am going to sing first the 'Mad Scene' from 'Lucia'; following that, 'Some Day He'll Come' from 'Madama Butterfly.'"

The girl was gracious and simple in her manner and really possessed a wonderful soprano. It needed more training, naturally, but there was the voice, feeling, and charm. Nan Neely had far to go once she started in her profession. No wonder she preferred a conservative, concert platform entrance into the musical world to the uncertain chorus-girl entrance. As the last notes of her second selection died away there was genuine applause. Even Julia conceded it.

Hardly had the enthusiasm subsided politely when Nan was singing with spirit the "Star-spangled Banner." In her uniform, her fervor was contagious, and I felt it as I stood up to join her in spite of my unfamiliarity with the people about me. But Jim held back. Never a note did he sing. At least, if he were young Jerry, he was clever enough not to betray himself through what he saw or what he said. His very aloofness now made me more certain he was the favorite nephew.

Nan was undiscouraged. She looked up brightly. "Let's have a good old-fashioned sing. Just the songs we all know."

She began with "Pack up your troubles in your old kit bag, and smile, smile, smile." Then she started, "Oh, how I hate to get up in the morning."

Everybody joined in and enjoyed it with the exception of Jim. Most of the tune he was silent. At other times his lips were merely moving mechanically in the familiar choruses. It was the same with "Over there" and "Where do we go from here." Not a sound escaped his lips. Nan concluded for the moment with, "Hail, hail, the gang's all here."

I was watching Jim Camp closely now. He seemed tired. Sometimes his eyes were closed. I wondered what was the matter. I was surprised that Kennedy did not keep a closer watch and I wondered if covertly he saw what I saw. The man looked to me as if the old songs had sent him browsing back in memory's fields. Was he living over again the dangers, the thrills, and the hardships of the war? I was sure of it and felt a little sorry for him. But, then, why wasn't the man on the level? I began to think that the singing was not working any better than our appeal to his sense of sight in our outrageous uniforms.

In a pause, Kennedy pulled from his pocket a packet of French cigarettes that were smoked a great deal over there by our boys when they couldn't get the American brands that the war made famous. I hadn't smoked one for a long time, but I recognized the aroma of them the moment I took the first puff after Kennedy had offered them around.

Jim Camp took one lazily, only looking at it with mild curiosity. He lighted it casually and began smoking. Now I was interested. Common as these cigarettes were in France, they were uncommon here. In fact, Craig had had to get them from an importer on Broadway.

Jim Camp smoked that fag with about the same amount of appreciation as if it had been cornsilk. In fact, no one seemed to comment on them, not even Julia when she calmly helped herself to one. I could imagine that the others set it down merely as a vagary of Craig's taste. But at least I would have expected Jim to pull out a "Fat" or a "Camel" when he finished. He did nothing of the sort; in fact, nothing. Smell didn't work, either.

So far, with each test, there had been no response, nothing apparently to excite recollection of the service. Yet I was still unconvinced that this was Jim Camp himself. He was certainly acting just as young Jerry Gowdy would have acted, I believed, under the same circumstances. I had a feeling, comparable to Nan's now, that this Jim Camp was posing, trying to make us believe that he was never over there, whereas, according to my idea, he was in reality a sort of reverse on Enoch Arden—had come back and married a girl as another man.

A moment later Julia asked us into the dining room. There the table was spread with sandwiches and cakes. There was coffee. It was, after all, just an old-fashioned party.

"I know what to do," exclaimed Nan, catching a glance from

Kennedy. "You men look lost. I can tell what is the matter. You need a little—smile."

Upstairs she ran, and a moment later returned with what I recognized as one of the packages Kennedy had sent to the apartment. As she unwrapped it I saw that it was a bottle of wine. But as she poured she carefully kept the label covered still.

"Now I want you to guess what this is," she cried. "It was given to me. I'll give you each a guess with your glass."

Some guessed port, others claret. In fact the crowd was banal. They showed how bootleggers can victimize the American public, selling them anything.

As a matter of fact, it was a light French wine used by the boys over there and very well liked in the many places where the drinking water was so impure that the drinking of this light French wine was almost a necessity. Kennedy guessed it right, but only after I had said I did not know and Jim Camp had hazarded that it was home-made elderberry.

There was amusement among them at that. But to me it showed merely that Jim Camp had exhibited another case of unusual ignorance for him. Either he was extremely cunning or an incredible boob. I was satisfied that my first surmise was correct. It looked almost to me as if he were going so far in his efforts to know nothing and to make mistakes, that he was ridiculous, no matter which man he was.

Well, I thought to myself, taste doesn't work, either.

"Maybe you don't care for that there French wine," now volunteered Jim. My hopes rose at his taking the initiative and doing anything at all—more especially this, as he added, opening the lower sideboard, "Perhaps you'd like a an orange blossom?" He gave a hesitant glance at his wife as we descried a bottle of gin in the dark recesses under the sideboard.

Julia unbent. "There are plenty of oranges in that dish."

Jim opened a drawer and began fumbling for a sharp knife as Julia produced a large jar and a strainer for the juice. He tried one or two knives, laid them back as too dull.

"What's that, a knife you want?" cut in Kennedy. "I can't oblige you exactly, but try this." Craig had reached over and slipped the steel bayonet from the case on my belt and passed it to Jim Camp.

"Thanks." Camp took the pointed metal ordinarily effective for thrusting with force back of it, but entirely useless as far as cutting an orange is concerned. He took it without comment, too. His face was absolutely innocent of guile, it seemed, as with apparent good faith in Craig's offer he tried to cut the orange.

"It's quite dull, Mr. Kennedy." He held the bayonet up and felt along its edge lightly with his thumb. "You'd oughter get it ground!"

Craig looked at the man sharply, but his eyes never flickered. Yet Kennedy himself had taken that bayonet and sharpened the edge a bit to make it a cutting edge. There was nothing wrong about that to this Jim Camp—except that it was not sharp enough! If he knew that bayonets depended on thrust, not a razor-like edge for their efficiency, he never showed it.

Each one of these more or less silent little dramas that Craig was staging with the able assistance of Nan to make Jim Camp reveal himself was mighty interesting to me. To me each confirmed my idea that the man was really young Jerry Gowdy playing a game. No one could be so absolutely stupid as this man pretended.

Nan relieved the situation by getting a knife from the kitchen and finished by squeezing the oranges while Jim fixed up the "orange blossoms" with what seemed to me a practiced hand, and thereby, also, betrayed something.

Touch, too, had failed. So, I thought Craig had been going through all the senses in the hope of getting something on this Jim Camp. To me it looked equally as if Jim Camp were using every sense he possessed to defend himself against Kennedy. I was actually wondering what was becoming of Kennedy's theory of the senses and crime. I was thinking that if he were going positively to identify this man he didn't have many more senses left with which to experiment.

I caught sight of Craig in a quiet talk with Nan, and for precaution I engaged Jim and Julia in conversation. Out of the corner of my eye, from the animation of Nan's face, I could tell that Kennedy was framing the plans for some further test. He had been virtually defeated so far. The guests were dispersing now, about midnight, and I wondered what next he would do.

As he said good-night to Nan, there was a little searching glance that passed between them which might be taken for many things—an understanding look between lovers or a significant exchange of signals between conspirators. I knew which it was.

"Is it a failure—or just a mystery?" I asked as we climbed into the car.

"It's still a mystery, Walter." He seemed in no hurry as we drove along, almost purposeless. "I'm just dropping back to the laboratory for a small package. Then, about two in the morning, when all is quiet, I am coming back to the Gowdy house. I have left your bayonet there purposely. Nan is going to let us in without their knowing. If anything goes wrong the old bayonet will be as good an excuse as we can find. You must go with me. I may need help."

"Surely. If it's really young Jerry, he'll likely be able to shoot."

We rode over to the city, uptown, and back, leisurely, avoiding the night life in these opera bouffe togs.

At last we were again approaching the Gowdy house. That part of Brooklyn was a quiet place in the middle of the night. There were few people travelling and everything we did seemed so conspicuous and noisy. Changing gears and jamming brakes sounded twice as loud as in the daytime.

Again we left the car a short distance from the house. That precaution had not been really necessary during our earlier visit, but neither of us knew just how this second visit would turn out.

Evidently Nan had been looking for us. As we walked quietly

up the low stoop the front door opened noiselessly. We could just glimpse Nan's face peering at us, white and scared, in the doorway. Her finger was on her lips, adjuring silence.

"They sleep in the front room," she whispered. "My room is in the rear. Another room is between us and probably you can hide there. There's a queer arrangement in the front and middle rooms—a space between them which is divided by sliding doors. When they're closed, it makes two private bedrooms. No one is in the middle room now. Sometimes when Jim takes a notion to snore, Julia gets up in the night and leaves that room to sleep in the middle room. But no change has been made yet to-night. Jim's nose seems to be behaving." Nan laughed impishly, quite like any youngster appreciating the humor to be had from a loud snorer.

How we ever trod on those old stairs without giving the whole thing away is beyond my explanation. We had both our weight and the creaking old boards to contend with. I breathed a sigh of relief as I made out the opened door of the middle room from the hall. It was unlighted and I slid into the dark room gratefully. I had no relish to be taken for a burglar in another man's house. I wanted to be where there was a window, some exit. Craig was right after me, and Nan followed.

"Did you unfasten the sliding doors?" whispered Craig.

"Yes; when they were still downstairs to-night after you left. I don't believe they would notice that the key had been turned. I heard Julia say she was so tired she was going right to sleep. Jim seemed just as dull."

"And you have the things ready I asked you?"

"Yes. They're under the bed. I couldn't find a flat piece of iron. But I got a dishpan and an iron fork. Will that be all right?"

Kennedy nodded.

"It's the best I could do." I could see that Nan was actually trembling over the prospects of the next step.

For the first time now, under Craig's flashlight, I saw that he had brought down from the laboratory a little hand siren that we had once had on a small motor boat. It was a simple enough thing to look at—but why in the name of sense bring a noise-maker like that when we were trying so hard to execute a silent house entry?

"What's the idea?" I whispered.

There was no answer at first. Had Kennedy thought of the neighbors? Had he considered the results of this tomfoolery? What was he to gain, anyway?

"Don't worry, Walter," he returned at length. "Nothing much can happen to us. I'm provided with a warrant. And I'm rather known at police headquarters." I smiled at the ironic answer.

Quietly he was preparing—something. Gently the sliding doors were opened, wide enough for us to get a glimpse of the sleepers in the waving street light, into the front room. Jim was not snoring yet. Julia had both eyes closed in a deep slumber.

Carefully Craig looked all about to be sure everything was ready as he wanted it. Then he signalled to step back into the shadow of the middle room.

He took the siren, muffled it in the folds of a bath towel from the rack. Nan did the same with hand towels partly over both dishpan and iron fork.

"Are you ready?"

"Yes!"

He turned the siren handle briskly. Muffled, it sounded the signal of danger. It moaned, rising ever higher to a crescendo of alarm, then falling, as of a motor boat or car coming.

Nan with the pan and fork also muffled had set up a resonant clatter.

I did not need to ask as I listened and looked at the three of us crouching in the darkness. I saw it now. It was brought back to me as yesterday. Just as the men in France would set up such an unearthly racket with sirens, tin pans, old iron, anything that would ring, vibrate, so were Craig and Nan arousing the stillness of the night. Over in France it could mean only one thing: "Gas! Put on your gas masks!"

The best part of Craig's serenade was its suddenness, the muffled clamor—the just as startling silence that followed—and complete darkness. I saw it all, the psychic preparation of the evening, then this shock to the unconscious mind, an actual taking advantage, turning to account of failure.

Was that a sound we heard in the front bedroom? Over each other's shoulders we peered. Some one was moving silently about, groping timidly, uncertain. Some one else was regularly breathing in sleep.

Whoever was moving so slowly was going toward the other door, the hall door in the front bedroom. Kennedy made sure his flashlight was still working and handy. The breathing continued, a little louder, perhaps, as if the person had been disturbed and in the disturbance had assumed a position difficult for respiration.

Breathlessly we tiptoed into the hall and stood by the other door.

The door knob rattled weakly, futilely, uncertain. Another effort brought no better result. Kennedy quickly flung the door wide open. There was the dim outline of the sleepwalker, as it were.

For just a fraction of a second, shaded, he swung the flashlight.

It was Julia Crandall!

She was not awake, by any means. Her face depicted terror, horror. One hand she held over her mouth and nostrils as if to shut off something, the other over her eyes. What did this apparition mean? We weren't after Julia Crandall. We were after Jim Camp!

"What's it mean, Craig?" I half whispered.

Kennedy motioned silence. We watched him go forward to her.

"You've been in these gas attacks before, nurse?" Softly, subtly his voice sounded. "This is my first!"

"Yes... many times.... Oh! I know them!" Julia murmured, hoarsely. Her voice sounded in guttural tones. She was not herself. Her hands now were fluttering aimlessly. "The gas mask, lieutenant, where is it?"

"Over here."

"Oh, it's awful these days up here in the receiving station, so near the front! We're always fighting the gas. Please—please get me my mask! Where is it?... It's frightful, all these wounded, suffering boys—and then those fellows gassed—dying! Hear them? Haven't they gone through enough—without this?"

"Let's get out of it now! Come this way. The masks... over here!" Kennedy had been thinking quick. "Did that Gowdy chap die yet?"

"Yes." A shiver. "He was telling me about leaving an uncle and two cousins back in the States. He'd been the heir in the will, supposes now that his cousins Jim and Nan will get his uncle's money. Oh, he said everything so coolly I could hardly realize he'd been wounded beyond help. Yes, his strength finally ebbed—and he died." There was another shudder. "Oh, get me my mask, before it is too late." She was clutching her throat. "I feel almost suffocating!"

In the darkness, listening to the terrified girl, I was piecing it together now by sheer logic. The whole experience had been so vivid in her memory ever since, was so indelibly associated with the sound of the siren, that when she heard it in her sleep she was living it all over again.

The semi-conscious girl seemed reassured for the instant, took a step with Kennedy.

Like a flash it filtered into my mind. She had been gassed, too, the night Jerry Gowdy died. That was why she was so frightened now. I imagined that when she was lying sick and helpless she had made up her mind to meet Jim Camp. When she got well she had gone back to nursing privately, had looked up old Jeremiah Gowdy, found he was ill, needed a nurse. Old Gowdy was dying. He was easy in her hands. But she had had to work quickly. She had found the will, copied it, changed the name, got him to sign it, perhaps he never knew what it was. Then she had made a grand hunt by telegraph for Jim Camp, and had located him. She hadn't wanted the girl to cut in. But Nan had heard, too. Julia had played Jim Camp, made him fall for her, married him.

"Oh, where are those masks? I'm choking!"

There was only a snore from the front room. Jim was sleeping through it all. It meant nothing to Jim.

"Then—it's Julia—not Jim!" Nan was whispering. "He hasn't reacted to the call, at all, It's the nurse!"

Kennedy bent over, nodded to Nan. By his manner I knew that he had made an instantaneous revision of judgment, that he had been as surprised as we. The nurse had responded, not Camp. Yet I could not help wondering if he had unconsciously felt just an inkling of something like this before. He seemed so prepared for the emergency. He was like a good football player, ready to take advantage of a fumble, any break in the game.

"Yes," he muttered. When you set a trap you don't always know just what game you'll catch—but if you're a good trapper you'll catch something you want!"

"Where am I?" Julia had opened her eyes wide, staring in surprise and fear. "What was that noise?"

She was now thoroughly awake and angry. Kennedy took her arm now, not quite gently. "That noise. It was the gas alarm you heard in your sleep. Sight, smell, touch, taste failed—but *hearing* has given Nan Neely her case to contest the will!"

THE SIXTH SENSE

"**HELLO, JAMESON! HOW** are you, Mr. Kennedy? Well, we're glad you've come out here to give us a hand! Come over by the fire. The old duffer hadn't laid in his winter coal. Cunningham and a couple of the other fellows went foraging around. Look what they found!"

The Rudyard house was situated in the Quaker Ridge region of Westchester and it and its sportsman owner had been first-page material for the past two or three days. All the papers were full of Reginald Rudyard's disappearance and every one of the newspapermen was eager to solve the mystery and get an exclusive story.

Kennedy and I had just come over from the railroad station in an open flivver, the only conveyance we could find.

"Br-r-r!" I shivered in the door as one of the boys addressed us. "It feels like snow, soon. By Godfrey! Craig, let's get over where it's warm."

Logs were blazing merrily away on the old bent andirons. About the hearth were gathered, on a huge, well-worn divan, in chairs, and standing, a group representing most of the big dailies of the city. Beside the fireplace, which with its ingle nook occupied the entire end of the huge library, was a pile of logs to which the speaker pointed.

"Who is host or hostess here?" inquired Kennedy, looking about with a smile as he warmed his back at the blaze. "You all look mighty comfortable. Jameson's brought me out here. I'm willing to help you out with your stories for the day. But I wish you'd tell me something more about this disappearance. Have you fellows learned anything new?"

About that fireplace I felt that our whole trip had assumed more of a holiday air than a search that seemed to have the shadow of tragedy hanging over it.

"Host? Hostess? Just wait until she comes back. She's a little queen—and her name's Martha Mix—goes in for interior decorating and all that. She says she has gone all over the house from top to bottom, when they first learned that her uncle Reginald had disappeared. She can't find a thing, she says, and admits that she'll be glad when everything is quiet again and the estate settled. She would like to live in this beautiful old house. She's already talking about the curtains she is going to have in the living-room windows. I think she's more interested in the future of those windows than the present whereabouts of the owner."

"Are there any other heirs?" asked Kennedy, simply.

"Two, besides this niece, a cousin named Burroughs and a nephew, Tom Ashley. They're more interested in the settlement of the estate than they are in the whereabouts of Reginald Rudyard, too." It was Jim Deering of the *Record* whose information about the family details seemed greatest. "They've all been here scouting around and trying to keep an eye on what we find. Not difficult, so far. We haven't found very much. It all looks pretty hazy to me."

There was a camaraderie in that little group about the fireplace. They had all done their level best to solve the mysterious disappearance and had failed.

"When are these heirs going to show?" I asked, looking about.

"They've promised to meet us here at two o'clock," Deering explained.

"Why aren't they staying here?" asked Kennedy.

"Why, it seems, at times, as if Rudyard contemplated going away. All the servants were dismissed at the end of the last month. The amount of supplies in the house indicates to me a premeditated absence. I suppose that's the reason; it's cheaper and less trouble to stay where they are. Sometimes when I think of that, I conclude that Rudyard has gone on some trip and that he took no one into his confidence."

Kennedy nodded thoughtfully. It seemed plausible with a man like Rudyard, famous for his roving habits. "Where are the rest of the fellows?" he inquired. Evidently he felt that there should have been more newspapermen at the announcement that the heirs would meet and talk to them at two.

"Well, you know we're a curious crowd. Once in a while an idea comes to some one here. He leaves the bunch, explores the old house, or the grounds, or something. If you see some one get up suddenly and leave without a word, don't think he's crazy. He has only got a hunch." It was a quiet little fellow from the *Sun* who volunteered this explanation.

I watched Kennedy with amusement. He was quiet—very quiet. He was now leaning back in a chair before the fire, toasting his feet, eyes half closed, apparently dreaming. But I knew there wasn't a word said, a motion made, that he didn't hear and see. He was deep in the mystery. We were not distracting him; we were just a part of the picture.

"Some one wired in to the *News* last night that Rudyard had been seen hunting ducks out at Montauk Point. That seems likely for a man of his tastes. And this year is a great year for ducks. I'm waiting for word from the office. They sent a man out there immediately to investigate." Cunningham of the *News* looked about him with an air of importance. At least he had an idea, something to tell. That was qualifying better than most of the fellows. Besides, it was all right to tell it now. It was too late for anyone else to start out on that angle.

Jim Deering stood up, yawned a bit, stretched, and left the room. There was a sort of silence for a few moments—an expectant silence. We were ail waiting for Deering to come back.

"There are many gunners and many places out there to go for

ducks," I considered, speaking to Cunningham. He nodded. "I was glad to pass up that job and come here, cover this end."

I fancied a shrewd look on the face of George Rule of the *Press,* but he said nothing yet.

It was not so long before Deering rejoined us. "I wouldn't be surprised, Cunningham, if you were right. I've looked in every closet and wardrobe I could find in the house. I haven't found Rudyard's hunting coat, not a trace of it. He was wearing it in that picture of him we ran into to-day."

For the moment Kennedy seemed interested in Deering, scrutinized him carefully, then seemed absorbed in his own thoughts again. I was a trifle disappointed. I had expected Craig to jump into the thing, make the fur fly, clean it up with a rush.

"He might have stuck it in a chest or box," I observed.

Deering shook his head. "I'm afraid you're wrong, old man. Some one else has opened up all the boxes, pulled everything out. There's nothing hidden. There's no hunting coat—and there's only a week or so left in the duck season in this state."

"That's reasonable," I nodded. "He hadn't been duck hunting this season. No sportsman like Rudyard is going to pass that up for the year. Very likely he took his coat and went gunning."

It was more than George Rule of the *Press* could stand. "Yes—but not out to Montauk Point—and not necessarily ducks. Somebody up in the Adirondacks is equally sure he is up there. We've started a man out from Plattsburg on a rumor."

Now that the thing had broken, Davenport of the *Express* seemed to feel as if a ban were lifted. "Well, he isn't everywhere. We just had a report that he was seen with a party down on Bamegat Bay. It's not likely all these rumors are correct. They can't be. One is just as likely as another. Shall we make a book on it?"

The third rumor seemed to take the thrill out of the absence of the hunting coat. Nor was there any thrill in laying a bet.

"What a house old Rudyard had!" exclaimed the little chap from the *Sun,* looking about, by way of changing the subject. "I can't imagine why anyone would leave such a place. Can you, Walter?"

"No; I'd like to go through the house. What do you have to do to get permission?"

"Take it," replied Deering. "Same as I did. We can't do any more to it than the heirs must have done some time before we arrived. Every has been pulled out, in the greatest confusion."

"I'll go with you, Jameson," Cunningham spoke up.

"All right," I agreed. "Let's go!"

Kennedy did not even get up to look about him. I knew some of the men were disappointed, too, to say the least, at his inactivity. He seemed to care nothing about their critical looks, was absorbed only in his thoughts, as if piecing things together. I felt that I would have liked him to accompany me. But he did not offer to go and I did not suggest it.

Cunningham and I went first to the kitchen and pantry. There seemed to be nothing in them, or in the dining room, only the evidence of a cleaning up, a lick and a promise, by Mary, the cook.

Out in the hall I noticed a heavy ulster, rather worn, hanging with some other wearing apparel. But nothing I saw so far meant anything to me in the way of a clue.

Down cellar we went next, gingerly and expectantly. But we were here also doomed to disappointment. We could find no traces of the man. Only, we discovered his wine cellar was empty. Cunningham jumped to the conclusion that Rudyard had been imbibing too freely, had strayed away, was lost, although there was no reason to suspect that the effect of the wine cellar would last so long. It was a long, narrow room, very dark except when artificially lighted, and I could see row after row of empty little racks large enough to put in a bottle on its side in each compartment.

All over the cellar we searched. I looked even into the furnace. The cold room and the storage room had neither the man nor a clue to where he had gone.

From the cellar we mounted up into the attic, with the idea of working down thence to the library again. Such an attic! Everything was there, from a quaintly interesting storeroom built out under the eaves to a huge unfinished portion that would have been the delight of any small child. I could even make out the aged wasp nests in the crevices between the beams. There was a ceiling over one large end, leaving a space between it and the ridge of the roof, which served a purpose of making the house warmer in winter and cooler in summer. This was reached by a ladder and a locked scuttle door.

From the attic down we searched each successive floor. It was a beautiful and well-appointed house. Wonderful paneling on the main floor in the more important rooms comported with the well-chosen furniture. Heavy doors to match the paneling, beautifully grained and lustrous, reflected our presence as we passed them. Floors of white mahogany gave dignity to the drawing room and rare paintings and old china showed the owner's discriminate taste.

It was a beautiful home, but, as I passed through, it seemed as if there were a desolate touch in it. Something seemed missing. If I had owned such a place I wouldn't be leaving it so unceremoniously. Such a house deserved a bit of courtesy. Was I getting reduced to the sob stuff, or was it just the cold house and morbid excitement?

As I entered the library again and observed the many rows of books, I could not help thinking that Reginald Rudyard was something more than a sportsman. He was a bibliophile. When the geese and ducks, pheasant and partridge, even big game were not calling, the famous characters of romance and history were beckoning.

I thought I would write up a brief description of the library and this little-known side of the missing man. It would make a good human-interest story for the *Star*.

I had been making notes for some minutes at a beautiful old Spanish table used as a desk. Under it was a quaint paper basket made of some highly polished metal, a relic of the past when things to be beautiful must be ornate.

A draught of wind, and my paper scattered. I leaned over to recover the sheets. In the basket I noticed an old blotter. I couldn't fish it out fast enough.

My enthusiasm got the better of me. "Look, Craig! This was in the basket. Perhaps there's some clue!"

There was a laugh from almost all the fellows except Kennedy. He maintained his kindly silence, was interested, as he had been in everything. I held up the blotter with its writing and figures and lines all blurred into each other as in any over-worked blotter. Much of it seemed to be in red ink.

Both Kennedy and I looked at it closely, but neither of us, it seemed, could make anything of it. Did I imagine I heard some of the other fellows snickering again? I looked up with a challenge. What right had they to laugh at what might turn out to be an important clue? I was holding up the blotter, twisting it around at every angle and in every light, hoping to get some idea of the words it had blotted, when Jim Deering entered the room after some new mission. It was all illegible. Deering laughed.

"Did you get fooled with that blotter, too? Everyone of us has been. We must all be as good as each other. I thought I had the whole case when I first picked that up off the desk. But I couldn't make head or tail of a single thing on it. Cunningham got so sore when he couldn't decipher a thing on it that he threw the blamed blotter into the waste basket."

The men thought it was a joke at our expense as Kennedy quietly passed the thing back to me and I laid it on the table. I didn't mind their laughing at me; what made me furious was the laugh by implication, perhaps, on Kennedy. However, as he said nothing about it, I gathered that he either didn't attach any importance to it or, at least, felt the better course was to ignore them. Well, I reasoned, if it meant nothing to him, there was no reason for me to be excited about it. Still, as I saw a small mirror on the wall, I took it down and, in spite of the chaffing

of the others, I tried vainly to determine what had been written on it. But the letters were too blurred together in a mass for
me to be able to make out one word, either in the black or the
preponderating red.

Kennedy was still sitting by the fire, calmly pulling at his
favorite pipe. I know he had watched me use both the mirror
and a magnifying glass I had picked up on the table, without
result. He seemed to be showing no further interest in the blotter or me. His mind was busy, probably, by this time on other
phases of the mystery.

"Did anybody see him leave the place?" asked Kennedy at
length.

"They haven't found anybody yet who saw him leave. But he
might have left after dark. People are indoors mostly at that time
of night in the country. Or he might have got up very early to
go for ducks."

"Or," Cunningham rejoined, embarking on another new
theory for him, "he might not have gone out at all!"

Kennedy had picked up a pair of tortoise-shell glasses on a
table back of the divan. "When people suffer from astigmatism
as it seems Rudyard did, they aren't going out without their
glasses." He held them to the light. "I don't believe he could see
much without these."

Cunningham was delighted at this corroboration. As for me,
I reacted to it, could not help thinking of Cunningham's theory
just a few minutes ago down in the cellar. "That may be true.
But he has gone—gone completely, in spite of his thick lenses
and his astigmatism."

"Or," said Craig, with a quiet smile, "perhaps he had more
than one pair of glasses. Most men in his circumstances do."

Cunningham's face clouded. Was Kennedy making sport of
us by setting up men of straw in order to knock them down? Or
was he getting back for that snicker over the blotter?

"Let's get down to brass tacks," bustled Deering. "Here's
something I found. I was going to bring it out when I saw Jame-

son so blooming interested in that bloody blotter. I didn't want to interrupt." Deering had disclosed in his hand a small piece of white paste-board. "It looks like a price tag and seems to have come from Riddel's hardware shop in White Plains."

"Have you been there or called up?" asked Craig.

"Been there. Looked new, as if it might have been a recent purchase. I picked it up by his bedroom door, inside. Seemed to me as if it might have been a last-minute purchase for his trip, whatever it was, ripped off hurriedly and dropped on the floor carelessly. I found that Rudyard had called at Riddel's three days ago and bought a file—No. 8A."

"A file?" I repeated. "Why in the devil did he need to take a file away with him?"

"What about his automobile? He might have broken a file in his tool kit and replaced it with a new one," Deering joked with me.

"Well, if you know so much, Deering, how long is an 8A file? I grant he might have been starting out on a trip and would want a full complement of tools."

"About six inches."

"Well, how thick is an 8A file?" I persisted in spite of the joshing tone of the answer.

"Say, Jameson, how thick are you? For Heaven's sake, what has the thickness of an 8A file to do with solving this disappearance or even getting news for our papers? A sixteenth of an inch!"

I glanced over toward Craig. Generally people who do the scoffing know least. Craig's face was quite serious, even thoughtful, but he said nothing nor did his expression betray anything.

I turned to the others, feeling a bit sore. "What's the matter with you fellows? If a man who disappears buys a file, hasn't one a right to inquire the exact size of it, even if he doesn't know what probable use there might have been for a file of that size? I am sure those questions are justifiable—even though they may prove to be useless. Have you fellows got a monopoly on useless questions? Anyway, I'll always remember what an 8A file is like!"

Cunningham, who had left the library a few minutes before, burst in unceremoniously, out of breath. "I've been down to the garage. He's taken his car with him."

"Is that so?" asked Rule. "Which one?"

"They're all gone—or did he have more than one?"

"Why, I've been talking to some of the people around here and they have spoken about his roadster, his limousine, and another mentioned his flivver sedan that he used to keep for the use of the servants. Everybody seemed to like him and he was mighty generous to his help, it seems."

"Suppose Deering, you get in touch with those relatives of his," advised the little *Sun* man. "Maybe they might have taken the cars from the garage. You know Martha—she fell for you and would talk to you, if she had one of the cars."

"There's no need to do that," put in Cunningham, his eyes puckered as if recollecting something. "In my opinion there has been only one car there for some time, or at least recently. The floor in front of two of the doors shows the grease and oil pretty well soaked in. In front of the third door I noticed that the grease and oil had dropped freshly,"

We had come to an impasse there, too. "Evidently," I remarked, "the thing that no one dares to talk much about or even hint in the papers is the strange attitude of his relatives toward him at this time of his disappearance—and the suggestion of foul play. Can't some of you fellows let us in for a little more information along that line? They are queer, these heirs." Kennedy smiled quizzically and I felt that at last I was leading the conversation around to an important phase of the case. "Just who is this Ashley, for instance? What is his business, if he has one?"

"He's a horticulturist over on Long Island, has some big greenhouses out near Easthampton." Deering of the *Record* assumed a posture of importance as if about to furnish a perfectly good suspicion. His tone was confidential. "From what I hear, he indulges his hobby of raising hybrids to satisfy his own inclinations, to the neglect, sometimes, of those flowers that the trade really wants. He's broke most of the time. We've made inquiries out there at Easthampton and he has some big notes at the bank due shortly. I am not saying anything, but that is how the wind is blowing from that quarter."

"And there's that Montauk rumor—out that way, too," noted the little *Sun* man.

Kennedy was leaning back, eyes closed, but alert. A smile played about his lips.

"What about these others," I asked—"Burroughs and the girl?"

"I know Burroughs, too," pursued Deering. "For a chap who is supposed to have a lot of money he is the limit. He's always broke. You see, he can't spend his principal. The old folks were on to him and fixed the will. Besides, he has the gambling fever. His allowance is spent before he gets it. Otherwise he's a pretty decent chap. It would be hard for me to think of him as a thug or a poisoner—but he always needs money." Jim Deering spread out his hands with an expressive gesture of suspicion.

"What about this Martha Mix, Jim, the one interested in you?" I couldn't help getting back at him.

"Oh, she never had any money. Her mother married a poor man who proceeded to invest nearly all his wife's money. When Martha came along, the family fortune was what hadn't been invested—not very much. I rather hope when Rudyard kicks off—if and when, as the lawyers say—that he does leave her this house. She's so crazy for a nice home and rather hates the idea of selling herself to the highest bidder to get one."

"How do you know so much. Has she refused you and your offer for a home?" I asked, impertinently.

"I know better than to ask. I have something else to do with my hard-earned money than to buy curtains for all these windows." He waved his hand about at the huge plate-glass panes of the library that afforded such a wonderful view of the surrounding hills and woodland. "And then, you know, Walter I met her only yesterday. I'm not a fast worker."

"There's this awful silence from *him*," commented Cunning-ham, with a scowl over our kidding, groping desperately for his theory No. 3. "It looks like foul play to me. Surely if a man read the papers he would let somebody know, to stop this hue and cry."

"It's quite possible he doesn't know," objected George Rule. "One can be buried in the Canadian woods or, for that matter, in any wild place, hunting, for weeks, without hearing what is going on or even being able to get in touch with the outside world."

"Or," the *Sun* man suggested, "he might be on a steamer sail-ing in midocean by this time."

"Well, wireless would get him there," I objected.

"Not necessarily. I believe that has been done, but there's been no information from that source. A great many captains have sent messages back that he hasn't sailed with them."

So it went with every theory or idea as soon as suggested. As fast as a new lead was developed, it would be shattered, would go the way of a dozen others previously. There seemed to be clues—too many of them, perhaps. But none that was any good. There was absolutely nothing to hang the reason for his disap-pearance upon.

As for me, I could not help thinking of Kennedy's theory of the senses. Which one was it that this case hinged upon? As far as I could see, none of the senses, of all the five, seemed to apply here. Suddenly a bright idea flashed through my mind. But I said nothing of it to anybody, least of all to Kennedy, Here was indeed a case for telepathy or something psychic or supernatu-ral I had heard of television—the faculty some are supposed to possess whereby they may touch some article belonging to a dead or missing person and forthwith obtain a vision of the owner. Kennedy was uncanny to me. Might he not possess, might he not develop, this sense of television?

I fancied I could see how it was with Kennedy. He wasn't

offering much in the way of ideas. He was busy knocking out our ideas. "What he was really doing was to interview us, eliminating the impossible and keeping quiet as to the rest.

Frankly, I myself was spinning in a whirlpool of possible conjectures. It seemed as if we had flitted lightly from one clever theory to another. Even the best of them, the most plausible, had been one after another knocked into a cocked hat. One idea I held and could not forget. It seemed to me that one or perhaps all of those heirs might clear the whole thing up if they could only be tricked into talking, cornered into a betrayal.

Some of us, too, were getting discouraged. Managing editors had hinted at the necessity of a good story for the third day, or the mystery might die on our hands. But there didn't seem anything new to find out. At first I had been hoping for a good thrill that could be sent out in time for the evening papers. It was now a question of the morning papers. Is it any wonder one gets the philosophy: Why spoil a good story for the want of a few facts?

We entered upon a discussion of the probability of a woman being mixed up in the disappearance, falling back upon the old stand-by, *Cherchez la femme.* But no woman had disappeared lately to our knowledge. Besides, Quaker Ridge gossip had it that Rudyard had been living very quietly for the last few months, almost the life of a recluse. His only diversions seemed to have been his books and tramping or riding about the country roads and lanes. Rudyard had been a man to whom other men were sufficient. The opposite sex had rather bored, even annoyed him. It is true, he was always courteous to the ladies. It was his nature to be so with everybody. But women he avoided, actually seemed to be ill at ease in their company.

"When we drove in," I ventured, "I saw that Rudyard had built a gas tank beside the garage. Maybe that may show something about his car—or cars—or even about his trip, if he took one."

It was an idea, at least. I went over to the garage. There seemed to be no bills or statements as to gas. And the tank was dry. In fact even the vapor of gas was not in evidence. It was as though it had been dry and unused some time. Again I was disappointed. It seemed as if everything I thought of turned out to be nothing, or at least something quite indefinite.

I was leaving the garage when I noticed Deering of the *Record* waiting as if to walk back to the house with me. He was holding up an old, rusty saw. From its condition it had not sawed a piece of wood in years.

"What do you make of that, Kennedy?" Deering passed the saw over to Craig. "Anything?"

I leaned over Kennedy's shoulder with the rest. Now I noticed that the very end of the saw, a thin, narrow saw, had been cut off straight and clean, perhaps three-eighths of an inch. While the saw was old, the cut was recent. It had not time to rust.

"Why was that done? What possible reason could Rudyard have for mutilating a saw in that fashion?"

"Maybe it was done by some one else."

There was our usual babble of remarks. I looked at Craig, but obtained no insight into his real feelings, whether it was of any importance or not in his estimation. His countenance was immobile. If he had any suspicions, one would never have known it.

"This is the case that puts the mist in mystery," I punned, desperately. "At least it's all misty to me."

Kennedy turned indolently. "While you were out, Walter, I thought I noticed a picture of the house. I can't see it clearly. It is there over on that table."

I picked up the picture, glanced at it in admiration, and passed it on to Kennedy. It was more than a photograph. It was the work of some talented etcher. It was one of the most beautiful little etchings I had ever seen.

The great entrance of this huge brick house was outlined boldly in this artistic bit of work. Four columns rising above the second floor seemed whiter than ordinarily through the etcher's artistry. Slanting down through the open spaces in the leaves of the trees, the sunlight filtered through. It seemed quite real as the sunbeams clung to portions of the portico, and the shadows softened it all. The dormer windows of the third floor stood out boldly.

One thing I liked about the other windows. The tops were curved and in the very middle was a white keystone. It was a dignified house and would have been called a mansion even if it had possessed neither wing. One wing, as I had gone through the house previously, I noted was the servants' quarters. The other was a huge solarium, marble tiled. Over it on the second floor was a large sleeping porch, part of the master's suite.

In the etching one noticed the beautiful shrubbery, the old evergreens, spruces, cedars, pines, and hemlocks. There seemed to be many kinds of shrubbery about the place, but the house itself was the jewel that seemed architecturally perfect, fitting its site harmoniously, yet retaining all its gracious dignity.

Under the picture, as if written in a pensive, tender mood, was an inscription by the owner, "Here lies my heart."

"No wonder Rudyard felt that way," I exclaimed. "I can't imagine his staying away from such a place so long at a time as he often does. But I suppose he's always glad to get back to it at the end of the journey, probably wrote that little thought some time on returning after a long absence."

In my enthusiasm I launched into a complete description of the interior for Kennedy's benefit, from the wine cellar on up to the very attic scuttle. If he would not accompany me about the house I would take him on a verbal tour of it.

"That etching ought to be up where one can see it," I exclaimed as Craig handed it back to me. "That's art."

I looked about, but could see no desirable place to put it on the paneled walls. So I stood it up on the mantel, where it occupied the space between two old Chinese vases. I let my eyes wander up toward the ceiling. By the side of a piece of paneling was a quaint little copper hook. On it was a key ring and a flat key, small and thin. I reached up and took it down.

"What do you suppose this key fits?" I looked at it curiously, flat and small, in my hand. Then I looked about the room. There were several cabinets, two huge closets, and many bookcases, but they all seemed to have keys and none of them looked like the little key I had found.

By this time Craig was examining it carefully. But he, too, put it down on the table beside the divan without any comment. It might not have been used for years or the thing it had fitted in that room may have been removed. Of one thing I was now sure. It did not fit anything there at present.

I was getting peeved at the way everything, even the smallest things that ought to have been evidential, was turning out. In any other case I would have felt sure that the key would open something that would unlock the mystery of Rudyard's disappearance. But now nothing was any good, not even a hunch.

In disgust I pulled my hat down hard, jammed my hands into my coat pockets, and started for the door. "I'm going to give this place another once-over. If I can't find anything this time, I'm going to write a story that will make the city desk rave and tear their hair. There won't be a fact in it; nothing but human interest." I slammed the door and could hear the laughter of the others as I made my retreat.

Down toward the fields I walked. Perhaps I expected to locate the remains, or some evidence. I don't know. But there were not even the remains of anything that had been raised there. There was no indication, even, that the field had been plowed. Actually it seemed not to have been tilled in some time.

Over to the flower gardens I strode. The soil was dark and rich, with all the evidence of fertility. But it had not been cultivated this year except for those plants which seed themselves year after year. As I walked about, poking first in one place, then in another, I thought that Rudyard's heart may have been given to his house, but his garden had not received much of his time

or attention. But then again, there were those trips. Possibly he
didn't think there was much use in a garden if he were away so
much.

I strolled over to the kennels. There were no dogs, and had not
been for a long time. That was strange for a hunter. It was the
same with the chicken yard—no chickens. Not so strange. But
the fact remained, the disappearance of the master seemed to
mean the disappearance of everything with life about the place.
More and more I became imbued with the idea that Rudyard
had gone either on a long hunting trip or on an ocean voyage.
Still, I had nothing to substantiate that view.

Not being able to find anything of interest, again I went
toward the house. What splendid walks were these! Before, I
hadn't noticed the many beautiful details of the place, irregular
blue stone laid in cement for walks, and white-columned pergo-
las. It was a dream of a place, but just now a little wild. To many
that would prove an asset rather than a liability.

It had begun to snow. Already I could see stretching out in
beauty and tranquility the white covered fields and trees dressed
in ghost-like array. Would this pall of white somehow, somewhere cover some last undiscovered clue? I turned back to the
house.

There had been a lull in conversation caused by the dearth
in new ideas, I found as I rejoined the group about the fire. In
silence we were raking over slumbering thoughts in the desperate need for copy.

Outside there was a jamming of brakes, the silvery sound of
a woman's voice accompanied by men. The noise of the arrival
made me curious. I walked over to a big window overlooking
the entrance.

There was a girl, two men, and an aged woman, the last
dressed rather plainly in black. She was the only quiet one in
the party. To the others the occasion of the visit seemed more
like a family reunion, but the old woman was red-eyed from
weeping, and sad.

"Come on in and we'll see what all these clever men have found out. You can't go home just yet, Tom." I surmised that the young lady was Martha Mix and that it was to Ashley she spoke. She certainly possessed a blithe and happy spirit over the prospect of a death or something worse. "Don't talk too much, Mary. They'll ask us all sorts of questions."

She glanced over, saw that we heard. Looking up at Jim Deering, who had joined me, she laughed teasingly.

"Mary. That was the name of the old cook fired last month," Deering explained, smiling back good-naturedly at the lively girl through the window.

In a moment the little party entered. The newspapermen all stood up, and Martha calmly seated herself and Mary in two of the easiest chairs by the roaring wood fire.

"Have you found out anything?" she asked, rather brusquely.

"Not much," Deering answered.

"Did Mr. Kennedy arrive? You told me he would be here. I guess he didn't come," Martha added, "if the disappearance hasn't been explained."

Craig smiled and bowed. Deering made a hasty introduction. I rather enjoyed the girl's momentary discomfiture. She had one of those rapid, feminine minds that jump at intuitions.

At the same time I took advantage of it. We would do the interviewing, not Martha. "We'd like to ask you folks," I hastened, "to tell us more about Mr. Rudyard. Were you acquainted with any of his intimate friends, people whom he might visit for any length of time—or any hobbies, other than hunting, that might keep him away?"

"I don't know much about him in that way," returned Martha, unabashed. "You see, I never visited here much myself, because he was never home when I wanted to come. How about you, Jim?" She turned toward Burroughs.

"Well," he began, with a drawl, "he rather avoided me, afraid I'd put a nick in his bank roll, I fancy. I was always trying to borrow from him in the old days when we were friendly. I think

Tom was the only one with whom he was friendly. I haven't seen him in two years.

I wondered at that remark. Burroughs was a gambler, broke all the time by his own admission, and Rudyard avoided him. Was Burroughs trying to mislead us about the last time he saw his cousin? The man's reputation caused me to look with disfavor at everything he said or did."

"He used to come out to see me sometimes," remarked Ashley. "I should say to see my plants. He was fond of flowers. His roving spirit never gave him much opportunity to cultivate them, though. But mine he enjoyed in his quiet way."

Several times Mary, timid, shrinking old lady, acted as if she wanted to speak, but was afraid to say anything before so many strangers.

Kennedy seemed to understand the cause of her indecision. He leaned over, touched her arm gently. "Feel badly over things, don't you, Mary?"

She looked up at him with a drawn, haggard face, nodded abruptly, and two tears streamed gently down her cheeks. Old Mary was the only one of them all who seemed to show any emotion.

"I want to know that he is safe—no harm come to him! I've known him a long time. He's been so good to me. I can't bear to think of him suffering or needing help. I tell you, Mr. Kennedy, when you've cooked for a boy until he grows to be a man you know something about him. I've known him from the time he would steal from the cooky jar as a boy until he grew old enough to go away on long trips, and he always took as many of my goodies away with him as he could pack!"

Kennedy reached over to the table, took up the small thin flat key and swung around quickly. "Miss Mix, do you recognize that?"

Martha looked at it sharply, shook her head. "I never saw it before. Where did you get is? I've opened about everything in this house that can be opened, hunting for a clue to Uncle Reginald. But I never used that and I have no idea where it might be used."

He turned to Ashley. "Nor I," he said, simply.

"And you, Mr. Burroughs?"

"Never saw it before."

"Sure?"

"I know nothing about it, and care less." Burroughs was angry at the insistence.

"Have you seen that key before, Mary?" Kennedy held it up so she could see it plainly. "Do you know what it's for?"

Mary looked at it and smiled wanly. "Sure I do. It's the key to that scuttle to the roof, the only one that locks and unlocks it." She became reminiscent. "Mr. Rudyard used to keep it hanging up there," pointing in the direction over the mantle. "It isn't so very old. Just a few years ago the squirrels ate through the cornice, under the roof, nested there, and became a nuisance, the destructive little pests. Mr. Rudyard wanted to get rid of them, but he couldn't get at them. They were between the roof and the ceiling of the attic. So he had a carpenter, old Mr. Work, come, cut the scuttle door through the ceiling, one he could lock up when he went away. Then they were able to get at those destructive squirrels. It was easy to get up there, lock and unlock it."

Kennedy nodded sympathetically. Martha seemed impatient and bored for a moment, then stood up suddenly.

"Well, how long are we going to sit here discussing squirrels and keys—and all the time getting farther and farther away from any explanation? That fire's hot, I must have a drink of water."

I started forward, ahead of Cunningham.

"No, don't trouble yourself, thank you."

Nevertheless Deering insisted on going with her to the kitchen.

"How would you catch a squirrel, Walter?" asked Rule, irrelevantly.

"Go under a tree and make a noise like a Press reporter!" I retorted, testily.

Martha and Deering returned.

"Did you get it?" asked Kennedy, casually.

"Yes," Martha was on her dignity.

"The wine cellar's dry," smartly added Deering, "but the drinking water here is excellent."

"Not frozen up, then."

"No, not yet," replied Martha breezily, "but it will be if a cold spell follows this storm."

"What's the use of staying here and talking about the water freezing?" exclaimed Deering, wearily. "I'll run down to town with you. Miss Mix, see that a plumber comes out to shut it off. I'm going to file a story that this case is baffling and to-night looks as if it would go down in criminal history as one of the unsolved mysteries. I'm ready to go. What do you say, fellows?" Deering turned to Kennedy. "I suppose you'll agree with me at last, Kennedy, give it up and wait for some real news?"

Craig eyed Deering calmly, very quietly for a minute, never moving from his chair. "Yes, I'll give it up"—he leaned over and knocked the ashes from his pipe into the fire—"because I have solved it!"

"Solved it?" There was a general exclamation from all of us about the fire.

"Yes." He picked up the key. "Take that. Go upstairs. Open the scuttle door. You'll find your answer there!"

All of us except Kennedy, even the heirs, wasted no time. I grabbed the key, took the steps two at a time. Up the ladder I climbed. There was some difficulty fitting the key. It seemed as if something on the other side had to be pushed out of the lock. It fell at last. The lock was not a spring lock; just a bolt that had to be opened and closed by the flat key.

I flung open the scuttle door. There in the dead space between the attic ceiling and the roof was the body of Reginald Rudyard, clad in his old hunting coat.

"Facts first, next motives, then clues." Before the fire Kennedy was climbing into his huge ulster. "My first point was that blotter you tossed away in the waste-paper basket."

He was staring at the bent andirons, out of keeping with the other things in the house, yet not replaced. He warmed his hands as he glanced out at the flurrying snow. "He hadn't laid in his winter's coal. There were figures on that blotter, many of them, too many to read, all in red ink. You know what red-ink figures mean to an accountant? Losses! Rudyard was a ruined, bankrupt man. I think you are going to find that his cars one after another have been sold or quietly seized, that the house was next to go to his creditors. He had nothing left to live for."

Kennedy turned to me. "My second point, Walter, was your question. How thick was that file? A file, so thin, was no earthly use for anything but to make a key. You found it, a flat key to that door. The indentations in the key were just a sixteenth of an inch. Then the piece of the old saw, just the thickness of that flat key. But the key was hanging as usual in its place. That was palpably a blind."

No one now, of all this smart group, was interrupting the monologue.

"In his accounts, nothing but red figures—losses. No money even to bury him. He had a sentiment about this old house to which he always came back after his wanderings no matter how far they took him. 'Here lies my heart!' In death he could not leave it.

"Rudyard contemplated no hunting trip. Besides, no such man goes out into God's country to commit suicide. And he had not premeditated suicide, either. The water was not even shut off. The winter's coal he could not afford. While the fit was on him, he did it here in the house he loved, with some quick poison, like cyanide, no doubt."

"And he never once moved out of his chair here in this library!" exclaimed the little Sun man, eyeing Kennedy. "It's—

it's uncanny! Gad! Jameson, this man is wonderful! He has a sixth sense!"

Deering, Cunningham, Rule—all of them—were too flabbergasted at the moment even to write or to grab a telephone.

"How thick is an 8A file!" I was ruefully regarding my own fool question, a fool question only to me. It had started the solution of the Rudyard case. I had not seen the forest for the trees. "Yes," I muttered, "a sixth sense—COMMON SENSE!"

ABOUT THE AUTHOR

IT WAS NOT so many years ago that the man who set out to catch a criminal was forced to rely, in large measure, on such uncertain and haphazard factors as natural shrewdness, personal bravery, intuition or—and this was his main bulwark against failure—on pure, blind, unadulterated luck.

Today, however, the detective who depends too much on getting the 'breaks' in solving a crime is going to find himself slated for almost certain failure. For—though luck, nerve, and all the rest of those intangible qualities which used to mean everything, still have their undoubted value—it is the laboratory, with its chemical and mechanical innovations, which has come to the fore and made crime-detection a science indeed, rather than the uncertain gamble of the past.

The police, or detective, headquarters of a modern city today has more of the atmosphere of a college chemistry or physics building than of a jail. And it is the white-coated experimenter with his test-tube and lens who is the terror of the law-breaker, rather than the flat-footed precinct dick of an earlier era.

Great strides forward in such fields as ballistics—the science of bullet identification; toxicology—the science of poisons; fingerprinting; photography; graphology—the science of handwriting; chemistry and physics, and electrical research, have all contributed to the broader field of crime solution as a whole.

Nor have the criminals been any less quick to seize on the newest contributions of science to aid them, than their natural enemies the police. For every advance that has been made by the safe and vault manufacturers the bank robber has developed a new way of getting through the time-locked, concrete-walled manganese steel which guards his loot. Fingerprints and bullets have both been forged; and the criminal who keeps pace with the times tries to have at his command just as advanced information from the laboratory as the detective.

Arthur B. Reeve

Naturally, to avoid remaining static while the processes of crime and crime-detection were changing so rapidly, detective fiction had to take into consideration the various developments of the laboratories. In England, Sir Arthur Conan Doyle, in his Sherlock Holmes stories, was perhaps the first author to utilize science as an integral part of his crime fiction. Who can forget the picture we invariably got of the sleuth of Baker Street holding a pipette in acid-stained fingers over a Bunsen burner, while Doctor Watson watched the master at some careful analysis? And we know of at least three technical monographs which Holmes is supposed to have written—one on the detection of bloodstains on cloth; one on the differences between various varieties of tobacco ash; one on the preservation of footprints.

And in this country Arthur B. Reeve became famous almost overnight after creating Craig Kennedy, The Scientific Detective.

Let's let Mr. Reeve tell us something about Craig and his creator.

Born 1880, Patchogue, Long Island. Princeton, '03, where he created the name "Craig Kennedy" and used character first in *Nassau Literary Magazine.*

Studied about everything with an 'ology or an 'onomy on the end of it—which accounts for the scientific in, Craig Kennedy.

Went to New York Law School and was fascinated by criminal law. Hence conceived the incongruity of combining science and law with a Nick Carter who should have both the University and Third Avenue Theatre melodrama in his make-up. Suped in Third Avenue melodramas often after coming to New York from college.

Wrote first story ever to have Maxim silencer in it; first story ever to mention the dictagraph; first story with the Freud theory before Freud was even translated. In fact created the modern type of scientific detective. Over two million Craig Kennedy books alone have been sold in America and a million abroad mainly in Great Britain.

Wrote "Exploits of Elaine," starring Pearl White, which ran a record of 36 episodes, never exceeded in serials, and was shown in almost every country in the world. Also wrote Houdini's pictures, *Master Mystery, Grim Game, Terror Island.* Sponsored N.B.C. Crime Prevention Program.

www.ingramcontent.com/pod-product-compliance
Lightning Source LLC
Chambersburg PA
CBHW020636030726
47498CB00002B/248